TAKEOVER

A HART DAVIS ADVENTURE

BY DUNCAN MCGEARY

The FBI couldn't even do a blockade right.

We emerged out of the gully with only a few hundred feet to go. The second we stepped out onto the flats, we heard yelling.

"Go!" I shouted to Derrick. "Go get Jerry!" I wasn't sure the cops wouldn't catch me, and I didn't want to slow down the boys.

The boys took off like a shot. I stumbled after them, trying not to fall on my face, and within seconds they were dozens of feet ahead of me. I wasn't even halfway across before the boys came up on the camp.

The shouting was loud on both sides, but even louder from inside the camp. I thought they were cheering us on. I couldn't make out the words.

The first bomb blew Jared and Cameron into the air.

I couldn't make sense of it. Bodies flying, and parts of bodies, and missing things, Cameron's body falling flat, Jared sliding in the dust. I remember all this in my memories, but I couldn't understand what I was seeing when it was happening.

Justin kept running and hit the second mine. He disappeared in a red mist, nothing left of him but bones and shattered meat.

My boy Derrick stopped dead in his tracks. He turned toward me, his face white. He started moving toward me and I knew. The moment he took that first step, I knew.

"Stop, Derrick!" I screamed. "Don't move!"

I was still twenty yards away when the bomb went off under my son. At almost the same moment, my legs went out from under me. I screamed and didn't stop screaming. Not because of the pain but because I knew.

My son was gone.

I don't remember anything after that, until I woke up in this hospital bed. A few blessed moments when I forgot, and then...I screamed and screamed.

CHAPTER 1

HART DAVIS

Nicole and I parked on the side of the highway a quarter mile away from the Johnson ranch. Cars lined the road, parked randomly, like pick-up sticks. The concrete abutment of an unfinished highway jutted out over the flat desert land. Transmission towers paraded through the middle of the spread, mechanical robots marching toward the low hills on the horizon.

"I'd be pissed too," Nicole said as we got out of our pickup and joined the throng walking toward the confrontation. "Harry is probably livid."

Even from a distance, I could make out the black uniforms and bristling gear of the Feds, while across from them, the crowd was amorphous, changing shape with the shifting moods of the mob.

"Can't stop progress," I said, though I agreed with her opinion. "You sure you want to do this?"

She didn't answer, just kept marching toward the old ranch house at the end of the red gravel driveway. The heat that rose from the ground was like that of an oven, the heavy breath of summer without shade. Nicole walked faster than me despite being a good foot shorter. I had to hustle to keep up.

I still couldn't believe that she wanted to be with me. I was pretty sure she'd figure out the real me and take off.

We walked under the power lines. The wires thrummed. The crowd vibrated as well: from excitement, from happiness, from fear. The event was attracting the best and the worst kinds of people: Friends who wanted to support Vanessa and Harry Johnson, strangers who sincerely believed in the cause, and others…well, political ghouls hoping it would all blow up.

As soon as I saw the signs and banners, I wanted to turn around. "Leave Our Land Alone!" "Live Free or Die!" "Land and Liberty!" The protesters may have looked like regular folks, but most of them were weekend ranchers, enticed more by the animus of rebellion than caring what happened to the Johnsons.

A long picnic table was set in the middle of the dry tufts of grass in what, in the High Desert, passed for a lawn. The Johnson family and their neighbors were bunched around the table, looking around at the crowd with annoyed expressions on their weathered faces.

Leaning against the house, Joshua Calley was rolling a cigarette and ignoring the commotion. Nicole had told me about him. Members of both sides of the confrontation cast curious glances in his direction, surprised to see a black man working for the Johnsons.

Jerry, the eldest Johnson boy, was yelling at some protesters who were trampling Vanessa Johnson's vegetable garden. Irrigated with canal water, the garden patch was infested with weeds, and what little harvest escaped the deer was usually fed to the hogs. Meanwhile, the younger boy, Derrick, not yet in high school, seemed to be trying to rev up the crowd, jumping up and down, taunting the police in his high-pitched voice. The other boys, four of them, were too young to truly understand what was happening.

The traditional ranch house had been expanded on and given a recent coat of paint, but it was still a humble abode compared to the homes of most of the wealthy ranchers in the area. Harry stood at the head of the picnic table, apparently too riled up to sit. Vanessa, his stout and petite wife—made even more so by the hunch in her shoulders—had her arm around his waist. She looked angrier than her husband. What I didn't realize until later was that they were upset about completely different things.

As Nicole and I approached, Harry scowled at us; then his granite face split into a tired smile. "Nicole! My gosh, the last person I expected."

"Hello, Mr. Johnson," Nicole said. She backed up a step and put her arm around me. "This is my friend, Hart Davis."

The old man barely gave me a glance. "Welcome to the rodeo." He waved his arm. "Goddamn protesters think they're proving something."

His wife squeezed him so hard he winced. "Now, honey, you know what they're doing...exercising their constitutional right to protest."

"Yeah, OK, fine, but do they have to do it in our front yard?"

"Why not?" his wife answered, and I could tell it wasn't a new argument between them. Vanessa Johnson may have been short, but she looked immoveable. "These people are on our side."

"Are you all right? Anything I can do?" Nicole asked, her voice so soft she could barely be heard above the shouting demonstrators.

"What's that?" the old man said, and then softened when he saw the concerned look on her face. "I'm doing fine, considering, thank you for asking. Not that any of *these* people care. They look right through me when I talk to them. I might as well not be here. I've asked them—politely—to leave, but they ignore me."

The Feds were edging closer to the borders of the property, dressed in full riot gear, looking more like soldiers than government agents. Their appearance couldn't have enraged the protesters more if they'd tried.

A man emerged from the bristling cluster and approached the picnic table. He wore a brown suit, well-worn boots, and a broken-down cowboy hat. His calm, fearless manner was enough to part the crowd. He gave Nicole and me a puzzled look, and then I saw the recognition in his eyes. He pointed to the badge clipped to his coat. "I'm Special Agent Rod Adams. What's going on? I thought we'd resolved all this."

"I remember you, Special Agent," Harry said. "Hell if I know what's going on. This bunch of yahoos just showed up. They aren't none of my doing."

The agent nodded. "I told my bosses it was probably something like that. Look, we can end this quickly peacefully. Get these guns out of here. Tell them to go home. Maybe they'll listen to you."

"Why should they?" Vanessa said. "They got a right to defend themselves. They can carry all the guns they want—it's their Second Amendment right."

"Agent Adams is just following orders, dear." Harry put his hand on her shoulder, but she shook him off.

Most of the protesters were openly displaying firearms, either guns in holsters or rifles being carried.

"Maybe we should give them some time, Agent Adams," Harry said. "Let them shout themselves hoarse. They'll most likely go home if you don't provoke them."

"I'd love to do that, Harry, but my bosses are insisting I do something.

"That would be a mistake, Agent Adams. These boys are looking for trouble. With all those guns, someone might get hurt."

"I agree," Adams said. "But see those news cameras over there? They're putting the pressure on."

"The same news cameras that are going to keep you from doing anything," Vanessa said.

Adams looked from Harry to Vanessa as if asking who was in charge. Harry flushed a little but stayed silent.

Adams turned abruptly and looked over at me. "What's *he* doing here?"

Harry looked around, puzzled, as if not sure who Adams was referring to. His gaze passed right over Nicole and me.

Adams nodded in my direction. "That's the man who shot it out with those guys up on Deadfall Ridge."

"Really?" Harry said. "I don't know him. He came with Nicole, who's an old friend of the family."

Adams stepped closer to me. Even through his strong cologne, I could smell the sweat under his bulletproof vest and jacket. "You looking to cause more trouble, Mr. Davis?"

"No, sir. I didn't know any of this was happening. Nicole wanted to visit Mr. Johnson, and I just came along."

Agent Adams looked skeptical. "If you don't have a good reason to be here, maybe you should get going before someone recognizes you."

Vanessa Johnson broke in. "If *you* don't want trouble, Mr. Special Agent, maybe you need to back off. It's your damn uniforms that's riling these folk up. It's like we're in Russia or something."

Adams merely nodded and shrugged. That's when I realized—and from the sudden lull, everyone else realized too—that Special Agent Adams wasn't really in control. No one was. It was as if everything was being dialed up by accident, as if a confrontation was inevitable because both sides were so certain they were right.

I put my hand on Nicole's arm and dared to pull on it slightly. "Let's get out of here." Ordinarily, I wouldn't have dared tried to move her where she didn't want to go, but I could tell things were about to get out of hand. She resisted for a moment, then gave in.

It was about that time that it all went to hell.

It was Nicole who'd insisted on coming. She'd known Harry Johnson since she was a child. Harry and her father had been best friends.

A few wealthy families owned most of the big ranches in the John Day area. A majority of them didn't live there during the off-season, but spent most of their time in Portland or Seattle or New York. They made their money by hiring rough young men who were willing to live in the old broken-down ranch houses or the double-wide trailers during the winter months, who rode their four-wheelers out to round up the cattle, or occasionally mounted up the old-fashioned way on horses they bought for a discount from rodeos. They made sure the livestock was fed no matter how deep the shit or the snow.

The Johnsons were different. They lived on their ranch full-time, didn't usually use four-wheelers, and spent a lot of their time in the saddle. The Johnsons lived the way their forebears had, and that's what got them in trouble. The tradition of burning the fields—and it didn't matter whether they owned the land or were only using it—brought them to the attention of the bureaucrats. The Bureau of Land Management had ignored the technically illegal practice for years, but some young wet-behind-the-ears official fresh out of college called them on it, and instead of apologizing, Harry got his back up and went ahead the next season and burned a few hundred more fallow acres.

Even that might have been ignored, as it had been for decades, except for the recent discovery of a Native American burial site on the Johnson property. The half of the pasture just north of the ranch house was sectioned off with ropes and signs.

Under new scrutiny, the Johnsons were served a cease and desist order on burning, and when Harry wouldn't—or because of Vanessa, couldn't—bend, he was arrested and hauled off to a Eugene jail.

After years of dormancy, the Sagebrush Rebellion was ignited all over again. Not so much by the local ranchers but by people from the outside, who'd been politicized by the internet and who made the Johnsons—against Harry's wishes—into martyrs.

Harry Johnson had already apologized; he was ready to get on with his life. The judge had been lenient. If left alone, the whole thing probably would have blown over. But Vanessa kept right on giving interviews to political websites that only inflamed the situation. Her two older boys took more after her than their father.

Vanessa had sent out a call for help, and a bunch of young men had shown up, looking for trouble.

I desperately wanted to get out of there before it all blew up. But one thing I'd learned about Nicole—she did what she wanted, and she didn't like taking orders from me. Or anyone, for that matter.

We started back down the red gravel driveway, but as we neared the highway, there was a roar of engines, and black smoke billowed out behind a squadron of jacked-up pickups with American and Confederate flags jammed into the corners of the truck beds. They came from the west, which meant they were most likely not locals from John Day. Rather than turn into the driveway, they slammed over the embankments into the north pasture.

Before I could really take it in, Nicole was sprinting in their direction. Nicole is fearless. I knew this because she'd saved my life when she didn't have to. She'd defied men she knew were killers—and this was before we were a couple, when we'd been on exactly one date. I'd sworn from the day I was acquitted that I'd keep out of trouble.

The pickups headed straight for the posts and ropes that sectioned off the Native American burial site. The archeologists had begun a few careful excavations. The hole the highway construction crew had created before discovering what they were digging into had been filled in with loose dirt.

The dirt went flying in heavy brown clouds as the first of the pickups roared over the posts and cut a deep, wide donut in the dirt. Another pickup bounced over the excavations. Something white that looked like bone flew into the air.

"Stop!" Nicole shouted. I could barely hear her over the revving engines. The final two pickups followed their brethren, cutting deep divots in the graveyard.

Nicole ran straight for the nearest pickup, and before I could catch up, she slammed into its door, barely slowing down. The driver jammed on his brakes. Nicole had her key out and was slashing at the paint and adding dents by kicking out with her boots. The door flew open, and Nicole went backward, landing on her ass and sliding a few feet. She jumped up immediately.

I was past her by then, holding out my arms as the driver jumped down from the pickup and marched toward Nicole.

"Whoa!" I shouted. "Just back off, buddy."

"What the fuck?" he roared back. "It's that bitch that needs to back off."

I saw red. That's about all I remember. The next thing I knew, I was crouched over the guy, my fists raised. I'm not sure if I actually hit him or not. He had his arms over his face. Apparently I'd tackled him.

If nothing else, the confrontation had stopped all four pickups from doing further damage. Two of the drivers were smart enough to clatter up the embankment and back onto the highway. They roared off toward the west.

One of the pickups was trying to follow them but was

mired in the soft dirt. The fourth driver was prostrate at my feet when Agent Adams and three other Feds arrived to put him in handcuffs.

By the time I looked around for Nicole, she was halfway to our truck. She hopped into the driver's seat of her old, battered pickup, put both hands on the steering wheel, and glared at the horizon. When I got in, she drove away without a word.

She shushed me several times on the way home, and I finally gave up. As we reached the city limits of John Day, she said, so softly that I could barely hear her, "I'm going back to school. I'm finishing my degree in paleontology."

My heart dropped, and I felt the blood drain from my face. "What about Nelson/Davis Wilderness Tours?"

"You and Granger can keep it going."

"For how long?"

She hesitated, then gave me an apologetic look. "A couple of years if I go for my master's, longer if I go for my doctorate."

"Can't do much with a master's these days," I ventured.

"No," she said. "You really can't."

"So the truth is…you aren't really ever coming back."

She didn't answer. This time, I joined her in silence.

CHAPTER 2

HART DAVIS

I thought the standoff at the Johnson ranch would be the end of it, that Nicole and I would be left alone to sort out our differences. I didn't realize that, three years later, I'd see many of those people again under more dire circumstances, and this time, cooler heads would not prevail.

My lawyer, Marie Jenkins, wants me to write down what happened. I'm sitting in the county jail, reading over the witness statements. Marie is very forthcoming with discovery material.

"Read it all over," she urges. "See if anything stands out. Look for exculpatory context."

"You mean an excuse?"

"Yeah, that. I mean, you are half-hero, half-scapegoat. Let's build up the hero part."

They're calling me "the man in the middle." At least, one of the columnists is. Marie brought in a newspaper, circled the phrase, and said, "That's good. That's very good; we can work with that."

"Write down what happened in your own words," she said. "Don't show it to anyone else, but *try* to appear sympathetic. The camera likes you already, but try to back it up with words. I might be able to get one of the national magazines to publish it. But keep down the polemics, OK?"

So here's my excuse: I never intended to be part of any takeover or occupation.

I know the jury will have no reason to believe me, except through my subsequent actions, but I honestly thought it was going to be a peaceful protest. No one was more surprised than me when guns were drawn.

Believe it or not, I stayed to keep the whole thing from spiraling out of control.

I stayed because I thought I could do some good. Truth is, I was never a true believer in the cause. I had already begun to suspect that my anger toward the IRS and the government came as much from my breakup with Nicole as it did for any legal actions taken toward me. I'm not sure what I was thinking—it was just about the worst way in the world to try to win her back.

But I'd already backed away from the Eastern Oregon Freedom Coalition in the months previous to the takeover. If my car hadn't broken down, if the IRS hadn't just taken every cent I had, I might not have hitched a ride when the EOFC announced they were heading to the John Day Fossil Beds National Monument.

I stayed because Nicole refused to leave and I thought I might be able to protect her. Whether that was a good decision, you'll have to decide.

But I'm also guilty. Guilty of being an idiot. Of being the kind of guy who couldn't take no from a woman and tried too hard to win her back. Who fell in with the wrong folks even though a part of me was telling me the whole time that it was a terribly stupid idea.

I'm writing this account for Nicole, to try to explain myself, to try to excuse the inexcusable. I'm going to tell the whole truth and nothing but the truth. (Though I doubt that's what my lawyer really wants.)

The following account is compiled not only from my own experience, but also from public testimony, media interviews, and trial transcripts. These are the first-person accounts of those who were there, including me.

It's up to me to tell the story. I'm probably the only one who can piece together what really happened.

CHAPTER 3

NICOLE NELSON

Garth Perkins found me in working in my office, which was filled with papers and fossils and smelled of sun-warmed dust. He was there to save me.

"Someone's been digging in the north quadrant," he said. He made it sound urgent, as if war had been declared. "I need you, Nicole."

I sighed. "I'd love to, but my shift starts in ten minutes."

Garth stared at me, and I realized that the top of my shirt was unbuttoned. I knew he had a thing for me, but I'd told him I was taken. Which wasn't quite true. It was over between Hart and me, but the little lie didn't quite seem like a lie if there was still a chance we might get back together.

If only Hart hadn't given me that ultimatum.

"Let Ashley take your shift," Garth said. "I'm your boss, right?"

"Well…technically," I allowed. He was senior paleontologist at the John Day Fossil Beds National Monument. I was supposed to be his assistant, but there really wasn't enough for me to do, so I helped out at Merriam Hall, the official visitor center, whenever I was needed. "I'll see if Ashley's around."

It would be good to get out onto the desert. This late in the season, it was starting to cool off. There were rain clouds on the horizon.

Garth followed me out the door as I surreptitiously buttoned my shirt to the top. After wearing it all summer, the tan ranger shirt was finally softening up. I'd be sorry to leave it behind, but it was my last year before—hopefully—getting my doctorate. It was unlikely I'd be assigned to the John Day Fossil Beds again.

I put on my round green ranger's hat. It always gave me a little bit of thrill, wearing the uniform. It was what I'd always dreamed of, though I'd put it off for a few years to take over my father's wilderness guide business when he'd had a stroke. That's when I'd met Hart.

The two of us had combined our businesses, and I'd been happy enough, especially with Hart—but there was always something missing. I was disappointed when Hart didn't back me up on my plans to go back to school.

Garth and I stopped at the office of the big boss, Perry Campbell, who was dressed in a suit and tie even though there was a good chance that not a single tourist would see him all day.

"Sure. I'll get one of the other girls to watch the counter," Perry said when I asked if someone could take my shift. His face went slack for a moment, and he caught himself. "Women, I mean." We'd been given a lecture by a senior ranger at the beginning of the season about how to address each other.

I smiled. It had never bothered me to be called "girl," but I appreciated the effort. And I knew it legitimately pissed off some women.

Garth led the way out the door. He was wearing his ranger's clothes—technically. His hat was turned up on one side, Aussie style, and he'd added a strap. His tan shirt was so pale from repeated washings that it was almost white. He wore dungarees rather than ranger slacks, and heavy boots with his cuffs tucked in. With his jangling pack, laden with tools, and his beard, he looked more like an old-time gold miner than a park ranger. Perry had tried to get him to shape up, and Garth would try, but a week later, he'd be back to his slovenly self.

Jessica was still on duty, and she looked stressed. A teenager was leaning over the counter with a grin on his face.

"So where are the dinosaurs?"

"No dinosaurs," Jessica said.

The teenager tried again. "Come on...you got a T-rex here?"

"We don't have *any* dinosaurs, sir. Oregon was under water

at the time. Mammals only."

"Mammals?" The kid pushed back his hat and scratched his head, looking around in dismay. "Who the hell cares about mammals?"

"Well…they are *big* mammals," Jessica said.

I knew how Jessica felt. I got really sick of questions like that. As if the only fossils that counted were freaking dinosaurs. It's a thrill to open a rock and find a leaf or a shell, but some people don't get that.

"No dinosaurs? Well, that sucks."

I could tell my fellow ranger was about to say something she'd regret. Jessica could be blunt.

I paused by the desk, letting Garth go on ahead. "Have you seen the saber-tooth tiger yet?"

The teenager hesitated, then decided to take an interest. "No, where's that at?"

I waved to Jessica and kept going. Garth was already making his way around the side of the parking lot. For being overcast and late in the season, it was a relatively busy day. I tried not to look anyone in the eye, knowing from past experience that if I made eye contact, I'd be asked questions. Garth was getting ahead of me. He was overweight, but after traipsing up and down the Painted Hills, he was also in good shape.

Garth would make an interesting boyfriend. He was funny and geeky, and even-tempered. But, despite everything, I wasn't over Hart. It wasn't me who had ended it. He couldn't seem to get over my "abandoning" our wilderness guide business, though I'd told him that I'd help whenever possible. For him, it was all or nothing.

I'd gotten a message from him that morning but erased it without looking at it. To keep on nurturing the relationship if he wasn't going to bend would only break my heart—again.

We reached the wooden walkway that wound through the colorful ravines. There were tourists at first, but the higher we climbed, the fewer we encountered. Garth didn't slow down, and I found myself huffing.

"So when's your boyfriend going to visit?" Garth asked. "Summer's almost over."

"I told him not to come."

"Man, if it was me, nothing would keep me away."

He stepped off the walkway and into a narrow cleft, at the end of which someone had started digging a hole.

"Can you believe it? As if they would find any fossils here." Garth shook his head.

"Why'd you bring me up here, Garth? It looks like they gave up."

"Oh, I just thought you'd like to get away from the tourists for a while."

I laughed. "I like to help out the other girls when I can."

Garth grinned back. "You mean *women*, don't you?"

I realized he was standing awfully close. I moved to one side as if suddenly interested in something on the ground. Once I started the motion, I really did notice something unusual.

It was a chunk of dry red mud, but there was something black and almost square embedded inside. I brushed off the encrusted mud.

"Is this what I think it is?"

Garth nearly snatched it out of my hands.

"Man, oh, man, I think it is! Dude! I can't believe it! I'll bet you anything it's an Ekgmowechashala!"

He pronounced it *Ig-a-moo-we-cha-sha-la*. I'd never said the name aloud, only read it in papers. The *Ig-a-whatever* was a primate—a squirrel-sized lemur that had preceeded humans on this continent. Its remains had only been found once before, in 1997.

"You got your doctorate, baby!" Garth said, wrapping me in a bear hug. There was nothing sexual about it, so I returned the hug.

By the time we got back to Merriam Hall, it was dark. Perry was locking up his office to go home, but when he saw what we had, he turned on the lights, and we gathered the employees who were still around and had a party. Perry even allowed us to get drunk.

I went to bed that night with my head spinning, knowing in my heart, without a doubt, that I'd made the right choice to go back to school.

If only Hart could see it that way…

CHAPTER 4

HART DAVIS

The ranch house was old and worn, paint peeling off the corners, a dry, musty smell coming off the exposed wood. The porch steps were rickety, and the front door barely opened because it was so warped. It was a working ranch. Cowboy boots, mud, and motor oil weren't gentle on surfaces. The mudroom was dusty, the grooves of the flooring clotted with mud.

But like an earthly airlock, the rooms beyond were pristine and shiny. The dark wood glowed along the walls; the floors were smooth from generations of socks and slippers. It was cool and dark inside, as if we'd been transported to another time and place. It was a reminder to me that, despite the modesty of their homes' exteriors, some of these Eastern Oregon ranchers were anything but poor.

Lois Carpenter met us in the living room and motioned for us to sit on the white sofas and chairs despite our dirty jeans and T-shirts. There were portraits of pioneer families on the walls. I had little doubt that they were Lois's forebears.

I'd expected a little old woman, radicalized by radio and TV. Instead, she was a striking, willowy woman in her midforties, long dark hair with small streaks of white at the temples. She was also dressed in jeans and a tight T-shirt, but they had been bought in a downtown boutique for more money than I currently had in my bank account.

"So you boys are on your way," she said. Her voice was deep and husky, with a rasp as if she'd already smoked three packs of cigarettes that day.

"Yes, ma'am."

I was a little surprised that it was Peter Sterns who answered her. He was the youngest of us: a real cowboy with shit-kicker boots, a battered cowboy hat, and a Western drawl to his voice.

Lois tilted her head a little and said, "Let me guess, you're from Boston."

Peter blushed and turned away.

"Don't tease the boy, Lois," Jim Marston said. "He's on our side."

Marston was our leader, if we had one. He owned a string of used car lots in the small towns east of the Cascade Mountains. He'd lost so many campaigns for Wheeler County commissioner that it was embarrassing, and all because he'd been denied a zoning change for his lot in La Grande.

"We're going to take it to 'em, ma'am," Jules Francisco piped up in his high voice. A scrawny little man with a prominent Adam's apple and buggy eyes, he was Marston's sidekick, the one who made himself a nuisance at the county commission meetings.

Jerry Johnson and his pal, Brad Patterson, sat on the sofa, eyeing Lois curiously. The only reason I'd even met the members of the Eastern Oregon Freedom Coalition was because of Jerry, who'd remembered my visit to his parents' ranch during the standoff with the Feds three years before. Brad was a Johnson ranch hand who'd come along to keep Jerry out of trouble, if that was possible. Jerry took after Vanessa Johnson and was a bit of a rabble-rouser.

Off in the corner was John Carver, a tall and silent type, who was rumored to have had a past romance with Lois. Meanwhile, it was obvious Mark Simons would have loved to have a past— any kind of past—with Lois. A quiet, chubby man, he couldn't keep his eyes off her.

"I'm going to regret this, aren't I?" Lois said. "Put seven good old boys under the same roof and you got trouble. But now that you're here…you boys can use the sofas and chairs or camp out on the floor."

"We're going to take back the Fossil Beds Monument, Mrs. Carpenter," Jerry said.

Lois was heading out of the room, to get the blankets, I suppose, but at this, she turned around. "You know, they hanged the lady who owned the rooming house where the Lincoln assassination was planned."

Whoa.

"It's nothing like that, Mrs. Carpenter," I said. "It's a peaceful protest."

"You taking your guns along?"

None of us spoke for a moment. Then Jules said, "Oh, well."

"Yeah, I thought so. Good luck with the 'peaceful' part."

She stood stock-still for a few moments, and I figured we were going to be back on the street but finally she nodded and left the room without another word.

I snagged one of the couches, falling onto it fully clothed, thinking I'd fall asleep instantly. Instead, like every other night, I couldn't help but think about Nicole.

I don't remember who suggested the John Day Fossil Beds National Monument as the site of our protest, but it may have been my idea. The Fossil Beds were where Nicole was working her last summer before receiving her doctorate. We'd broken up. She wasn't answering my phone calls anymore. I'd been an idiot, given her an ultimatum, and she'd called me on it.

I wasn't in a great frame of mind. I blamed it on my problems with taxes, not recognizing that I was angry at Nicole. She didn't know about my tax problems—*our* tax problems, because she was still a partner in Nelson/Davis Wilderness Tours—because I hadn't told her. I'd made the mistake of letting my former wife do the taxes, which she'd assured me she could handle.

I didn't know that she was the White Widow then—and the White Widow *don't do taxes.*

At the end of the last hunting season, I'd borrowed Granger's Harley and started traveling around the West, attending foreclosures of ranches and making a nuisance of myself. That's where I'd met the Eastern Oregon Freedom Coalition.

As with every night, the more I tried not to think about Nicole, the more I saw her in my dreams. It was no use. I was wide-awake.

A soft light came from the kitchen. I got up and headed that way. Behind me, Patterson got off the floor and took my couch. Fair enough. I hadn't called dibs.

Lois sat at the small table in the corner, drinking coffee and smoking a cigarette. The ashtray, in the shape of a horseshoe, was full of butts. It was a completely modern kitchen, angular and flowing, with bright blue trim and an industrial design. Sticking out among all the modern equipment was an old wood stove, probably the hippest thing of all.

She looked up at me as I entered. "I can't sleep since Mathew died," she said. "Too damn hollow a house. Not haunted…the opposite of haunted, like it's been abandoned."

"Huh," I said.

She smiled tiredly. "Another talkative guy."

"Sorry. I never know what to say when someone dies."

She pointed to the chair opposite her, and I sat down.

"It happened two years ago," Lois replied. "I'm getting over it." She got up and poured me a cup of coffee. Even though I usually drown my coffee in flavored creamer, I drank it black. *No sleep tonight.*

"Whose idea was it to go to the Fossil Beds?" she asked.

"Pardon?"

"Your little protest. Because John Carver and the other boys couldn't scrape two ideas together with a shovel."

"I may have said something…"

"Well, you'd better be sure you want to do it," she said. "You could all end up in jail."

"I keep hearing them say, 'The tree of liberty must be refreshed…'"

She broke in, "'With the blood of patriots,' yadda yadda. Did you ever hear the next line?"

I shook my head.

"'It is its natural manure,'" she finished. "Jefferson got that right. It's pure bullshit."

"They're about to take my business," I said.

"So pay your damn taxes."

"With what?" My voice was loud enough that I heard some-one moan "Shut the fuck up!" from the living room.

Lois was less than sympathetic. "Boo hoo, you're broke.

Aren't we all? As you guys are fond of saying to the less fortu-
nate, get a job."

I felt the anger rising, but I pushed it down. I was a guest,
and I was tired, and this woman had taken us in. "This isn't
about me," I said.

"Oh, right."

She stubbed out her cigarette and stood, the chair making a squealing sound on the tile floor. "I think I'll try to sleep.
Thanks for filling the hollow for a while."

I stood too. "We really appreciate you taking us in, Lois.
Truly."

"You're welcome," she said. "But forget you were ever here."

I finished my coffee, trying to shake off the bad feeling I'd
gotten from the encounter. She'd seemed so disdainful, though
I knew that she was the money behind our little group. She'd
made it sound like I was some kind of tax dodger, unwilling to
pay my way.

I could ask Nicole for help. *Hell, no. This is my problem.*

Back in my sleeping bag, on the floor, I was sure I wouldn't
be able to sleep, but somehow I drifted off.

CHAPTER 5

MARK SIMONS

All the way to the Fossil Beds, I wondered if I should say something. To this day, I still don't understand why I didn't. It would have been so easy, and I think it might have changed everything. The guys would have been on the lookout; they might have even saved me from myself.

Yeah, but that never happens. I'm on my own; always have been.

The night before, I'd watched Hart Davis go into Lois's kitchen and overheard them talking in low voices. I really wanted to join them, but I've never been any good at joining conversations. Always awkward, that. I got up and approached the doorway, then hung back and listened.

"Forget you were ever here," I heard Lois say finally, and then silence. My heart sank, even though she wasn't saying it to me.

She hadn't recognized me at all when we arrived. After all the times I'd trailed along with Carver when he came to visit. She'd always smiled at me, then ignored me. Didn't matter. I'd felt high being near her, enough to daydream for months. Just looking at her made my heart swell.

That may have been a few years ago, but hell, my looks hadn't changed all *that* much. I was a little heavier and had a little less hair and a goatee, but you'd have thought she'd at least know who the hell I was.

I stepped back into the shadows when Davis came out of the kitchen, then waited until he'd rolled up in his sleeping bag.

I went through the kitchen and down the hallway. Lois's door was partly open, and I nearly went in. Shit, I don't know what I was thinking. She'd have probably screamed "Rape!" at the sight of me. Then again, knowing what I know now, maybe not.

She was talking to someone, so I hesitated to knock.

"Yeah, Hart Davis," she was saying. "The Strawberry Mountain Killer. He didn't seem that imposing to me, but we shouldn't underestimate him. From what I've heard, he was up against some ex-Special Forces types. I'll keep an eye on him."

A short pause.

"I couldn't talk them out of it. I think they're going to muck it up."

She was talking about us. I stepped back another couple of inches, and a floorboard creaked. I held my breath, but she kept talking. "I'll keep an eye out. You know, this might be for the best. We were looking for a trigger event. Depending on how stupid these idiots are, this might just be it."

Silence. I could hear my own heavy breathing and tried to hold it in, but then I gasped for breath even louder. She still didn't hear me and spoke right over my huffing.

"Hell if I know why they picked the Fossil Beds. Has to be more than a coincidence. Someone might have said something around Carver when he was here. Maybe he gave the others the idea by accident.

"I'll give it a couple of days and then scoot on up there. Pretend to be Little Miss Helper." There was a pause, and then she laughed. "I am, aren't I? Anyway, give them time to set up, see what happens, maybe nudge it along. Meanwhile, you guys get ready. When I give you the go-ahead, come on in with everything you got."

A long silence, then, "Yeah, love you too."

I heard her taking off her clothes, humming to herself. I fought temptation for a moment, then put my eye to the opening. I managed not to gasp. She was beautiful in the dim light, slender, with small but full breasts and long legs. She lay down on the bed and put her hands between her legs.

I stepped back, managed to avoid the creaking floorboard,

and got back to the living room without anyone noticing.

It was hard to sleep that night, trying to make sense of what she'd said. I knew that it had sounded suspicious. I also knew that she'd said "I love you" to someone else. It was only then that I realized I'd been harboring some kind of illusion that with John Carver no longer in the picture, I had a chance.

Maybe that's why I didn't say anything. I was pissed. Not at Lois, though that's who I should have been pissed at, but at everyone else. Men like Davis, who could have a conversation with her.

So I kept it to myself, and Lois got her way, and we all got screwed.

CHAPTER 6

HART DAVIS

I didn't pay much attention to my friends' chatter on the way to the Fossil Beds. I was busy rehearsing what I was going to say to Nicole. A simple apology wouldn't be enough. I'd known she was strong-willed from the moment I met her. She was the only reason I'd survived my jam in the Strawberry Mountains. I'd been hunted by skilled mercenaries, and she'd help lay down a false trail to lead them away from me, risking her own life.

I should have known that I couldn't make demands of her. I'd made the classic mistake of trying to change the one I loved—I could see that now. I needed to make her believe that I'd seen the error of my ways and that I was willing to support her with whatever she needed.

Words wouldn't be enough. I'd have to follow through. I would let go of my hunting guide business, if need be. I'd go wherever she went, be a house husband if that's what it took. After all, wherever we ended up, I could learn the territory and start all over again.

But without Nicole, none of it mattered.

I was slowly waking up to the realization that I'd confused my anger toward the IRS with my feelings toward Nicole. I'd been angry, and when the chance came to express anger toward something—anything—I took it. I felt self-righteous for a few days or weeks, and joined up with some people whom I really didn't agree with on most things. It didn't take long before I realized that I couldn't go as far as these guys in my political views. They didn't know that. I simply stopped attending meetings or responding to posts on Facebook.

I hitched up with them for the trip to the Fossil Beds, because I needed a ride to get to Nicole, to explain things to her and ask for her forgiveness. Obviously, that's not how it worked out. In fact, I couldn't have done anything worse.

I grew progressively more nervous the closer we got to the Fossil Beds. The political arguments in the van were getting heated. It wasn't so much that my companions disagreed—they were spouting the same talking points they heard every day on the radio, saw TV and online. But they were unsure about how to express their displeasure with the government. Jules sounded like he wanted to shoot it out with the Feds and die a martyr. But I figured the others had more sense.

I knew that a couple of them—Jim Marston and Jerry Johnson especially—had been radicalized, but I didn't think they'd do anything about it. Jim always struck me as a big talker, and Jerry was young, just spouting whatever he heard his mother say. I didn't realize that they thought it was a spiritual crusade, that the world would turn on their actions.

It was all background noise to my thoughts.

I wish now that I'd been listening a little closer.

The scenery brought me out of my funk. The Ochoco Mountains were beautiful this time of year, in full evergreen glory. We passed a couple of meadows with herds of deer grazing like cattle. In another month, hunting season would begin and the animals would escape into the higher elevations. We crossed over the pass and down into the dry Eastern Oregon canyons. Two pointed buttes came into view as we came around the last corner, seeming taller than they were against the flat landscape.

We passed through the little town of Mitchell, which had recently suffered one of the periodic flash floods that curved down the narrow valley. Tents spotted the hillside—a portent of what was to come. We stopped for soda, and as soon as we stepped out of the car, the heat of midday blasted us. It had rained the night before, so there was an unusual fog of humidity rising from the pavement.

The eastern part of the state isn't what people think of when they think of Oregon. It's dry and unpopulated, and what few people do live there are conservative and rural. I was a confirmed desert rat—I loved the dryness, the juniper trees, and the sagebrush. I felt a pang at this thought, because I knew there was a good chance that if…*if*…Nicole took me back, we'd be moving away. She'd be at the beck and call of the same federal government we were on our way to protest.

I started to wonder how I could get out of the protest, which was bound to cause trouble.

That ought to go over well with Nicole.

I felt a little queasy at the thought. Maybe I'd hang back, not really be part of it. My anger over my tax situation seemed less important now. I was starting to admit that much of it was my own fault. Because of my anger at Nicole, the government had been an easy target.

We started to pass the exit into the Painted Hills section of the national monument, still a good distance away from the visitor center. Jules Francisco slowed down the van and started to turn.

"What are you doing?" Marston asked.

"I've never been here, man," Jules said.

"You've lived in John Day your whole life and you've never seen the Painted Hills?'" Simons said.

Jules hunched over stubbornly and kept turning onto the road. "Never had no reason, but as long as we're here…"

"I wouldn't mind seeing them again," I said. *Anything to avoid the inevitable confrontation with Nicole.*

Brad Patterson was following us in his pickup, with Jerry Johnson as his passenger. I looked out the back window in time to see him slam on the brakes, swerve, and almost miss the turnoff.

As the rolling hills came into view, I was glad we'd made the detour. The rains had deepened their colors, and the bright sunshine seemed to find every little change of texture. It was as if the hand of God had poured down mountains of colored sand and swirled them into layers. No one said anything, but once we got out of the car, no one was in a hurry to leave either.

I walked by myself up the wooden walkway to the first viewing site.

If only Nicole would come back to the Strawberry Mountains, we could have views like this every day.

I sat there until Jules honked the horn below me.

Reluctantly, I rejoined my friends. I had a strange feeling that everything was going to go wrong. I wish now that I'd stayed on that wooden bench, maybe hitched a ride into John Day with some of the tourists. I wasn't ready to face Nicole, and certainly not with my nutty friends along.

I should have listened to my instincts.

It all went to hell in those first few minutes.

The Thomas Condon Paleontology Center was relatively new. The last time I'd visited, the headquarters had still been in the old James Cant ranch house, with tiny rooms and a musty odor. This new place still had some rough edges, as if the construction wasn't quite finished, and the landscaping, such as it was, still had some ways to go before it would be attractive.

Merriam Hall, the visitor center, was a modern structure that looked almost like an A-frame, with concrete statues of extinct animals and stone benches lining the covered walkway to the front doors. It had rained the night before, and there were puddles in the desert sand, but the morning sun was already drying the ground.

We piled out of the van and the pickup. That's when I saw Jim Marston and Jules Francisco pull out pistols. Brad Patterson and Jerry Johnson lifted rifles out of the back of the truck.

The moment seemed to last forever, as if I was seeing my whole future.

Then I started running. They were already entering the visitor center before I could reach them. From the corner of my eye, I saw tourists recording the event on their cellphones. A few of the more prudent parents were hurrying their kids to their cars.

We're already screwed, I thought. *No matter what happens next.*

I'd known my companions were bringing weapons along, but that wasn't uncommon among Eastern Oregon ranchers. I grew up seeing a gun rack in the back window of every pickup.

It had simply never occurred to me that they might actually carry them inside.

I slammed into the automatic doors, which were opening too slowly for me. I backed away, embarrassed, and waited for them to slide open. By the time I entered the cool air of the lobby, Jim Marston was marching up to the front counter, followed by Jules, who had his gun pointed at the ceiling, as if he was going to fire a warning shot.

Please, God, don't do that.

Nicole was behind the counter, wearing her green-and-tan ranger uniform. She was a little puzzled, not yet understanding what was happening. She's small and blonde, a little chubby, but pleasingly so. Despite working in the desert all summer, her skin was still pale. The moment I saw her face, I wanted it all to stop. With a sinking heart, I saw her flush, then, as the implications of what was happening struck, I watched her already white skin turn even whiter. She looked over Marston's shoulder toward the entrance, and her eyes passed over me—at first. Then her gaze rocketed back to mine with an expression of "What the fuck?"

"We reclaim this land!" Marston shouted. "In the name of the American people!"

The words didn't make any sense. For a second, I thought it was a joke. It sounded ridiculous, like Wyatt Earp putting an end to a barroom brawl. The revolver in Marston's hand seemed too heavy for him to hold steady.

"What the hell are you doing?" I shouted, sliding to the stop in front of Marston, almost losing my balance. It probably appeared comical to the shocked tourists. A young family was staring at us in alarm. The father grabbed his kids around the shoulders and guided them out the door, the mother acting as rearguard, looking scared.

"Get out of my way, Davis," Marston said. "You knew this was coming."

"The hell I did!" My mind was spinning through the last couple of days, wondering how I could have missed the signs. "I thought this was going to be a peaceful protest!"

Jules laughed shakily. He seemed both excited and scared.

His Adam's apple seemed to be trying to escape his throat. "As if that would do any good. We're giving this place back to the people who should have it."

By now, the other members of the Eastern Oregon Freedom Coalition had entered. All of them had guns.

All but me.

"So you're giving the land back to the Native Americans?" Nicole asked in a far steadier voice than I would have thought possible.

"What?" Jules asked. "What do you mean?"

Nicole just laughed. Jules turned red, and I thought I saw his finger tighten a little on the trigger.

A scream came from one of the side rooms, and I jumped.

Nicole finally looked me square in the face, her expression neutral. It was as if she didn't know me.

"That's a saber-tooth tiger," she said. "Or what we think one sounded like."

Now that I was attuned to the sounds, there was a cacophony of animal noises coming from the darkened display rooms that ringed the lobby. Somehow, what was happening was completely appropriate. Nature, tooth and claw…and guns.

"Nicole. I didn't know. I'm sorry."

She raised her chin slightly and looked away. Her shrug made me want to go behind the counter, grab her by the shoulders, and shake some sense into her. Then I realized how that would sit with her.

Having made his proclamation, Jim Marston stood there awkwardly, as if uncertain what to do next. Nicole decided for him. She lifted a microphone from the counter. Her voice came over the speakers.

"Visiting hours are suspended temporarily. Please exit the visitor center as swiftly as possible. Our apologies if you have traveled a long way to get here, but I'm sure the situation will be quickly resolved."

She set down the microphone and turned to Marston. "Right?"

Jules answered instead. "Not until you give the land back to us."

"And how do we do that?" Nicole asked. "What exactly do you expect us to do?"

"Well…give us the keys," Jules said, "and get out."

Nicole laughed again and flung out her arms in an expansive gesture. "This place is open to everyone already. So what you're saying is that you're going to lock people out?"

"Maybe…a bunch of…Mexicans. Easterners. People who don't belong here."

I thought she was going to jump over the counter and grab Marston's gun.

Before I could move, the door at the back of Merriam Hall opened. A tall older man in a tweed suit marched with long strides to the counter. He stood next to Nicole and put a calming hand on her shoulder.

His voice was surprising deep. "I'm Perry Campbell, director of the Thomas Condon Paleontology Center. What's going on here?"

Marston looked scared, as if suddenly realizing how much trouble we were in. "We're reclaiming everything you-all took. This place, the Painted Hills…all of it."

"You already own it. This national monument already belongs to the people," Campbell said.

"Don't give me that crap. You Feds don't belong here," Marston said. "The federal government isn't supposed to own land. It's in the Constitution."

"How about we talk this over in my office?" Campbell's voice was reasonable, calm. For a few seconds, I thought it was all going to be resolved, that Marston and Campbell would come to an agreement. Maybe the authorities would overlook the guns. After all, no one had made a threat yet, and open carry was common enough in Eastern Oregon to be an excuse.

"You'd like that, wouldn't you?" Jules said. Marston looked as if he was trying to quiet his friend, but Jules wasn't having it. "Tell us a bunch of lies and then arrest us."

That's when Campbell came around the counter and it all went sideways. He loomed over the smaller man. "Leave now and we won't press charges."

I doubted that was up to the director, but I kept quiet.

"You're crazy, man," Jules said.

Perry raised his eyebrows, as if to say, *I'm not the crazy one here*. He put out his hand. "Give me the gun. I can tell you don't want to hurt anyone."

Jules glanced at Marston. With a quick movement, Campbell swept the gun out of his hand.

I was surprised. The director didn't seem like the hero type. More like a professor, with his horn-rimmed glasses and tweed coat.

Jules turned red. I think if he'd had the gun then, he would have shot Perry dead. Instead, Jim Marston marched over and pointed his pistol at Campbell's forehead.

"Give it back."

Damn and hell. We're screwed.

Perry hesitated for a long moment, then let the revolver swing down on the trigger guard and slowly extended his hand.

Jules snatched the gun back. "Fuck you, man. Don't try doing that again."

Perry shrugged and walked back behind the counter. In a low voice, I heard him say, "Get out of here, Nicole. Don't argue with me."

"I'm sorry, Perry. I've seen guys like these before. I'm not leaving the Fossil Beds to their tender mercies."

"I'll stay," Perry said. "I'll make sure they behave." He turned to Marston. "I assume we aren't hostages here."

Marston shook his head as if trying to clear it. I suddenly realized that he'd never really expected this to happen and hadn't thought past that first dramatic declaration.

"Of course you're not hostages," I said, seizing my chance. "You and your staff are free to leave."

Marston looked relieved that I'd taken the decision out of his hands. *We can still get out of this, as long as no one is threatened.* I gave Nicole an imploring look, but her expression only hardened.

"I'm not going anywhere," she said.

I stepped around the counter and grabbed Nicole's arm. "Don't be stubborn. Let's go."

She followed me for about four feet, then stopped cold.

"I'm not leaving. I don't trust these guys not to make a mess of things."

"They've got guns, Nicole!" Every instinct I had told me that now was the time to get out. "Someone's bound to do something stupid."

"All the more reason to stay. Someone needs to take care of the place."

We stared into each other's eyes. For the first time, she didn't seem angry with me. "You can go, Hart. You aren't part of this, I know that much."

She couldn't have said anything that would have stiffened my resolve more.

"I'm not leaving without you," I heard myself say.

And that's how it happened. I figured it would all blow over within a day or two.

But I couldn't shake the image of Jim Marston pointing his gun at Perry Campbell's head.

CHAPTER 7

HART DAVIS

Merriam Hall was cleared of tourists within the hour. The rest of the rangers and staff, about fifteen employees altogether, were convinced to go home. They packed up and left by midafternoon; everyone except Campbell and Garth Perkins, the staff paleontologist, who both refused to leave Nicole.

I couldn't see any way of getting them to leave without pointing guns at them.

It became clear that neither of the two rangers knew about my relationship with Nicole, and for some reason, we both kept quiet about it. I was already planning to be a middleman, someone who could negotiate for both sides. Nicole must have had her own reasons for keeping quiet. Maybe she was embarrassed; I don't know.

Marston and I went off behind Merriam Hall to argue it out. It was a barren place, littered with chunks of concrete left over from the construction that no one had bothered to pick up, even a length of rebar or two. It felt more like the desert than the desert did. There was some kind of weird stuff piled up almost in dunes, chalky green. I tried to poke my fingers into it and found that it was rock hard, though it looked soft. There were mounds of the stuff, like melted mint ice cream.

The hills were colorful, even outside the Painted Hills. Sheep Rock loomed over Merriam Hall, a rocky pinnacle, with greens and reds and browns and yellow layers below. There was green farmland in the little valley, which contrasted with the grey-green sagebrush and juniper trees.

I remember the smell of fresh-cut timber. The visitor center was a few years old, but it felt new. The fancy architecture was out of place there.

The John Day River was a half a mile east, with the highway running in between. The road ran through a valley, starting at Picture Gorge and passing on through the towns of Fossil and Spray. The building was nestled between low hills, filled with high yellow cheat grass and low-lying sagebrush, spotted with scraggly juniper trees. There was a brick enclosure around the center, almost like a defensive wall.

There was a flagpole with an American flag near the doorway, and—ironically—stickers on the door saying "No Firearms."

"We've got to get the park rangers to leave," Marston said. He looked scared and excited. He knew that he'd blown it by pointing his weapon at the director. But he was also standing straight, as if proud of himself.

"Believe me," I said, "if I could get them to go, I would. I don't think they'll leave until we do."

"This is bad. They'll be watching us. They're going to testify against us someday."

I felt a bit of a chill at that, right there in the shade of the building—which really didn't protect us from the heat at all. It was hot that first day, and I think that's what made the cold that night so much more…cold. The mud from the previous day's rain had already dried, leaving a layer of dirt that cracked when you walked on it, and seemed to turn instantly into dust.

"If they see us being respectful, it might count in our favor," I said.

"Respectful?" Marston laughed. "You don't know Jules and Brad and the rest like I do. They're a bunch of yahoos. They'll be busting things up before you know it. And that's before the military types start showing up."

"So we stop them."

Marston gave me a suspicious look. "They're impressed with you because of what you did up in the Strawberry Mountains. Like somehow that means you know stuff. But I think that's bullshit. I think you got lucky."

"You're probably right," I said.

Marston kept talking. "These people work for the federal government, Hart. They aren't on our side. They're going to spy on us, and they're going to talk to outsiders, and it's going to be one big mess. Let's keep it simple. We kick everyone out, take over the place, and stay until we make our point. We stay until they let us go without charges."

"That isn't going to happen," I said. "We're in for it now. We're in over our heads. We're all going to jail."

"No, we aren't. The Feds are afraid of us, afraid of setting off a revolution. They'll wait us out."

"Marston…you pointed a gun at a man's head. Do you even know if they have security cameras here?"

From the way the blood drained from his face, he obviously hadn't thought of that. Then he shook his head stubbornly. "They'll give in when they see how many people come to our side."

"God, I hope not," I said. "I don't think this place can handle too many more people. It's the fucking desert, Marston."

"Yeah, well, we'll call for help. Believe me, they'll be coming from everywhere."

I shivered again. As soon as he said it, I knew it was true. It wouldn't be long before word got out and every yahoo from miles around started showing up.

I didn't realize that Marston had big plans. That he thought he was George Washington and this was the new revolution. If I'd understood his grandiose plans, I'd have grabbed Nicole, thrown her over my shoulder, and marched on out of there.

But I was still in my little bubble, not realizing how the rest of the world would see our little rebellion.

That first night at the Fossil Beds, we froze our asses off. We had come in our street clothes. Jerry Johnson didn't even have a coat. I was wearing a fleece-lined vest.

I slept in the back seat of the van, and I don't think I've ever been that cold. Ever. I shivered all night, slipping in and out of a thin blanket of sleep. I didn't know that the yahoos were already at work. John Carver was breaking up furniture from

Merriam Hall, burning it in a giant bonfire in the parking lot.

We started off on the wrong foot and never did get back on the right one. But everyone was excited. Most were certain that we were going to be attacked at any time—that feeling never did go away. But those first protesters were giving each other hugs, telling each other how much they loved each other and how great they all were for standing up to the FBI.

"They'll back off," Patterson said. "They'll see, we're good people."

First thing in the morning, I went into the visitor center. Nicole was standing behind the counter as if it was a normal day. She flushed when she saw me, and then shook her head ever so slightly. If I didn't know her, I probably wouldn't have caught it.

I turned around and went back out.

I thought the takeover would last a couple of days, maybe a week. By early that afternoon, people started showing up, some of them with guns. Most of them were locals looking for excitement, but a few of them were hardcore believers in the cause— whatever that was.

At first, there were more news people than protesters. They were clustered on a slight rise in the road near the roadblocks, with telephoto lenses. Jules sat on a lawn chair in full view, blanket on his lap, rifle on the blanket, battered cowboy hat scrunched down over his forehead. He became the face of the rebellion.

I decided it was my job to keep things calm, to make sure that neither side did anything drastic. The occupiers were accepting me as one of them, and I was careful to keep my doubts to myself. To be quite honest, I was more worried about law enforcement; that they would take a simple occupation and turn it into a bloodbath. But I figured the FBI's aggressive tactics had burned the Bureau in previous confrontations and that they'd hold off this time.

But the longer we were there, the more could go wrong. Especially when everyone was armed. The thing about weapons is they tend to get used.

That second night, as soon as it got dark, I went back to

Merriam Hall. Nicole was sitting on one of the couches, watching a TV that someone had installed in the lobby. Half the occupiers were there, doing the same thing. No one seemed to notice when she got up and went toward the back of the room, toward her office. She gave me a tiny wave, and I followed.

She shared the office with Garth. I liked the place a lot. The walls were lined with bookshelves, with a ton of Western-type knick-knacks: arrowheads and wooden statues of Native Americans, cowboys on bucking broncos, a Billy the Kid toy, his right boot up on a coffin, looking mean and gripping a Winchester.

I felt immediately at home. Until I looked into Nicole's eyes.

CHAPTER 8

NICOLE NELSON

After the initial confrontation, a strange uncertainty filled the air. Now that they'd actually taken over the place, the occupiers didn't seem to know what to do. We were all in shock that first night, both the occupiers and the occupied. I went back to my office and slept fitfully on my sofa. More than once, I woke wishing that Hart was there.

He approached me the next morning with an uncertain smile. I shook my head at him and turned my back. When I turned around again, he was talking to Marston. I don't know what made me do that; some instinct that it would be best to let others believe Hart and I were strangers rather than an ex-couple.

It wasn't until later that night that I saw Hart again. I motioned him into the office.

He looked so chagrined, so down in the mouth, that I almost forgave him then and there. Then I remembered what kind of people he'd allied himself with and my sympathy dried up.

"What were you thinking?" I asked. It came out calmly, though I was furious.

"I didn't...I didn't know they were going to pull guns."

"You knew you were going to protest, right? How did you think that was going to go?"

"I didn't think a protest would do any harm. I thought maybe the Bend TV stations would show up, take a few pictures, that's about it."

Hart stood in front of my desk with his head down, as if

being lectured by the principal. There wasn't an available chair for him to sit in. Garth and I shared the office, but my supervisor did most of his work in the tent he'd set up in the desert. Meanwhile, I'd filled every open space in the place with fossils and papers and books. I got up from behind my desk, transferred a stack of books from one of the chairs to the floor, and motioned Hart to sit.

He still looked like a guilty schoolboy. It's strange now to look at the news coverage and realize that the rest of the country thought this was a big deal, the sign of future upheaval, and dangerous as hell. I thought it was a bunch of nonsense. I was mad at Hart for being so foolish.

"Why did you do this?" I asked. "Were you really so angry at me?"

Hart's head came up, and I could tell by his expression that he hadn't thought of that. "It wasn't about…" he started to say, then trailed off. He stood up and started pacing. "I got into trouble with the IRS. I was pissed off about it, so I attended some meetings with these guys. But really, I only came along because they were headed here. I didn't know they were going to actually take over the place."

"Oh, Hart," I sighed. "Did you forget who you are?"

"What do you mean?"

"You're the Strawberry Mountain Killer. You were front-page news a few years ago."

"They dropped the charges!"

I leaned forward. "Some people will always believe the worst, Hart. Once charged, you're guilty as far as they're concerned. What they'll remember is that you're dangerous. What do you think is going to happen when the authorities find out you're here?"

"Jesus. I never thought of that."

"It doesn't sound like you thought much about anything."

He plopped back down in the chair and shook his head. "I really blew it."

"More than you seem to realize. Your very presence makes it more dangerous for everyone, Hart. You need to get out of here. Go to the authorities. Explain what happened."

He didn't answer. He was looking around the office, but not really seeing anything. He leaned over and picked up the fossil of a leaf off of my desk. It happened to be the very first fossil I'd uncovered at the monument. "This...this is really what you are about now, isn't it?" he said. "I'm sorry. I should have supported you."

"Yes. You should have."

"I came here to say you were right. I want to start over. I'll go anywhere you go."

It was what I'd wanted to hear, but now that he'd actually come around, it felt like it was too late. I'd already moved on without him.

As if reading my mind, he came around the desk toward me. He looked so hangdog that I gave him a hug. All the memories of our days and nights in the Strawberry Mountains came back to me.

"When this is over..." I started to say. The words brought me back to reality. I tried to disentangle myself. "You need to leave, Hart. Get out of here before something goes wrong."

He held me firmly. I could have broken away, but when it came right down to it, I didn't want to.

"I'm not going anywhere without you, Nicole. I'm only leaving if you come with me, so if you're really worried, that's what we should do. Your boss has already said he'll stay. Besides, if Marston and the others decide to do damage, there isn't much you can do about it."

This time I did push away, turning my back and straightening my desk chair before sitting in it with an upright posture. I looked Hart in the face, and I knew that the stubbornness I saw there was mirrored on my own.

I slumped and closed my eyes. "Well, I doubt they'll stick around for long. The Feds will hang back, let you guys become colder and dirtier and hungrier. Won't take long to run out of toilet paper. Things are about to get miserable."

"I'm not so sure," Hart said, returning to his own chair. "Marston thinks word will get out and people will come streaming in. I'm not so sure he isn't right."

"Then it will all go to hell that much faster," I said. But

despite my words, I had a sudden insight that the bigger this takeover got, the bigger it would get. These things tended to take on a life of their own. "What's the endgame here?"

"Endgame?"

"What's your...their goal? You know the government isn't going to just hand the land back. What are they hoping to accomplish?"

"I don't know, really. Who knows?"

"Well, then, how does this end?"

He shook his head. "I don't think the guys thought that far ahead."

"It might be up to us to solve this thing," I said, feeling as I said it that it was right. "We're the intersection, the two people who can meet in the middle. How much do the others trust you? I mean, it's obvious to me that you didn't know about the takeover in advance."

He sat thinking for a few moments. "I may not have been paying much attention. Jules said something when we were at Lois Carpenter's house, but I didn't realize what he was getting at. They know I'm not a complete convert to the cause, but...I think they trust me."

"Do they know about us?"

"Us?"

"Our relationship...our former relationship."

Again, he sat for a long moment in thought, then said softly, "I'm not sure I actually said anything to them. Jerry would know, but he's so self-absorbed, he probably won't say anything. But everyone heard me call you Nicole when we first came in."

I shrugged. "We both come from the same small town. Meanwhile, Garth knows I have—*had* a boyfriend, but he doesn't know it's you. I think we need to keep our distance from each other, not look like we're conspiring or something. I'd hate for both sides to distrust us when we want the opposite thing to happen. So we should stay away from each other."

"I don't think I can do that."

The pleading in his voice made me realize how impossible it was. I wasn't sure I could do it either. "At least when we're out in public, we should try to stay across the room from each other. No lingering glances. But…when we're in my office, that's different."

He looked relieved. "Thank you, Nicole. I promise I won't fuck up again."

"You surprised me, I admit," I said. "I thought you had more sense. But let's give this a try. If nothing else, we need to figure out how to resolve this thing. Because this situation is likely to escalate pretty quickly. So it's up to us, Hart. You ready for that?"

He smiled, and it was like nothing had changed. I remembered why I'd fallen in love with him. When he stood up and came around the desk again, I greeted him with arms open. When he kissed me, I returned his kiss. A beautiful lassitude overcame me; his smell, his touch… That's when I knew I loved him as much as I ever had.

Despite everything, all seemed right with the world.

Little did I know.

Then I remembered why he was there.

Summoning all my willpower, I pushed him away. It was too damn soon to forgive him. I was pissed at him for playing mind games…but here I was doing the same thing.

With a businesslike tone, I said, "You'd better get back to the others before they miss you."

Hart opened his mouth to object, but then, to his credit, he turned around and left, closing the door quietly behind him.

That was the day we decided that, come what may, we'd stick it out to the end. And though I might not have believed it at the time, Hart and I would stick it out together.

CHAPTER 9

JOSHUA CALLEY

I was on the other side of the Johnson ranch when Harry called me. I hopped on my four-wheeler and rumbled back to his office. The old man's gout-swollen foot was propped up on an ancient rolltop desk packed with decades' worth of ranch papers. Harry probably didn't even realize I was running the ranch from my laptop. Damned if he was going to let go of twenty-year-old gas receipts and out-of-date electric bills.

He told me about the mess Jerry had gotten himself into at the John Day Fossil Beds.

"You gotta go help them out, Joshua." Harry stumbled to his feet and put his hand on my shoulder, his way of showing how much he trusted me. "All kinds of weird stuff is going down, and it's nuts. Vanessa's worried about Jerry. If I could go myself, I would."

"Bad idea," I said. "You being there would really bring down a shitstorm."

Harry stared me. Sometimes I wonder if I'm too blunt, but the thing about Harry is that after he steps back from his initial gut reaction, he tends to give things some thought. "Harry's better nature," I called it. I don't blame a man for his lizard brain if he can overcome it.

I don't think Harry knew how famous he'd become. The Feds had come to take our cattle, but Vanessa had gone on YouTube or some such thing and blasted out a challenge, and idiots from all over the country had shown up, most of them carrying guns.

Once Vanessa got on TV, I could see her head swelling from

all the attention. I wanted to walk up to her and say, "Just stop, ma'am. You've won, but the more you rub it in, the harder they'll come back at you and Harry, and your sons, and all these nuts you've pulled into your orbit. Leave it be. Sell the cattle and leave it alone."

Unfortunately, she'd already infected her eldest son with her politics.

I told Harry, "I'll grab Jerry by the ear and haul him home."

"He's gotten too big for that," Harry said, though his tone said he wasn't so sure. Jerry had always been a little isolated, spending most of his time in his room, playing video games.

"I don't like it," I said, being blunt again. "When they came for our cattle, that was one thing. They were coming at us. But this is yanking on the bull's balls for no good reason."

I stayed out of politics as much as possible. Which is a good stance to have for a black man in Eastern Oregon. But I'd watched the divide widen, just as it did in the rest of the country, only out West, the divide was symbolized by public land. There was a yearning for a simpler time, when a man could do what he wanted with his own property.

"Just do the job" was my motto. I believe in doing what needs to be done. Walk in, pick something off the desk, and fucking do it. Step on toes, hell, *break* toes—and fingers and legs—if it needs to be done. I was a blunt tool for a blunt business.

Harry frowned. When he did that, when his granite face creased, he looked like a Founding Father.

"You know that, and I know that," Harry said quietly. "But Vanessa has the boys all worked up."

I was surprised. I'd never heard him criticize or disagree with his wife, or vice versa. That was one of things I admired about him.

When Harry looked at me, he saw a friend and colleague. Vanessa? Even after all these years, she saw my skin color first. Like I said, I don't blame people for their reptilian brains, but Vanessa had never changed her mind about me, she'd just learned to cover it up better.

Nevertheless, Vanessa and I had an understanding, for Harry's sake. I didn't step on her toes and she didn't step on mine.

"Please do this for me, Joshua," Harry said. His voice wavered. I couldn't stand that he sounded like an old man. "Take care of Jerry. You're the only man I trust."

"OK, Harry. If that's what you want."

The next morning, I loaded up the big ranch truck with supplies and headed for the John Day Fossil Beds National Monument.

By the time I got there, things were a mess. The original occupiers had been joined by dozens of men and woman from the surrounding area. I wondered if bringing provisions was the right thing to do. I might be helping extend the occupation. The authorities had surrounded the area with big trucks and bulldozers; news vans lined the road, and spotlights were being set up everywhere. It was weird to see that many people. It didn't take much to increase the population of Wheeler County by a fair margin.

Some of the men were already raiding what little goods the Fossil Beds had, hoarding food, starting to barter for things they wanted. I put a quick end to that, moving all the reserves into the storage shed out back and posting a guard.

I didn't kid myself: I realized many of the newcomers were racists.

It didn't matter. Harry had sent me to make sure everyone was fed and hydrated, had a place to sleep, and had somewhere to shit that wasn't the floor of the visitor center.

Most of all, I was there to watch over Harry and Vanessa's kid, and to keep the whole thing from blowing up. I'm six foot four, two hundred fifty pounds. When I stare a man in the face, that man usually backs down.

The food I brought was distributed under a single canvas canopy, and the space underneath soon sported tables and chairs. It became known as the mess tent. Other supplies were filtered through there as well.

The main thing I remember was the air of paranoia. Some occupiers were sure the FBI was going to come in hard any minute. Others were just as sure the Feds wouldn't do anything. There were rumors of drones flying overhead.

There was a lot of grumbling, but in the end, the occupiers

did I what told them. Confederate flags dotted the camp, which put my teeth on edge, but I tried to ignore them.

On my second day there, someone unfurled a Nazi flag.

Here's the thing. If you hang out with a crowd that flies a Nazi flag and you don't do something about it, by my reckoning, you're a Nazi. I marched right up to those boys and demanded that they take the banner down.

I'd already discovered that some of these guys made a big deal out of not giving their names, as if they were captured soldiers in an enemy country. The leader of the peckerwoods was a scrawny guy, wearing a beat-up cowboy hat and cowboy boots with cow dung on them. He looked me up and down, and to his credit, he didn't back down, though he was half my size.

"It's a free country," he said. "As I'm sure *you've* heard."

The guy's friends were fatter versions of him, with trucker caps instead of cowboy hats. I knew he wouldn't back down in front of his friends. Typical macho bullshit.

"Fine," I said. I walked over to the pallet of bottled water by their tent and picked it up.

"What are you doing, man?" the scrawny guy said.

"I brought this water to the camp. I'm willing to share with people who aren't Nazis and racists. You're either on my side or you aren't."

"No need for that," one of the other guys said to me, then turned to his scrawny friend. "Take down the flag, Billy."

Billy wasn't having it. "We got tap water, last I heard. Don't need your bottled water."

I nodded. "Good. I'll be taking that case of beer, too."

"I *brought* that beer," Billy said.

"Yeah, what brand is it? Don't be looking. Tell me what your favorite brand is."

"Uh...Miller," the guy said. He turned around and saw the blue and red Budweiser labels. His hand went to his belt, but he wasn't carrying. I had a feeling he usually was. If he had been and he'd tried to draw, I was close enough to bash his brains in before he had a chance.

The other two peckerwoods didn't wait for Billy to decide what to do next. They were already rolling up the swastika flag.

I put down the water. They'd taken too much of it, probably before I'd had the chance to institute rationing. *One battle at a time*, I decided.

I turned around and walked back to the mess tent. The next morning, walking around, I realized something was different (besides everyone tracking me out of the corner of their eye), but I couldn't quite put my finger on it. Then I got it. There were greens and blues and every other color of flags and signs, but there were no reds—not only had the Nazi flag disappeared, but so had the Confederate flags.

After that, the only people I had trouble with were some of the locals, people from Bend, Redmond, Madras, and other small towns around there. They'd set up in a little encampment of their own, apart from the rest. It was clear they thought they should be in charge. A guy named Kerry Lawrence led them. He was a city commissioner in one of the local towns, though I was never sure which.

When they saw that I had the lion's share of supplies, they gave in. But I found it necessary to keep Lawrence in the loop.

By the third day there, I figured I had a handle on things. Pretty clearly, we were going to run out of food if more wasn't brought in. Marston and Davis seemed to be in nominal charge, if anyone was. Marston put out a call, and for a few days, food flooded in, the out-of-date cans you find in the back of the pantry; shit no one wanted to eat, like beets and brown rice and baked beans. I wasn't sure what stunk up the place more, the trash lying around everywhere or the gas everyone was passing.

I tried to lasso some of the occupiers into cleaning up the trash, but the peckerwoods would wander off after a few minutes of work. The one item all of them were willing to pay for was the beer and whiskey that some of the more enterprising souls brought in and started selling for inflated prices. The rowdiest would be drunk by midday. Then the heat would hit them and they'd start puking all over the place.

There was a fair amount of random destruction going on. I'll tell you, if there is one thing I can't stand, it's vandalism. It seems completely pointless to me. Robbing a bank? Hey, that's where the money is. Murder? I can see getting angry enough to kill someone. But tearing shit up just to tear shit up? That is beyond the pale.

Every year, the Johnson ranch sold access passes to a limited number of hunters. It was a nice, lucrative sideline, paid the feed bills for a month or two. But when I caught any of them shooting up signs or anything other than the animals they were supposed to be hunting, I kicked them right out of there. Didn't matter if they'd been there for hours or days.

They screamed about it, and some threatened to sue, but there it was in the contract, in nice big block letters: NO VANDALISM.

So, right away, I put a stop to the defacement of government signs and equipment.

Everyone saw the need for latrines, and I managed to get some dug by rotating men in and out of the job. Hell, most of these guys, I'd never hire at the ranch; bitching about blisters after ten minutes of digging.

Lazy city boys was what they were.

I made them save every container, fill 'em with water, and stash 'em away. It was obvious what the authorities' next move would be.

CHAPTER 10

VANESSA JOHNSON

The first time Derrick and me tried driving in to the Fossil Beds was a few days after the takeover, but the Feds had already blocked off the road.

"They need food," I said to the squirt of a cop at the barrier, his vest and camouflage outfit looking bigger than he was. "Blankets and stuff. My son left behind his medication." It was just his cholesterol meds, and Jerry could do without them for a spell, but I wasn't going to let them know that.

"If you'll give me the medication, Mrs. Johnson, I'll make sure he gets it," the officer said, a young guy, Jerry's age if half his size, polite as can be, but he knew my name and I hadn't told him, so he was ready for us. They all were, like they'd been expecting us.

"He's *my* son. I'll take it to him myself."

"I'm sorry, ma'am, orders."

Harry wasn't able to come along. The newspapers reported that he had sprained an ankle being thrown from his horse. Sounded romantic. But my husband's horse-riding days were long over. He rides the ranch ATVs these days, most often a four-wheeler, a three-wheeler if he's feeling daring.

What he really had was a bad case of gout. Pissed me off, the number of times I told him to lay off the sausages. He'll kill me for telling you that, but I'm here to tell you the truth. *All* the truth.

So my youngest son, Derrick, came along instead. I didn't think anything would happen; otherwise I wouldn't have brought him.

Derrick started getting ticked off at the cop. I could see that clenched-jaw look he got when he wouldn't do what he was told. Before I knew it, the boy was climbing the barrier. I saw it in the agent's eyes first, then turned to see Derrick climbing and the agents pulling out their guns, and then I was screaming and hollering.

I *never* scream like that. I think screaming women in movies are annoying. "Stop hollerin' and frickin' do something!" I always wanted to shout at them. But I never been so scared in my life. Derrick was only fourteen, but he was big for his age. Really big. Six foot, two hundred pounds. They'd have shot him as a man, never knowing his age, I was sure of it.

"He's just a boy!" I shouted. Derrick was tackled halfway over the barrier. That little runt of an agent flew through the air and hit my son square in the back. I saw Derrick's back bend in half...in *half*.

I don't remember running at them. Another agent stepped in front of me, something bright red in his hands. My eyes started burning like they were melting. And then wires curled out at me, striking me in the chest. A shock went through me. And then I was blinded, the pain shooting into my brain.

I stopped screaming then, dropped poleaxed to the ground like a bolt-gunned cow. The sudden silence made the video all the more dramatic: the red pepper spray, then the Taser and the flop to the ground. Everyone saw them beating up a fourteen-year-old boy and pepper spraying and Tasering a fifty-four-year-old woman.

I wasn't going to give up. I was coming back.

I thought that was the worse they could do to me.

I was wrong.

Listen here. The men would never have done it if I hadn't shamed them into it. They would have sat around the tavern and talked it to death and talked it to death.

I know I'm going away for a long time, but I'm not just falling on my sword here. Or my kitchen knife, rather. I'm telling you that I'm at fault.

I wanted it to happen, and I'm glad it happened. You can do

the opposite of blaming me. You can—like, what is it?—praise me or brand me, because I willed it to happen and it happened. My father lost his land because of some stupid tortoises, because some judge decided they were more important than people. It was like the Constitution didn't exist anymore. The government just did whatever it wanted.

Jerry had wanted to leave the guns behind, and I told him that was stupid. Really stupid. No one was going to listen to us if they weren't staring at a bullet.

So right there, you bastards, you can blame me or praise me, 'cause I did it.

No, I take it back. Don't blame me. Blame those damn turtles—sorry, *tortoises*. They've always been there. I played with them when I was a kid. There aren't any less of them than there ever were; they're all over the place.

The cattle and the turtles don't even inhabit the same places. Actually, the cattle are afraid of the damn things. So no problem.

The Feds want to close off the land because of a bunch of turtles? That's crazy. We've lived here forever. My family and Harry's family, we've been here for as far back as anyone can remember. If the Indians were objecting, I could maybe see it. But they don't care either.

It's an excuse to take our land, a big phony excuse, and no one here believes it, you know. Outsiders, people who never been here, they get all mushy about a bunch of turtles, but who cares? They don't really care.

It's not like we eat the damn things. The turtles taste terrible, even in soup. Terrible.

So we leave them alone and they leave us alone. They can crawl around forever, those turtles—tortoises—and no one will care. Leave them be. Leave *us* be.

CHAPTER 11

HART DAVIS

Right from the beginning, I was the man in the middle. Neither side knew what to make of me. I decided to pretend to be one of the occupiers because I thought I could influence them more from inside instead of being some random guy sticking around because his girlfriend was in trouble.

In the first few days, the Feds stopped letting people in, which meant we were running low on supplies almost from the start. I mean, all we'd come with was the clothes on our backs. The park rangers shared their food with us, so we weren't starving, and most of us camped inside the Merriam Hall, except Jules and a couple of others who chose to sleep outside "in case they try to sneak up on us," so it was uncomfortable but not too bad.

In the first negotiation session—Marston handled that—the Feds gave those of us who were already at the Fossil Beds permission to come and go, and in return, we promised to not accept any new occupiers. Neither side held to the bargain, of course.

The stupid part was bringing guns and then waving them around. But then, as Marston kept pointing out, if we hadn't, the Feds probably would have just swooped right in and arrested us. When I was interviewed, I tried to make it clear that no one was in danger, but a few of the guys couldn't help but make vaguely threatening statements. And I was trying to blend in.

"They shoot at me, I'll shoot back," Jules said, over and over again. A reasonable statement, on the surface, but all everyone heard was "I'll shoot."

"I love this country," Jules rhapsodized. "I love the warmth of the sun, the smell of the desert, the open horizon as far as I can see. This is my country, and no one can take it away from me."

"We quit now, we go to jail forever," Jim Marston said. He raised his voice so that half the camp could hear him. His voice was confident, almost smug. "But we wait, and they'll start offering us deals."

I hated to admit it, but I thought he was right. But I also thought that with the two sides in a standoff, both armed, things could blow up at any second. But even if the occupiers wanted to give up, it was too late by then. At the same time, it was kind of exciting. Like we were living in a momentous time.

Protesters came pouring into camp over the next few days. The Feds reversed course and started letting them in. They kept doing that: opening the camp, then closing it, then opening it, as if unsure what to do, like parents who couldn't figure out how to discipline their kids.

The newcomers had seen the pictures of Mrs. Johnson being pepper sprayed and Tasered, her young son brutally tackled. Jerry Johnson denied medicine! I knew those two and thought that short of lethal force, that was the only way the cops could have stopped them, but that's not how it looked on TV.

So in came a new gang of protesters, some of whom I knew, most of whom I didn't. The ones I didn't know weren't ranchers, as far as I could tell. Most came from the city or suburbs or small towns. I'd never seen so many American flags and pickups. They brought horses in big old trailers that circled the parking lot like a wagon train. They saddled up their horses and went out on patrol, a flag in one hand, an AR-15 in the other.

They piled firewood near the road, started a campfire, and stood waiting for what they were sure was the coming assault. Meanwhile, they posed for the cameras.

But none of these dumb fucks thought to bring their own food or toilet paper or clothing or sleeping bags or anything else. If not for Joshua Calley, we would've starved. Marston shrugged it off. "God will provide," he said. "Have you seen how many local ranchers we've gotten? This is really happening."

Right from the start, Marston and the original occupiers treated the local ranchers with more respect than the militia types, who all dressed and talked the same. Marston and Jules wanted to accomplish something and not just parade around self-importantly.

The Feds were lying low, and at first, the only sign of them was drone flying over every few hours.

After a couple of days, Nicole volunteered to go into town for supplies. I encouraged her for ulterior motives. I thought she wouldn't be allowed back in. But she must have realized what I was up to, because she gave me an odd look and decided not to go.

She still didn't want to be around me publicly.

It took all my willpower not to follow her around like a puppy.

It was strange. Maybe the authorities thought we would change our minds, be so overwhelmed by the overfilled toilets that we'd give up. Maybe they figured we were putting all the bad eggs in one basket. I doubted they wanted another confrontation, especially with the TV cameras rolling. For sure, they didn't want an escalation, because while the original occupiers had brought a few hunting rifles and pistols, the new protesters had come loaded for bear—and moose and elephant—toting AR-15s and even some M-16s.

The Feds finally did block the roads again, and then it was just us idiots. There were several dozen men and about a dozen women, including, surprisingly enough, Lois Carpenter. One morning, she was just there, nodding to me from across the parking lot. I was surprised to see her after our conversation in her kitchen, but I was glad she'd come. I thought she was level-headed, and we needed that. She took over the cooking and cleaning, ordering everyone around. No one challenged her.

Pretty soon, Lois and Joshua were running the place between them.

Joshua didn't hide his disgust much. The media gravitated toward him, but he ignored them, didn't so much as look at them. The Johnson ranch foreman took over logistics, rationing the food, finding places for people to sleep, getting latrines dug, that kind of thing.

At one point, he confronted Jules. "Fuck you military types. You're all posturing and standing around, and it's bullshit. You want to make a point, listen to people like him."

To my surprise, Joshua pointed at me.

After a week, it looked like we were settling in for the long haul, which surprised the hell out of me, 'cause I thought the whole thing would be over by then. After that first freezing night, I tried sleeping inside the museum, under murals of ancient mammals, with fake trees and concrete pillars. But every few minutes, there would be the electronic screech of a mastodon or some other creature, and I'd sit bolt upright.

Finally, I grabbed my sleeping bag and went outside and slept on the concrete walkway. Or tried to sleep.

We'd all fucked up royally, and damned if I could see a way out.

CHAPTER 12

CARLTON MANNING

I was visiting my parents in Portland when I got the call from my editor at the *Washington Post*. I was a little surprised, because I was a new hire and this looked like it might be a big story. But I was the closest, apparently.

I drove over the mountains the next day, passed through Bend, which has grown beyond belief since I was a kid, and then on into the desert of Eastern Oregon. It wasn't an easy drive; about as far from an interstate as you can get.

I reached John Day and decided to stay the night. Of course, all the rooms were booked, but I took a chance and asked if there were any cancellations. It seemed unlikely, since the town was full of rented SUVs and police cars from all over Oregon.

The desk clerk, a young Hispanic woman, winced and said, "Yes, one of our regulars decided not to come because of all the fuss. So there's a room available."

"What do *you* think about what's happening?" I asked.

"I know why they're doing it, but it's stupid. It's only hurting us, and what good is that?"

I took the room, even though it had two double beds. I deposited my stuff in the room and went for a walk. There was no need to drive anywhere. I could walk the circuit of downtown within a few minutes.

The desk clerk's opinion was pretty much universal. The locals mostly agreed with what the takeover people were protesting but thought it was a dumb way to go about it.

"I'm seeing outsiders with guns everywhere I go," said a

girl at a fast food restaurant I stopped at. She looked like she was barely out of middle school. "What happens if there's violence out there? Will they start shooting here, too?"

A middle-aged woman at the next table over said, "We are all friends and neighbors here. This is a tight-knit little town, and this protest is a disruption to our lives. None of these guys are from around here, you know. Not one. They've canceled school, which is a pain in the ass because my kids are running loose, and they've even canceled the football game."

The football game was mentioned quite a bit, as if canceling it was the worst thing coming out of the takeover.

At the hardware store—which was fun to browse, by the way; it was the good old-fashioned kind of store that sold individual nails and screws, the kind I remembered from childhood, before Walmart came along and drove them all out of business—the young man working there said he was worried because he lived just a few doors down from the sheriff's department.

"The militia guys are driving by every few hours." He shivered dramatically. "Gives me the willies."

I walked to the sheriff's office. Wire fencing and yellow crime tape surrounded it, because it had been turned into the operations center. A gaggle of reporters was waiting outside, and I joined them.

Walt Halligan, the mayor, came out and told everyone to go home, that he had nothing to say, that it was a nonevent and would be over soon. He wasn't very convincing.

None of the sources I talked to except the mayor was willing to go on the record.

I stayed the night in John Day, then headed out to the visitor center at the Fossil Beds the next day, amazed that I wasn't stopped at any roadblocks. The Feds were anything but consistent about access, which only lent credence to the idea that they didn't know what they were doing.

I'd thought I might be the only national reporter there, but I saw some familiar faces.

This thing was blowing up.

CHAPTER 13

HART DAVIS

We opened a can of worms, and a lot of hate and anger spilled out. I wasn't all that comfortable with that, but there I was, right in the middle of it all.

It was weird. Here we were, the protesters and the media, neither of which would have been there without the other. And each side thought the other was phony. Well, it was all artificially created drama from the beginning, and I can see how it would annoy the local residents.

Marston became our spokesman, and when you watch video of him now, you can almost see him puff up. On TV, he looked bigger, more serious. Weirdly enough, Marston's sidekick, Jules, had taken me aside at one point and asked me to be the spokesman.

"*You* should talk to the reporters," Jules had said. "Marston is too full of himself, and I'd probably say 'Fuck' at the wrong time, and the rest of 'em? Who the fuck knows what would come out of their mouths?"

Jules was an odd duck, but when he insisted on something, the rest of us usually gave in. He was a true believer, not a doubt in his mind. Still, I declined the spokesman job, so it was Marston who stood in front of the cameras and spoke for all of us, trying to sound reasonable. I missed it when it was happening, but the whole thing was replayed that night on the TV in Merriam Hall.

The moment those microphones were shoved in his face, Marston froze up as stiff as a ventriloquist's dummy. He was staring into the camera lights, his mind blank. But if you didn't know him, you might have thought he was simply waiting for the reporters to settle down.

Marston has a slight Western drawl that he sometimes slips into when he's trying to fit in. Sounds a little Southern to me and fake as hell.

Right from the start, the reporters were antagonistic. There was one lady reporter who was really aggressive, looking like a mannequin with her caked-on makeup.

"What's your name, sir?" she asked.

"James Marston...Jim." There was panic behind his eyes, as if he'd been thinking about lying.

"And where are you from, Mr. Marston?"

"Everywhere and nowhere," Marston said. His eyes darted around as if he realized that the statement made him sound homeless, a drifter. "I own car dealerships in several towns."

"Why are you doing this? What's your agenda?" the reporter asked.

"No agenda," Marston answered. "What does that word even mean? No, we just want freedom. We want to do what we've always done without interference. We want to work the land as we always have, as God intended."

"What do you *want* specifically?" she fired back.

"We want the federal government to return these lands to Grant and Wheeler counties. The Constitution is hanging by a thread. There is no right under the Constitution to take this property away from the ranchers and loggers who make their living on it. We won't go home until it is returned."

"Do you believe in the federal government, Mr. Marston?"

Marston laughed. It sounded pretty good, genuine. He waved his arm at the line of federal agents surrounding them. "Pretty hard not to."

Sounding peeved, the reporter rephrased her question. "Do you recognize the federal government's authority?"

Marston paused. "Sure...when they're in the right. Look, I don't speak for everyone. There are people here who think only the county sheriff has jurisdiction. Others only recognize the state. What we all want is freedom. We took care of this land for many years, neighbor watching out for neighbor."

"But what if your freedom infringes on that of others?" She got closer to Marston and the camera, close enough so that you could see her pores under her makeup.

Marston stepped back a little, then realized what he was doing. His voice rose.

"When was the last time you walked out into the desert, lady?" Marston dropped his Western drawl, sounding angry. "Yeah, I thought so. Never, and you never will. It's all sagebrush, dust, and juniper trees out there. You'd spend five minutes out there and run back to your condo. But those of us here *like* it. We want to protect it more than you do. We take care of the land; we don't just let it sit there and rot, good for nothing. We don't want the desert tortoise to disappear anymore than you do. We'll look after them, like we always have.

"But you want to shut down working ranches, ranches that have been with families for generations, because you might, once in a million years, want to go for a walk in the desert and pet a tortoise."

"Are you talking about yourself, Mr. Marston?" the reporter asked. "We understand you were denied a zoning change for one of your car lots. Is this a personal grudge?" She shoved her microphone in Marston face like she was going to shove it up his nose. You could see the anger flash across his face.

"Screw you, lady."

There was a glint of triumph in her eyes.

It all kind of went to hell after that, Marston rolling his eyes and throwing up his hands, the reporters yelling questions. It made for pretty good TV.

Jules loved it. Jules—hero, martyr of the Juniper Revolution. Some people thought Marston was the instigator. They thought Jules was a joke. Marston, especially, treated him like the village idiot, his little Igor.

The media had fun with the image of Jules putting a tarp over his head to escape the heat.

But from that day forward, I saw iron under those buggy eyes and in that scrawny bantam frame. His political views were shallow, maybe an inch thick, but they were iron, unbreakable.

He led the charge and the rest of us followed.

I've often wondered if any of the violence would have happened if Jules had still been around at the end. He was crazy enough to take on all the anger all by himself. Without him as the focal point, the hate spilled out in every direction.

I wish he was here to tell his story.

Strange how quickly it becomes about personality, isn't it? Drama queens, the media. They don't care what it's all about, they just like the conflict. Funny little Jules, pompous Marston, laconic Peter, black cowboy Joshua, middleman Hart: all of us caricatures they can pigeonhole into their stories.

Who cares what it's really about, right? Forget the history, forget the nuance, forget the legitimate grieves.

There are good guys and bad guys.

Simple.

CHAPTER 14

JOSHUA CALLEY

The media has made the takeover people out to be a bunch of crazies, and it's true that eventually the more radical fringe took over, but in the beginning, they were just protesting. I should know. If there weren't some good people there, I wouldn't have survived for long.

If I thought I'd banished all the racist elements, I was wrong. Well, truth is, I knew that they were still there, but they'd been driven underground. The outright malignant bastards weren't showing their faces.

I heard later about what happened to Mrs. Johnson and her youngest, Derrick. But I saw the results of it within a couple of days. I was still setting up the mess tent when one of the guys who was helping me came rushing in. "You'd better come see this," he said.

I'd heard engines revving in the background while I was working but hadn't paid much attention. Now that I focused on them, it sounded like the German army was approaching. The dust cloud was still swirling in the air when I emerged from the tent, coating everything in the camp with a gritty layer of dust. Right from the start, these guys were assholes. Most people slowed down when they came in over the desert, as a courtesy.

Three brand-new, enormous Hummers were sliding to a stop near the entrance of the parking lot. They'd come in overland to evade the roadblocks. The Feds were letting people in, but I had a feeling they would have drawn the line at these guys. They poured out of the vehicles, fully armed, dressed in fatigues, looking cocky. There were about five men in each vehicle.

On their shoulders, they were wearing the lightning bolt patches of the SS. My blood went cold. I felt the calm anger that came over me when I knew I was in for a fight. I marched up to the guy who was waving the other men into some kind of order.

"Where the hell did you come from?" I demanded. I got as close as I could to him without actually bumping up against him.

He gave me a glance, trying to hide his surprise, then his gaze went over my shoulder. "Who's in charge around here?" he asked, dismissing me.

"Just tell me you brought enough supplies to feed yourselves," I said.

By now, half the camp had come out to watch. Most people were hanging back to see what was going to happen.

He reluctantly looked me in the eye. I didn't see a smidgen of fear there, which was unusual when I was up in someone's face. This guy was maybe an inch shorter then me and a bit less thick around the middle, which probably meant he was in better shape.

Jim Marston finally stepped up beside me.

"What organization do you represent, sir?" he asked, his voice friendly.

"I'm Carl Lundgren," the big guy said, looking glad to be talking to someone other than me. "Knights of the White Sword."

"The KKK?"

"We don't call ourselves that anymore," Lundgren said. "But sure."

Marston looked over at me, alarmed. Then he surprised me. "We're going to have to ask you to leave."

"Says who?" Lundgren demanded, his voice low and threatening. His men were lining up behind him. I watched their fingers, which were outside their triggers but too close for comfort.

"I'm Jewish, Mr. Lundgren. My grandparents died in the Holocaust."

One of the men behind Lundgren snorted. That's when Hart

Davis joined us. "I grew up Catholic. I hear the KKK has a problem with that, too," he said.

"Hey, fellas," Lundgren said. His tone had moderated. He let go of his rifle, letting it swing from the shoulder strap. "We're just here to help the cause."

"Your cause is not our cause," I said.

Lundgren flushed and whirled on me. "What the fuck are you even doing here? We don't need your kind here."

There were fifteen armed men facing the three of us, and not one of us had thought to bring a gun. I thought we were screwed until Lois Carpenter arrived. She joined us with a smile, as if we were having a nice chat. Benson and Smith were at her side, and they *were* armed. The crowd behind us separated a little, and Kerry Lawrence and his crew moved to the front.

"Fellows," Lois said. "We appreciate that you came, but this protest is about land, not skin color or religion."

I thought at the time that Lois was on our side. Now I realize she was just protecting her turf.

"It's the other way around, buddy," Davis said. "*We* don't want *your* kind here."

"You all feel that way?" Lundgren voice rose. "What the hell is wrong with you people?" Despite the opposition, he didn't look like he was going to back down.

I spread my arms out to either side, gently nudging the others back. I moved in even closer to Lundgren, staring into his eyes. For the first time, I saw doubt.

"How about the two of us figure it out," I said. "Man to man."

I'd put him on the spot. I figured he wouldn't back down with his men watching.

He managed to grin at me, though it was pretty clear he wasn't happy about what was happening. But as I expected, he took up the challenge. "Give us some room, boys."

He handed his gun to the man next to him.

We faced off.

Then, out of the crowd, Jules Francisco walked up to the big Klansman and spit at his feet. Lundgren looked over at me, confused. Jules was half his size and looked like he could be broken in half with one twist of the wrist.

"My name is Julio Miguel Francisco," he said, though I'd never heard him called anything but Jules. He gave me a squinty look. "You want me to take care of him?"

Lundgren laughed in disbelief, but amazingly, no one else did.

"I've got it, Jules," I said. "But thanks."

Jules shrugged. "Oh, well." He spit again and walked away.

It was a huge gamble I was taking. If Lundgren was ex-special forces or something, a trained fighter, I wasn't going to stand much of a chance. I had fifty pounds on him, but I figured he'd be quicker. He was also a good twenty years younger than me, so the fight needed to be over fast.

It grew quiet. Suddenly there were only two people in the world, and one of them was my enemy.

He made the first move, a feint to my head, but the real strike was for my belly, which he must have thought was my weak spot. I managed to dodge both blows, though enough of his second strike hit me hard enough in the midsection for him to realize that I wasn't all fat.

He backed away, recalculating.

I didn't give him time. I closed in on him, and his fist glanced against my cheek hard enough to hurt, but not enough to stun me. I wrapped him with both arms and we went backward, falling flat to the ground. His head hit the concrete with a thump.

Dazed, he barely warded off my blows, but as I'd thought, he was quicker than me. I couldn't get a solid strike in. Already, I was grunting, and he could sense my stamina was nowhere near his.

But I'd gotten the measure of him. He wasn't trained. He was a bar brawler, a street fighter.

Inside, I was already certain I would win. Street fighter, my ass. He had never met a street fighter like *me* before.

He managed to squirm out from under me, and we scrambled to our feet. He thought he had me. I could see it in his eyes. Blood ran down my cheek, and I reached up and purposely rubbed it around my face, making it look worse than it was.

Overconfident, he began swinging wildly, half landing his

blows, but it must have looked like I was in trouble. I caught a glimpse of Davis's face. He looked worried. I smiled at him, and he raised his eyebrows.

The calmness that came over me was complete. It was as if I could see every little movement, hear every little sound. I waited, looking for my moment, and the more he flurried blows down on me, the more openings there were. But I wanted the right one.

He flagged slightly after a particularly fast flurry. I was backing up, looking like I was on my heels.

Then I stepped forward.

It took one solid left to his chin to end it, after my right fist had knocked the breath out of him. He went down, his legs giving out, folding in sections: legs, trunk, head.

He lay on his side, unmoving.

"Get back in your damned Hummers and get out of here," I said to the other assholes.

They picked up their fallen leader and pushed him into the back seat of the lead vehicle. A few of them looked uncertain, but a small guy with tattoos on his face, who was a little older than the rest, waved them on.

The tattooed guy got in the driver's seat and gave me a momentary glance. For a second, I thought he was going to nod at me, but he managed to resist.

They drove out of parking lot and off down the road.

CHAPTER 15

MARK SIMONS

Obviously, we should have planned ahead a bit more. Those first nights were rough. The bigwigs slept in the building, but the rest of us slept in cars and froze our asses off. I'll give Jim Marston credit, he slept in one of the cars like the rest of us.

It got better after Joshua showed up. Some of the others vouched for him, so I gave him a chance, though he was bossy as hell. But it turned out he knew what he was doing. Still, there were those on the inside and the rest of us on the outside. I thought the original guys should have stuck together, but they let a bunch of outsiders in. Marston hung out with us and was kind of the go-between, but still...

The media found out Hart Davis was the Strawberry Mountain Killer and suddenly that's all they could talk about. I never trusted the guy. He cozied up to the pretty blonde ranger girl right off. And he didn't use plain English like the rest of us.

Marston was the only one who seemed to notice my suspicion. He came up to me and started a conversation, which surprised me because he usually ignores me. "You know, Hart would be on the other side if things had worked out a little different," he said. "It's not in his blood like it is for us."

"Where did he even come from?" I asked. I'd been thinking some of the same things, but nobody ever asked my opinion. Marston, for once, looked like he was interested.

"You think..." Marston looked me in the eye. He lowered his voice. "You think he's a plant?"

I hadn't even thought of it, but the minute he said it, I

wondered if it was true. I mean, later I realized Marston was trying to stir up trouble, but at the time it seemed possible.

"Could be."

Marston said, "Makes you wonder, don't it?"

"So you think the Feds wanted this? You think that it's a setup?"

He shrugged. "Doesn't mean we have to do what they expect. Maybe we do exactly the opposite."

"Davis has gotten real friendly with that lady ranger."

"Pretty strange," Marston said. "Pretty *damn* strange if you ask me. You know, you ought to talk to Lois Carpenter. She thinks like we do."

I must have frozen or something, because all I remember is Marston patting me on the shoulder and saying, "Well, think about it." There was no reason for Marston to know about my thing for Lois.

I couldn't think about much else for the next couple of days.

There was a teacher I had in high school, Mrs. White. Looking back, I realize that she was only seven or eight years older than me, younger than I am now, but back then, the difference seemed huge. Anyway, there was something about her. She wasn't even all that pretty, but if she even looked at me, I swear to God, I'd get an immediate hard-on.

She knew it, too. She called me in for a conference and I sat there like a lump while she talked to me, acting real friendly. I've always wondered, you know. Just wondered.

Anyway, Lois Carpenter had that effect on me. I couldn't take my eyes off her. Oh, I didn't dare look at her directly, because I was afraid she'd catch me looking, but if she was anywhere near, she's all I'd notice.

Didn't take much for her to wrap me around her little finger.

CHAPTER 16

PETER STERNS

It had rained a few days before the takeover, and there was mud everywhere.

It's the mud I remember. Which is weird, because most of the year, it's the dust that's the problem. But something about the High Desert makes you remember when it rains. Maybe because it happens so rarely, you really take notice. The mud wells up from the ground, swelling and filling everything in a caked layer that dries like concrete. The ruts in the roads are two feet deep, and they stay there all year long, hardened and tough, something you have to drive around. I imagine the trenches from World War I were like that, baked runnels that became part of the landscape.

Then there're the mudrooms, stomping your boots, the broom right there by the door because clumps of dry red mud drop away and roll into every nook and cranny. And doormats that become so encrusted they're useless, just slippery and slidey.

So my first memory of the Johnson ranch is the mud.

I'd been working for Harry Johnson for only a few days when the first standoff happened. I had no idea what I was in for. In the past, I went from ranch to ranch. When I got tired of whatever ranch politics were happening, I moved on. An experienced ranch hand has a job any time he wants it. Most people try it for a little while and then quit because it's hard work for small pay.

I like the big meals most ranches feed you, the responsibility they give you, and that they only casually mention if you get something wrong, expecting you'll get it right the next time. I like the cowboy boots and the chaps and the hat. I like the heat beating down so hard that the sweatband rimming your hat can't handle it anymore and droplets land on your cheeks, cool and wet. I like the dust and the dried grass sticking to my jeans and the juniper pollen floating through the air.

I like the horses, especially my own horse, Lucy, and the smell of cow shit in the baking sun, and the horizons as far as you can see.

I like the rain when it comes, and the mud that follows.

I like everything about it.

A few months before the takeover, after a desert rainstorm, Joshua Calley, the foreman, turned to me and said, "Smells like fucking freedom, don't it?"

My lawyer told me to write down my story, tell the court and jury why I was there, what I was thinking. It's supposed to make me a sympathetic figure, I guess. So I'm going to tell you exactly why I was there.

I went to see a so-called cowboy poet at the Deschutes County Library. He wore a beautiful hat, not a crease or a smudge on it. The kind of hat I always wanted to wear to the dances but couldn't afford. Instead, I go to them bareheaded because I don't want to gross out the ladies with my funky workaday hat.

Anyway, this guy had a magnificent handlebar mustache (I can barely grow one) and a belt buckle that would've covered my whole belly. I wondered if the guy had ever even been on a horse.

Then he started performing—and it was more a performance than a reading—and I was captivated. The words really spoke to me. I went home that night and tried to write a poem, but I never could come up with anything worth anything.

But sitting here in jail, remembering, I suddenly got a hankering again, and I sat down and wrote a poem about the last time I went riding.

What's it got to do with what happened?

Everything. Because if you don't understand this about me, you don't understand anything. Besides, if this makes it to the court transcripts, I figure that makes me published. Smiley face and all that.

In Cahoots

The moonlight in cahoots
to keep me riding
the dusty trail
on the banks of the canal,
a calf astray in the weeds.

Blackbirds dive-bomb me,
pretending to be wounded,
leading me astray,
in cahoots, I reckon
with the lost calf.

Be safe, I murmur.
The water rushes through
the narrows, in cahoots,
spraying the soft green
amidst the brown.

In cahoots,
the bounding rabbits,
the scurrying lizards,
to keep me wandering,
no hurry to find the calf.

Dark and quiet,
until the calf bellows,
lost in the reeds,
needing its mother,
in cahoots to end my sojourn.

I rope the calf,
it quiets and follows,
the blackbirds ignore me,
the darkening trail
in cahoots to lead me home.

That way of life is disappearing. Someday it will only be in poems. Though I figure robots will be running everything by then, and they don't write poems.

It was writing that bonded Michelle and me.

Michelle came right up to me, in the first couple of days at the Fossil Beds, and stared at me while I was eating an apple. At first, finding something to eat during the occupation was pretty random. You grabbed whatever food you brought or could beg off someone, sat wherever, and hoped you wouldn't go to bed hungry.

From the corner of my eye, I thought she was a guy. She was slender, wearing cargo pants with full pockets, and heavy boots. Her black hair was as short as mine. The only color she wore was her deep purple T-shirt, which she wasn't wearing a bra under. I realized later that she always wore something purple, even if it was only her socks. She had dark brown eyes and a mischievous smile.

I offered her the half of the apple I hadn't eaten yet. She grabbed it and said, "Thank you. None of these other pricks will share."

She plopped down next to me. I tried not to overreact to her proximity. I wasn't used to it, but it was also nice. I never did talk much to girls back in school, and hardly at all once I became a cowboy. I'd found that when I went to county dances, women almost always approached me, and I barely had to say anything, just live up the laconic image of a cowboy, but those relationships never turned into anything.

"Michelle Foster," she said, reaching over to shake hands. "But call me Mich."

That was the start of it. We hung out together after that. I got comfortable with her right off the bat. I figured she was gay and wouldn't be interested in me. But we talked about stuff—never politics, mostly books and art and things that I'd never talked about with anyone before.

It was the last place in the world I would have expected to find someone like that.

CHAPTER 17

NICOLE NELSON

I could tell that the occupiers had no idea how to end the take-over. Their demands were all over the place, most of them impossible. I mean, wanting the federal government to give up all jurisdiction over public lands? To give back national parks and forests and monuments? Ridiculous.

The FBI was equally clueless. I listened to some of their conversations, and even I could tell that what they were say-ing was bullshit. They were going by some kind of negotiat-ing handbook or something that sounded totally disingenuous. Everything had a cost, like offering sleeping bags and stuff in exchange for…what? For letting me and Garth and Perry go?

"I'm here of my own volition," I'd told them straight out, but they acted like they didn't believe me, like I was being held cap-tive. At the time, I thought I was a free agent.

I also thought the whole thing was all out of proportion. The John Day Fossil Beds National Monument was going into the off-season, with a few dozen visitors a day anticipated; that's all we were being put out. The wear and tear on the facilities? That could be fixed.

I figured that the coming snows, the wet and cold, the lack of snacks and beer, and sleeping on the floor would discourage them and the whole thing would sort of die with a whimper.

But I didn't think the Feds—sorry, that's what the takeover people called them—I didn't think the Feds would wait around forever before they tried coming in. The guy they had talking to us, Special Agent Rod Adams ("Call me Rod"), had a genial demeanor, but it was difficult to miss the hard-faced looks of the agents standing behind him.

Negotiations went nowhere, because there were as many agendas as there were protesters (what they called themselves).

Hart and I met in my office whenever we thought no one was looking. He finally seemed open to my explanations as to why I wanted to pursue my degree in paleontology. I told him about my love of the Painted Hills and the Fossil Beds. "Not like my boss, Perry, though. He *loves* the fossils."

"Makes sense considering he's a fossil himself."

I laughed, feeling a little like a traitor. "Perry is a good man. He can be talked to, once you get past his absent-minded professor ways."

Perry was rarely in the office. He generally patrolled the grounds, picking up cigarette butts and litter, scolding people, and was pretty much ignored by the occupiers.

"What about Garth? He keeps traipsing off into the desert as if nothing is going on," Hart said.

"Yeah, I think he forgets that there is anything going on."

"Well, he'd better be careful. He's been ignoring some of the occupiers, and they think he looks down on them. They might take it out on him."

"Garth? He's harmless," I said.

I wish now that I'd listened to Hart's warnings.

CHAPTER 18

PERRY CAMPBELL

Rod Adams, the FBI special agent in charge of negotiations, took me aside about a week after the takeover. The FBI had entered the camp unarmed.

"Just dial any number, Mr. Campbell, and you'll get us," he said in a no-nonsense tone. He'd maneuvered us out of sight of others so he could slip me a dedicated cellphone. "Dial 1, that's all you have to do. If you're in trouble and need immediate help, call 911 and we'll come in after you right away."

"I don't think that'll be necessary," I said. "I don't think these guys are violent."

"We've spent years and millions of dollars trying to figure out who is dangerous and who isn't," Adams said. "These things can escalate fast. People get killed. We'd prefer to pull you out. Frankly, it would make things easier for us if things go south."

"I won't leave without Garth and Nicole," I said.

"Try to talk them some sense into them, Mr. Campbell. Remember, the occupiers are carrying guns. All it takes is one mistake, and bullets will start flying. Every bullet fired is a regret in these types of situations. You can't call back bullets after you calm down."

I moved closer to him and leaned in. "I can keep an eye out from the inside. Tell you what's happening."

"I appreciate the offer, Mr. Campbell, but we'd prefer you not do that. Stay away from the occupiers as much as you can. Don't let them think you're spying on them."

The special agent hadn't blinked an eye at my offer, and I

suspected from then on that they already had someone inside. They didn't need me, which was strangely reassuring.

Agent Adams wasn't finished. "I can't begin to tell you what a bad idea your staying is. You're the adult here, Mr. Campbell. You need to leave, and you need to talk your charges into leaving with you."

I shrugged helplessly. "I'll try."

"Please do. And hide the phone. Not all these people are good people, Mr. Campbell. Some are dangerous."

"Which ones?" I asked. "I mean, give me some names."

"I'll tell you as soon as you're away from them. But until then, you're safer keeping your head down. If you start treating people differently, they'll notice."

For a moment, I wondered if the FBI agent didn't trust me. But I was the most boring citizen ever, not so much as a traffic ticket in thirty years, and they had to know that.

I'd been getting almost used to the idea of the takeover, but after this conversation, I decided to try harder to talk Nicole into leaving. But every time I saw her, she was with that Davis fellow, who was one of the original occupiers. For a few days, I wondered if she was going over to their side.

Garth Perkins wasn't much help. He'd stayed originally to protect Nicole. He had an obvious crush on her, though she seemed oblivious to it. But after a few days, Garth was completely entrenched.

I thought if they came for anyone, they'd come for me, and I was willing to accept that. But maybe…maybe because everyone expected it, my death simply wouldn't have meant as much.

Everyone is calling me a hero, and I don't mind if this recounting of events disabuses people of that notion. I should have seen it coming, and it is this blindness more than anything else that I regret.

CHAPTER 19

JOSHUA CALLEY

I was expecting the Feds to attempt something sometime soon. I was just finishing an inventory when the cry went out, "They're shutting down the water pump!"

The pump house was about three hundred yards away, in the middle of a meadow. I looked over and saw three men opening the door to the little wooden building and going inside. My people started running, guns in hand. Several guys jumped on their horses and spurred them toward the pump house. It would have been an almost stirring sight if it hadn't been so stupid. One of the guys had a big American flag on a tall pole, which he jammed into his stirrup, and he went riding off, hollering, the red, white, and blue flapping in the wind.

There was only one operational four-wheeler that anyone had thought to bring along. I walked up to Jack Cantrell and said, "Give me the damn keys."

He frowned at me, clearly thinking about refusing. I got closer, looming over him by a good foot. He handed them over.

I managed to get there right as the first horsemen were arriving. They were having so much fun that none of them got off their horses, just circled the pump house like a bunch of rampaging Indians in an old Western.

I pulled right up to the door.

"You people best get out of here," I shouted. I glanced over my shoulder to check how close the others were.

A Fed poked his head out. He had a buzz haircut, dark horn-rimmed glasses, and a pasty face. "This is federal property."

"Not the right thing to say." I tried to catch his eye, to drill into him what kind of trouble they were in. "That isn't going to cut it with the good old boys that are about a hundred feet away, guns in hand."

He stepped out, examining me curiously, as if a black man was the last thing he'd expected to find out here. Then he saw the horsemen and the crowd surging toward us and his face went even whiter, if that was possible.

I turned, putting both hands palms out toward the crowd. "Slow down!" I bellowed. "I've got this!" I turned urgently to the Feds. "These fellows are just leaving, right? And you're leaving the water on, right?"

The other two men emerged reluctantly from the pump house. These guys looked more like maintenance men than Feds. They looked scared, too. "We didn't have time to do anything," one of them said.

"Good thing for you," someone said. Mark Simons stomped toward us, ignoring my signals. He wasn't a tall man, but he had some girth, and he almost butted that girth right into the first Fed. "Now get out of here before we tar and feather you!"

The Fed ignored him and turned to me. "What's your name, sir?"

That brought me up a little short. They wouldn't have needed to inquire very far before they figured out who the big black man was. But then, I figured we'd all be identified soon enough. They probably had cameras on us right now.

"None of your fucking business," Simons answered for me.

"I only ask so that I may properly address you. Both of you."

"'Sir' works just fine," Simons said.

"All right, sir. This has nothing to do with what's happening with you folks. We are checking the water quality, like we do every month."

"Bullshit," Simons said. "It takes three of you?"

"These men wanted protection, and you can't blame them. Let us take our sample and we'll get out of here."

"You'll get out of here now, without no sample. It's all bullshit."

"Very well, but if anything happens to your water, remember

that we tried to help. Your latrines aren't safe. You're probably contaminating the aquifer."

"Sure, whatever," Simons said. He looked around for support, and someone said, "Hell, yeah!" He turned back. "We'll take our chances."

The two maintenance men, if that's what they were, started walking toward the barricades in the distance, followed reluctantly by the Fed. You could tell it was taking all their willpower not to hunch their shoulders or look behind them. I watched carefully to see that none of our people aimed their guns at them. I didn't know if I could stop them, but I planned on trying. But they all seemed to feel that they'd won, and they slapped each other on the back, whooped and hollered, and went back and broke out the whiskey, which they actually shared for once.

Within a week of that incident, half the people in the camp got sick, and not another day went by when someone didn't seem to have intestinal troubles of one kind or another.

Of course, they were all certain the Feds had poisoned them. I wasn't so sure. The stink from the latrines assaulted me every morning when I woke up and sent me off every night into some messy dreams.

Besides, all the Feds had to do was turn off the electricity. Which they did, just one day after the pump house incident. One of the portable generators was dragged down to the pump house, but that meant a bunch of the trailers went without electricity. Gas was siphoned out of the pickups, and I figured that some of them would be unmovable lumps of metal when it came time to leave.

It made things harder, for sure. It was a good strategy on the Feds' part, because I could see the occupiers' excitement fading as the days went by. For once, the Feds were being coy, not pushing things. I was rooting for the takeover to end, frankly. It was all pretty pointless.

And it would have, too, if the new guys hadn't showed up.

CHAPTER 20

MARK SIMONS

Man, the adrenaline rush of facing off with the Feds at the water pump! I've never felt that way before. Everyone was standing around doing nothing, except the black guy, Joshua, who seemed more on the Feds' side than ours.

The intruders gave us a line of bullshit about "testing for water quality," but they backed down pretty fast when I challenged them.

I was still jazzed up by the time I got back to the camp. I got some slaps on the back and attaboys from some of the others. Bunch of fucking cowards, all talk and no action. Nothing was happening. The energy was leaving the camp, and I could see where this was headed. Something needed to change.

I crashed about five minutes later, the oomph draining out of me. I collapsed into the lawn chair outside my tent, pulled my hat down over my eyes, and listened to the sound of others talking, not really hearing what they were saying.

Someone tapped on my knee. I pretended to be sleeping. They tapped again. I took off my hat and snapped, "Leave me the fuck alone."

Lois Carpenter looked down at me with a strange smile, like she'd expected my reaction and was amused by it. It was the first time she ever touched me, just a little tap, and I still remember the feeling of it. I sat bolt upright, almost breaking the lawn chair under me.

"Careful, cowboy," she said. "Don't fall on your ass."

My mind went completely blank. "You surprised me,"

I managed to say. "I'm good." I was trying to be cool, but I was as flustered as I'd ever been. I thought of all the nights I'd dreamed of her, and here she was, standing inches away.

"I'll bet you are." She sat in the chair next to me. "I heard about what you did out there, facing off against the Feds. I was beginning to think nobody in this camp had any balls. Are *you* the guy who's going to step up?"

She turned toward me, so close I could smell her breath. A sweet tincture of wine. I forced myself to look into her eyes, not to look her up and down. "I'll do whatever needs to be done."

"Good," she said in a near whisper and scooted even closer. I could tell some of the other guys were looking at us out of the corner of their eye. I put my hand over my throat as if scratching, but really I was covering my nervous swallow.

"I'm scouting around," she said, "trying to figure out who really means business and who's here for show."

She put her hand on my knee and squeezed encouragingly. I was sure I'd embarrass myself by getting a hard-on, but I was too damned scared. But later, in my tent, all I had to do was replay it in my mind.

"I didn't come all this way to play around," I said. I sat up and stuck my chin out. "We should be making demands or something. If we're just sitting around like this, they're going to win. Everyone is getting tired and bored. These folks are going to head home with their tails between their legs."

"What do you think we should do?"

"Tear down some of these fences, to start. Get rid of the 'No Trespassing' signs. Let them know that the owners of this land are taking it back."

"Let's *do* it then," said Lois. "I know about three other guys so far that want to do more than yap. We're meeting tonight in my trailer, about seven o'clock, right after dark. You want to come?"

I nodded, trying not to act too eager.

"But don't tell John Carver about it," she continued. "I think...no, I *know* he's a plant."

"He's a spy?" I said. Carver and I'd joined the Bakersfield

Freedom Coalition about the same time. But if anyone knew what Carver was really up to, it would be Lois. They'd lived together for months.

Then again, I didn't think Carver was all that political. "I'll fucking kill him," I said anyway.

"Slow down, cowboy," she said.

I was embarrassed. *What an asinine thing to say.* "I didn't really mean it," I muttered.

"You didn't?" She raised her eyebrows. "Well, something will need to be done about him, you know, if we're *really* going to take action."

I stared at her. I couldn't believe what I was hearing. She was really talking about killing someone. I should have stood up and walked away right then.

Then she laughed and pushed her shoulder into mine.

"I'm just joshing. I wouldn't want to hurt Carver."

She put her hand on my leg again, this time on my thigh. *Damn. Damn. Damn.*

She whispered, "But you know, if we did want him out of the picture—not actually kill him, you know, but some kind of accident ought to be easy enough to arrange."

"I, ah...I thought you didn't like politics."

She laughed, and everyone looked our way. I pretended I'd said something funny.

Lois brushed her hand against my shoulder. "Like I said, when you're serious, you do something. You don't talk about it. The more serious you are, the less you talk about it."

My God, that touch...

Look, I'm not stupid. I knew what she was doing, but I was glad she was doing it. *Manipulate me all you want*, I wanted to say, *but keep touching me like that.*

She stood, and I lurched up after her. Standing this close, I could see that she was a good three inches taller than me. She was wearing some kind of intoxicating perfume. When was the last time I was close enough to a lady to smell her scent? My first wife hadn't even used deodorant. Jamie had been slender too, but in a scrawny way. Lois was all woman.

"The Feds aren't going to take the incident at the pump

house lying down," she said. "My guess is they'll be coming in after us tomorrow."

"You really think so?"

"I'm betting. We'll need to be prepared." She stood up and put her hands in her back pockets, smiling.

"I'll see you at seven o'clock then," she said. She nodded to me and walked away. I watched every little movement of her body, and she knew I was watching, too. Then, unbelievably, she glanced back and winked at me.

I slumped back in my chair, closing my eyes, trying to catch my breath and slow my heartbeat.

"What were you two talking about?" The voice was right beside me. I jumped a foot and yelped.

"Sorry, I tried to make some noise." John Carver eyed me, as if he already knew what we'd been saying. I tried to think of an answer.

When nothing came out right away, Carver said, "Be careful with Lois. She isn't what she seems."

"It's none of your business, is it?" I said. "Besides, I wouldn't hurt her for anything."

Carver looked surprised. "Oh…you thought I meant… No, buddy, *you* need to be careful of *her*. She uses people and throws them away."

"I thought you left her," I said. I wanted to walk away. I didn't want to hear what he was saying.

"I'm an idiot when it comes to women, but I do have a well-defined sense of self-preservation. Besides, it was only a matter of time before she found a way to get rid of me. She has a habit of doing that."

"I'm supposed to take your word for it?" I said.

He shrugged. "Have it your way, Mark. I'll hate to see you go down." He turned and walked away.

I believed him. Every word. But it didn't matter. It would be worth the cost, whatever it was, to have a woman like that for even a day.

CHAPTER 21

CARLTON MANNING

I'm not sure why you're deposing me. I have no damning information, and if I did, I wouldn't tell you. I have to protect my sources.

As a journalist, I spent a grand total of two days at the site of the takeover, wandering around, trying to get a sense of the place.

The minute I walked through the line of campers circling the parking lot, a bearded fellow came up to me and said, "Hi, I'm Mohammed. Take all the pictures of Mohammed you want."

I pretended to take a picture of him, then asked him where Hart Davis was. If nothing else, getting an interview with the Strawberry Mountain Killer would make sure the trip wasn't a disappointment.

Mohammed shrugged. "Davis hangs out inside, writing shit. Or he comes out and talks to you guys, saying shit."

I nodded and started to walk away. He called out behind me. "You want to talk to someone who really knows what's going on, come to Mohammed."

I turned on my heel. "All right, Mohammed, what's *really* going on?"

He appeared flustered for a moment, then said, "Wouldn't *you* like to know?"

That's pretty much the way all the interviews went: People going by absurd nicknames, spouting vague slogans, and acting mysterious. I don't think any of these guys or gals knew what they were going to do in the next second, much less having grand a plan. Everyone was toting guns—they didn't go to the latrine without them strapped to their belts, or slung over their shoulders, or just carried around.

The overall odor was of shit, horseshit, and more shit, cigarette smoke, and fumes from the portable generators. The heat itself seemed to have a smell. It crowded in on you, and pinpricks of sweat popped out within seconds of leaving an air-conditioned vehicle. That first night, I walked outside the perimeter to get a picture of the camp from a distance, and the sights and sounds and smells were completely different; sage-brush and juniper pollen and the trill of birds, and bare, rocky ground that stretched out for miles.

The camp was made up of people who professed to love the land, but I never saw them looking outward. They had a little circus going, and it fascinated them all. It was the apocalypse as far as they were concerned, the end times; it was all coming to a head. Things in this country were intolerable, according to them, more intolerable than they'd ever been, and this was the moment when heroes stepped forward and did something about it.

I'd read the same stuff online before I'd arrived. Everyone there had already imbibed the Kool-Aid or was taking their cues from those who had.

If I tried to ask a rational question, they'd pause and, more often than not, they'd give me a considered, even reasonable answer. Then someone would yell out something racist or crazy, and whomever I was interviewing would raise their fist and repeat the slur, contradicting everything they'd just said to me.

So it was all a big show, and despite all their talk, none of the occupiers really expected anything serious to go down. They half hoped it would, but none of them was going to fire first. There were a couple of folks who talked that way, but the others shunned them, and they left after a few days when no one would listen.

There were ten or twelve dogs running loose through the camp, and didn't I know it. You had to watch where you were walking. But these dogs had about as much organization as the protesters did, and they acted pretty much the same, running around in packs, sniffing each other's butts.

It all would have faded away if the Feds hadn't tried to act like hardcases.

I wasn't there when the real troublemakers showed up. I saw no sign of them when I was there. If I had, I would have tried to talk to them, get a sense of what they were planning. But I wrote my little piece, and all I could glean was some colorful flavor and anecdotes, nothing very substantial.

By the second day, I was ready to pack it in. I was heading to my car when I saw a big, bearded fellow leave the campground and start heading straight toward the hills in the distance. Curious, I followed him.

I was wearing the deck shoes I always wear, long trousers and a long-sleeve button-down shirt. Not the most comfortable things to wear in the desert. I'm scared to death of ticks, to be honest. Lyme disease, you know.

By the time I caught up to the guy, I was covered in brown dust up to my knees, and my throat was already tickling from thirst. Well, not really thirst, but the anticipation of thirst, which is worse.

He turned curiously at my approach. "Can I help you?"

"What's your name?" I asked. "What are you doing out here?"

"Garth Perkins," he said, sticking out his hand.

I took his hand, which was dry and solid, unlike my sweaty palms. "Garth…one of the park rangers who stayed behind?"

He nodded. "I saw no reason not to keep working. I thought I caught a glimpse of some pictographs last time I was out this way. I figured I'd check it out."

Pictographs. That sounds interesting. I thought it would embellish my story. All I had was my cellphone, but I'd illustrated my articles with cellphone pictures before. "Can I come along?"

He eyed my striped dress shirt and me. "You can't tell anyone the locations of the pictographs. Not a hint, or I'll leave you out here for the coyotes."

"Agreed," I said.

He took off his backpack and pulled out a thermos. "You'd better hydrate, then."

So if you're wondering if the rangers were really hostages, this pretty much proves they weren't...at least, not then. Garth could have kept walking a few miles to the nearest ranch house if he'd wanted to.

I decided to follow him.

We seemed to trudge on forever at a steady incline that I didn't notice until my thighs and calves started burning.

"How far have we come?" I asked, panting.

"About a mile."

"No way," I said, nearly stopping. "We've gone farther than that."

"Way," he said. "Almost exactly that. That tree over there is what I call the Mile Tree." He turned and pointed to a hill that was cone shaped. "That's Two-Mile Hill over there."

"How far to the pictographs?"

"Past my usual markers," he shrugged. The bastard wasn't even sweating. "I'm guessing about three and half miles."

I repressed a groan. That was seven miles round trip. I consoled myself that the return would be mostly downhill. Garth rummaged around in his pack a little more, pulled out a folded-up safari hat, and handed it to me. It was thin, but I immediately felt the difference.

"Thanks," I said.

After a few more minutes of trudging, I ventured, "What do you think of all this?"

"What do you mean?"

"I mean, what do you think of the ranchers taking over the Fossil Bed Monument? Do you think they have a point?"

"These land-use issues are complicated. The federal government is a long way off, and some of their rules really don't make sense locally. On the other hand, the local governments are prone to let the ranchers do whatever they want. But really, neither side is right. If there was any real justice, this land would be returned to the Paiutes."

"The Native Americans?"

"It's why I became an archeologist as well as a paleontologist," Garth confessed. "I'm not into digging stuff up; I'm into avoiding that as much as possible. It's pretty rich for these guys from Arizona to come in here and take over. See, that's what the white men always do. Tell us how the land once belonged to them, when what really happened was that they took it from the Natives. Actually, even the idea of owning any of this land is missing the point. The land and the Native Americans are the same. Dig up a foot of soil, and you're digging up their past."

"So what's the answer?"

"Beats me. I do know that some of these protesters get a bum rap. I mean, stuff that looks like environmental disasters are actually things that work in the environment's favor. Setting fire to the fields, for instance. The locals know what works—except when they don't.

"But ultimately, the federal government has a duty to protect this land for future generations. The irony is, these folks are being manipulated by big business. If this land became private, it wouldn't be the small ranchers who took it over, but the megacorporations. I doubt the takeover people even realize that it was outside interests who were stripping this land a hundred years ago. The Malheur National Wildlife Refuge, for instance, exists because outsiders were hunting birds to extinction so people in Europe could have fancy hats."

"But you think the federal government has gone too far?" A little late, I pulled out my back-pocket notebook and started writing, trying to catch up.

"Here and there, but it's better than letting these guys pillage the land. They've got their own bullshit cowboy mythology. The end times are coming, they figure, or they just don't care. This whole idea of guaranteeing their grazing rights— there's no mention of cows in the Constitution. So...no way. I figure the BLM and the Forest Service are doing the best they can. But I do see how the ranchers might be pissed off about it."

It's ironic, isn't it, that of everyone I interviewed on the government side, Garth Perkins was the most sympathetic to the protesters. Fucking ironic.

We never found any pictographs.

"They're rare," Garth said, shrugging when we got to outcroppings and saw that what looked like writing from a distance was lichen filling the cracks in the stone. "Which is why we need to protect them."

I took some pictures of red rock pinnacles standing out from the desert sands like worn sculptures of long-dead kings. On our way back, the light of the setting sun slanted almost parallel to the desert floor, bathing it in a golden light that our shadows cut into a hundred, maybe two hundred feet. I'd never seen that before. I'd never been in a place where the sun wasn't blocked, where some wall or another didn't cut off my shadow.

This was everyday wonder to these folks: the light; the landscape; the quiet, soft wind, scented with sage. It occurred to me that these folks might just think differently than those from back East, that they might just have a different take on things.

I wish I'd stuck sentiment into my article instead of the using the snarky, cynical tone that's expected of me.

CHAPTER 22

BRAD PATTERSON

I'm in jail because of that picture. You know, the one where I'm lying down on top of the overpass that crossed the Johnson ranch with my Winchester poked between the concrete partitions. Got my "Live Free or Die" cap on, my military boots, a bulletproof vest.

Makes me look like a badass, but I was shaking like a leaf, man. I was scared to death. Scared I'd have to pull the trigger. I remember my mind going blank, me thinking over and over and over again, *Don't make me shoot. Please, God, don't make me shoot.*

And then one of those slick national magazines interviewed me later and I bragged that I would've fired if the Feds had attacked my people, because it would have been self-defense. Even though I doubted I would have done any such thing.

"We were just a few patriots, and they had the whole government on their side," I said. "The Feds have tanks and tear gas and all the rest. My little rifle against all that."

But when I see that picture, I still get shaky. I'm not that kind of guy. I was just staking out a little place for a little freedom, a little place to make my stand. I might have died that day. It was all a big mistake.

Since the incident on the overpass, I carried my Winchester XPC around with me everywhere I went. I figured that someday they'd work out who was in that picture, the one of me sighting down on the federal agents in the arroyo. They'd figure out who I was and come and get me and my rifle.

I wasn't sure what I'd do when that day came. Carrying the rifle never became completely natural, though. I was always conscious of its weight, of what it could do.

A couple of weeks into the takeover, a new group started showing up. They were different from the earlier militia types, who'd carried their racism and white supremacy on their sleeves. I saw Joshua examining them, but the newcomers were courteous to him and he let it go.

I couldn't put my finger on it, but they were rougher somehow, and more fit, hard like I figured a Seal Team might be hard. The women were hard, too, but not like the tanned, leathery ranch women like Lois Carpenter. They were more like what I figured college athletes would be like if they kept up their training.

I started calling them hard-asses, and that's how others began to refer to them behind their backs.

Anyway, they weren't like the first batch of protesters. Most of us knew each other, knew one another's strengths and weaknesses. Let's face it, we were a bunch of misfits in the modern world. But I always figured the Founding Fathers were like that: Adams, Jefferson, old Ben Franklin.

This new group, you could put them in suits and ties and they'd fit in on Wall Street.

"What do you think?" I asked Marston after I told him how uncomfortable they made me.

He glanced over at them and nodded. "I've wondered too. I thought maybe FBI. But have you talked to them? Hard to fake that level of commitment."

"Committed to what, though?" I said. "I didn't sign on to be part of some militia."

Marston gave me a sideways look and snorted. "Better not read the newspapers, then, because you're already there as far as the public is concerned."

I hadn't even thought of that. Of course that's how people would see it. I rocked back and forth from my toes to my heels, which I did when I was nervous. Like I couldn't decide whether to run or fight. "Can't we just ask them to leave?"

"I'll have a talk with them, see what I can do." He gave me

a reassuring pat on the shoulder, like he was going to take care of it.

People brought in newspapers when they visited, and I'd been using them to start my campfire at night. Now I started reading them before burning them. Turns out these new guys came from a whole bunch of groups, half of whom I'd never voluntarily associate with. Joshua's pounding of the KKK guy had driven away the worst of them, or at least the more overtly racist, but these new guys definitely had an agenda. I just wasn't sure what.

There was this one guy. He told us his name was Smith. Fucking Smith. We should have tossed him out right then and there. But...well, there was always a chance, I guess, that his name really was Smith.

The guy gave me the creeps, and I didn't know why. He didn't do anything, just stood around like he was on guard or something, but—unlike me—he looked like his rifle was part of him, like it was another limb.

I served time in the county jail for some DUIs, and they had these romance novels lying around. Guys would get them from their girlfriends because they weren't allowed porn and these books were pretty filthy.

Smith looked like one of the guys the heroines lusted after in the books, all chiseled features, muscles, and glossy hair.

I didn't trust him one damn bit.

This may sound strange coming from the guy who's semi-famous for sighting down on Feds from an overpass, but there was no fun in it, I got nothing but grief from it, and I still have nightmares where I actually pull the trigger, and I wake up sweating.

I worked a ranch once where something terrible happened right before I arrived. A cowboy was out riding, like I used to do almost every day. Sitting on his horse on a ridge, drinking some water.

Someone shot him from a long distance, right in the head.

They never caught who did it. I always wondered who would do such a thing and why. There was another guy, in my hometown, who shot a lady jogger in the head from the top of a hill. He said he did it to see what it felt like, to see "her head pop."

Like I said, I always wondered who would do such a thing.

Well, Smith would do such a thing. That's the feeling he gave me. He's the guy who would do that.

CHAPTER 23

MARK SIMONS

Iwaited until dark before getting up and walking to Lois's trailer. I took a roundabout route, coming in from behind, looking over my shoulder. I'm pretty sure no one saw me.

Why I was being so cautious, I wasn't sure. But I had a sense, even that early on, that what we'd be talking about and doing wouldn't be things we'd want other people to know about.

Lois had made the little trailer almost homey. There were a couple of houseplants beside the steps, some nice chairs and a table outside under an umbrella.

She opened the door before I got to the steps and gave me a big, welcoming smile. At the top step, she leaned down and gave me a hug. It was an awkward angle. I felt her breasts brush against my chest.

"I'm glad you came, Mark," she said. "Come on in and meet the others."

I wasn't surprised to see Jules sitting by himself in a lounge chair. On the small sofa were two men I'd seen around but didn't know.

"You know Jules, of course. And this is Curt Smith and Conrad Benson from Idaho. I've been communicating with them for quite a while."

I sat down between the two men on the sofa, feeling like a little boy squeezing in between adults. They were tall, in good shape—they had a military look to them.

Lois stayed on her feet, pacing a little, going over to the kitchenette counter, fiddling about with coffee and drinks. She didn't ask me what I wanted, just brought over a cup of black coffee. I took a sip and almost spit it out. It was laced with rum. I wasn't much of drinker. The mixture burned down my throat. I glanced over at Benson, and he was wearing the ghost of a smile.

I never did see Smith smile. There was something about him that was familiar, like I'd met him before, but the more I looked at him, the more the feeling faded. Maybe it was just that he was a hard-ass and I'd run into enough of them to get a pretty good sense of what he was about.

Finally, when everyone had a drink in their hands, Lois stood in front of us. It was nice to have an excuse to stare at her, to be able to look directly into her face, even better to examine her head to toe. But it was a little hard to concentrate on what she was saying. She blew me away. My heart raced, and I felt sweaty. I heard my name.

"…Mark and I were talking about it earlier. Take my word for it, the Feds are going to regard the pump house confrontation as a provocation. My guess, they'll try to roust us out of here tomorrow, first thing. We need to be ready."

"They wouldn't dare," Jules said.

"They don't think we're serious, Mr. Francisco. They think if they catch us off guard, we'll give up. So we'll need a couple of lookouts and to tell as many people to be ready in advance as we can. If we meet the Feds with a united front, I think they'll back down."

"They better," Jules said. He'd picked up his rifle and was cradling it.

I couldn't believe what I was hearing. I'd always figured we'd get arrested as protesters. But facing off with loaded guns? That was a whole 'nother thing.

"Just standing there glaring at them won't work," Smith growled.

"What do you mean?" Lois asked. She posed the question in such a way that I figured out later it was a plant. They'd arranged the whole thing in advance. Jules couldn't see it, but I could.

"We need to get those rangers out there with us," Smith

said, "make sure that anything that happens to us happens to them. Benson and I will make sure they're there."

"How?" Jules said. "They aren't hostages."

There was a long silence after that. My heart fell, and I could see that Jules was also starting to get a glimmer of what the real situation was.

"We'll make sure they're there," Benson said.

"Good," Lois said. "Why don't you take first watch, Mark? Benson, you relieve him in six hours or so, and then you, Smith."

I nodded, trying to hide my relief. If Lois was right, the Feds would come in the daylight. If she was wrong, they'd come in the small hours of morning. Either way, my shift would be over.

As the meeting broke up, there was a sense of purpose—for the first time in a long time.

On my way to the front of the camp, I passed by other occupiers, and I wondered how many of them realized how serious things were getting.

I took my spot near the entrance and stared at the bright lights across the way.

I made it through my shift, doubting the whole time that anything would happen. Benson came and relieved me at three in the morning. I stumbled off to my tent and barely made it to my sleeping bag before I was out.

Some idiot had brought a damn cowbell to camp. Its insistent clattering woke me. Someone was clanging that thing as hard as they could.

I checked the time.

Six-thirty in the morning, which meant Benson was still on watch. The bright light of early morning lit up the blue walls of the tent.

I groaned and rolled over, pulling the pillow over my head. I could still hear the clanging, but I figured if anyone asked, it was plausible that I could've slept through it.

Wasn't it? Did I really want to face off with the Feds? They'd all been trained, and they no doubt were itching to take us down. At six-thirty in the morning, reality was sinking in.

But then I realized that Lois would take one look at my face and know what a coward I was.

I crawled out of the sleeping bag. The cold morning air nearly froze me into a statue, the crawling statue of a man who couldn't stand up for himself. I slipped on my jeans, grimacing as I realized how much they stank. My socks...I almost sniffed them and then thought better of it. I safely encased them in my mud-encrusted boots.

Once outside the tent, I realized I'd left my rifle behind.

My heart isn't in this, I thought. *I should get back into bed. Let this play out without me.*

It was as if Lois was standing right there next to me, frowning. I didn't have to imagine it at all. I ducked into the tent and grabbed my rifle. I didn't put a round in the chamber, though. I didn't take off the safety. I had no fucking intention of shooting anyone.

Word must have gotten out about the possible invasion, because almost the entire camp was in front of Merriam Hall. Lois was nowhere to be seen, which I thought was strange, but later on, of course, I realized she was never where the action was actually happening. She just instigated it all.

The park rangers weren't there, and I breathed a sigh of relief, but just as I was beginning to think it was going to be all right, Perry Campbell and Nicole Nelson showed up, with Benson and Smith accompanying them, and joined the crowd.

Across the way, directly in the glare of the morning sun, a troop of black uniforms came out from behind the barricades. I was blinded for a moment by an intense glare, as if the Feds were carrying mirrors. Then I realized that they had clear plastic riot shields. They were fully armored, wearing vests and helmets. Each was carrying a billy club or a stun gun, but none of them appeared to have firearms.

The Feds formed in a skirmish line, shields so close together that they seemed almost locked. Other Feds were behind them, ready to push forward when they met resistance.

That's when Smith took charge of the occupiers. He started moving people around, forming our own skirmish line, a wall of resisters two and three thick surrounding Merriam Hall. Somehow, he maneuvered Perry and Nicole to the middle of the front row without them realizing it.

Then he and Benson took their places behind the park rangers, rifles held at chest height.

It became eerily quiet. The two sides stared at each other, one at attention, in ordered rows, the other a ragtag group, milling around.

A loud whistle blew across the way, and the Feds started marching toward us in lockstep.

It was thrilling and frightening at the same time. It felt more like a battle of the Revolutionary War than a modern skirmish. And maybe it was…a Second Revolutionary War. Maybe this was our Bunker Hill, our Concord.

Apparently, I wasn't the only one who thought so.

"Don't shoot until you see the whites of their eyes!" someone shouted.

"For God's sake, don't shoot at all!" someone else—I think Hart Davis—shouted.

I laughed. It was a nervous reaction, not appropriate at all, but it was catching, and I heard several people around me also bark out a laugh.

Most people unconsciously stepped back, but a few leaned forward, rifles lifted almost to their shoulders. *This could really end up badly,* I thought. Up to now, the Feds had treated us like protesters, but if a gunshot was fired, we'd instantly turn into domestic terrorists, and there wasn't a lot that the American public wouldn't countenance when it came to fighting terrorism.

By some miracle, no one fired.

But then the Feds escalated things.

Two tear gas canisters landed a few feet in front of our line. Our group began to lose its cohesion. I held my breath. But instead of anyone firing, Jerry Johnson picked up a fist-sized rock and heaved it ineffectually at the advancing line. It fell ten feet short. Others quickly followed his example, and seconds later, the sound of rocks thudding against shields filled the air.

Other than that, it was strangely quiet. Neither side was shouting, but each seemed intent on watching the other side. The line of Feds kept coming, and two more tear gas canisters landed among us. Brad Patterson picked one up and threw it back at them. It was windy, so the gas wasn't as effective as it could have been, but my eyes still watered, and I felt my throat swelling up like it did when I cried.

This time I was certain someone would fire their weapon.

I looked back at Benson and Smith.

There was no mistaking it, at least to my eyes. Their rifles were mere inches away from the backs of Nicole and Perry's heads. Alone among the crowd, the two men were unmoving, staring into the distance, as if they could see something no one else could see. I followed their gaze.

Bright flashes of something reflected in the morning sun. Binoculars or scopes, I guessed.

Whoever it was probably saw the same thing I was seeing, because seconds later, whistles started blowing and deep voices sounded the retreat. They didn't call it that, but that's what it was.

Cheers rose from our side. The people around me gave each other fist bumps, even hugs. They thought they'd fought off the advance.

But I knew what had really happened. I glanced around the crowd to see if anyone else had seen what I'd seen.

Hart Davis was staring at me with a grim expression. I felt myself shrugging, as if to say, *It's not my fault.* He ignored me and pushed his way through the crowd, trying to reach Perry and Nicole, but they'd already left.

Smith and Benson stood with their rifles at their sides. Then they turned and gave each other a slow high five.

CHAPTER 24

HART DAVIS

Had no one else seen it?

I'd glanced at Nicole at the most critical moment of the confrontation, when I thought it might break out into an all-out battle. Smith and Benson were standing right behind her and her coworkers. The men's rifles weren't pointed directly at their heads, but close enough to read their intentions.

I almost turned around and challenged them myself, but at that moment, whistles and shouts signaled that the Feds were retreating. I'm betting whoever was in charge of them, who no doubt had scopes trained on us, had seen the same thing I did.

I don't think anyone in the camp saw it but me, except maybe Mark Simons, and I never could read him. Even Nicole seemed unaware of the danger.

When it was over, I went straight to her office and entered without knocking. She turned around, shocked, and looked like she was going to kick me out; then she saw my expression.

"We have to leave now," I said.

I wondered whether to tell her what I'd seen but decided I didn't want to worry her. It was best that she remain her cheerful, smiling self.

"That bad?" she asked with a little grin.

"I think it is."

Her smile faded. I think she saw my fear and intuited what had happened, though she never asked.

"Hart…I've told you…"

"No, this is different. These new people, they're different.

They aren't Marston or even Jules. Patterson is calling them hard-asses. They're ex-military, from the looks of it. They have a different agenda."

"Even if I wanted to leave, I won't go without Garth and Perry. It's my fault they're here."

"Then let's go get them…now."

I went over to her, intending to take her hand. She stepped back, searching my face, and then said, "OK. Let's go."

We left the visitor center and headed toward the entrance of the camp. Perry seemed to hang out there a lot, as if hoping it was all going to end soon and he could just leave. Instead of Perry, we were met by two of the hard-asses, Benson and Smith.

"You folks going somewhere?" Smith asked. He stood relaxed, but his rifle was in his hands.

"None of your business," Nicole said.

"Because if you're intending to leave, we'd rather you didn't right now."

"Why not?"

"Well, we're all in this together, aren't we? Best not make it look like we're splitting up. Just for a day or two, you know. I'm sure everything will have settled down by then."

I started seeing red. I would've marched right up to the man, but Nicole slipped her hand into mine and gently pulled me away. We didn't say a word until we were back in her office.

I closed the door. "We've got to end this takeover."

"I agree," she said. "But how do we do that?"

"I don't know, but we'd better figure out a way. And fast."

"OK, Hart, let's figure out a way," she said.

CHAPTER 25

NICOLE NELSON

Hart's urgency confused me at first, but slowly, by the things he said and didn't say, I figured out that he thought I'd been in danger.

I hadn't registered it consciously at the time, but I'd felt a tingling behind my back. I'd looked around to see what was causing it. There were two large and rather rough-looking men behind me. One of them nodded and smiled, but the cold look in his eyes contradicted the smile.

I would have missed the whole confrontation if someone hadn't banged on the office door that morning. "You're going to want to see this!" they shouted.

Most of the camp was already awake and shambling in the direction of the parking lot. I have to admit, I was surprised to see the FBI taking action. It seemed reckless to me. All it would have taken was one hothead taking a shot and it would have been a massacre.

Thank God, the Feds retreated.

I was shaking by the time I got back to my office. It had been a mistake to stay at the Fossil Beds. It was so clear to me now. I'd put Garth and Perry in danger.

So when Hart came bursting in, insisting that we needed to leave, I believed him.

By the time Benson and Smith turned us away at the camp entrance, I felt a calm come over me. I realized that we had to end the stalemate, one way or another.

"We've got to end this takeover," Hart said.

"I agree. But how do we do that?"

"I don't know, but we'd better figure out a way. And fast."

"OK, Hart, let's figure out a way," I said.

Easy to say, but it was clear from the ensuing silence that neither of us had any ideas.

"Why don't you original occupiers surrender?" I said. "If you give up now, at least no one gets hurt."

"No one's going to listen me," Hart said. "No one's ready to give up. They don't see the danger. We've been trying to resolve this for days, but settle with one group and you piss off another." He stood up and stared at the door as if he expected someone to come in.

"All right," I said, shaken by his certainty.

We sat in our chairs, not looking at each other. It seemed hopeless. I'd made a huge mistake, putting us all in danger. I didn't care about myself, but Hart never would have stuck around if not for me. He'd been stupid to bring his friends here, but I'd been equally stupid in making my friends stay.

"But what if we come up with a statement that everyone can agree on?" I asked. "Something general."

"That would be toothless, and these guys want to use their teeth, if you know what I mean."

"So we make it sound, you know, all fangy and ferocious, but make the actual content tame. I'm pretty sure Special Agent Rod would understand what we're doing."

Hart sat thinking about it. He was clean-shaven, groomed, unlike most of these cowboys, who were beginning to stink. I liked looking at his profile.

"That might actually work," he said, finally. "The guys smart enough to see through it, like Joshua and maybe Peter Sterns, they want to end this as much as we do." He frowned. "Some of the others might be a problem, though. Benson and Smith and people like them *want* something to happen. They probably think they're going to spark some kind of revolution or something."

"So we'll outvote them," I said. I didn't really think it would work, but it was better than doing nothing. Better than letting this whole thing explode like I knew it could.

"So…" he said, his gaze drifting to the ceiling. "Something like, 'When in the course of human events things turn to shit, you gotta do something about it. Cut the ties, don't let others tell you what to do, because BY GOD, we know as much as they do, dammit…'"

"Something like that," I said. "Maybe break out a thesaurus for a bit more style."

"Let's do it," Hart said.

We spent the rest of the afternoon working on it.

The Juniper Proclamation, we ended up calling it.

I think we almost pulled it off. It sounded like we…they… were willing to go down fighting. But if you read between the lines, they weren't really asking for anything. I mean, it really was more in the way of a proclamation:

"Now is the time to act.

"*Whereas,* the federal government no longer works for the people, but against us, it is our duty to defy its authority.

"*Whereas,* the federal government has ceased to listen to the legitimate concerns of the people, we refuse to follow its dictates.

"*Whereas,* the federal government denies our inalienable constitutional rights to life, liberty, and property, we reject its power over us.

"*Whereas,* we have been deprived of our rights to free assembly and free speech, we must fight for those rights.

"*Whereas,* our rights are being taken away from us little by little, we will no longer allow that theft to continue at the hands of the federal government.

"*Therefore,* it is our duty and honor to defy the federal government's overreach into public lands, which the Constitution does not allow without the consent of the local governments.

"*Therefore,* the Juniper Coalition will recognize only the authority of the county sheriff within whose jurisdiction we protest. We will not leave until he asks us to leave."

When Hart added that last sentence, I was puzzled. "Sheriff Hammond supports the takeover."

"That's the tricky part, the face-saving part," he said. "I'm pretty sure the others will agree to the stipulation because of that. But I'm betting the Feds will work on the good sheriff until he gives in."

"Have you ever *met* Sheriff Hammond?" I asked. "He's more radical than half of you protesters."

Hart nodded. "That's why there's a loophole." He looked very pleased with himself.

"What loophole?"

"Most of the Fossil Bed Monument is within Grant County, but a small portion is in Wheeler County. So we just have to make sure the sheriff of Wheeler County realizes that. Once we've all agreed to the statement, we'll have to abide by it. If Sheriff Lopez asks us to leave, it will give us an excuse to get out of here."

"God, I hope you're right. I like deviousness of it. I hope Lopez catches on to the loophole."

He looked down at the scribbled document that had so many crossed-off lines and corrected stuff that if you didn't know what it already said, you'd never guess. "It isn't strong enough."

"Good," I said. "That will give the others something to bicker about. Whatever you give them, they're going to change anyway."

He grunted, leaned back in the office chair, and pulled his hat down over his eyes, thinking hard. I loved his look, the civilized rancher thing. For a moment, my heart did the same strange loop-the-loop as the first time I'd seen him, in the Strawberry Mountains.

After a moment, Hart sat up, pushing his hat back. "I just realized. It can't be me who proposes it."

"Why not?"

"I don't think these guys trust me. They don't think I'm really one of them." He let that hang there, then said, "It's got to be one of the others."

"Marston?"

"Like I said, I want to keep this document away from him for as long as I can. He'll mess it up somehow."

I ran their faces through my mind, trying to attach names to them, eliminating them one by one. Patterson? Too quiet. Jules? Too loud. "What about Peter Sterns?"

"Peter? He's just a kid."

"The others like him, and everyone can see he's smart."

He frowned, then smiled. "You're right. They might accept it from him. I'll talk to him tonight. This is good."

He leaned over and kissed me. I gave in for a moment, then pushed him away.

"Are you ever going to forgive me?" he asked softly. "I don't want to push myself on you. If you want me to give up…"

I should have answered him. The truth was, I'd already begun to forgive him. I hadn't exactly handled things right either. But something inside me still wanted to punish him a little.

The silence extended too long, and whether I wanted it to be or not, it became a rejection.

The door creaked open a crack behind us. A woman poked her head in. I'd seen her around, joshing with the guys but giving me cold looks every time our eyes met. A dark-haired woman, nice-looking in a hard way, like she washed down every day with a couple of shots of whiskey and a dozen cigarettes.

If I thought I'd gotten cold glances from her before, I was practically frozen solid by the look she gave me now. I realized that I was sitting on the footstool at Hart's feet, my eyes about waist height. Hart pushed the office chair back and stood up as if he realized how it looked too.

"That reporter from the *Washington Post* is outside, and he won't talk to anyone but you," the woman said to Hart.

"Thanks, Lois. I'll be out in a second."

Lois shot me another killer look and closed the door. Hart picked up the Juniper Proclamation. He was blushing, and I realized it was because of my rejection, not because we'd been caught smooching.

"I'll show this to Peter," he said, rushing his words. "Let him put some style into it. He writes poetry, did you know that?"

It seemed like he couldn't wait to get out of there, so I shook my head silently in response, and he gave me a weak smile and left.

I wish I'd said something. *I'm just not ready, Hart. But...soon.* Maybe if I had, he wouldn't have...

I wasn't there when Peter presented the proclamation that night. I wouldn't have been welcomed in that crowd. But from what I understand, it almost worked. It *would* have worked, dammit, if things hadn't gone south.

Instead, the Juniper Proclamation became a call to battle.

Writing it turned out to be a big mistake.

A very big mistake.

CHAPTER 26

PETER STERNS

They must have made a clerical error this morning. They put Hart Davis and me in the exercise yard at the same time. It was a small courtyard with a postage-stamp lawn, a line of concrete picnic tables, and a concrete walk within the perimeter. It didn't look like jail until you noticed the razor wire along the top of the walls.

Hart was walking the circuit, and I joined him. First time I've seen any of the others.

"Have you seen Mich?" he asked right away.

"She's not allowed to talk to me," I said, my heart speeding up at the sound of her name. "Or I'm not supposed to talk to her, I'm not sure which."

He nodded. "Hang in there, buddy. I don't think she was faking her feelings for you."

It hurt to even think about it, so I tried not to. I was spending most of my time scribbling down lines of poetry, most of which I'd never show anyone. I might not be able to talk to Mich, but I couldn't stop thinking about her. They were love poems, something I'd never thought I'd write in a million years. It was embarrassing.

But there was one poem I thought I could show Hart and that he might like.

I asked him to read my cowboy poem.

He hesitated, then put out his hand.

I've never been so scared in all my life. I thought he'd laugh in my face, but he read it seriously, folded it up, and handed it back. "A little elegant and refined for cowboy poetry, don't you think?" he said.

I felt the blood rush to my cheeks. I hated blushing; it made me feel like a ten-year-old again. Thing was, he'd confirmed my suspicions. See, while I'd started by reading cowboy poets, I'd stumbled across a few others since: Yeats, Frost, people like that. And no matter how I tried to ignore their voices, they tended to creep into what I was writing.

I tried to laugh it off. "You calling me elegant and refined?"

"Why not? That's how your poetry strikes me for sure."

"But I use the words *cahoots* and *reckon*," I said.

"Yes, but very elegantly."

I hadn't planned on showing him my new poem, but at this, I pulled it out.

Walking in twilight,
The day's garments drop away

The north breeze
Sweeps the sunlight

The soft light of the mountains fades
The moonlight glows

Sleep the worries, the frenzied flow,
Rapids left behind, the river slows

The trees stand unmoving,
Forever twilight, forever silent.

He read it and shook his head. "Were you an English major, Peter?"

"I didn't even finish high school," I said.

"Well, maybe you should have. I bet some college would take you on. I mean, there wasn't a lot of poetry in the classes I took, but hell, Peter, you write *poetry,* and that's got to mean something."

Not at all the response I'd expected, but after he said it, I realized that secretly I'd sorta hoped for it. I don't know why. I wasn't going to college. I was going to prison.

It was like Hart read my mind. "They aren't sending all of us away, Peter. You got more of these poems?"

I think I blushed a little, and he seemed to guess why I was being reticent.

"Show your poems to your lawyers at least," he urged. "Let the jury see the human side of you. No one will think less of you if the poems are a little...sentimental. How old are you, anyway, Peter?"

"Twenty-five," I said.

"Give me those poems," he said. "Damn me if you're going to jail."

CHAPTER 27

HART DAVIS

I couldn't look at Lois Carpenter; I was too embarrassed. Until that scene in Nicole's office, I'd harbored the illusion that she would forgive me. By why should she? I'd acted like an idiot.

Part of me wanted to keep walking, straight out of camp. Let Benson or Smith shoot me in the back. Put me out of my misery.

But then what would happen to Nicole? And the others? I was going to protect her, even if from a distance. The truth was, I still loved her and I always would.

Lois was talking to Mark Simons. Mark looked like a hulking football player who was being reprimanded by a teacher. I hadn't seen much of him since the takeover started. He talked big when nothing was happening, but now that the real deal was here, he'd blended into the desert sands, or so I thought at the time. Turns out, I couldn't have been more wrong.

Lois pushed herself away from the wall and gave me a raised eyebrow and a knowing smile. She turned her back on Simons like he wasn't there. He flushed a little, glared at me, and walked away.

"Sorry, the reporter took off," she said.

Lois's off-kilter smile told me she suspected that Nicole and I were up to something.

Lois said, "What are you two cooking up in there?" She glanced at the Juniper Proclamation in my hands.

Should I tell her? I wondered. *Should I let her in on it?*

Lois had a good head on her shoulders. At the same time, she was cynical about the whole thing. Which raised the question…

"Why are you here?" I asked. "I thought you said this was foolishness."

"I love foolishness in all forms," she said. "Besides, a lot of my friends are here. I figured you men would be helpless without a few of us women around to take care of you."

She stood a few feet away from me, a woman who knew her mind, who usually got her own way. After the soft presence of Nicole, it was kind of jarring, and yet...I was pulled toward it. The certainty of it. There was no game playing, no doubts about what she wanted.

She was tall whereas Nicole was short, and dark-haired instead of blonde. It was like she was a different species. It wasn't really their looks that made them so different, though, it was their personalities, equally dark and light.

"So what have you got there?" she asked.

"I thought we needed a...a mission statement, a proclamation of some kind."

Lois laughed. "You serious? Did you know that the guy in the camper next to me is certain the Feds are experimenting with coyotes to make them deadlier?"

"Why would they want to do that?"

"You're asking for logic? A mission statement? Try getting all these guys to agree to *anything*."

I lowered my voice. "Then how do we get out of here, Lois? I mean, there has to be an end goal."

She reached over and patted me on the arm, her hand lingering a little too long. I glanced at her, and she looked away. "It's all going to peter out anyway," she said, "when people stop sending food. Already, we're down to Spam and Top Ramen. I heard this morning that the Feds aren't letting any more people through again, and those who leave aren't being allowed back in."

"There are some hard-asses here," I said. "They'll go on a hunger strike if they have to."

"So let them," Lois said, shrugging. "As long as the Feds don't try anything, I think this whole thing will be over pretty soon."

The lights in the hallway flickered, and we both looked up.

"It's only a matter of time before they turn the electricity off," she said. "We can guard the water pump all day and night, but without electricity, we're screwed. Portable generators aren't going to cut it with this many people. If we thought we were roughing it before…"

As if to reinforce her words, someone opened the front doors, and the smell of garbage and overflowing latrines wafted through the building.

"See what I mean?" she said. "I give it another week, if that."

I didn't say anything. I thought it would last a lot longer.

"Can I see what you wrote?" she asked.

She didn't wait for an answer but pulled the papers out of my hand. I watched her read the scribbled proclamation, expecting her to laugh. Instead, she squinted and pursed her lips, bringing out the wrinkles around her eyes and mouth. For some reason, that made her even more attractive.

She handed it back, looking thoughtful. "Nice. The Juniper Proclamation. The language may be a little fancy for these guys. But…well, we wrote it, so it counts, right? It's pretty vague; that's good. Not nearly radical enough, but I'm sure you realize that. The others will want to add some blood and guts."

"That's what Nicole and I thought, which is why we kept things…general."

"She's OK with this?"

"She wants the takeover to end, and there isn't anything in the proclamation that doesn't have some truth to it."

She cocked her head at me and winked. "I especially like the part about the sheriff. Kind of puts us in a box. Either we think the county sheriff is the ultimate arbiter or we don't, right? Turns us into a bunch of hypocrites if we don't obey."

I nodded, a little worried that she'd seen through it so quickly. But then, I had the feeling she was smarter than just about anyone in the camp.

"You want me to type that up for you?" she asked. "Is there a working printer around here?"

"I thought I'd let Peter Sterns take a look at it, see if there was anything he can add."

"Smart. Everyone trusts Peter. Not everyone trusts you." I

winced, and she snorted. "You know that already."

"Something has to come out of this," I said. "Even if it's some vague generalizations. Otherwise we're going to look like a bunch of fools."

"Too late," she said cheerfully. "But let me know if I can help. I'll back you when the time comes. Meanwhile…I need to get back to my trailer and water the plants."

We stood awkwardly for a few moments, trying to think of something to say. Then she leaned in and gave me a hug. "I'm glad you're here, Hart Davis," she said and walked away without looking back.

CHAPTER 28

MARK SIMONS

At the next meeting, Lois was pumped about the way the Feds had retreated when faced with a united front.

"That was fantastic." She paced back and forth in the narrow corridor of the trailer. "The whole world saw the Feds backing down. Now we need to push a little harder. We need to do something people will notice."

"Damned straight," Jules said.

"What do you suggest?" Benson asked.

"Well…we can start with pulling down all the 'Do Not…' signs," she said.

"Yean, *fuck* those," Jules muttered.

"Maybe tear down some of the fences," Lois continued, "that kind of thing."

"Oh, *that* will impress them," Smith said. His voice was so deep it was like I needed to adjust the volume of a TV set to hear him clearly. "Tearing down signs and fences, how fucking radical."

"What do *you* suggest?" Lois asked.

"If it were up to me, I'd burn down the whole damn place," Smith said. It was like he was talking to himself and didn't care if anyone overheard him.

That was met by silence. I glanced at Lois. To my surprise, she seemed to be considering the idea. Then she shook her head.

"We want to spin this whole takeover thing as long as possible," she said, sounding thoughtful. "We start setting fires and the FBI will be on us. No, we start with something small and then escalate. Make sure each thing we do isn't enough of a stretch from the last thing to make them want to take the chance of confronting us. Maybe, at the end, when we're done and we don't care anymore, *then* we burn the place down. So, people...what's the sweet spot?"

Benson and Smith sat unmoving, but Jules pushed himself to the edge of his chair, almost slipping off in his excitement. "Anyone else sick of having to walk a quarter mile to take a shit?"

It wasn't a really quarter mile, maybe half that far, but it was farther than I liked. Once, I almost didn't make it. On the other hand, I thought keeping the smell away from the main part of the camp was a good thing.

"I stepped in some shit today," Benson said. "I'm hoping it was dog shit."

Jules nodded, his scrawny neck wobbling. "People are pissing outside their tents. I wouldn't be all that surprised if some of them are shitting on the ground, too."

"Explains the stink," Smith said.

Lois laughed. Everyone shut up and looked up at her. "I like it. It's good. The Feds are already freaked out about all the sanitation stuff. Maybe we can dig a garbage ditch while we're at it."

"Where do we dig?" Jules asked.

Lois looked around the room as if she wanted one of us to decide. She glanced at me. I swallowed and stared down at my feet. I wasn't sure about any of this.

"We dig right there to the north of the visitor center," Smith said. "Why not make it easy?"

I found myself speaking before I knew it, somewhat to my own surprise. "That's the Native American graveyard section. There's a sign there saying it's a Native heritage site."

"Who fucking cares?" Benson said.

"I got nothing against Indians," Jules said. "Can't we dig somewhere else?"

"No," Smith said. "That's the point. It'll shake things up, but the Feds won't do anything. They'll fuck the Indians over like they always have."

That's when I remembered where I'd heard of Curt Smith

before. I'd read about him in the papers, one of the few times I actually read a paper. I was in a diner, bored out of my skull, and the words "Native American" and "grave robbing" had caught my eye.

Curt Smith had been convicted of looting Native sites and selling relics online. If I remembered right, he'd gotten five years, which had seemed like a lot to me at the time. He'd been called "incorrigible" by the judge. Told he needed to be "taught a lesson."

I turned to Lois, intending to object, but she was nodding enthusiastically.

"That's perfect," she said. "It'll be all over the news."

"Yeah," Jules muttered. "It'll make us look like assholes."

But it was clear that Jules and I would be outvoted, even though we'd tried to argue the point—assuming that Lois would even think to put it to a vote. She shot a triumphant look at Smith. It made me wonder. Lois had said she'd been communicating with Smith and Benson for "quite a while." Was all this arranged in advance? Had Lois and Smith already made the plans and just wanted some stooges for cover? And I wondered if it was pure vindictiveness or whether they had plans to sell any artifacts that were unearthed by the digging.

Smith said, "We'll meet at Merriam Hall tomorrow morning, at seven o'clock. Won't be many people awake then to try to stop us."

"No," Jules said.

Everyone turned to him, surprised. There was no mistaking his disapproval.

"Tomorrow's Sunday," he said, his big eyes glaring at us. "I ain't doing nuthin' on Sunday, especially if it's breaking the law."

"There's a higher power at work here," Lois said.

Jules stared back at her, jaw clenched. "Oh, well," he said.

Lois turned to Smith, looking flummoxed, and made a disgusted sound. "First thing Monday then, if that makes the lawbreaking easier."

Jules nodded, his head bobbing unenthusiastically.

Lois stood up and started toward the door, then hesitated.

"I think we need more people. Think about who we can ask to join our group, and bring them here tomorrow night at seven o'clock. Make sure they're reliable. Is that all right with you, Jules? Can you come to a meeting on Sunday?"

"Talk never hurt no one," Jules said.

"No?" Lois said, looking amused. "If you say so."

We all got up to leave, but at the door, Lois took my arm. "Stay a minute," she said softly.

I might never have come back if she hadn't asked me to stay just then. I was starting to have some real doubts. But with those three words, all my doubts were forgotten.

After everyone left, she closed the door and turned to me with a smile. "I'm counting on you, Mark. It's hard to know what these other guys want. Jules is a bit of a loose cannon, don't you think?"

"He talks big," I said, "but he's all right."

"Well, *you're* my point man, Mark, and I appreciate it." She gave me another hug, this time a full-body one. She felt so slender and fragile. She held on long enough for me to put my hand on her back, and then long enough for me to think about nuzzling her neck. She pulled away then, and I flushed, thinking what a mistake that would have been.

"See you tomorrow, then," I said. "You going to be with us Monday morning?"

"I'm going to take a step back for now. I've got some of these idiots like Hart Davis fooled. I can learn a lot by talking to them. So you and the others, you go ahead and do what we talked about. We'll get together soon."

I wondered, the way she said it, whether she meant the group or her and me. Everything was a double message from her.

I was helpless to refuse her. I ain't excusing myself for what happened, I'm just saying.

CHAPTER 29

HART DAVIS

Around 8:30 that night, I made my way to Lois's trailer. As I approached, I saw Mark Simons leaving. He seemed to be transformed from the guy who had accompanied us to the Fossil Beds, standing taller, his chin high. I caught a glimpse of Lois closing the door, and I wondered if Mark was making some headway on his obvious crush. I sorta hoped so.

Lois must have seen me coming, because she opened the door and ushered me in. It was like I'd stepped into another world, a feminine world. Outside was dirt and grit and denim-clad men and women carrying guns. Inside the trailer were frilled curtains, a tablecloth, and a quilt along the top of the small built-in sofa.

Lois grabbed the proclamation out of my hand. "You want me to type this up?"

"If you don't mind," I said. "I can't type to save my life. Even with spell check."

She laughed as if I'd said something funny. "Come on in, then," she said. She led me to the second room in the trailer, which consisted of a big bed and, along one wall, a small desk with a computer, a printer, and some electronic equipment I didn't recognize.

"I borrowed a printer from the office," she said, sitting on the edge of the bed. "I figured you might come by."

"I've called for a meeting tomorrow at noon at Merriam Hall," I said. I stayed standing. "I'm hoping you'll help get the word out."

"I've already heard. Noon is a great idea. It will be so hot by then, everyone will want a little of that sweet air conditioning."

She typed up the proclamation rapidly, played with the font a little, made the title THE JUNIPER PROCLAMATION stand out with some old-timey lettering, put in some bullet points, and otherwise made it look official.

She made a couple of copies. "Mind if I keep one? Might be valuable someday, like having an original copy of the Declaration of Independence."

"I'm no Thomas Jefferson."

"Oh, I don't know about that. You got *something* going…"

Her words hung in the air for a moment. I wasn't sure what to say to that.

She stood up from the bed and scooted over to the door. "Come on, let's have a drink to celebrate."

To my surprise, she brought out a bottle of wine. She sat down across the table from me, stretching her legs out on the bench. She reached over and filled two plastic cups to the top. "It's Two-Buck Chuck. Do you mind?"

"Not at all," I said. "I'm just surprised that anyone has wine in this camp. I can't walk ten feet without kicking an empty beer can."

"So…because we're all rednecks?"

"I didn't mean…"

She laughed. "Like I said, you've got *something*. You're not a reflexive snob. Your egalitarianism comes with thought. But there is that moment when you're broadcasting 'I'm better than you' from behind your eyes. And then there's a second moment where you say, 'No, I'm not.' For some of us, that second moment is your saving grace. But for others, they won't see past that first reaction."

"Egalitarian," I said. I could feel heat rising in my face. "Big word for a redneck."

"We're not all yahoos," she said. "But I prefer men who don't think too much."

"Like Mark Simons?"

She looked away, frowning. Then she shrugged. "He's sweet."

"Sweet like a puppy dog?"

"I'm hoping there's a little pit bull in there," she said. "I don't know… I've thought about it."

She refilled our cups to the top. I'd noticed she was belting it back and felt it polite to mirror her.

"You've thought about what?" I teased. I was starting to relax. Until then, I'd been stuck in Nicole's office, replaying my last interaction with her over and over. To my surprise, Lois answered my question.

"Finding a lover," she said, not the slightest bit embarrassed. "I haven't had any action since Mathew died." She looked me in the eye as she said it, and I felt a stirring. I almost got up and left then and there. It had been a long time since I'd had any action, too. That plus the wine was dangerous.

"That's hard to believe," I said.

She rolled her eyes. "I'll take that as a compliment."

"I mean…"

She laughed and poured another cup of wine. "You're *so* serious, Hart Davis."

I took a big gulp of wine. "If you don't mind my asking… what happened to your husband?"

"Mathew was shot standing behind the counter at his feed store," she said, looking down at the table then taking a drink. "He always used to joke that I'd find him slumped over the cash register someday, but I don't think he was envisioning it quite that way." She looked up at me, and there were tears in her eyes. "All for fifty bucks in the register. I used to tell him not to work so late, and especially not to let people in after closing, but he just laughed and said I was paranoid."

"I'm sorry," I said. "Did they catch the guy?"

"Never did. Some dirtbag off the street, so they said. What a waste." She eyed me speculatively. "What about your wife? Was she like Nicole?"

No, she was like you, I wanted to say, but I was afraid it would come out too bitter. My ex-wife was also known as the White Widow, a psychopathic killer, but I couldn't tell Lois that. Amanda was still on the loose.

Lois picked up her glass. "To the Second Revolution," she said.

"Don't you know that you can count me out," I answered, but drank anyway. She gave me a puzzled look. I shrugged. "You know, like what Lennon said?"

She looked even more confused. "Like Lenin?"

"The Beatle, not the communist."

She paused to think it through and then started laughing. "You really are too serious, Davis." She fiddled with her phone, then set it between us. "Revolution" began playing, and before I knew it, we were both belting it out.

We talked until after midnight. Lois was easy to talk to. She got all my references, even the dated ones. With Nicole, I was never sure she understood what I was talking about.

The image of Nicole's smile floated before me, and I realized that Lois and I had been sitting companionably for several minutes without saying anything.

I felt her hand on my shoulder. Lois had moved to the bench on my side of the table and was sitting close to me. There was one empty wine bottle in front of us and another bottle that was half full.

"I need to go," I heard myself saying. Even drunk, I knew this was a rebound reaction. But then, in my mind, I saw Nicole pushing me away, a forbidding look in her eye. *Nicole is never going to take me back.*

Lois was sitting between me and the door and showed no intention of moving. Her hand moved down my back.

"Stay," she murmured. She leaned over and kissed me on the cheek. I kissed her back, on the mouth, the taste of wine on both our tongues. She broke it off and said, "We're a lot alike, Hart. Too much so. It would never work out. But…I need someone tonight. Just for tonight."

Just for tonight, I thought.

She took my hand and led me to the big bed.

CHAPTER 30

JOSHUA CALLEY

I almost got Jerry out of there. He'd never been away from his family for this long, and he was kinda lost. Mrs. Johnson had tried to get through the blockade several times but kept getting turned away. Harry was apparently still laid up, his gout worse than ever.

Jerry was drinking like a fish. He was a good Mormon boy, and it was his first time away from the strictly regimented life of the ranch, and he was going a little crazy. I've never seen anyone take to booze so quickly. Makes one wonder if it runs in the family, and whether some grandparent or another had chosen the Mormon faith for that very reason—"lead us not into temptation" and all that.

If I could get Jerry out of there, I could leave too. Then the whole takeover thing could fall apart as far as I was concerned. I was barely holding it together as it was. I was using every little trick I knew to stretch the supplies, but donations were slowing down to a trickle, nothing was making it through the blockade, and it was only a matter of time.

I could tell things were about to go south. New people were showing up, and they weren't much like the first batch. These guys were humorless, standing around watching everyone as if we were cattle about to be gleaned for the slaughterhouse. I wasn't sure if they were Feds or something worse.

The way they looked at me...

When I was a kid in Tennessee, I slipped away from my parents to watch a Klan march. I watched from a rooftop, with an easy getaway route that I was sure no adult could possibly follow.

Some of the Klansmen didn't wear hoods. They were the true believers, not caring what anyone thought. One of them looked up at me. He smiled, as if he wasn't surprised to see me. But I remember the look in his eye. If he'd mimicked having a noose around his neck, he couldn't have been any clearer.

That was the day I decided to head out west. I figured it might be better out here, and it couldn't be worse.

But now the diehard racists had found me. I had to wonder: Who would support me if it came to the crunch? Jerry, who was drunk all day? Hart Davis, who was losing his influence day by day? Jim Marston, who swayed with the winds? Peter Sterns, who was only a kid?

Lois Carpenter was taking over, I could see that clearly. She was friendly as hell to me, because we had to work together to get people fed, but I wasn't fooled. I didn't know if she was a racist, but I doubted she'd put up much of a fight for me. I was useful, taking care of the day-to-day details. But the day was quickly coming when my usefulness would be at an end.

I started planning a way out for Jerry and me

So Jerry wanted to get drunk? I'd make sure he got so drunk he could barely stand, and then I'd put his arm over my shoulder and we'd stumble right out of there, right into the desert, even if I had to drag him. I'd call Harry, make sure someone was waiting for us on the highway with a fast car. I thought about calling Vanessa, but I wasn't sure she'd go along with it.

I didn't care about any of the rest of that bullshit. I owed it to Harry to get his son out of danger, and that's what I intended to do.

CHAPTER 31

HART DAVIS

I awoke early the next morning. It wasn't quite dawn, but there was a soft glow on the horizon. And then it hit me. I'd cheated on Nicole.

Wait, you don't owe Nicole anything. She made her feelings clear.

The thought didn't banish my guilty feelings.

I disentangled myself gently from spooning Lois and got dressed. She moaned and turned over but didn't wake.

The two copies of the Juniper Proclamation lay on the table where I'd left them. One of them had a wine stain on the corner, so I left it behind.

I poked my head outside the trailer door, hoping everyone was still asleep. There was half an inch of snow on the ground, which hid the mud and grime. The world seemed quiet, peaceful.

There was no one in sight. I clambered down the steps and out into the open area between the trailers, and breathed a sigh of relief. Anyone who saw me now would have no idea where I'd come from.

I took one last guilty look behind me. Someone was standing in the shadows, just below the window of the trailer's back room. John Carver emerged into the light. I tensed, though I wasn't sure why. I knew that Carver was Lois's former lover, but I'd thought it was long over.

"What do you want, Carver?"

"I'll tell you what I told Mark," Carver said in a low voice. "Watch out for her."

"Watch out?"

"Lois isn't what she seems."

"I didn't know you still cared."

"I'm don't, though I've slept with her every night since I got here—except last night, of course."

"You've *slept* with her...?"

"Let me guess, she told you she 'needed someone tonight. Just for tonight.'"

I turned away, feeling sick. I'm not sure what was worse, the hangover, the guilt, or the sudden stab of suspicion that I'd been played.

"I'm on *your* side, man," Carver said. "She's... Just stay away, that's all I got to say."

I nodded. "I intend to, but not because of your warning. It was a mistake. I won't repeat it."

He looked down at the ground and spit. "Good idea."

I turned and walked away, feeling like shit.

I didn't go to the mess tent for breakfast that morning. I knew Nicole would be there waiting for me. I figured she was as interested in the unveiling of the Juniper Proclamation as I was, though she wasn't going to attend. She wasn't welcome by the others.

I didn't think I could look her in the eye.

There were stale graham crackers in my tent, and I ate those, washed down with a thermos of lemonade. I put on fresh clothes and splashed some water on my face and headed out.

People were beginning to stir, stumbling about, brewing coffee over open fires. I nodded to them, certain they could all see the guilt on my face.

Peter Sterns was camped at the far edge of the tent area, the rising sun behind him. He was already up and dressed. I handed him the manuscript without explanation.

He read the Juniper Proclamation silently. This was the first test. If Peter thought it was wrong, then it didn't have much chance of succeeding. But in the end, he nodded and handed it back.

"It's good. A little vague, maybe."

"Less vague than nothing at all."

"I'll give you that," Peter said. "It's a good starting point. Gotta figure everyone's going to want to put in their two cents' worth."

"I'm expecting that. I'm hoping for something unanimous when we're done, though."

"Unanimous? Good luck with that," he said.

"I was wondering, actually, if you'd mind presenting it. Everyone respects you, Peter. And I don't know everyone the way you do."

"Really?"

He was more pleased than I'd expected. He put out his hand. I slapped the proclamation into it. He read the paper again, his lips moving as if he was already practicing.

CHAPTER 32

BRAD PATTERSON

Walking around camp, I didn't recognize anyone. The ground was wet from melting snow and the gravel shifted under my boots, mud welling up. It was a sloppy mess.

My pal Jerry Johnson was in one of his funks. Missing Mommy and Daddy, I guess. He barely emerged from his tent these days, just sat in there drinking a horrible brand of local beer and reading Louis L'Amour novels.

The others in the original group were getting lost in the mix.

Peter Sterns spent most of his time scribbling in his notebook. Hart Davis was holed up in the visitor center with that female ranger, planning big things, I guess. Marston was chasing whatever cameras showed up. John Carver wandered around camp like a ghost, rarely talking to anyone. I'd passed him in the mess tent the other day and it was like he didn't even recognize me.

Jules, I saw everywhere. He could be heard talking at all times of the day and night. He didn't drink—a good Mormon— but damn, he could talk. I was just one of the boys to him now, no more important than anyone else, never mind that I'd known him for years and the rest of these guys were strangers. He was soaking up the attention from the media, who seemed to think he was a colorful character. He was, I suppose.

None of this is an excuse for what happened later. I should have sucked it up. So I was a little lonely and homesick, big deal. But I will say, it made me easy prey.

I was scarfing up breakfast in the mess tent with a bunch

of guys I didn't know sitting all around me. It was the cleanest place in the camp; Joshua insisted that everyone clear their plates and use the trash cans, on threat of expulsion. We were all strangers to each other, but it didn't stop the rest of them from making new friends. I just couldn't figure out how to begin.

Someone sat down beside me, but I barely paid attention to them.

"You're that guy, aren't you?"

"Pardon?" I turned. It was Curt Smith. I tensed up instantly, my fork full of scrambled eggs barely making it to my mouth.

"That guy in the picture on the overpass," he said, nodding in affirmation. "I admire your style, man. Are you a veteran?"

"No," I said, though I was tempted to lie. I wanted to impress this guy. He scared me, but I sensed he was the real deal, not pretending like me.

Smith seemed unfazed. He nodded. "Well, you handled it like a pro."

Damned if I didn't swell up with pride at that, like a high school nerd being complimented by the star quarterback. I knew I was being manipulated, but it didn't matter. I hadn't had a real conversation with anyone for days.

Smith leaned over, lowering his voice. "Listen…we're recruiting guys who really mean business. Not like these posers." He nodded to everyone else at the table. Most of them had fallen silent at his arrival, and none of them challenged what he was saying. Which did make them posers, I guess.

"We hold a meeting every night around seven o'clock in Lois Carpenter's trailer. Invitation only," he continued. "I asked the other guys about you, and they seem to think you're a perfect fit. You want to come around?"

"Sure," I said. "That's cool."

Jesus, I remember how lame that sounded. In my defense, I immediately regretted saying yes. Even then, not knowing any of the details, I knew it wasn't good. But no one else was inviting me anywhere.

I thought I could just check it out…but once I was in, I was in. No one ever said it, but I knew that they'd consider my leaving a betrayal. I wasn't sure what they'd do to a traitor, but I wasn't willing to find out.

Trouble is, I roped Jerry into it, too.

"Mind if I bring Jerry Johnson along?" I asked as Smith started to get up.

He didn't change expression. In fact, I don't think he showed any emotion whatsoever through the whole conversation. "Johnson...as in Harry Johnson?"

"His son."

"I think that would be great," Smith said, "if he's anything like his old man."

CHAPTER 33

HART DAVIS

I'd scheduled the mass meeting for noon, but I had no way of reaching everyone short of approaching them one by one, and there wasn't enough time for that. I went to Marston, who was hooked into the grapevine, and he seemed a little envious but promised to put out the word.

I'd hoped for a big turnout but was surprised when the entrance hall of the visitor center filled up. It was the only room large enough to fit everyone.

Sunlight glinted through the high windows, refracted by melting ice, sending rainbow colors across the floors and tables. The snow was gone, but the moisture had frozen overnight. It was such a peaceful place; no sound of traffic in the distance or any other signs of civilization, only the low hubbub of curious occupiers.

I climbed up on the front counter, and everyone quieted down. Lois was in the exact center of the crowd, an anticipatory smile on her face, which widened when she saw me looking at her.

"Peter Sterns has something he'd like to present to you," I said. "He'd like to know what you think of it."

I looked down at Peter, who was standing in front of the counter. He looked scared. I reached down and pulled him up to my side. He nervously clutched the proclamation and cleared his throat. "This is entitled The Juniper Proclamation," he said, his voice cracking.

He started reading, his head down.

"Speak up!" someone shouted.

Peter looked up, surprised, his face reddening. *"Now* is the *time* to *act…"* he shouted, then modulated his voice.

His voice became stronger, stanza by stanza, as he read the proclamation. I scanned the faces of the listeners, half of whom seemed puzzled.

"…*Therefore,* the Juniper Coalition will recognize only the authority of the county sheriff within whose jurisdiction we protest. We will not leave until he asks us to leave."

Peter's voice trailed off as he finished. He looked out over the crowd.

I don't know what I expected. Cheers, maybe? Jeers? It was met with complete silence. Puzzled, I searched out Lois in the throng to get her reaction. She was whispering something into Mark's ear.

Mark nodded and turned toward us. "What do we need all that for? It doesn't say shit."

I was stunned. It was Lois speaking through Mark, I was sure of it. Why was she sabotaging us?

"What do you mean?" Peter asked.

"I mean, we're defying the federal government, everyone knows that. The county sheriff tells us to leave, and we just go? Well, that depends, don't it? I won't take no orders from that traitor Lopez. I don't see any demands here. Nothing for us. Like…well, like the federal government needs to give us back our land; they need to quit charging us for grazing our cattle. They need to let us cut down our own trees and mine our own soil."

"Or what?" I said. I was dismayed. The little trick of complying with Sheriff Lopez had already been blown out of the water. "You won't leave? Are you planning to spend the rest of your life here?"

"Well…we need to demand *something.*"

"Mark's right," Marston said. "The authorities will ignore that proclamation. As soon as we leave here, we've lost all leverage. We should at least ask for amnesty."

Benson spoke up. "I don't mind going to jail, but not without getting something in return."

"They won't just *give* us anything," I said. Now I heard jeers. I looked over at Peter, who was still standing on the counter, still standing tall. He put up his hands.

"This isn't about the land!" Peter shouted. That quieted the crowd. "It isn't about cows or trees or minerals. It's about principle. This declares what we stand for. If we're right, if we convince enough people, the rest will follow. But first we need to be clear about what we're fighting for. We're fighting for *freedom*."

"Fuck yeah!" Jules Francisco shouted.

Peter was just getting started. "This is our declaration of freedom: that we few men and women, banded together in a righteous cause, ask our fellow citizens to join us in throwing off the shackles of the federal yoke; that we be free from their interference in our sacred lives; that we are the owners of our rights. We demand freedom!"

Jules came out of the crowd and stood in front of us. He pumped his right fist in the air. "Freedom!" he shouted.

Everyone flinched a little and looked at each other as if trying to figure out what everyone else was going to do, but Jules was undeterred. "Freedom!" he shouted again, this time pumping both fists. One by one, a few of the others joined in, halfheartedly at first and then, as more people got on board, louder and louder, until the din was deafening.

Just like that, Peter, the youngest of us, and Jules, the craziest, became our new leaders. I tried not to stare at them. Peter's words had been a clarion call, as I imagined the Declaration of Independence had been when read to the crowd in Philadelphia.

Oh, shit, I thought. *What have we done?*

This was the kind of talk that got people killed—worse, got *innocent* people killed. This was the kind of fervor that made people blow up federal buildings with daycare centers on the first floor, that got federal workers who were only doing their jobs assassinated.

I suddenly realized that not only didn't I believe in this cause, this takeover, but thought it completely wrongheaded. I'd been angry and drunk, and it had been a stupid impulse to ever start associating with these people, but now it was too late to stop it.

Peter held up his hand, and the crowd slowly quieted. "Brad and Mark are right about one thing. We need *something* in return. We should demand that this proclamation be published in all the newspapers."

In a tone only he could hear, I whispered, *"All* the papers?"

Without missing a beat—the kid was a natural—Peter added, "At least the *New York Times* and the *Los Angeles Times.* If they publish it, so will everyone else."

I wasn't so sure about that, but it was a way out. The government had given into such demands before. The Unabomber had his manifesto published—it had even led to his capture. I tried to shake off my unease at the comparison. I raised my hands.

"We'll present this proclamation tonight at the five o'clock news conference," I said. "If anyone wants to discuss it, talk to Peter Sterns here."

Peter looked at me in surprise.

"Hey, it's your responsibility," I said in a low voice as the crowd began to break up. "You want to be an inspiring leader, you gotta own it."

CHAPTER 34

PETER STERNS

When Hart Davis first asked me to read the proclamation, I didn't have the heart to tell him that I thought it was a pretty unimaginative document. This kind of thing should be stirring, poetic. But when I racked my brains trying to improve on it, I kept running into the same problem; everything sounded like a hackneyed version of the Declaration of Independence or the Constitution or the Gettysburg Address.

I wondered whether to show it to Mich. We'd developed a friendship that wasn't about politics—weirdly enough, considering where we were and what we were doing, we barely mentioned it.

The third time I saw her was in the mess tent that Joshua Calley set up in the center of camp. I was working on a poem, making sure that no one could see what I was writing. She came right over and sat across from me. I was self-conscious about it and closed the notebook. Jerry Johnson, sitting at the next table, sensed it.

"She don't look interested in boys, Peter," he shouted.

Mich stared down at the table, her face turning bright red.

"Forget him," I said. "He's a Neanderthal."

"What are you writing?" she asked.

"Oh, nothing. I suck."

"Do you mean what you write?" she asked seriously. I nodded. "Then it can't suck," she said.

I smiled at that, almost tempted to show her.

She looked up at me with a smile. "Why are you so different,

Peter Sterns? Why the hell are you even here?"

"I came with my friends," I said. Which was mostly true. I suppose I believed, in some theoretical way, that the federal government ought to stay out of the private Western lands, but the longer I was at the Fossil Beds, the more I doubted the wisdom of the takeover.

I *liked* that the Fossil Beds and the Painted Hills were part of a national monument and couldn't be torn up. I suppose that was one of the reasons I avoided talking politics with Mich. I was afraid I'd find out she was a Nazi or something. It wouldn't be that strange. Half these people were racists, though none of them would admit it.

Why *was* I here?

I let the comment pass. We talked about other things, as usual. I told her I was a "desert rat" and she laughed. "Oh! I've got to write that down!"

She pulled a notebook out of one of her big cargo pockets, and I finally learned why all her pockets looked stuffed. She had notebooks, scraps of paper, and pens and pencils in them. She scribbled down what I'd said.

"What's that?" I asked.

"Oh, I'm trying to be a writer too," she said in a dismissive tone, as if it was the most ridiculous thing a person could do. "Just dabbling, you know. Everything here is so dramatic."

"Dramatic?" To me, everything in the camp was boring and smelly and dirty, and, worst of all, there wasn't much going on.

"Well, consider the possibilities," she said.

"Can I see what you wrote?" I asked and put out my hand like I wouldn't take no for an answer. She hesitated, then handed over the notebook. I couldn't make the slightest sense of her chicken scratches.

"Sorry," she said, taking the notebook back. "It's a personal shorthand. Here, let me read you something."

"'Once upon a time,'" she began. "'A little girl climbed out her bedroom window and into the mountain meadow beyond. The meadow was covered in a white blanket like snow, though it was the middle of summer. As the little girl went on, she saw that the ground was covered with white butterflies, and on each undulating wing was a marking in the shape of an eye. The butterflies rose into the air, circling around her head, and she realized that beneath them were the half-eaten bodies of her family.

"'They surged down upon her...'"

"Carnivorous butterflies?" I asked when she paused.

She blushed and closed the notebook. "Like I said, I'm just dabbling."

"No, keep reading! I love it!"

"Maybe someday, Peter," she said, looking away. "When this is all over."

After that, I hadn't seen her for a couple of days, though I'd been looking.

Now, with my reading of the Juniper Proclamation just minutes away, I sought her out. I found her near the entrance to the camp, staring off across the way at the barricades. She turned at my approach.

I told her about the Juniper Proclamation, and she asked to read it. She handed it back with the comment, "Interesting."

"*Something* needs to be presented," I said defensively. "There has to be something we can rally around."

"But why *you*, Peter? You could get in real trouble with this."

"That's why it needs to be good," I insisted.

I figured Mich was a writer and that if anyone could freshen up this manifesto, she could. She pointed out a few spelling errors and then begged off.

I was disappointed when she hurried away.

I understood why Hart wanted me to be the one to read it aloud. He wasn't one of the true believers, and that was becoming clearer with every day that passed. He was spending more time with Nicole Nelson than he was with his buddies. He obviously didn't have his heart in this, and the national media was starting to pick up on that as well and was pressing him. He was by far the most famous—or notorious—of the occupiers; the Strawberry Mountain Killer.

It was only a matter of time before Hart broke down in front of everyone and said out loud what a mistake he thought it all was.

But then, maybe that needed to happen. I was homesick,

and I was sick of the yahoos who had come in later and started throwing trash around and who were loud and drunk half the time.

The other occupiers accepted me for some reason, even though I wasn't really one of them either. I was allowed to be different. I was allowed to be the artist in the group.

The poet.

They kind of liked it, I think.

Something happened to me while I was reading the proclamation. I got into the spirit of it. When it fell flat, it sort of irked me. So I added some of the poetic stuff I'd been trying to come up with, stealing liberally from the Founding Fathers, and it worked. I thought for a second that the crowd was going to carry me out of there on their shoulders.

I ain't no one's prophet. I ain't no guru. I had no more idea what to do than anyone else, but all of a sudden they were listening to me. I admit, it went to my head a little. I guess maybe I thought I could end the takeover peacefully, get something in return from the Feds.

But obviously, I overestimated my influence.

Everyone seemed to like my speech, but I cared about only one opinion. It wasn't until late that night that I finally saw Mich again. I was in the mess tent surrounded by admirers. When I saw her enter, I immediately got up and went to her side.

She was wearing a purple Aussie slouch hat. *Where does one find a purple slouch hat?* I wondered. It also seemed to me that she was wearing more makeup than before. The other men in the room were eyeing her too, where in the past they'd pretty much ignored her.

"You're an idiot, Peter Sterns," she said. "You've really messed things up."

"Huh?" I don't know what I'd expected, but it wasn't a scolding.

"Really, Peter, you should be putting your writing to better use," she said, picking up her coffee and leaving the mess tent without looking back.

CHAPTER 35

HART DAVIS

I made my way through the crowd, getting congratulatory claps on the back. But most of the people were surrounding Peter, so I was soon able to get away.

The door to the office was open. Nicole was sitting there facing the door as if expecting me. I came in and sat down opposite her. She looked grim. For a moment, I was afraid she knew where I'd spent the previous night. Fortunately, she didn't notice my unease.

"What have we done?" she said.

"You heard?

"How could I not? Peter's got quite the voice. Thought I was listening to a Founding Father there."

"Yeah, that caught me off guard too. Peter got a little ahead of us."

"What have we done?" she repeated, sounding dismayed and a little dazed. "We've made it worse."

"It'll die down," I said.

"This isn't the sort of thing that dies down. Everyone in that room got radicalized. *More* radicalized." She looked me full in the face. "I tried to get ahold of you last night," she said. "I was having second thoughts. I wondered if we weren't just stirring things up. I thought I'd see you this morning, at least. Where *were* you?'

"Just walking around, clearing my head," I said. I glanced at her and gave her a tired smile, not liking myself for my ability to dissemble. Amanda had always said I was a better liar than anyone knew, probably because I so rarely lied. "There's a good chance that the newspapers will publish the manifesto. There's nothing really alarming in it."

"It doesn't matter, don't you see that? Your people are all riled up. No way they're leaving anytime soon."

"We should just leave," I said. "Dare Smith and the other hard-asses to shoot us."

Nicole's gaze went over my shoulder.

From behind me, someone said, "Your scheme kind of got away from you there, didn't it?"

I froze. It was my worst nightmare: Lois and Nicole in the same room. I felt a sense of foreboding.

Lois came into the office and looked around for somewhere to sit. When I didn't get up from my chair, Nicole frowned at me, but Lois shrugged it off and leaned against the doorjamb.

"You always looked down on us, didn't you, Hart? Never took us seriously. You'd rather spend your time with someone like *her.*"

I stood up and grabbed Lois's arm. "We need to talk," I said, trying to guide her out the door. She shook me off.

"This is the start, the Second Revolution. I wasn't joking about that," she said.

"I thought you didn't believe in *any* of this," I said, still trying to make sense of her words. "That you thought it was all silly."

"I thought what we needed was true believers, not squishes like you. We've made plans, and I was afraid your impulsive action would blow our chances. But I was wrong. This is where it starts. Without meaning to, you've made it happen."

"Lois, you don't really mean this."

She laughed. "You think you know me because you've slept with me? You're just like all men, led by their cocks."

I sensed Nicole stiffening behind me. I wanted to disappear, teleport back to Bigfoot Ranch, or into the middle of a highway, or as deep into the desert as it was possible to get. Anywhere but here.

Lois had meant to expose me, I could tell. Out of sheer meanness. Until then, I'd tried to ignored the warnings, the feeling that she wasn't really on my side.

I couldn't look at Nicole. I wasn't sure I was ever going to be able to face her again.

"You'd better get some sleep, Davis," Lois said, her voice so sympathetic that it was mocking. "You look terrible. I did keep you up pretty late last night, and it's clear you can't handle your alcohol." She laughed and casually pushed off from the door. "I'll leave you two lovebirds alone."

She left before I could say anything. I turned reluctantly, but I didn't need to worry about looking Nicole in the eye. She was staring at the wall, her face stony.

"Lois is right," she said, her voice sounding like it was drifting to me from across a deep valley. "You look terrible. You should get some sleep."

"Nicole…"

"What?"

"It didn't mean anything. I was drunk."

"What are you talking about?" She finally looked me in the eye, and I think my heart stopped for a moment. Her eyes were glassy, like frozen ice.

"I was drunk."

"Oh, *that*." She shrugged. "You're a grown man. I have no hold on you, remember? Now, if you don't mind, I would like to get some rest. I think you're right, though. I think it's time I left."

She got up and held the door open. I hesitated, then realized I had no choice but to leave.

She closed the door behind me.

CHAPTER 36

JIM MARSTON

Well, wasn't that a kick to the side of the head! Little Peter Sterns giving the speech of his life and getting everyone all riled up. Well, maybe Peter wasn't so little anymore, but I couldn't help but think of him as a kid, since I'd known him from the time he was born. Hart just sort of stood there next to him and seemed to go invisible as Peter shone.

I was the first one to slap Peter on the back. I could see the new power in him, that he was the guy who would get it done. He needed a little guidance, that's all. None of this Mickey Mouse shit that Davis came up with, or his little girlfriend, who I figured was the real impetus behind that limp-dick proclamation. Wasn't worth shit until Peter added his declaration of freedom.

I didn't leave the kid's side for the next few hours. I doubt he would have done anything else without me whispering in his ear. We almost got there, too. Almost got the Feds to back down, maybe even make a few concessions, give us all amnesty.

Let me state right here that while I knew who Lois Carpenter was, I was in no way part of her cabal. I had no idea what was coming. If I had, I would have done everything in my power to stop it.

Anyway…

Even better, people were looking up to little Jules Francisco too. My roommate, as it happened. We'd ended up together in a single tent when it started getting too cold. Before the takeover, I thought Jules had the mind of a fifteen-year-old, if that. But we started having long talks in the dark of the tent. Wasn't much else to do at night. Turned out Jules was kind of thoughtful. He told me all about his childhood in Mexico, how he'd come over the border all by himself when he was ten.

"When did you become a citizen?" I asked.

Silence. Deafening silence, except—I kid you not—crickets outside the tent.

"Jesus, Jules. What are you doing here? Half the people here would haul you down to the border and kick your ass over it."

"I like the U.S.," Jules said. "Mexico was corrupt; the federal government didn't help us. I don't want that for this country. I'm...I love freedom, man. Real freedom."

So even before the proclamation was read, I'd already changed my mind about good old Jules. I thought he'd listen to me.

I thought we could get some things done, by God.

CHAPTER 37

HART DAVIS

Most versions of the Juniper Proclamation floating around these days include Peter Sterns's verbal additions. By the time Marston held the next news conference, the press already had copies. Since I doubted anyone in the crowd had transcribed the speech, Lois must have gone back to her trailer, added Peter's words to her own copy, retyped it, and made duplicates.

Marston read the manifesto with far less fanfare than Peter, and it fell flat with this more cynical crowd. Reporters started shouting as soon as Marston finished, but none of the questions were about what he'd read. The questions they asked were routine, and he answered them in a rote fashion.

I don't even remember the end of the press briefing. I do remember seeing Lois standing at the far edge of the clearing, looking as though she was trying to get my attention. I turned and walked in the opposite direction, though it was the long way around to my tent. I went behind the trailers and stopped dead in my tracks.

There wasn't a soul in sight. The sun was hovering over the horizon, the light slanting across the sands, desolate and peaceful. The sounds of the people in the camp behind me were muffled, and I could ignore them. The air was fresh, with a faint hint of sage.

I leaned back against a trailer, catching the last of the afternoon's shade, and closed my eyes, taking deep breaths, trying to calm my nerves. No luck. I was still shaking from the way Nicole had dismissed me.

Nothing had clarified how I really felt about her more than seeing the disappointed look on her face. I'm sure that she thought she was broadcasting a neutral expression, but I saw through it. She'd been on the edge of tears.

I don't cry, not but once a decade, but if I could have, I would have then. My impulsiveness had once again ruined something good. I moaned aloud.

I don't know how long I stood there, soaking up the silence. Then I heard a rustle and my eyes popped open. Near the closest small hill, three deer were standing, staring at me as if trying to figure out what kind of strange creature I was.

The rest of the world is just beyond, I thought, *most of it paying no attention to what is happening here.*

I could simply walk off. I'd hit the curve in the highway in about four or five miles, get a ride into town, check into a motel.

The Feds would catch up with me eventually, I supposed. There would be consequences to all this. But right then, I didn't care. Any motivation I'd had to be there was gone.

If I hadn't been so exhausted and hung over, I'd probably have done exactly that. But I needed to sleep.

The trailer I stood behind was a long one, parked next to another one even longer. I made my way down the narrow space between them. A shadow at the end of corridor blocked what little light there was. I couldn't tell who it was except that it was a he and that he was tall.

If I could have turned around without being obvious about it, I would have. I really didn't want to talk to anyone. But I keep trudging ahead, trying to regain the alertness that my sojourn into the desert had washed away.

Somehow I wasn't surprised that it was John Carver. He was probably there to gloat.

"I saw what she did to you," he said.

"Who?" I asked, wondering if he'd overheard my conversation with Nicole.

"That bitch Lois, who else? She used Mark Simons as her cat's-paw. That's what she does. Don't you see? She undercut what you were trying to do."

"She did more than that," I muttered.

He looked triumphant for a moment, then seemed to realize how much I was hurting. "Sorry, man. I tried to warn you."

"You did," I said. "You sure as hell did."

"There's more going on than you realize, Davis. A lot more. And she's right in the middle of it. She gets other people to do the dirty work, but she's the spider, spinning her web."

"What do you mean?" I didn't know if Carver was nuts, but he'd been right about Lois so far and I was willing to listen.

But he wasn't looking at me anymore. His face had gone pale. He was staring over my shoulder. I turned around. Lois was sitting in a lawn chair by a campfire across the way. For once, she was alone, none of her retinue with her. Seeing her like that, she stood out, a singular charismatic figure.

She wasn't looking at us, but I sensed that she'd been watching us, that she had positioned herself so that she could see me when I re-entered the camp.

"We need to talk in private," Carver said. "Somewhere *she* can't see us."

"She can't hear us," I said. "Just tell me now."

"Oh, hell, no." He ran his hands over his face, thinking. Then he turned to me and said. "Say something funny."

"Something funny," I said.

He laughed, slapped me on the back, and walked quickly away. I plastered a smile on my face, which might have even fooled someone from a distance, someone who didn't know me.

But it didn't fool Lois. She stared at me and shook her head slightly. She stood up, waiting expectantly.

Screw it. I turned and went back between the trailers. By the time I returned to my tent, it was fully dark. I was hungry and thirsty, but most of all, I wanted to close my eyes, if only for a few moments.

I flopped down on my sleeping bag and went to sleep instantly.

CHAPTER 38

NICOLE NELSON

I was mad at Hart, but I was even madder at myself. Could I really blame him for seeking solace somewhere else? Wherever Lois Carpenter walked, she left ripples that were undetectable unless you were looking for them. I'd seen how Hart's head had turned to watch her, but I hadn't thought anything of it. She was dark and slinky, the way I wish I could be. There always seemed to be men around her, doing her bidding.

Tears filled my eyes every time I thought of her and Hart together. Well, I'd been willing to give him a chance, but he'd made his choice.

Somehow, some way, Lois Carpenter was directing things. She hadn't even been part of the first takeover group. She'd come in later, at first a sort of a den mother to them all. Now, all of a sudden, they were hopping to her orders. Her lackeys concerned me, those who would do anything she asked, like Mark Simons, and others whose motives were murky, like Curt Smith.

After the issuing of the Juniper Proclamation, things got a little dicey. I decided that Hart was right—it was time to go, no matter what. Leadership had changed. Oh, Peter Sterns was the figurehead, and a decent man, but he didn't have any real power. Marston blustered and issued commands, but no one listened.

I tracked down Perry and told him it was time to leave, no excuses.

He agreed with me. "They've gotten meaner," he said.

"Some guy tried to kick me when I bent over to pick up a cigarette butt. Probably should have expected it. It's not like these guys are all that stable."

My boss was looking a little worse for wear. He'd always been a neat dresser, his hair combed so that not a single strand was out of place. Now he looked a little like Albert Einstein on a bad day.

I knew he was implicitly disapproving of my original decision to stay, and who could blame him? It was clear to me at that point that there never had been a chance of resolving this peacefully.

Perry said, "I'll track down Garth tonight when he gets back. I never quite know where he is."

"He won't want to go," I said. "But we have to convince him."

"He'll leave," Perry said. "Or he won't ever work in a national park again."

I was disappointed in myself. I'd read these the protesters all wrong. I'd thought a few of them were honorable, but then, honorable people don't take public property and claim it for themselves. They don't try to wrap it in the word *freedom*. Freedom to do what? Take away the land set aside for the general good and keep it for themselves? Dig up beautiful landmarks and hunt species to extinction? What kind of freedom is that?

There was no talking to most of them. They didn't believe in science, or education, or facts.

Honorable men didn't sleep with the first woman who became available.

I was disgusted with the whole thing and wanted out.

But I didn't realize how quickly things were changing. If I'd known, I'd have left my stuff behind and gotten the first ride out of there.

CHAPTER 39

BRAD PATTERSON

The shit started coming down on me. Fuck it; I let it. Crap started piling up, but I didn't see it. Like always. I can look back and say, "Yeah, you should have walked away right then and there, and why the hell didn't you? I mean, it's not like you haven't done it before." But I never see it until later.

I have what I call outsider dreams. I'm always the outsider, and when I'm invited into the inner circle, it always ends badly. Always. I wake up and I'm a fucking mess. I always wonder: *Why did I stay? Why didn't I try to get away? It would have been so easy.*

But I never see it until too late.

So that Monday, I woke up from a bunch of nightmares. The sleeping bag was almost inside out, my pillow twisted into a corkscrew.

The night before, I'd been sitting at the campfire minding my own business when the guy next to me nudged me and offered me a joint.

I could've just shaken my head, but I knew that everyone sitting there would think less of me, especially if I walked away, or worse, if I stayed straight while they all got stoned. So I smoked weed with those guys, none of whom I knew very well or cared about what they thought.

I mean, I stayed, so I guess I *did* care what they thought.

The sharp edges of the world blurred, the leaping fire slowed, and I felt myself nodding off. Then I heard laughter and "Man, he ain't here anymore.

As usual, the stuff made me paranoid as hell. I was filled with shame, and I got up and staggered away, but it wasn't any help, and the paranoia went with me, all the way to my sleeping bag, my head a rat's nest of doubt and fear. I thought I was losing my mind.

So I'm just saying, it pretty much ruined my day. I woke up with that feeling still all over me. I couldn't shake it.

I thought about hiding in my tent, and if it hadn't been so damn hot I would have. What the hell? It had snowed the night before, and now it was sweltering. I lay on top of my tangled sleeping bag, naked, trying to cool off.

Finally, it got so hot inside the tent that I threw on my clothes, unzipped the front, and stepped out.

Ever since I'd arrived, I'd been getting respectful nods from outright strangers. Word had gotten out that I was the guy in the picture that was splashed on the cover of *Time Magazine* and all over the internet. So they'd nod or smile, and I'd try to nod or smile back, and I'd get it all wrong, you know. I never did know how to do that simple thing of smiling at a stranger or relaxing around people. I was on guard every moment I was awake and there was the slightest chance anyone was watching me.

Jerry's tent was next to mine, and I scooted into it before anyone could see me. He was on his back in his underwear, big mouth open and snoring, asleep despite the heat. The tent stunk from a week's worth of farts.

I opened the vents and left the front flap open. There was a cooler by Jerry's head, and I fished out the only soda can in the melted ice. It was lukewarm. There were still two beers in there, which surprised me. A near case worth of empty beer cans littered the tent.

I looked down at my oldest friend. I'd tried to get away from people after high school, and that had led me west, always west. The fewer the people, the better. I was all right one on one. I'd landed at the Johnson Ranch. Jerry was my age, maybe a little younger, and he was an odd guy. He'd been homeschooled, kept away from other kids his age. Which had made him kind of strange, because he was a real extrovert.

We became friends right away. I hung around with him,

letting him do all the talking, and it was perfect. I know other people thought something was going on between us because we were always together, but there was none of that. His mother had pulled me aside one day and grilled me, and though she never asked outright, she circled the question until she got the picture. After that, she left me alone.

As if…

Jerry was a mess, flabby and frankly a little smelly.

No, I daydreamed about women, and I got jealous of guys like Hart Davis who could arrive at a place like the Fossil Beds and within days be hanging out with the prettiest girl in camp. Not only was she pretty, but she was from the other side! How does that happen?

I think maybe that's why I didn't walk away. I had to choose sides, and I was too jealous to take Davis's side.

"Wake up, asshole," I said. I splashed a handful of water from the cooler on Jerry's head. He sat up and swung feebly at me, and I dodged the blow, laughing. I was feeling better already. "You going to turn into a drunk?"

"Maybe," he mumbled. He moaned and put his hand to his forehead. "Fuck no… This hurts. What time is it?"

"It's past noon. Come on, you idiot, let's get some food into you. You'll feel better. Eat some cereal and toast. Might want to stay away from the bacon and eggs."

He turned a little green at the thought. *Uh oh.*

He crawled to the entry, stuck his head out, and puked. He stayed there on his hands and knees for a while, puking every few minutes.

"Damn, Jerry. I'm going to need to cut another exit out of here."

He finally pulled himself back inside and flopped back on his sleeping bag. "Just let me die."

"No can do. We've got a meeting to go to tonight."

"What meeting?"

"Some of the guys and Lois are getting together to talk about the Juniper Proclamation and what to do next."

"The Juniper *what*?"

"Did you even leave the tent yesterday?"

"Yes…no…I don't remember."

I realized that I'd been letting my best friend rot away. If I'd had doubts about going to the meeting—and I think I was leaning toward not going—this changed my mind. Jerry needed to get out among people again.

"Come on," I said. "Clean yourself up. I'll be back with some food."

I went out the tent flap and stepped into the puke. I cursed all the way to the mess tent, dragging my foot in the dirt. In a way, having to take care of Jerry was a blessing. It overrode my paranoia. It took a couple of hours to help get Jerry back on his feet. We walked around the camp until he stopped shivering. I steered him away from the guys who were selling cases of beer for four times the normal price.

I'd never seen Jerry drunk before. It wasn't a pretty sight. Eventually, the afternoon passed and it was time to head for Lois's trailer. We passed the mess tent, and I saw John Carver staring into his mug of coffee. Seemed like I'd barely seen him since we arrived. I waved at him when he looked up.

Carver had always seemed like a self-sufficient loner to me. He'd never looked lonely. But now his cheeks and eyelids seemed to be drooping with some kind of crushing sadness.

He got up and came over. "Tell me you aren't going to one of Lois's little conspiracy meetings," he said in a near monotone.

I didn't answer. The way he said it brought back my paranoia all at once.

"Jesus, Brad. Don't you see what she is? She's a witch, and she's fucking dangerous. Stay away from her and her little cult."

"That's a little…strong, don't you think?" Jerry said.

"That's not even the half of it, you twits. You two are babes in the woods."

That wasn't exactly the way to win us over. In fact, had the opposite effect. Carver was like one of those guys in my dreams—there was always one—who tried to give me an out, but I never took it, not in my dreams and not in real life.

"So she ditched you," Jerry said. "Get over it."

Carver gave him a disbelieving look and laughed. "Is that

what you think? Hell, I barely got out alive." He walked away, shaking his head.

We made it to the meeting right as it was starting and listened to their crazy plans. I knew right away that we'd made a mistake in coming and that I didn't want any part of it. But I sat there, paralyzed by doubt, sure everyone would hate me if I got up and left. It turned into one of my nightmares, and like I always did, I stayed and did things I was ashamed of. But unlike my dreams, I couldn't shake it off or pretend it wasn't real.

The worst thing was, I dragged Jerry in my nightmare, and he paid the price.

CHAPTER 40

MARK SIMONS

The trailer was crowded for the next meeting. Mud had been tracked into Lois's nice clean kitchen, smeared along the bases of the chairs and table. There wasn't room for everyone to sit, and people were standing in every empty spot. I had to push my way through them to get to Lois's side. She gave me a distracted smile.

There was a whole bunch of people I didn't know, but also people I did know. Jerry and Brad showed up, Jerry looking like hell and Brad trying to blend in with the woodwork.

Curt Smith and Benson had some new friends. Guys like them, tough and unsmiling. They meant business. I didn't joke when they were around. Jerry tried to say something funny and it fell flat. These guys were serious.

I sat between them and my friends. It was like a high school football team sitting in with the Chicago Bears, acting all grownup but not quite pulling it off. I sat nearer the big boys, trying to be one of them. Thing was, I was way more angry and resentful about the politics than they were. I couldn't figure out where they were coming from—it was almost like they'd been hired, but who the hell could afford that? Lois? I didn't think so. Marston? He was too cheap.

They were there for some reason, though, and I guess maybe the politics went deep down with those guys, like they'd already made up their minds so long ago that they never even thought about it.

Brad tried to talk about the Juniper Proclamation or whatever they were calling it, and everyone just stared at him.

"Don't mean shit," Smith said, and that ended that.

"Are we on for tomorrow?" Benson asked, looking around the room. Jerry and Brad looked confused, so I explained it to them. Jerry thought digging up the Indian graveyard for latrines was a great idea. Brad shut down, just went blank, which meant—I think—that he wasn't so sure. But it was going to happen, that was pretty clear. Smith and Benson and the other hard-asses wanted it.

Even more, Lois wanted it. And if she wanted it, so did I.

"Shouldn't we wait to see what the proclamation does first?" some guy asked. He wasn't part of my group or the hard-asses. I wasn't sure who'd brought him.

"Wait for what?" Lois asked. She got up and stood in the center of the circle. "For the Feds to give up power? For them to hand over the keys and give in to us? No, we need to push them. We need to do something that will set the world on fire."

World on fire? Holy shit, what was she talking about? I wasn't sure, but I liked it. I liked her talking that way.

She caught herself, as if thinking she'd gone a little too far.

"You know what I mean. We need to make a statement. Not words, but action. So we provoke them. And then we provoke them again." She turned in a slow circle, looking us all in the eye, one by one. I swear she almost smiled when she saw how into it I was. "Don't you guys get it? We need people behind us. That isn't going to happen until everyone sees the Feds overreacting. Like they did at Ruby Ridge and Waco. Then the word *freedom* will fucking mean something. The Johnson ranch was only a partial victory, and they almost got away with it at Malheur."

I was surprised when Brad actually spoke up. "So someone has to die?"

"No, I didn't say that."

Yes, you did, I thought. *And you're right.*

"I'm just saying we need for the Feds to do something stupid. Otherwise they can sit there behind their barricades and wait us out. So we'll dig up the graveyard, and they'll have to act," Lois said.

I looked around at the faces around me and saw a lot of uncertainty. Suddenly, I felt crowded, as if I was going to be crushed. I had a sudden impulse to get up, leave the trailer, and keep walking. But Lois was close enough for me to smell her perfume, and it was like a tractor beam keeping me in place.

There was a brief silence. I wanted to laugh. Why were we even talking about it? Lois was going to get her way. She always did. I wasn't so sure she was right. I thought it was bad public relations to be digging up an Indian graveyard, but I wasn't about to say anything. I figured it was Curt Smith's idea because he wanted revenge. He was stone-faced through the discussion, but I wouldn't have wanted him to be looking at me.

"I don't like it," Jules said. His Adam's apple bobbed, and his eyes flicked about nervously. "I like Indians. I wouldn't want anyone digging up *my* grandparents. Why don't we dig up that native plant plot? I mean, that's just stupid, right? Native plants are native. Who needs a fucking garden of them?"

I almost laughed. Leave it to Jules to speak his mind. He was either fearless or dumb, and I'm still not sure which. The other guys weren't laughing, though, so I stifled it.

"We decided that it was closest to the camp, remember?" Lois said. "You were bitching about having to go so far to take a leak. Let's just do what we planned, all right? We'll meet there tomorrow morning, at first light. We'll be halfway done before anyone notices."

And that was that.

I lingered, hoping Lois would ask me to stay again. The trailer emptied out pretty quickly, with Smith the last one out the door. He glanced my way, then at Lois. Something passed between them, and he left.

"Sorry about all the mud," I said, as if it was my fault.

"You want a drink?" she said, giving me a smile.

"Sure, anything is fine."

"I've seen you drink whiskey, wasn't sure if it was on the rocks."

"Don't matter." *Jesus, Mark. Say something clever.*

She poured us both half a glass of whiskey and sat down at the table. I sat opposite her, wishing I had the courage to sit next to her. It was like my first dates in school, all awkward and fumbling and embarrassing. I wanted to remember it all, to remember it for later, so I could go over it again and again. I fingered the phone in my pocket, and on a sudden impulse, I hit record.

To this day, I'm not sure why I did it. I just knew that I would want to play our conversation over again. I don't think it was because of her scheme, but maybe a part of me already understood what was happening.

"Someone is turning into a problem," she said after taking a big chug of whiskey. I tried to match her, then tried not to start coughing.

"Davis?"

"No, I can handle him. John Carver. He's been hanging around the trailer, talking to people when they come in or go out, trying to tell everyone what a bitch I am."

I flushed, knowing I should say something but not able to think of anything that didn't make me sound like an idiot. "He approached me," I said. "I blew him off."

"Blew him?" she said.

"I…I mean…" *All you have to do is laugh*, I thought, but I acted flustered, like a moron.

"Is that why you haven't tried to kiss me?" she said.

"Do you want me to kiss you?" It was stupid, but at least it was direct.

"Not many guys ask first. But yes, Mark, I'd very much like that."

I got up and slid in next to her, bumping her against the trailer window. She laughed. Before I could grab her, she put her hands to both sides of my head and gave me a full-on kiss. She held me there for what seemed an eternity, then let me go. She turned and took a drink of whiskey.

"That was nice," she said.

I couldn't say a word. Part of me realized that by holding my head like that, she'd controlled the whole thing. But most of me didn't care. Even with that, though, I didn't have the guts to go in for a second helping.

"I need to get up, Mark. Do you mind?"

I scrambled off the bench. She scooted by me, patting me

on the arm, went to the refrigerator, and rummaging around. I stood there stupidly for a few moments, then slid back to my side of the table.

In hindsight, it's not hard to see how she manipulated the whole thing. A little kiss, that's all it took to make me do something that I'll regret forever. Yeah, she played me, but to be honest, I knew it even then, in the pit of my stomach.

I didn't care, then or now. It doesn't make me innocent. It makes me a sucker.

"So, what do we do about John?" she said, sitting back down with a plate of carrots. *Carrots and whiskey?* I wondered. I took one politely and started munching on it.

"Ignore him," I said. "No one's listening to him. They think he's a jealous ex-boyfriend. What can he say?"

"He knows something about me," Lois said. "Something I'd rather people didn't know."

"What?"

She shook her head. "I don't want people to know…especially people I like," she said.

"Nothing he could tell me would change my mind about you."

Her eyes widened a little, as if that surprised her. She put her hand on top of mine. "I think we should do what we talked about. I'm in charge of the meals next Friday. I'll give him something that will give him indigestion so bad he'll think he's dying. He'll need to go to the hospital. No one will think anything of it. It's not like conditions around here are exactly sanitary. A lot of people have already gotten sick."

"What do you want me to do?"

"When he starts getting sick, get him out of the mess tent. Take him somewhere and call for an ambulance. Maybe even lead him over to the barricades and let the Feds take care of him. But give it an hour or so. Take him into the desert until he's *really* sick."

"What time?" I asked. I felt something in the pit of my stomach, like I was really crossing some line this time. I mean, I'd already broken so many laws, you'd think one more thing wouldn't have mattered. But so far, I hadn't hurt anyone. I'd never planned on hurting anyone.

"I've watched John for a week or so," Lois continued. "He almost always gets to the mess around six-thirty or so. So if you're there from then on, it should be good. John has meals earmarked for him because of his allergies, so that's taken care of."

"What about the meeting?" I asked. It would be the first time I'd missed one of the seven o'clock meetings in Lois's trailer.

"I'll tell you what happens later," she said. "Best not to postpone it."

"OK," I said. "I'll do it."

She smiled and stood. I got up too and walked reluctantly to the door. She was there, waiting to be kissed. This time I got to put a little something into it, hugging her. She huffed and murmured, "Wow," and then sort of pushed me out the door.

It wasn't until later that I realized that she'd created a nice little alibi for herself. While she was in a meeting, I'd be with Carver. There'd be no witnesses. It would be her word against mine.

Except...

I reached into my pocket and turned off the phone.

CHAPTER 41

BRAD PATTERSON

By the next morning, I was ready to bail on the whole idea. Digging up an Indian graveyard was wrong in every which way.

I woke up at first light, though I'd rather have slept in. I heard Jerry in the next tent over moving around, his lantern on full blast. I drank some cold coffee to clear my head, leaned back on my sleeping bag, and wondered how to get out of this.

Jerry was real enthused after the meeting, going on and on about the Juniper Proclamation.

"It didn't say enough," he said. "I could do better than that."

As soon as we got back, he popped a beer, sat down with a notepad, and started scribbling. I joined him for a while, but he barely looked up. I don't think he even noticed when I left. Three beers and I was out on my feet. Jerry was still lost in his writing.

The next morning, I poked my head out of the tent, saw Jerry's big shadow hunched over, and had a feeling he hadn't slept at all, that he'd been up all night trying to write something *better*.

I crawled out of my tent and into his, five feet away, avoiding the dried puke in the dust that had been shoved aside, probably by my leaving the night before. I looked down at my jeans and sure enough, there were brown stains at the knees.

Screw it, I wasn't changing my pants. I had one clean pair left, and I wasn't going to put them on until I was ready to leave.

"Hey, Jer," I said, poking my head into his tent. "You been at this all night?"

He didn't even look up from his notebook. The tent was littered with beer cans, but it didn't look like many more than the day before. He had a new obsession. "I've got it, man," he said, his voice cracking. "This is the real deal. Listen to this:

"Declaration of We the People,

"Signed by I, Jerry Johnson, exempt for all your laws, and the following citizens of the free states…

"This is the truth, and shall stand until that time that a rebuttal is made, and said rebuttal shall be truth of our claims.

"I, a man, who the union of flesh and spirit, endowed by the Creator, if not disproven, is so.

"I, the son of Abraham, given dominion of the land and the animals,

"I, who was created equal, shall have no man tell me what is mine,

"I, who shall represent the beloved, my children and my wife, and all who believe, through eternity, created by God, shall not have others rule over me.

"I, who am a citizen of Heaven, shall not give authority to those who represent Earthly powers.

"I, who is free of all powers but those of God, Who is not the creation of the Legislature or of Congress or of Judges appointed not by my Creator…"

Oh, boy, I thought.

It went on and on like that, to a nice even one hundred "I's." It was nonsensical, not to mention delusional. It sounded crazy to me, the sort of thing a homeschooled Mormon boy would write in his fevered dreams.

"That's a whole lot of 'I's,'" was all I said.

He frowned and flushed a little. "Should I change them to 'we'?"

"It won't matter, Jer. They aren't going to accept that. The law is the law. They have the cops and the army and everything else."

"The *people* are behind us," he said. "The *real* people."

I didn't think so. I'd gone into John Day on one of the requisition runs. The clerks and the people on the street had acted anything but friendly. But there was no reasoning with Jerry when he was like this.

He kept talking. "There is a higher law. I am answerable only to God above…and to my family. I answer to them. No one else."

"Leave it be, Jer. We're already in enough trouble."

He looked at me blurrily, as if he hadn't heard what I said. Then he looked toward the eastern side of the tent where the morning sun was lightening up the green fabric. "What time is it?"

"I don't know," I said. "Too early."

"Come on, man. We've got to hurry." He rose, and his head hit the top of the tent, shaking the whole structure. He cursed, pulled on his pants, and turned toward the entrance.

"Let's not go to the protest," I urged. "Let's stay here, sleep in a little more. Go get some coffee and donuts." *Day-old coffee and stale donuts, but anything to get him to stay.* "They don't need us, Jer."

He wasn't listening. He stumbled out of the tent and lurched toward Merriam Hall. I followed reluctantly.

My heart was pumping big time by the time we got there. My fingers felt numb, my face dry and tight, the thumping in my chest so hard I was sure everyone could hear it. Jerry's eyes were shining. He was high stepping now, not galumphing along as he usually did. It was like we were marching to war. Only one of us knew what war could really do to a man, and it wasn't Jerry.

The rest were already there, clustered in the shadow of the corner eave of the center. They had picks and shovels, and for a moment I thought we would get out of it, because we hadn't thought of bringing any tools. I kicked at the ground, which was so full of rocks that I thought it would be impossible to dig it up without a bulldozer.

But Lois, damn her, had brought extra shovels, which she wordlessly handed us.

Jerry pulled out his manifesto. "I got something better than that Juniper Proclamation," he said.

"Really!" Lois said, stepping back and looking him up and down.

He handed it to her, and she opened it and quickly read it. I have to give her credit, she kept her face straight.

"Interesting," she murmured. "We'll have to talk about it later." She shoved the paper into her back pocket and turned to face the rest of us.

"Let's see how much we can get done before they notice us," she said in a low voice. She looked us each in the eye and then nodded. Curt Smith heaved his pickaxe and dug into the gravel on top of the soil. The rest of us spaced ourselves out every five feet or so and started digging. There was lots of clanging and dust flying into the air, but it took some effort to get below the impacted surface. It wasn't but a few seconds before something white came flying out of the red soil.

Bone. A fucking bone.

That's when I knew we were wrong. Even if our cause was just, this was a terrible thing to do. Jules was still standing in the shadows, leaning on his shovel, shaking his head. I straightened up and walked over and joined him.

"Get to fucking work, you two," Benson said, looking over his shoulder.

Man, every fiber of my body wanted to obey, but for once my conscience actually overrode my need to fit in. I felt sick to my stomach. I closed my eyes, feeling a moan coming up my throat, and then...*bam*, the struggle was over. I was released. For once, my conscience won.

I was doing the right thing and I knew it. It was weird how liberating that was. It might have been the first time since I was a kid that I'd actually gone against the group. I'm thankful for the revelation now, because even though I was as much to blame as anyone for the takeover, from then on, I tried to do the right thing.

More fragments of white bone spotted the piles of rocks and dust, along with something that looked like rotted leather and a few beads, the vibrant colors peeking out from the layer of clay that covered them.

"We're going to regret this," Jules said, standing straight and wiping away sweat. He left a big muddy streak on his forehead. "But might as well get hung for a sheep as a goat." He stepped to the end of the line and started digging.

That was the true test. I was alone in my defiance. Jerry turned toward me and motioned at me urgently. He looked worried. He couldn't help but shoot a look at Smith who, so far, had ignored me. Then the big bastard slammed his pick into the dirt and turned toward me, slapping the dust off his hands with a loud clap.

"Get your lazy ass over here," he said.

I might have given in right there, but I could tell he was reaching for my name and couldn't remember it. *Fuck him, and fuck everyone who ever pushed me around without caring a damn how I felt.*

"No, man. This is wrong."

"Who the fuck asked you?" Smith growled. "You came along on this. Now pick up your shovel and start digging."

"Fuck you."

Before I could react, Smith was in front of me, pushing me against the wall, knocking the breath out of me. I don't know what got into me. Not self-preservation, that was for sure. I tackled the guy around the knees, catching him off guard, and he went down under me. I loomed over him, my fists raised.

But I couldn't do it. I didn't punch the guy's face in when I had the chance. He flipped me over and then he was on top of me, and his fist came down hard, smashing into my cheek. My mind exploded into stars and void, and I lost track of where I was and what was happening.

Blood dripped down my chin onto the sand, the droplets quivering in the wind.

The voice I heard came from somewhere else. Somewhere far away.

"What the fuck are you people doing? Can't you read the signs? This is a restricted area."

Garth Perkins saved my life. It wasn't on purpose, he didn't mean to, but it was still pretty ironic. I'd seen the ranger from a distance but never met him. But after that, I felt like I owed him.

It gave me courage when I needed it.

CHAPTER 42

HART DAVIS

Distant shouting woke me up. I was still dressed, my jeans adhering to my skin, and I was out of the tent and pulling on my boots before I could have second thoughts. I figured the Feds were coming in at last, and suddenly it felt really important to me to try to stop anything violent from happening. There were too many guns and hot feelings around.

It was a blessing, in a way. I didn't have time to think about Nicole.

By the time I got there, most of the camp was already up, surrounding the two men at the center of the shouting match by the corner of Merriam Hall.

My heart fell when I saw what they'd done. A three-foot-wide and three-foot-deep trench severed the middle of a restricted zone. Dust was still floating in the air.

Just like that, the protesters had lost any moral high ground they had, if they'd ever had it.

Garth Perkins was facing off against Curt Smith, a good six inches shorter but fearless in his righteous anger. Smith appeared calm, while Garth looked furious.

"You've desecrated holy ground, you shithead!" Garth shouted. "We promised the Paiute Nation we would never touch this place!" His bushy beard and long hair were wild, as if he'd just gotten out of bed and rushed over. He had on his big boots and his floppy hat, but otherwise was wearing only underwear.

"*You* promised?" Smith asked calmly. "And who are you? What gives you the right to give away our land?" It was more threatening to me that he was so calm and collected. Most people get a little shaky when confrontations happen, but he didn't seem fazed in the slightest. He was a big guy, but he seemed compact and dangerous, as if he could explode.

The anger radiated off Garth. It would have made me and almost anyone else back down. But not Smith. Off to one side, I noticed Brad Patterson looking on with a cut lip, hatless for once, looking like he was ready to get in the middle of it all.

I figured I was more Smith's size, even though I also suspected he had the experience to best me in a fight. I thought I might be able to get a few licks in, take his attention off Garth. As I stepped forward, I felt Nicole approaching, not so much seeing her as sensing she was near. The crowd parted, and I turned and watched her walk toward me. She was dressed in her ranger uniform, green and grey, with her Smokey the Bear hat on.

Everyone else faded from my vision. I hungrily soaked up the sight of her. She caught me looking and veered away, ending up about a third of the way down the circling crowd from me, and then I couldn't see her anymore.

I froze in place, unable to move, my insides all twisted up. I wanted to fall at her feet, I wanted to run and hide, I wanted to be anywhere but there. How long I stood there, I don't know.

Too long, that's for sure. Too long for me to do anything to help Garth.

As Garth raged at him, Smith calmly stepped forward and slammed his fist into Garth's stomach. You could hear the air whoosh out of the ranger. He groaned and fell to his knees. But Smith wasn't done. He grabbed Garth's head firmly in both hands and slammed his knee into his face.

Garth flopped boneless to the ground, blood spurting from his nose. Smith shoved his boot under Garth's belly and kicked him into the trench. He stood over the unconscious man and drew his 9mm pistol. "You like those old bones so much, why don't you join them?"

I was too far away to stop him. I didn't carry a gun around, unlike most of them. (I was thinking *them* by then instead of *us*.) I wasn't sure I could have fired a gun if I did have one, which I suppose was why I wasn't carrying.

Brad looked like he was ready to do something, I don't know what. But I saw it in his face. It was that look that gave me the idea to approach him later and feel him out. It looked to me like he was as sick about what was happening as I was.

"Hey!" I managed to shout. And then a blur came out of the crowd and landed on Smith's back, a flurry of fists and feet and teeth and hair.

Nicole barely budged the big man, but he flinched and lowered his pistol. He reached back, grabbed Nicole by her shirt, and threw her over his shoulder. Her hat went rolling away on its rim. She tumbled onto the dirt and then into the ditch. She scrambled to her feet and tried to climb out of the hole, but was so angry that she fell backward with a frustrated shout.

By that time, I was finally moving, running full tilt at Smith. He heard me and turned, aiming his pistol right at my face. A hand came down on his arm as he fired, and the bullet slammed into the dirt at my feet, sending dust into my eyes and mouth. I slid to a stop.

"No one is getting shot today," Lois said, her fingers digging into Smith's arm, reinforcing her words.

Most of the people in the crowd had stepped back, but a few were gathered around Smith and Lois. A few others were clustered together opposite them. I took note of the uncomfortable looks on their faces and tried to remember their names. Not everyone was down with this. Kerry Lawrence stood with his local people, looking as though he was getting ready to intervene. But on whose side?

But Lois had it under control. Smith muttered an obscenity and stepped back, holstering his 9mm.

"Benson, get on the phone to the FBI and tell them not to worry about the gunshot," Lois said. "Tell them there was an accidental discharge. Hurry up before they start storming the place. The rest of you, you need to cool down. What's done is done and we aren't about to undo it, so get used to it or leave. This is the way things are going to be around here. This isn't some vacation, so if you aren't serious, get out of here."

She turned and searched the crowd until her eyes landed

on me. "The *New York Times* and the *Washington Post* both published the Juniper Proclamation. So if that was all you wanted out of this, then you have no reason to stay. But the rest of us have decided to do something concrete. We won't leave until the president rescinds the Ochoco Monument designation."

The Ochoco Mountains were due west of the John Day Fossil Beds National Monument, between Prineville and where we were standing. It had been a hard fight to gain the federal designation for them, so it was actually a pretty savvy move on Lois's part, on the surface. Truth was, these things rarely if ever got changed back retroactively. Too many vested interests.

Still, it wasn't a completely outrageous goal. It was just possible enough to keep people there.

It didn't matter for me. I was done. I wanted nothing more to do with any of it. I walked over to where Nicole was bent over Garth, tears streaming down her face. I looked through the crowd, caught Peter Sterns's eye and motioned him over. I looked around for more help, but most people avoided my gaze. Marston was wavering, I could tell, but in the end he turned away. Brad took a step toward us, but then Jerry grabbed his arm and pulled him back.

I put my hand on Nicole's shoulder, leaned down, and whispered in her ear. "We've got to get him out of here."

She nodded and stood up. Between Peter and me, we lifted Garth out of the trench and carried him to his hut behind the visitor center, a refurbished toolshed that Garth had made into a cozy little nook. His boots dragged on the ground, and a plume of dust followed us.

We rolled him into his cot. "Should we get a doctor?" Peter asked.

"If they'll let us," I said. "I doubt they will, because Smith and the others will be paranoid that it isn't a doctor but a Fed."

"Or both," Nicole added. She still hadn't looked me in the eye. Nothing had changed, apparently. I was ashamed that it wasn't me who had stopped Smith. It didn't matter. I was going to help her and Garth whether she wanted me to or not.

"I think he's got a concussion," I said. "One of us needs to stay with him, monitor his condition. If he looks worse, we'll carry him out of here on our backs if we have to."

"Where's Perry?" Nicole said. "Did any of you see him?"

"I wasn't looking for him," I said, then realized how snippy that sounded.

She ignored me and turned to Peter. "Will you stay with Garth while I go looking for my boss?"

Peter glanced over at me, puzzled, unaware of the change in Nicole's and my relationship. "Sure."

"We're leaving as soon as I round up Perry," Nicole said. She bowed her head, and I realized she was crying. "I should never have stayed. If it wasn't for me, Perry and Garth wouldn't even be here."

I wasn't sure that was completely true. Garth hadn't even been around when the decision to stay had been made. He'd been off on one of his field trips. He'd returned, taken in the situation, and never shown the slightest inclination to leave.

Nicole stood desolately at the center of the shed. Her blonde hair was scraggly, her eyes red, but she'd never looked more beautiful to me. I took a step toward her.

She whirled, arm outstretched, index finger upright, as if it was a wand warding off unwanted magic. "Don't you dare," she said. "You shouldn't be here. Go join your terrorist friends."

Peter stared at the two of us, shocked.

"I am sticking with you," I said, "until I'm sure you and Garth and Perry are safe. You don't have to like it. You don't have to like *me*. But that's what I'm doing."

"Then make yourself useful and find Perry," she said.

"You've got it," I said. I left the hut without looking back.

CHAPTER 43

BRAD PATTERSON

I didn't think I'd be welcome at Lois Carpenter's nightly meetings anymore, not that I wanted to go. I was leaving the camp. I'd be sorry to leave Jerry there, but he was a grown man, dammit; he could make his own decisions.

It was one of those sunny days when light pierced every corner and even sunglasses couldn't keep out the glare. As I walked back to my tent, my phone dinged. At first, I ignored it. Somehow the press had gotten ahold of my number, and I was getting so many texts and messages that my phone was always overloaded with them. But then, for some reason, I dug my phone out and looked at it. There was a missed call and a text that said, "Call me, Bradford."

There was only one person in the world who called me Bradford, and I didn't dare ignore her. I called back, standing there at my tent entrance. The camp looked deserted. I wondered how many people were leaving, had already left.

"Hello?" came the familiar voice.

"Who's this?" I asked, just to be ornery.

"This is Vanessa Johnson, Bradford, as you well know. What was that gunshot?"

"Nothing," I said, wondering why I was lying. A man had nearly been shot. Shouldn't the world know about that?

"Bullshit. I've always known when you're lying, covering for Jerry. What was it about?"

I told her about the confrontation at the Indian graveyard.

"Traitor," Mrs. Johnson said. For a second, I thought she was talking about me. "I never did trust that Hart Davis. You say that Lois Carpenter is running things now? Good. She's a hard-headed woman."

Not so good, I almost blurted. Someone was going to get killed, I was sure of it, and Lois wouldn't care. In fact, I thought she wanted it to happen. And if it was me who got shot, there'd be many crocodile tears shed, but I'd still be dead.

"I want you to watch after Jerry, Bradford," Mrs. Johnson said. She wasn't my mother, but I was as cowed as if she had been. "I'm depending on you."

"He's a grown m—"

"No, he isn't, and you know it. I admit I made a mistake keeping him home too much. He's too naïve for his own good. You've lived in the real world. You've got good instincts. I've known that ever since Jerry blew up the outhouse in the south pasture and you covered for him."

Damn. She knew about that?

"So you never leave his side, you hear? You take care of him." She clicked off before I could agree or disagree.

But, of course, she knew the answer. Just like that, my momentary freedom went poof. Because a woman whose will was stronger than mine, or Jerry's, or anyone else's in her extended family—and it extended up and down and sideways—had told me what to do.

In a way, I suppose it was good that I stayed. But it didn't help Jerry much.

CHAPTER 44

PERRY CAMPBELL

I didn't see the fight between Garth and Smith. At first light, I'd wandered into the desert, looking for a place to use the phone Special Agent Adams had given me. The pressure of the heat gathered around my body, pulling the sweat out of my pores. It's weird how far you have to go in the desert when you need some cover. Like, if I had to take a piss, I'd have had to do it right there in the open. Not that anyone would have cared.

In fact, the first juniper tree big enough to hide behind was disgusting. People had been coming out there and voiding their bowels.

Sorry, that isn't what this record is supposed to be about, is it?

Anyway, I finally found a place to bring out the phone. Despite how early it was, Agent Adams answered immediately.

"I'm glad you called," he said, interrupting my "Good morning." "We want you out of there. No arguments. All three of you."

"What's going on?"

"Some troublemakers the Bureau is worried about have managed to sneak into the encampment. That original group, they seemed like idealists and bumblers, and we figured we could talk them down, but these new guys...they're more radical. Militia types. Violent backgrounds."

"That's what I'm calling about. I think we're ready to leave. I just have to talk Garth into going, if I can track him down."

"No, you'll *order* him to leave, Campbell. You're their boss. Act like one."

That's not how it worked. If I got bossy, the people under me got pretty passive-aggressive. It wasn't a military or a police-type situation, after all. But…he was right. It was time to assert whatever authority I had. I'd gained some goodwill, I figured, by not being bossy all these years.

"All right," I said. "We'll pack up today. We'll leave first thing tomorrow."

"No, you'll leave now," Adams said, his voice flat. "You'll give no indication of your plans. Leave everything. Just get out of there."

I hesitated. During the Malheur standoff, the occupiers had dug through the files and the storerooms, disrupting everything. That's one of the reasons why I'd stayed, to keep that from happening here. I thought I could pack up the most important stuff in a couple of boxes, though it would take time to sift through it all.

"Are you hearing me, Campbell?" Adams asked. I wondered how long I'd been standing there staring at the sand. "We want you out of there by the end of the day. No questions."

I agreed and hung up.

Someone had piled up some rocks nearby in an impromptu sculpture. I usually knocked those stupid "art" cairn things down because they weren't natural to the landscape, but this time, I lifted the top rock, put the phone under it, and replaced the rock gently. Like I said, even then, I had the sense that things were going off the rails.

It would be just my luck if it rained for the first time in days, but I took the chance. I hurried back to camp. Now that the decision had been made—and made by people higher up—I didn't have to feel guilty about it.

Instead, I felt immense relief that it had come this. I hadn't realized until that phone call how worried I was.

But of course, all hell had broken out at Merriam Hall by the time I got back. Really, it should have been the perfect excuse. Garth was injured, and it was one of the takeover people's fault, and he needed medical attention.

I wasn't sure who to approach, or whether I should approach anyone at all. "Just get out of there," Adams had insisted, and I was inclined to agree.

Nicole was in the hut, taking care of Garth, who was still unconscious.

"Why haven't you called the FBI, gotten medical help?" I asked.

"The others won't let us," Nicole said. "They're worried that any medical people will actually be Feds."

"Then we'll carry him out ourselves," I said.

"We were planning to," she snapped. "But suddenly you were missing. We were waiting for you."

"Oh…sorry," I muttered, though I wasn't sure what I had to be sorry about. "Well, I'm here now. Let's get out of here." I looked down at Garth, who wasn't a big man but was a little thick around the middle. I figured he was at least two hundred pounds. We weren't going to get very far carrying him. What were we supposed to do? Dump him into a wheelbarrow?

"We're going to need help," I said. "Will Davis help us?"

Nicole rolled her eyes. "He's out looking for you, actually. But yeah, he'll help us if he has any integrity left."

"What happened with you two?"

"There is no 'you two,' Perry," she said. "He's an idiot, just like the rest of them."

OK, then. But it was probably a good thing, as long as Davis was still willing to help us. I thought maybe if Davis grabbed Garth's shoulders and I grabbed his legs, we could carry him on out. I was pretty sure they had gurneys at the barricades. They could meet us in no man's land. In fact, I would call Adams and tell him to do that.

I thought it was over. But by then, our chances of any kind of peaceful resolution were already gone.

CHAPTER 45

JIM MARSTON

I've been told by my lawyers to be completely honest, and that no one will see this statement but them. I trust this is so because, though I took a prominent role in representing the Juniper Coalition, I had nothing to do with the violence that followed.

I'll admit, I thought the new demand of removing the Ochoco Mountains' monument status was brilliant; just what we needed. Most people in America didn't care about it, or if they thought about it at all, they probably thought the Feds were overreaching.

Peter Stern's reading of the Juniper Proclamation had struck a chord with the public, and the tide was turning in our favor.

So I stuck to my guns, refused to budge, and slowly, I felt things changing.

"I'll tell you the truth," I said to Agent Adams when I was on the phone with him and alone for a few moments. "I know you aren't going to give us back the Ochocos, but we need something solid, you know? We need to feel like we're getting something."

"How about if we say we'll put it up for review?"

Secretly, that's what I'd hoped he'd say. I thought it was the most we were likely to get. At least it wasn't abject surrender.

"And of course, we'll need to be given amnesty," I added. This was a deal breaker for me.

Adams didn't hesitate. "For those of you who haven't broken the law, that is certainly doable."

Well, that was the trick, wasn't it? But I thought I could get a commitment from him to agree that *I* hadn't broken any laws, and maybe Peter Sterns and a few of the others. It was public land, after all. We had a constitutional right to congregate and to protest.

Curt Smith and Lois Carpenter came back into the room, so I said loudly, "I think we'll need a little more than that," in a very firm tone. I ended the call and turned to them with a smile. Lois might take some convincing, but I was certain we were on the right path.

I do believe everything would have been resolved if the hard-asses hadn't gone and dug up the Indian graveyard. The reporters had been almost friendly up to that point. The whole camp had been kind of festive, people coming and going, not much tension in the air. After that morning, everything changed.

Worst of all, public opinion went against us. The Indians weren't shy about telling the world how we'd desecrated their ancestors' remains. It was hard to convince anyone that the land belonged to us originally, as Jerry Johnson was proclaiming, when the Paiutes had been roaming the area for thousands of years.

In their eyes, we were just one more group of white guys coming in to take over.

I was ambushed that night at the news conference with one question after another about the Indians, no matter how much I tried to change the topic back to the Ochocos. Smith and his pals had fucked it up royally.

Luckily, no one had actually seen Smith's confrontation with Garth Perkins and Nicole Nelson, or we'd have been run out of there within hours. That Garth was injured was a secret that Lois made clear was not to be leaked on punishment of… what? No one wanted to find out.

"It was a mistake," I heard myself saying, but of course, one interview with that Benson fellow and it was clear that it wasn't a mistake, that they'd done it on purpose. "We needed sanitary facilities, and that was the closest place to dig."

"So you're defecating on the graves?" Kari Martini asked in mock horror. It looked good on TV.

"Of course not," I said. "We will restore the site to its original condition." I wasn't sure about that, but I had to say something. In the end, I closed down the news conference, just walked away with all the reporters still yelling questions. It felt like knives were being sunk into my back.

I almost quit then, but when I talked to Special Agent Adams later that night, he said, "We're the reasonable ones, Jim. Let's keep this on track. Try not to dig up any more graveyards and we'll get past this. I've talked to my superiors, and they've told me that they'd be willing to give you special consideration since you've tried so hard to end this peacefully. I don't think jail time will be necessary, as long as there's no violence."

"What if…" I hesitated, then decided to say what had been on my mind from the beginning. "What if some of these guys don't give up without, you know…"

"We'll deal with them separately," Adams said. "If you and Davis and Sterns and some of the other leaders leave, we think it will all fall apart. We can hold a joint news conference telling the world that we've decided to study the feasibility of removing the Ochocos from monument status."

"No, we can't announce it together," I said. That would have been a disaster. I could picture Smith and Benson and some of the others yelling treason. "Maybe if you announce it first, and then we take credit?"

"That's fine," Adams said. "We don't really care who takes credit. We're ready any time."

I started to believe that it might work. We'd get the government to make a concession, even if it wasn't real, and those of us who were blameless would stay out of jail. A victory for both sides. Peter Sterns could write a book, I'd run for county sheriff back in La Grande, and no one would be hurt.

That's why I was so alarmed when I saw Davis and Campbell emerge from the hut carrying Perkins. They were carrying him in his cot, with the aluminum tube legs still down. Nicole was right behind them, looking worried. It was pretty obvious they were leaving. I should have let them, but…

Thing is, though they were never hostages while I was in charge (I will fight the kidnapping charges to my last breath), there had been an implicit sort of deal. The FBI was less likely to storm the place if there were civilians there. I mean, until that day, no one ever said they had to stay against their will.

I hurried over, blocking their way. "You can't leave yet," I said. "We're about to make a breakthrough."

They set the cot down. Davis had his back to me and didn't say anything, but Campbell marched up to me. "I don't give a damn about a breakthrough. You people are all insane. You nearly killed Garth. You expect us to stay?"

"But...but you insisted on staying, and it's part of how this is all going to work."

I wasn't really sure what I was saying, but I was certain that if they left, all our leverage would be gone and we'd all go to jail for the rest of our lives.

Davis finally turned around and looked me in the face. "Get out of our way, Marston," he said. "If you had any brains, you'd come with us."

"They'll arrest you as soon as you step over to their side of the barricade."

"I *should* be arrested. This takeover was a dumb thing to do, and I'm sorry I ever went along with it."

"Went along with it? You suggested this place, Davis. And I'll testify to that fact."

"Do what you gotta do," Davis said. He turned back around and lifted his end of the makeshift stretcher. "You ready?" he asked Campbell.

Campbell lifted his end, and they went around me. It wasn't smooth going. Perkins looked like he was going to roll off at any moment, and sure enough, within a couple of feet, Campbell stumbled and Perkins landed face first in the dirt with a *thud*.

Lois Carpenter arrived before anyone else could react, followed by her toady, Smith. She motioned to the men who'd gathered around to watch.

"Block the view," she said. "We can't let the Feds see this. They'll come in guns blazing, and we aren't ready yet."

I thought it was too late already. I figured the FBI had binoculars on us. Hell, they probably had sniper scopes zeroed in on our heads.

I'm not sure what would have happened then, but Garth Perkins decided it for us. He opened his eyes with a loud groan. Everyone's eyes went to him as he got to his knees and then unsteadily to his feet.

"I'm not going anywhere," he said. "I'm not leaving until these assholes leave."

"They almost killed you, Garth," Nicole said.

"All the more reason to stay. Who knows how much damage they'll do?"

"Let others handle it," Davis urged. "You can't fight these guys. What are you going to do, shoot it out?"

"If I have to," Garth said. "I've handled a gun before."

"Garth…" Nicole started to say.

All this was going on with Lois Carpenter and her followers standing right there watching. She had a strange smile on her face. It wasn't just Smith and Benson behind her, either. Or just Jules and Brad and Jerry. There were three or four new guys I hadn't seen before, rough-looking guys, wearing camouflage, with semiautomatic rifles strapped to their backs. Lois looked back at Smith, and he stepped forward.

"You aren't going anywhere," he said.

Complete silence fell. Everyone understood the ramifications of that statement.

"To be clear," Davis said, "are you saying you won't let us leave?"

Smith glanced at Lois, and she shook her head slightly.

"Let's just say we're requesting that you stay for now," Smith said. "We can discuss it in the morning."

I held my breath. I was praying no one would use the word *hostage*, because I figured as long as that specific word wasn't used, there was still wiggle room. We could claim it was all a big misunderstanding.

"I'm not leaving anyway," Garth said. He looked like he could barely stand. His voice was slurred, but no one doubted he meant it.

"Well, there you go," Smith said. "Listen to the big man. He's got more balls than all the rest of you put together. I'm sorry I hit you, man. I misjudged you."

"Fuck you," Garth said. "I'm pressing charges when this is over."

Smith laughed. "You do that."

Davis looked like he was ready to challenge the ultimatum. He glanced at Nicole, who shook her head. His face fell and he turned away. I don't know what had happened between them, but the way her eyes followed him, I knew she still had feelings for him. She shook it off and went over to Garth and put his arm over her shoulder.

Campbell hesitated a few moments longer. I think if he'd walked away then, Lois would have let him. I remembered her words, "We aren't ready *yet*." Even now, that sends chills down my spine. Then his shoulders slumped and he went to Garth's other side, and the three of them stumbled back to the hut.

Peter Sterns stepped out of the crowd, grabbed a corner of the cot, and followed them. So did that girl who called herself Mich.

I wish now that I'd joined them, but I just stood there. Everyone was looking at me to see what I'd do, and I just stood there.

None of this was planned, at least not by me. I didn't want it to happen. I swear to God, after that, I was as much a hostage as any of them.

CHAPTER 46

JOSHUA CALLEY

There were big doings back at Merriam Hall, but I wasn't there to see them. I was in John Day picking up supplies. Harry Johnson had sent me a cashier's check—they were still letting mail in—and it was enough to supply the camp for another week or so.

I was a little surprised the Feds let me leave without arresting me, but I think the negative publicity of starving the takeover folks was something they weren't willing to risk. The Feds followed me every step of the way, and I could tell they were itching to jump me, but I suspect that they wanted the whole basket, not just one egg. They certainly didn't want the one black egg. How would that look?

The people on the street were distinctly unfriendly, and who could blame them? I found out later that sympathizers were patrolling the streets, parking outside the houses of city officials, and that would be enough to make anyone mad. It sure would have me.

I also heard later that some of the local teenagers were ready to pile into their pickups with their hunting rifles and put an end to the takeover right then and there. Lord, what a mess that would have been. A new crew had shown up out there, and they meant business. Luckily, the teens' parents stopped them from following through.

I expected to be waved through the barricade, but instead, a state trooper stepped in front of the pickup and motioned me to stop. I rolled down the window, feeling that old fear in the pit of my stomach.

Stop it, I told myself. *These cops aren't like the cops in Atlanta. No…they're worse.*

"Please step out of the vehicle, sir," the cop said in a flat tone. He looked like any other cracker, with a beefy face, red cheeks, and protruding eyes. He already looked angry.

That's when the old feeling really came down on me, anger and fear all wrapped up like barbed wire in my stomach. "Am I under arrest?"

"No, sir. Special Agent Adams would like a word with you. If you'll come this way."

I got out of the truck reluctantly, certain I was about to be arrested. I was almost surprised that my legs moved, that I maintained my outward composure. I followed him to a construction trailer, the kind I'd spent much of my life in, bare bones and functional. He opened the door and ushered me in, but didn't follow. The FBI agent was sitting at a small table piled high with paperwork. He motioned for me to sit and continued writing for a little while.

He looked up at me finally and smiled. At least, his mouth smiled; his eyes were dead serious. "Would you like a drink? Soda? Beer?"

"No, thanks," I said. "The back of my pickup is filled with the stuff."

"Right," he said, leaning back in his chair. "You look like a smart man, Mr. Calley. I can't believe you're part of this."

"You mean you can't believe I'm with these white supremacists?"

He nodded.

"What you really mean is, what kind of self-hating Uncle Tom am I?"

He looked surprised but nodded again.

"You don't know these people the way I do, Agent Adams. You probably see them as ignorant, racist rubes. Did you know they backed me up, ran the Klan off? These are good people when politics aren't messing with their heads."

"With some of them, messed-up politics all there is to them," he said.

"Sure, there're bad apples in every bunch. Just like the

bad-apple cop who shot my brother in Atlanta. But you know, I don't hate all cops because of it. I'm here to try to protect those who haven't gone bad yet. The innocents."

"The best way to protect them is to get them out of there," the agent said.

"I can't force a man to do something he don't want to. That's *your* problem."

"You want to see your friends dead? Because that's the way it could go down. What we need is someone on the inside who can tell us what's really happening."

Well, I guess I still had some of my Atlanta street attitude, because damned if I was going to be a snitch. He could see it in my eyes, too.

"You can go, Mr. Calley," Adams said. He looked tired, like he hadn't slept in days. He was under more pressure than I was. "When it all goes to hell, I hope you'll do the right thing."

"If you leave them alone, they'll get bored," I said. I felt almost guilty about it, like I was giving away a secret.

"I used to think that too, but that was before Smith and the others took over. You may not see it, Mr. Calley, but things have gotten more serious. Try to pay attention. You may only have one chance."

Agent Adams stood up and waited for me to stand too, then extended his hand. I took it and shook it, man to man. He was just doing his job, after all. I started out the door, but he called out to me. He extracted a card from his shirt pocket and wrote something on the back. It was embossed with the FBI seal and had his name, title, and a phone number on it. He'd written down his extension.

I took the card out of politeness, intending to ditch it before I got back to the camp. A card with the FBI seal wasn't something I wanted found on me.

I drove the rest of the way back with my mind in a whirl. I decided then and there that it was time to bring this little escapade to a close, whatever it took. As long as I got Jerry Johnson out of there safe, I didn't really care about the rest of it.

CHAPTER 47

MARK SIMONS

I wasn't sure how I was going to get close enough to Carver to see the effects of the drug, much less how I was going to convince him to leave the mess tent with me. I was pretty amazed when he sat down right next to me, solving both problems.

I watched him pop the lid off the Tupperware container that held his special meal, trying not to stare. Man, when he took that first bite of lasagna, I held my breath, wondering if he was going to keel over right then and there.

I'd never been all that friendly with Carver. He was my opposite—a lady's man, tall and slender, good-looking in a cowboy sort of way. Didn't talk much. I'd been surprised when he didn't join Lois's crew, because he'd been the one who'd led us to her in the first place.

So I asked him, "Why are you staying away from Lois? I thought you and she had a thing."

"A thing?" He laughed. "I don't know what got into me, taking you guys to her house. I was tired and hungry and I thought maybe, just maybe, she'd changed. Yeah, she changed all right. She's worse."

"Worse in what way?"

"She's a sweet bitch, Mark. Can't you see that? She's sweet to your face, but as soon as you turn your back, she sinks a knife in it. She uses people…men. Most women can't stand her, 'cause they recognize a sweet bitch when they see one."

I should defend her, I thought. But I knew he was right. She was using poison this time instead of a knife. Same diff.

And it didn't matter. I didn't care. I was totally hers, no matter what she said or did.

So there, I've just incriminated myself, not that it matters worth a damn. I remember thinking *poison*, not *drug*, because inside, I kinda knew. She wanted Carver out of the way, and Lois wasn't one to take half-measures. If I'd known the reason she wanted him gone, I would have had even less doubt. But I'd heard the underlying hiss in her voice when she told me what to do, the kind of hiss a woman makes when she really can't stand someone.

Carver was talking at me, and I hadn't heard a word.

"What?"

"How do you think this is all going to end, Mark? You think the Feds are going to give us what we want and we're going to walk away, free to live our lives? Even if we survive this, we're going to jail."

"Why? We're just protesting. We have a right to assemble and protest, don't we?"

"Shit, Mark, you drank the Kool-Aid. You don't march into someplace and take it over with guns and call it a protest. Although...if we can get even one juror to think that, it might work. But it won't matter. Our lives are fucked up from now on, no matter what else happens. And for what? Nothing's going to change."

"Lois says we aren't leaving until we get something."

"Lois says...Jesus, Mark."

I felt really defensive right then, and I wanted to spill out all the plans and all the goals Lois had detailed. I wanted Carver to understand. Then I realized it didn't matter. He'd be out of the picture soon enough.

"Shit," Carver said, pushing away his food half-eaten. "Why would they serve lasagna when it's so fucking hot?"

"You all right?" I asked. "You're looking a little green."

I can't tell you exactly what I was thinking then. I remember being alarmed, but also kind of excited. It was the power, I think. The rush that came with knowing I could do that to someone—just like that—and them not know I was doing it or able to do anything about it.

I had a flash of insight into Lois. She *always* thought this way. She'd do what she wanted to other people, and they were helpless to stop her. I realized that most people had no idea what was happening around them, that they assumed the best of others, even the most cynical of them. They counted on the Golden Rule. Someone like Lois, she could bulldoze her way through them like bowling pins, knocking them over and not looking back.

"I think I'm going to puke," Carver said. He tried to stand up, then plopped back onto the bench with a groan.

"Let me help you," I said. I hurried to his side, helped him to his feet, and held him steady. Once he was up, he seemed to stabilize, and we walked right on out of there. No one was looking our way. No one noticed. For once, I was happy I was such a nobody, because I've read all the witness statements, and not one person remembers me being with Carver in the mess tent.

Not that it matters. I hate to be the one to tell my lawyers, but my confession is going to be hard to deny, because I fucking meant it at the time. Even now, I'm pretty sure I deserve whatever they send my way.

We walked behind the mess tent. Carver fell to his knees and puked, sending a spray out onto the sagebrush. I still remember the liquid dripping off the branches, glinting in the twilight. It was desert beyond that, and so I kept walking, putting Carver's arm on my shoulder and practically carrying him. He was groaning, eyes closed, and muttered a few times, "What the fuck is wrong with me?"

I remembered what Lois had told me: "Give it an hour or so. Take him into the desert until he's *really* sick."

Well, he was as sick as a dog. We had to stop every ten feet or so while he retched. The last few times, nothing came up. It was terrifying. His mouth was open, his throat distended, his eyes bugging out. He turned white, then red, then white again, and he staggered one last time and fell forward into the dust.

I hauled Carver behind a juniper tree, looking over my shoulder to see if there was anyone around. To my surprise, he pulled himself up into a sitting position, his back against the tree. There was an anthill under the juniper's trunk, and the insects started swarming over him, but he didn't seem to even notice.

"Mark," he said weakly. "You see what she's done, don't you?"

I nodded.

He blinked. "So you knew?"

"She wants you out of the way, Carver. Just for a while. I'll call an ambulance..."

"Won't matter. She'll have made sure there was enough poison to kill me. I'm going to fucking die, Mark. Jesus, I'm going to die, and I fucking deserve it."

I pulled my phone out of my pocket, started dialing 911, then hesitated.

"Call them, Mark...for your own sake. I'm dead, but you can still save something of yourself if you try. You hang up and you're lost. Lost to this life and the next, if you believe in anything at all. I'm telling you, you don't want that. I ought to know."

I put the phone back in my pocket.

"You noticed how nice Lois's house is?" Carver said. "How well she dresses? Her goddamn stable of horses and her trips to Europe?"

I hadn't noticed or known any of these things, actually, other than the house, which hadn't seemed all that fancy. It had been a big house, nice, and I had wondered how she managed that on Social Security payments from her deceased husband.

"She had a million-dollar policy on Matt, and she collected. A mysterious robbery gone wrong. They didn't even question it. And now she's gotten rid of the only witness."

He closed his eyes, and his Adam's apple did a dance in his throat, as if he was trying to cough it up.

"Get out of here, Mark. Save your damn soul. She's the devil."

God help me, I watched him die. He fell silent, then leaned over and slid onto his side, the ants swarming over his face. He shuddered a couple of times and then went still.

I'd never seen anyone die, never even seen a dead person. It freaked me out how still he was. Not a twitch of movement.

The ants were crawling over his open eyes. I grabbed his feet and pulled him away from the nest. There was a lava rock outcropping a couple of dozen feet away. I hoisted Carver over my shoulder and staggered through the soft dust, ants crawling off his body and onto my face. I brushed them away, and Carver slid off and slammed into the rocks, face first. A huge gash opened on his forehead. Not much blood spilled out.

That's when I got the idea: I'd just leave him like that. Maybe they'd think he had fallen, smashed his head. Maybe they'd think it was an accident.

I walked away, trying not to think about the insects and the coyotes and the buzzards. Trying to forget I'd even seen what I'd just seen. Halfway back to camp, I felt my own meal rising in my throat. I leaned over and spewed all over the brown dust.

I stared into that puke for a long time, trying to interpret it. Did it look like what Carver had ejected? Did Lois get to me too?

But I immediately felt better, so figured it was my body rebelling against what I'd done. I'd gotten my meal from the food line. There was no way she could've known what I'd select.

Lois will be appreciative, I thought, and then, *She better be appreciative, because now I* know *something.*

I'd better watch my back.

The nightly meeting was over by the time I got to Lois's trailer, but she was waiting for me.

"Did you call 911?" she asked.

"No need, he's dead. But you knew that, didn't you." It wasn't a question.

"He's dead?" She looked genuinely surprised, which only confirmed what a great liar she was. "Well, damn. But with drugs, there's always that chance. Where is he?"

"He's out there," I waved vaguely. "He smashed his head into some rocks."

She nodded appreciatively. "Smart. Carver's been drinking ever since he got here. I don't doubt his blood alcohol level is sky high. Good job, Mark." She gave me a hug and then started to pull away.

I didn't let her go. "No," I said. "I want more." I kissed her hard, squeezing her until her breath huffed out of her body. She fought me for a few seconds, then she returned the kiss, just as hard.

It wasn't me. I knew that. She'd just killed someone and it excited her, and I was the guy who'd done what she wanted, and she'd probably fucked guys uglier than me.

I didn't care. I wanted it. I thought maybe if I got it out of my system, I'd get over her. But as she lay in my arms afterward, I realized it had only gotten worse. I'd kill anyone for her. I'd kill the whole damn camp if I had to.

And I'd die for her.

CHAPTER 48

CARLTON MANNING

After the occupiers dug up the Native American artifacts, my editors sent me back to Oregon. The story, which had been dying the slow death of nothing new happening, had come alive again. And apparently, to my editor, I was the go-to guy for all things Oregon.

I'd grown up east of the mountains, but I couldn't wait to get out of there. I went off to college in Boston, and I never looked back. My parents moved to the Willamette Valley, which was never home as far as I was concerned. I'd fly into Portland and out as fast as I could. I never had a reason to go back to Eastern Oregon.

Funny thing is, I don't remember it being so spectacularly scenic. I mean, it wasn't as if the Cascade Mountains suddenly popped up on the horizon. I'd even gone skiing on Mt. Bachelor most weekends throughout high school, but somehow, I'd never really seen the skyline, or I'd forgotten. I was gobsmacked when I came back to this side of the mountains.

As I drove over the Ochocos and down into the valley beyond, two huge cinder cones popped out of the flat landscape and, as always when I saw such sights, I wanted to climb them, to look down on the world from a place few people had ever been.

I was to meet Edward Summers in John Day and then drive over with him to the Fossil Beds, interviewing him along the way. A Native American archeologist, he'd been invited by some of the takeover people to come and examine the damage done.

But some of the other takeover people didn't want him coming.

The desecration of the graveyard had changed the whole dynamic of the takeover. Most of the occupiers were struggling to come up with excuses, and others were apparently embarrassed. Meanwhile, various Native American organizations were pressuring the federal government to do something. My sense was that the FBI had been willing to wait out the takeover, but now they were under pressure to end it.

All the motel rooms in John Day were booked, as usual, but I thought I might get lucky and snag a cancellation again. I was prepared to drive back to Bend if I had to. As it happened, Ed offered me the extra twin bed in his room, and I gladly accepted. Good thing, too, because there was a heavy snowfall on the passes that night, the kind of mid-October snow that would melt within days but cause chaos while it lasted.

But even more importantly, if I'd left that day, I would have missed all the action.

Over the phone, Edward Summers had spoken in a slow, deep voice, so I was expecting a large man who moved deliberately. Instead, he was small and quick of movement, and even quicker of mind. Only his words were slow.

I sat on one twin bed and he faced me on the other. I pulled out my notebook and pen. (I'm old-fashioned that way.)

"To start with," I said, "I'm curious... what Native tribes lived in this area?"

"Lived?" he said. "As in past tense?"

"I mean..."

"No, you're actually right. Not a lot of us live in Wheeler or Grant counties nowadays. We've got the Confederated Tribes of the Umatilla nearby and, of course, the Tribal Council of the Burns Paiute. To give you an overall view of it, you would probably refer to the original inhabitants of this area as the Northern Paiute. Though the pioneers referred to us by the derogatory term *diggers*."

"So when the takeover people dug up the graveyard..."

"Just more of the same. See, I don't think these guys have any idea of the history of this place. They think that we owned this land, the way the settlers think they own land. To argue with the federal government over ownership is pointless to us, because in our view, no one can own the land. We are part of this world. You can't dig very long before you dig up our past, our ancestors."

"There's no there there?"

"More like it's all there there," Ed answered. "Have you seen the YouTube video the protesters just posted?"

"I've been driving for the last six hours," I said.

He jumped to his feet and turned the computer screen on the desk in my direction. I recognized the man frozen on the screen; Jules Francisco. Ed clicked the video on.

Jules had a box in his hand, and he was sifting through its contents with his fingers. You could see fragments of white bone inside. "We didn't mean to hurt no one's feelings," he said. "We want to return this back to you. We're really sorry."

Ed froze the screen again. "See, he thinks he can make it all good by returning some old bones. But the bones aren't owned by us, they are part of the land." Ed waved his hand. "It's difficult to understand if you weren't raised in the culture. I'm sorry if I'm lecturing."

"That's why I'm here, Ed. Lecture away."

"There are about four hundred members of the Tribal Council of the Burns Paiute. When white explorers first came here, they described vast villages along the waterways of this land. We were systematically killed off, by disease and starvation and violence. We had our own Trail of Tears, and the current Native Americans living in this area are the few who came back."

He turned to his computer and turned on the video again.

Jules stared into the camera, goggle-eyed. "We would like to sit down with you and discuss this. Tell us what we can do to make it right. You deserve to have freedom too."

"Well, isn't that nice of him," Ed said, turning down the volume. "He's a real character, isn't he?"

"Yeah, but Jules is a character who open carries a Colt .45."

Ed considered this for a moment. "We Native Americans are not their enemy. You guys are."

He had a point. Jules had shown almost a reverence for

Native culture, even though he didn't understand it. To Jules and the others, the media were a bunch of liars, causing trouble.

"I've agreed to meet with Francisco," Ed said. "Though I must tell you, almost none of my people agree with my decision. They're afraid that negotiating with these people lends them legitimacy."

"Then why are you doing it?"

"I see it as a teaching moment. I never could resist a teaching moment. Lots of people are watching that stupid video. I'd like to bring some history and facts to all this."

Facts, I thought. *Good luck with that.*

He took a quick look at his watch. "I'm supposed to be there in an hour or so. We can talk in the car. I've got a Hummer, which will be handy in case we need to make a quick getaway."

I agreed to go in his Hummer, which was bright yellow and had the words "Tribal Council of the Burns Paiute" stenciled on the doors. He filled me in on more of the history of the Paiute, which turned into a sad and sordid tale with the arrival of the white man. It made the occupiers' complaints seem silly and petty. One of the people in the takeover, Jerry Johnson, had written a long treatise about how his family rightfully owned this land and how the federal government had taken it away illegally. What he didn't seem to understand, or even know, was that his family had taken the land forcefully from the Native Americans.

This truth was coming down hard on the protesters. You could see it in the videos like Jules's, where he was trying to explain himself and failing. You could see it in the reaction of the public, who were almost universally coming down on the side of the Native Americans.

We arrived at the barricades and were stopped. I expected we'd be let through. As far as I knew, they were still letting people in and out, except for a few who were on a no-entry list of some kind. A week before, some of the takeover's leaders had driven to a town hall meeting in Arlington, a small town to the north. It hadn't gone well, according to news reports. Some of the residents had tried to make citizen's arrests. Ironically, the FBI had stepped in to let the takeover people leave.

"I'm sorry," the state trooper said. "We've closed the roads."

"Since when?" I asked.

"As of ten o'clock this morning," the trooper said. "If you'd like to discuss it with Agent Adams, you can park over there. He's in the first trailer."

Adams seemed to know who I was and let me in. I introduced Ed, and Adams instantly perked up. "You were supposed to meet with Francisco?" he asked.

"Yes, sir," Ed said. "It was prearranged, so if you'd just let me in, I might be able to do some good."

"Sorry," Adams said. "Orders."

I knew the special agent in charge was pretty much the one who decided these things, but for whatever reason, Adams didn't look like he was going to budge.

"I need to call Jules," Ed said. He turned away and went to the corner of the trailer. I started to say something to Adams but he raised his hand to stop me, listening to Ed's end of the conversation. I didn't think much of it at the time, but of course, the significance of it is clear in hindsight.

Ed was saying, "If you'll meet me in Spray, I'll reserve the conference room at the motel. I'll bring pizza... You will? Thank you, Mr. Francisco. I look forward to talking to you and your friends. Yes, seven o'clock. See you then."

Agent Adams walked us to our vehicle, apologizing again for not letting us pass.

"Is something happening?" I asked in a low voice.

"Same old, same old," he said, shrugging.

"Off the record?" I offered.

My hand was on the door of the Hummer, but when he hesitated, I stepped away. We walked out of Ed's earshot.

"It's getting serious," Adams said. "There are people infiltrating the original occupiers who mean business. That's why I've closed off access. I'm hoping we can end this peacefully. Normally, the longer something like this goes on, the more likely they'll give up. I'm not so sure this time."

"Thank you for telling me," I told him.

I was disappointed that I wouldn't be able to get out of there as soon as I'd hoped, but I was intrigued by this new information.

CHAPTER 49

JIM MARSTON

Jules had to be the first to die. I can see that now. None of us were going to give up easy, and the government needed their pound of flesh, and Jules was the reckless son of a bitch who fit the bill. He knew it, too. He played his part perfectly, the Kabuki theater of reaching for his gun—or did he? Hell, even I don't know.

Like I said, he played his part perfectly, face down in the red snow.

I was a few feet away, shocked through and through, numb. Droplets of blood had landed on the crusted snow, and for an instant they kept their globular form, catching the rays of the sun, before bursting and spreading in a red stain. My face was frozen, my feet stumbled, my hands wandered around until they were clamped in handcuffs. Sitting in the back of the police car, my eyes closed, the red lights twirling behind my eyelids, I knew it had been inevitable.

Jules was the first.

Not me, I thought, relieved—to my shame. I'd thought it would be me. They weren't going to shoot Hart Davis, with his college education, or Carver, the lady's man. I thought maybe it would be Joshua, considering his skin color, but maybe they realized how it would look, shooting the only black man within a hundred miles.

No, it was going be either the fat guy or the geeky guy, and this time they chose the geek. When the time came, I didn't reach for my gun, I didn't run. I just let them take me.

Oh, well, Jules would say.

You guys blew it. I'm talking to you, FBI and DEA and ATF and whatever else fucking agency is reading this. I'm assuming you're all reading this, since my court-appointed attorneys are useless. (Yes, you.) I don't know what else I can expect from lawyers who work for minimum wage, or something close to it. They've been rolled over in every hearing I've been to, the prosecutors just flat-out doing whatever they want. Nice trick, freezing all my assets, making sure I have bargain-basement representation.

So I'm addressing you.

You blew it, people.

I had it all worked out. If you had left us alone for another couple of days...but you just had to pull the trigger. Jules is dead because you guys couldn't wait a little longer.

It was Jules's idea to go to the meeting in Spray. He was really bothered by the Indian response to the takeover. It had apparently never occurred to him that we were infringing on Indian territory, but once it became a big deal in the media, he really took it to heart.

That's the thing you guys didn't understand, will never understand. Jules was all heart (can't say much for his thinking), and he was the heart of the movement. You may have thought that when you cut out the heart, you were ending it, but all you did was make sure blood flew everywhere, infecting everything it touched.

Nice job, Special Agent Asshole Adams.

It was me, Jules, Margie Fineman (who went to the meetings and was our unofficial recorder), then Barry Peters and Carl Simpson. We were the nucleus at the Fossil Beds after Davis opted out.

Oh, and Peter Sterns, who was the face and voice of our little group. He decided at the last minute not to come along, thank God.

So you took us out, the very people trying to find a solution. And guess who that left? The extremists, Lois Carpenter's little clique. That's who you had to deal with, and look how that turned out!

Anyway. Back to that night.

We drove up toward the small mountain pass north of us, hitting snow after about a thousand feet. That should have been a sign. Snow arriving that early wasn't unheard of, but it was unusual. Then we hit more snow, and I was pretty sure we wouldn't make it. But the snowplows had been through sometime in the middle of the storm, so it wasn't impossible. It was just slushy and slippery, and the cliffs on one side of the road were pretty hairy.

Jules was driving the van, white-knuckled, and he wouldn't listen to the rest of us who wanted to turn around. He stared straight ahead, his jaw clenched. Occasionally, he'd mutter, "Oh, well." I don't think he even knew he was doing it.

Finally, Margie got really strident about it. "You're going to kill us!"

"I've got to talk to the Indians," Jules answered. "I got to make them understand."

Jules would have listened to that Indian professor, I'm pretty sure. He might have even come around. I figured if Jules came around, I could swing the rest of them. Jules was the key.

I didn't see the roadblock at first. Jules muttered a curse and I looked over at him curiously, then was pushed back in my seat as he accelerated. Two black SUVs straddled the road, with a half-dozen agents clustered behind them, all of them pointing their weapons at us.

Jules ignored the roadblock, driving straight for the five-foot gap between the blockading SUVs.

"What the hell are you doing?" Simpson shouted, and right on top of that was Margie's ear-piercing scream.

It's all a blur after that; the agents scrambling out of the way, gunshots being fired, the window shattering, spraying safety glass all over my chest and lap. I put my arm over my eyes, so what I remember is the grinding sound of metal, the *thud* of the crash, the compression of the airbag driving shards of glass into my cheeks.

Then we were through it. But Jules was out of control, accelerating at the same time that the van was sliding sideways.

We slammed into a snow bank and the still-inflated airbag knocked the breath out of me.

"You bastards!" Jules was screaming. "You broke your word!"

Through it all, I had a weird sense of inevitability. Of course, this was how they would do it. Get us separated and take us out. They hadn't actually promised us anything. They...*you* lulled us into a false sense of security, waiting until there were enough of us to make an impact.

But I could have told you Jules wouldn't take it lying down. He wasn't going to just surrender, get on his knees, and let himself be handcuffed. There was no way.

The van shuddered a couple of more times, and I realized that bullets were hitting us. Later on, it was claimed that all the shots were at the tires, but I swear I felt bullets whizzing by me. No way to prove it, since they came through the already broken windows.

Jules let out an animal sound, a near scream, and smashed his shoulder against the van's door, unhooking his seatbelt at the same time. He dropped down to the road, which was at a steep angle. I heard him grunt as his cowboy boots met pavement.

He hobbled away into the snow.

"Jules!" I shouted. "Don't do anything stupid!"

But that was an impossible request. Jules was nothing if not determinedly stupid. That was his curse and his blessing. He was sure he was right, and as long as he was sure, nothing could stop him. Nothing but a bullet.

I shouldn't say it. I should let you bastards dangle in the wind. But I saw Jules reach for his revolver. Thing was, that's all he did. Reach for it. Then he took his hand away and yelled something incoherent. Then he reached for it again.

If you'd just waited. Just another few seconds. If you'd talked to me, I could have told you that Jules was never going to draw his weapon, much less fire it at another human being. Jules talked big, but he wouldn't hurt a fly. Literally. I'd seen him open screen door and let out a fly.

I heard three shots, not two. One took Jules' arm off at the elbow. If nothing else, that would have ended it. Jules staggered and grabbed his stump. There was plenty of time to realize he was out of it, incapacitated. The next two shots (you say there was one, but I heard what I heard) hit him in the chest. He looked down, disbelieving. Then the disbelieving changed to full-on believing, like he'd been expecting it.

I ran to his side. I heard the shouts to get down, and I expected a bullet in the back, but I wasn't going to let Jules die alone. He was face down in the snow, a red halo surrounding his body. I turned him over.

I put my hand on the chest wound, felt the spurting blood against my palm, and knew it was hopeless. Jules looked up at me with the most peaceful expression I'd ever seen on him. He looked like a different man, the kind of man he could have been with a little luck.

"Oh, well." He sighed. He closed his eyes and stopped moving. The blood against my palm lost force. I lifted my hand, and blood trickled out of the gaping wound.

It was only seconds, but it seemed like forever.

Then three agents tackled me and threw me face down in the bloody snow. I still remember the cold and wet against my face. Did I cry? Or was it the melting snow? I don't know. I don't remember.

My arms were pulled back, hands cuffed tightly, and I was lifted and carried away, and thrown into the back seat of one of the black SUVs. I had it to myself. I figured the others were already in custody.

That's how it happened. Pretty much a cold-blooded murder, but they have video showing Jules reaching for his gun. Like, three times. No one ever mentions that he never actually drew down.

You killed the heart of the movement, but you didn't kill the movement. You created a martyr whose blood filled the hearts of others.

It's your fault, what happened. You'll all get off without so much as a reprimand, I know. Because of what happened later, there is probably nothing you could have done that would be second-guessed now.

But I'm telling you that it didn't need to be that way. I was there, I was a witness, and maybe no one will ever read this testimony, but it will be on the record at least.

Unless my worthless lawyers let it get buried, which I wouldn't doubt. I'm going to jail for a long time. I know this. But they can't keep me from telling the truth.

CHAPTER 50

MARK SIMONS

I woke in that narrow little trailer bed with bruises on my elbows from banging against the bolsters. Damn, once Lois gave in, she was a live wire; it was like an electric current connected us. She'd come and I'd come, and I'd come and she'd come, and… It was everything I'd dreamed of and more.

Someone was banging on the door. Lois was at the table, writing. She looked over at me with an annoyed expression. "Hurry up and get dressed."

"Afraid someone will see me?"

"I don't give a damn, Mark. No one will be surprised, they'll just think I took pity on your sorry ass. By the way, if I'd known what a fine ass it was going to be, I'd have done this a lot sooner. But if you plan on blackmailing me, do it now. Get it over with."

"Blackmail you about what?" I asked with as innocent a tone as I could muster.

She stared at me steadily for a few moments, then smiled. "Exactly."

I stepped into my pants while Lois yelled at whoever was at the door. "Wait a goddamn minute."

I took my time about getting dressed. I wanted the world to know about us. But despite her words, I could tell Lois would rather keep it a secret. I gave in, put on my shirt, and pulled on my boots. Not until I was sitting at the table did she get up to answer the door.

Not surprisingly, it was Curt Smith. He barely gave me a glance. Either he didn't care or I was beneath his notice. I wondered about the two of them. To be honest, from then on, I wondered about every guy who came near her.

"You need to answer your damn phone, Lois," Smith said.

"What is it?"

"Go ahead, turn your phone on. I guarantee it will be the first thing you see."

I reached in my pants pocket for my own phone, looked at the screen, and froze. I must have stood there for a full minute while the implications flooded into me like someone had opened the top of my head and poured adrenaline into it.

I ambled over as casually as I could and looked over her shoulder.

It was an aerial view of Jules Francisco getting shot. A media helicopter was hovering overhead, kicking up the snow and obscuring the scene they were recording. But it was clear to me that Jules was daring the cops to shoot him.

I heard once that the most common last words of a gunshot victim were "Go ahead. Shoot."

On top of the adrenaline rush I was already feeling, this was too much. I felt lightheaded. I tried to slide into the seat next to Lois, missed, and landed on the floor. I felt Smith's hand under my arm, pulling me up onto the seat.

"You all right, man?" Smith asked. He sounded surprisingly sympathetic. "You guys were friends, weren't you?"

I don't have friends, I thought.

"Where are the others?" Lois asked.

"Benson and…?"

"No, the *others*," she snapped.

Smith frowned and looked over at me. Lois put her hand on my shoulder. "Mark's with us all the way."

"They aren't arriving until after midnight," Smith said. "They think the cordon is too tight to slip through unnoticed in daylight. We don't want to start the firefight too soon."

"Shit." Lois pushed against me impatiently, motioning that she wanted out from behind the table. I scrambled to my feet, still trying to process the words "start the firefight."

Holy shit.

"Get as many of our people as you can to the visitor center,"

Lois said. "Tell them to come armed."

"They're always armed."

"Tell them to come locked and loaded then," she snapped. "The squishes are going to use this as an excuse to give up."

"Yes, ma'am," Smith said. I thought for a moment he was going to salute her. His hand went to his holster, as if he was already thinking about drawing his pistol. He snapped the clasp open and closed. "You got it."

Lois looked tired. I wanted to take her in my arms, but I knew that the previous night had been an anomaly. If anything was to ever happen again, it was going to be her idea.

"I didn't even know they were going," she mumbled. "Idiots. I could have told them what would happen."

"Sorry," I said.

She smiled at me. "Not your fault, big guy. By the way, I needed last night as much as you did."

Man, the pride I felt! She really seemed to mean it. "Big guy," she said, and I'm not—except in one department. I thought, at that moment, that she really had feelings for me. That was the pinnacle; that moment right there, even more than the sex.

A half hour later, I hit bottom.

CHAPTER 51

HART DAVIS

They didn't post guards outside Garth's hut, but I noticed that every time I looked out the grungy little window, a few of Lois's crew were hanging out nearby. The hut was getting stuffy, despite the numerous cracks in the wall. It was bare-bones, a workplace with a concrete floor, the cot, tables running along the other three walls, a hot plate and a microwave, and a couple of broken-down chairs.

The room was small. We were pretty scrunched together, but even so, Nicole had managed to maneuver herself as far away from me as possible. Between her and me were Perry and of course Garth, who was on his back on the cot, staring up at the ceiling. Peter and Mich stood to one side, watching but not saying anything.

"You should leave anyway," I said. "I don't think Lois is ready to confront you, not yet. Not where the FBI can see what's happening. But if you guys get locked in here at some point, they'll have no way of knowing what's happening."

"No," Garth said to the ceiling. "I'm not leaving."

"Garth…" I wanted to pick up the shovel in the corner and whack some sense into him. Not that it would have changed his mind. "Nicole and Perry won't leave unless you do. You're endangering them, too."

"They can leave. They *should* leave. I'm not keeping them here. But I'm not letting these bastards win," Garth said stubbornly.

"Win what, Garth?" Nicole said. "These guys have already

lost. They're like suspects who try to flee from the police in their own cars. The cops already know who they are. Everything they do only makes it worse."

Garth pushed himself into a sitting position and groaned, holding his head. "It's my fault. I failed to protect the things I was here to protect. I was out in the desert doing my thing and not paying attention."

"It is hardly your fault," Perry said. "These idiots are responsible for their own actions. You've already stopped them, Garth. I doubt they'll be stupid enough to try again."

Peter said, "We'll make sure of it, right, Davis?"

"Yes. We'll do everything you could do, Garth. There is no reason to put yourself in danger. Or Nicole, or Perry."

Garth looked up at me with an expression that was as stony as his fossils. He wasn't going anywhere, that was clear.

"Your choice," I said. I turned to Nicole and Perry. "You guys need to leave without him. Garth's being an idiot. I think Lois is going to turn this into something bad. But like I said, for some reason, she isn't ready yet. We should at least challenge them."

"Davis is right," Perry said. "I'll stay with Garth, but there is no reason for you to, Nicole. I'm ordering you to leave."

She stared down at her hands. I didn't think Perry's orders carried much weight with her.

"Nicole?" I prompted, unable to keep the pleading out of my voice.

She finally looked me in the eye.

If I'd seen anger there, or even hate, I could've handled it better than what I did see. Her expression was painfully sad, as if I'd broken her heart. Which I probably had. It wasn't the kind of hurt people got over quickly.

"Nicole, it makes no sense for you to stay," I said. I motioned to Peter. "We'll try our best to keep Garth and Perry safe."

"Oh, great," she said. "And now you're *so* reliable."

I realized that everything I said was hardening her resolve in the opposite direction. I turned to leave, uncertain what else to do. Someone followed me out. I expected to see Peter, but it was Perry Campbell, looking troubled.

"Can I trust you, Davis?" he asked.

"Yes," I said. "I'm done with all this. I want it over, and I want you guys safe."

"Especially Nicole?"

"Especially Nicole," I answered.

He nodded. "I've been in communication with Special Agent Adams."

"How?" When we'd allowed the three rangers to stay, we'd also taken away their cellphones.

"He slipped me a special phone during one of our meetings. I've hidden it out in the desert." He looked around furtively. There were occupiers all around us, some we knew, some we didn't. "I don't think I can get to it anymore without being stopped, but you can."

"Get back inside," I said after he told me where to find the phone. "Stay out of sight. I'm going to talk to Agent Adams."

No one paid much attention to me when I left, but to be sure, I went due south toward the mess tent before ducking between the trailers and heading east. I reached the desert behind the camp and poked my head out. There was no one around. I walked toward the small rock outcropping Perry had described, with the single large juniper, ambling as if all I was doing was taking a leak.

I lifted half a dozen flat rocks before I found the phone. It was blinking red, and when I turned it on, I saw that the inbox was full. There was only one number entered, and I dialed it.

"Perry, I'm glad you finally saw fit to answer your phone. I've left fifteen damn mess—"

"This is Hart Davis," I broke in. "We've got a problem."

"You think?" Not the response I'd expected. "Where's Perry?"

"That's part of the problem," I answered.

There was a long silence. I wondered if I should just start telling Adams what was going on. I opened my mouth, but before I could speak, he said, "How did you get pulled into all this, Davis? You've had trouble before. You should have known better."

"You going to lecture me?" I asked.

"The others, they don't really have the overall picture, but you do. In some ways, you're worse than they are. I have to tell you, my bosses wanted me to take you out, because of your reputation."

"Way to try to win me over," I said.

"Win you over to what?" he asked. "You aren't one of these yahoos."

"See, that's your problem. You think of them as yahoos, and they know it."

"You know what I can see from where I'm standing? I see beer cans littering the landscape. I see food wrappers and broken glass and cardboard boxes. The only thing missing is old tires. You want to tell me they aren't yahoos? They dug up a Native American graveyard, for Christ's sake."

"That was...unfortunate."

"You think?" he said again.

OK. Maybe I did deserve a little sarcasm. "Look, does it matter? We're here now, and we have to deal with the situation."

"I want to be sure who I'm dealing with, that's all. Are you crazy Strawberry Mountain Killer Hart Davis or the reasonable Hart Davis?"

"The idea that you are about to be hung in a fortnight concentrates the mind wonderfully," I said.

"That it does. Samuel Johnson, right?

"Paraphrased a little. Are you through testing me, Special Agent Adams?"

He laughed. "All right, Mr. Davis...Hart...what's the problem? And I hope to God it isn't what I think it is."

But it was. I told him about our confrontation with Lois Carpenter and her "request" that Nicole and the others stay until morning.

"They're hostages?" His question was sharp, no-nonsense.

"No one used that word, but in effect...yes. However, it's also a moot point, because Garth won't leave, and because of that, neither will Perry or Nicole."

"So that's what the fuss was yesterday?" Adams asked. "We saw a crowd, and one of my people swears he saw someone on a stretcher. Unfortunately, the one thing we can't see, where we can't tell what's happening, is in a crowd. But when I heard that,

I almost gave orders for the rescue."

The rescue. Put in those terms, I realized that I really was on the wrong side. I'd never thought it would come to this.

"Garth was injured," I said, quickly followed by, "but he's OK now. It's a concussion. It was an accident." I was pretty sure if I told Adams that Garth had been attacked by one of the hard-asses, all deals would be off the table. The Feds would come storming in, no matter the cost.

"We count six people in Garth's hut. Who are the other two?"

They must have state-of-the-art surveillance to see inside the hut.

"Peter Sterns and Michelle Foster are with us."

"Good. It's time to get you people out of there." There was an urgency to Adam's voice that sent a chill down my spine.

"Why? What's happening?"

"We removed your delegation to Spray from the game board."

I had no idea what he was talking about. "What delegation?"

"I thought you were part of the leadership there, Davis, otherwise, why are we talking? In fact, we were sort of hoping you and Peter Sterns would be part of the party."

"Let's just say I've taken a step back," I said. "I'm not without my influence, though. Tell me what happened."

"Jim Marston, Jules Francisco, and a few others were planning to meet with a Native American representative. We set up a roadblock to take them into custody. It didn't go as planned."

The moment he said it, I knew. Jules had said from the beginning that he wouldn't let himself be arrested.

Adams didn't try to hide it. "Francisco went for his weapon. He's dead."

"Oh...shit."

"It won't be long before that leaks. The media knows, and we've asked them to sit on it, but that never lasts. So you don't have much time."

"I'll try again to get them to leave," I said. Not only would I'd try, but I'd damn well carry Nicole out on my shoulders if I had to.

"You'd better do better than try. If our three people aren't out of there by morning, we're coming in after them."

"You mustn't do that," I said. "Lois and her friends are serious. I think they *want* a gunfight. They keep talking about getting ready. It doesn't sound good."

"That's why we're coming in," Adams said. "When you're ready, head straight for the main entrance to the camp. We have it covered on three sides. Don't let anything keep you from leaving. If anyone tries to stop you, we'll stop them."

"When should we go?" I asked.

"Now. Five minutes ago. Just get out!"

"All right...be ready for us," I said. I ended the call and turned toward the camp. I hadn't gone more than a couple of steps before I smelled something foul. There was a black, heaving mass on the far side of the rocks, and it took a moment before I could distinguish individual ravens.

Something was dead. The dread that had been filling my belly since I woke up became so powerful that I buckled at the knees. I reached out and braced myself against the trunk of the juniper.

CHAPTER 52

PETER STERNS

"I said, why are you here?"

I finally heard the words and realized that Garth Perkins had repeated them several times. I had been lost in thought, wondering if anything good was going to come out of this. Where I really wanted to be was home, sitting at my old kitchen table, writing poetry about birds or horses or anything else that was harmless. "What's that?" I asked.

"Why the fuck are you here? I recognize you. You're the guy with all the fancy talk about freedom. Well, where's *my* freedom, asshole?"

"Peter is trying to help, Garth," Mich said.

"Big man with a gun strapped to his belt. I don't need that kind of help. And who are you?"

"Michelle Foster," she said.

Actually, I think you might need my gun, I thought, but I said, "I don't like what they did to you, Mr. Perkins. I'll be damned if I'll let them do it again."

"Then why didn't you stop them?"

"I didn't get there in time," I said. Which was true. Garth had already been lying on his back in the ditch by the time I arrived. By then, Lois had restrained Smith.

And if she hadn't stopped it? Would I have had the guts to do what was right? Only way to prove that was to do what was right now.

"I'm sorry about what happened," I said.

"Nice and polite," Garth muttered, "but I don't see how I'm supposed to trust you."

"What the hell, Garth!" Nicole said. "Why are you antagonizing one of the two people who want to help us? Sometimes you're a real jerk."

I said, "No, it's all right. I totally get it. But Mich and I are going to help you whether you like it or not." I looked over at Mich, and she nodded. "We'll wait outside if it will make you feel better."

"Don't you dare," Nicole said. "Sit down, put up your feet. I'll fix us something to eat." She got up and went over to the table, where there was a hot plate and a microwave, a stack of Top Ramen, and some cans of chili. From the small refrigerator under the table, she extracted a couple of beers and handed them to Garth and me.

So we sat there in that hut, not knowing what was going on outside. Despite the danger, I finally felt like I was on the right side.

CHAPTER 53

JOSHUA CALLEY

When I heard about Francisco's death and Marston and the others being arrested, I called for a general meeting. Five minutes before it was to start in Merriam Hall, I got a call from Harry Johnson.

"Get Jerry out of there, Joshua. This has gone too far. Let's wrap this up."

"Yes, sir. I was just about to suggest that," I said. "I've called a meeting. I'm pretty sure the majority will go along."

"And the minority?"

"That's going to be more difficult," I told him. He knew already that Jerry would be among the resisters. No sense me going on about it.

"Vanessa won't say it, but she's scared. I mean, she talks big about making sacrifices for freedom, but Jerry is her favorite boy. She'll probably blame you, Joshua, if you surrender now, but I'm asking you to do what she *really* wants, not what she says. I'm pretty sure she won't insist I fire you."

Pretty sure? Thanks for the vote of confidence, boss.

I said, "This thing is either over or it's about to escalate. I'm not waiting for that. If Jerry won't come along, there isn't anything I can do about it. Have you tried calling him yourself?"

"Like I said, Vanessa won't let me. But never you mind that. I know what she wants in her heart, and that's to have her boy home safe. Try your best, Joshua."

"Jerry is his own man, sir. That's the way you raised him."

"He's a kid," Harry snorted. "A stubborn kid without a clue

about the world. That is my fault. I did raise him that way. But I never thought he'd have to face all this bullshit. I'm sorry I ever started the whole thing, but it's too late now."

"Yes, sir," I said, leaving it hanging there.

He grunted and hung up. I stared down at the phone, half-expecting it to ring again and it be Vanessa this time. She'd harangue me about never surrendering, but I thought Harry was right: Secretly, she wanted me to try to end it.

I sighed and walked over to the visitor center. By then, someone had turned off the displays, so instead of the unearthly sounds of long-extinct creatures, I could hear the scuffing of boots and low voices. Any loud sound echoed.

About two dozen men and one woman, Lois Carpenter, showed up for the meeting. The rest had already left camp or were packing to leave. These were the hardcore believers.

I looked for Jerry in the crowd and aimed my words in his general direction, trying not to be too obvious about it.

"It's time to pack it in, boys. This is over. We've made our point, and it's time to go home. For most of you, I'm betting the Feds will let you walk away. But don't kid yourself. Sometime in the future, they'll knock on your door, and you'll have to go in and testify. If you're honest and truthful, chances are, most of you, you'll be all right. Maybe get a little jail time or a fine."

"Then why give up at all?" someone shouted.

"If you walk away, you'll have a figurative target on your back, but if you stay, you'll have a literal one. I don't know about you, but I've been feeling a sniper's sight on my back for days now. We've pushed this about as far as we can. Jules Francisco is dead. If we don't clear out, there'll be more of us dead."

"Jules Francisco was murdered!" someone shouted.

So there it was. I'd expected this, and I wasn't surprised that it was Lois Carpenter who said it.

She stepped to the front of the crowd, her dark eyes flashing with fervor. "Have any of you seen the video? Jules wasn't even armed, and they shot him down."

"He was carrying," someone said. "He was always carrying."

"But he didn't *draw* his revolver," Lois said. "They shot him anyway. This isn't the time to give up. This is the time to step up and do something!"

"No," I said, my deep voice overriding hers. "No one else needs to get hurt."

Lois glared at me. She was surrounded by half a dozen guys, most of whom were dressed in camo, rifles at the ready, pockets bulging with extra magazines, whereas most of the others were dressed in jeans and cowboy hats. They were carrying too, but mostly pistols and a few rifles. It looked like someone had plopped a military unit right there in the middle of us.

"'The tree of liberty…!'" someone shouted.

"'Must be refreshed from time to time with the blood of patriots and tyrants,'" I finished the quote for him. I shook my head. "Come on. Let's get real, folks."

There's nothing like talking straight to people. They can tell when you mean it. Politicians ought to try it sometime. Most of these folks had come to this place thinking it was going to be fun, a spectacle, and a way to feel important. None of them wanted to die.

"Let's face it, people. We've done what we set out to do. We've told the world what the federal government is up to. People are listening. But if there's…if there's a disaster, if people die, that's *all* they'll remember. The whole point will be lost. Let's pack it in and go home. I don't know about you guys, but I'm looking forward to sleeping in my own bed."

I looked around, saw their chagrined expressions, and figured I had them.

"No!"

Jerry Johnson stepped out of the crowd, Brad Patterson doing his best to pull him back. They were like a single person sometimes. Jerry provided the motion and Brad was the rudder. I sensed that Brad was having his doubts about this whole venture. Jerry got into trouble because of his naiveté, but Brad had a knack for steering him clear.

But not this time. My heart sank.

Of all the people to turn the tide…

"I'm not going home with my tail between my legs," Jerry said. "Jules is a hero. He died for us. I'm not letting him die in vain. We'll get the Ochocos back or we'll damn well fertilize the soil with our blood."

Fertilize the soil? I thought, wondering if anyone would laugh.

No one cracked a smile. Lois's lieutenants picked their moment. They stepped forward, rifles in hand. They raised them over their heads. "Freedom!" Smith shouted, and Benson echoed him.

There were a few seconds of stunned silence, and I thought there was still a chance of overriding them, but then someone else took up the cry, and before I could stop them, the chant of "Freedom! Freedom!" overwhelmed anything I or anyone else could have said.

I looked around for allies, but Hart Davis and Peter Sterns were nowhere to be seen, and of course, Jim Marston was out of the picture. I was on my own, a black man trying to talk down a room full of angry white people. Not ideal. If I was the kind of man who was going to let that scare me, well, that would have been the moment.

"It's over!" I roared. The chanting faded. "Go the fuck home," I said. "Take a shower, get a good meal. You're making fools of yourselves here."

I don't know, maybe it was the idea of being ridiculed that finally sank in, but I saw a few men start to slip away.

Lois came toward me, and if looks could kill, I would have been dead on the floor, rigor mortis already setting in.

She pulled out her revolver and fired it into the ceiling of the visitor center. I winced, and half the crowd crouched defensively. I'm not sure I'd ever heard a gunshot inside, at least not without earplugs. I wondered if the FBI could hear it and whether it would bring them pouring in.

Plaster rained down on us. I looked up at the damage with regret. I really hated vandalism.

"Are you children?" Lois shouted. "Did you think this was a game? We're staying, damn it. If you've got any guts, you'll stay with us. If not, we don't need cowards like you around."

Well, that trumped their fear of ridicule. A woman telling these men they were chickens worked just as well as if they were ten-year-olds on the playground being taunted with "Cluck… cluck… cluck."

With a sinking heart, I knew I'd lost.

CHAPTER 54

MARK SIMONS

Lois was magnificent. A warrior goddess. Who knows what would have happened if she'd hadn't gotten her way? She wanted to be in charge.

From that moment on, she was in control of the whole thing. Even Joshua bent to her will. The tired woman of ten minutes before was now vibrating with triumphant energy. Her eyes were flashing. She gave me a smile.

And then Hart Davis walked in with a bundle over his shoulder. The crowd fell silent at his entrance, more from his manner than from what he was carrying, because it was hard to see what it was. I thought it was a moth-eaten sleeping bag at first.

Then I smelled it. The details of the bundle suddenly became clear; the gray jeans, wide leather belt, and cowboy shirt with tortoiseshell snap buttons, bloody and torn. Some animals had been at the corpse, but it was still recognizable, at least to me.

Without fanfare, Davis slid the body off his shoulder and managed to lay it on the front counter without dropping it.

"What's this?" Lois asked. "What have you done?"

Davis gave her a strange look, then turned to the crowd. "This here is John Carver," he said. "I found him in the desert."

There was a stunned silence.

I wanted to run out of there. I felt my legs starting to move of their own accord, but Lois's fingers clamped on my arm. She gave me a warning look.

"He was covered with ravens by the time I found him,"

Davis said, "and it looks like some coyotes has taken a few chunks out of him. From the condition of the body, it's difficult to say what happened. There's a nasty gash in his head, and part of his skull was plastered onto a nearby rock, so it could have been an accident. That's probably how it would have been ruled. Everyone knew Carver drank heavily; just another drunk falling down where he shouldn't. Happens every day..." His voice trailed off.

"But?" Joshua asked, as if he already knew.

"A few days ago, Carver approached me to tell me there was a conspiracy, that something was about to happen that no one was prepared for. I figured, you know, that he was nuts. But finding him dead kind of puts a different spin on things. I can't be the only one he talked to."

Davis glanced my way, but I made sure my face was neutral.

There was a rustle in the crowd, and another guy stepped forward, someone I didn't recognize. "He said pretty much the same to me. Vague as hell, but he seemed to believe it."

"Me too," someone else said.

"Not much proof of anything," Joshua said. "As you say, he was a drunk. A mean one at that."

"I found something else," Davis said.

I knew. I'd hoped my phone was lost in my jumble of dirty clothes or something, but inside, I knew.

Lois let go of me and I edged away from her, as much for her sake as mine. I stepped back into the crowd, trying to blend in. No one was paying any attention to me yet, not even Davis.

"I found someone's phone in the dust next to the body." Again, Davis paused, almost giving me enough time to get out of there. I'd head straight into the desert, and either the FBI would shoot me or I'd die of thirst, and I didn't much care which.

I reached the double doors of the center, but right as I did, Peter Sterns pushed away from the wall, looked me in the face, and shook his head. He had a Colt .45 aimed straight at my gut.

"Turn around," he said.

I almost didn't hear him, because there was a sudden uproar behind us. I hadn't heard Davis say my name, but I knew from the reaction that he must have. At first, the crowd didn't see me and Sterns, but someone finally glanced over their shoulder and noticed us.

Sterns motioned with the gun and marched me up to the counter. He reached over and removed my pistol and my bowie knife from my belt.

Joshua held up his hand to quiet the crowd. "The phone itself isn't proof. Maybe Mark dropped it while taking a leak. It's not like we haven't all done it. But running away...that would seem like an admission of guilt. At least enough to make a citizen's arrest, which I am now going to do."

He turned toward me, his face solemn as if he really hated what he was about to say. "Mark Simons, I'm placing you under custody until such time as I can turn you over to the proper authorities. And if even one of you damn fools tells me that there are no 'proper authorities,' I'll fucking arrest you, too, for obstructing justice."

There weren't any takers. Not that I expected anyone to come to my defense. I never thought I was all that well liked, and this only confirmed it.

Lois stepped to Joshua's side, giving me a look that made me feel small, as if I was a toad. An ugly toad. She was angry, all right, because I'd been stupid enough to drop the phone and ruin her plans.

"I agree, Simons needs to be detained," she said, "but it doesn't change anything. He's a loser who's been stalking me ever since I got here, jealous about me and John and our relationship, even though it was long over. But we can't let this stop us from doing what is right. It has nothing to do with what we're trying to do here."

I ought to have felt humiliated. She didn't have to call me a loser or put the motive on me. She could've just said, "If he's guilty, turn him over." But I knew what she was doing. She was trying to save the movement, and if it meant throwing me under the Hummer, then that's what she'd do.

Oddly, I was kind of awed by it. She was the strongest person I'd ever met. What she wanted, she got. Besides, by putting me down like that, she was trusting that I wouldn't turn around and blame her. Or maybe she was trying to set me up in case I did.

But it didn't matter. I wasn't going to pull her into it. What did they have, really? My phone at the scene? I didn't think that'd be enough. And would anyone I knew believe I'd poison a man rather than just shooting him in the head?

I decided that I wouldn't give her up, no matter what.

All this went through my mind, but for some reason, I forgot the real danger. Then Davis raised up my phone in his hand, and I knew I was screwed.

CHAPTER 55

PETER STERNS

Before Hart took Carver's body to the visitor center, he came to us.

He'd hurried into the hut but then just stood in the middle of the room, as if he'd forgotten why he was there. The skin on his face had shrunk to his skull. His eyes were wide, with dark circles under them.

"What's wrong?" Mich asked.

"I… You'll have to see for yourself."

He held the door open. We went outside, all of us, except for Garth.

The sun was going down but there was still enough twilight to see the body on the ground, face up. I knew whoever it was had been dead for part of a day because I could already smell the first stages of putrefaction. Because of the heat, it was happening fast. Working on a ranch, I was always coming across dead animals: deer, skunks, rabbits. This was similar, but some primitive part of my brain could tell the difference.

"Who is it?" Perry asked.

"John Carver," Hart said. Until that moment, my brain couldn't make the connection, but as soon as Hart said the name, I knew he was right. I was surprised that it didn't impact me more, but Carver had always been a loner, never saying much. We'd never been close. What I felt was dread and sadness, not so much a personal loss, but a feeling that the whole movement was about to be tarnished even more than it already was.

"He came with me and Hart," I added. "Part of the first group."

"I don't recognize him," Nicole said.

"He mostly stayed out of sight," Hart said. "I think he had doubts from the beginning."

She approached the corpse slowly, bent halfway over to get a better look, then thought better of it and stepped back. "What happened?"

"It looks like an accident," I said, kneeling down. "He's got a nasty gash on his head."

"Not enough blood," Garth said. "That kind of wound bleeds profusely." He looked around and shrugged. "I started off pre-med."

"I don't think it was an accident either," Hart said.

"Why would anyone—" Nicole started to ask.

Hart broke in. "He tried to warn me about Lois, but I didn't listen. He said something about her husband dying suspiciously."

Nicole noticeably stiffened at the mention of Lois and turned away. "She's in the middle of everything, isn't she?"

"This is big trouble for everyone," Perry said. "Don't you see? The FBI won't stand back if there's been a murder."

"Perry's right," Mich said. "This means they'll be coming in, whether we want them to or not."

"That's probably true," Hart said, "but if this was Lois's doing, then think about what her reaction is likely to be. She's got a whole cadre of followers willing to do anything she tells them."

"There's more," Hart said, holding out an iPhone. "I found this nearby."

"Nearby?" I asked.

"Maybe a yard away. I probably should have left the crime scene alone, but I picked the phone up before I thought of it."

"Let me see it," Mich said. She reached out, then retracted her hand. "Shouldn't we be trying to preserve any fingerprints?"

Hart shrugged. "Too late. I wiped the sand off it."

She took the phone and turned it on. "What do you know?" she said. "No password." Her fingers flew across the surface of the phone, and it lit up. "It belongs to someone named Mark Simons. Any of you know him?"

Hart and I stared at each other. We'd both seen how Mark had fallen under Lois Carpenter's sway. To me, it was confirmation that this was a murder. Mark might not have done the deed—in fact, I'd have been surprised if he had—but he'd probably dumped the body.

Mich was still working on the phone. Suddenly, voices emerged from it, and we fell silent, listening as a murder was planned.

There was very little discussion about what to do once we heard the recording. I told them about the meeting Joshua was holding at that very moment. Jerry and Brad had come by earlier, encouraging me to attend.

That had been a couple of hours ago.

"Calley wants to fold up the tents, I can tell," Jerry had said. "We need you there, man. We need all good men to take a stand."

We stood there looking down at Carver's body as if none of us could really believe it.

"What about the body?" Perry asked. "Shouldn't we do something? Cover him up? Call the cops?"

"I've got a better idea," Hart said. "We have a chance to blow this whole situation wide open. Everyone will be at the meeting in Merriam Hall."

Nicole put her hand on Hart's arm. He leaned into the gesture, closing his eyes for a moment.

"I'll come with you, Hart," Nicole said.

"Not a good idea," he said. "Simons will accuse me of being a turncoat as it is."

So it fell to me to help Hart carry the body to Merriam Hall, but once at the door, he stopped. "I'll take it from here. I want to shock the hell out of them."

We managed to get Carver's body over Hart's shoulder, and he pushed the door open and trudged to the front, Carver's head bouncing against his back, leaving a smear of blood on his shirt.

I decided to stay near the door and watch it play out.

The whole scene worked better than we could have expected.

Unlike everyone else, I had my eyes on Simons from the beginning. When he looked like he was going to slip away, I drew my gun and motioned him back. I thought Hart drew out the drama a little too much, but I couldn't argue that it got their attention. He waited until Lois made her condemnation of Mark. Then he pulled the phone out of his pocket and brandished it overhead.

Mark's face went pale. Lois looked puzzled. She obviously hadn't known that her lover was recording her.

"So...what do we do about John?" Lois voice sounded soft, seductive.

By contrast, Mark was gruff. *"Ignore him. No one's listening to him. They think he's a jealous ex-boyfriend. What can he say?"*

If anyone had any doubts that it was Lois and Mark talking, their reactions gave it away. Lois froze, closed her eyes, and put her hand on Curt Smith's arm to steady herself. Mark's face went from pale to a bright red, and his mouth dropped open and stayed open.

"He knows something about me. Something I'd rather people didn't know."

"What?"

"I don't want people to know...especially people I like."

"Nothing he could tell me would change my mind about you."

"I think we should do what we talked about. I'm in charge of the meals next Friday. I'll give him something tomorrow night that will give him indigestion so bad he'll think he's dying. He'll need to go to the hospital. No one will think anything of it. It's not like conditions around here are exactly sanitary. A lot of people have already gotten sick."

"What do you want me to do?"

"When he starts getting sick, get him out of the mess tent. Take him somewhere and call for an ambulance. Maybe even lead him over to the barricades and let the Feds take care of him. But give it an hour or two. Take him into the desert until he's really sick."

"OK. I'll do it."

Hart clicked off the phone and held it up. "There's more. It looks like Mark recorded several conversations he had with

Lois. Pretty clearly, she was setting him up all along…and he must have been suspicious."

The room was completely silent.

"I didn't mean for Carver to die," Lois said. "I was just trying to give him a little tummy ache."

"Like your dead husband?" Hart said. "Is that what happened to him? A bullet in the gut?"

"That's not fair," she said. "Listen, everyone. It doesn't matter what happens to me. I'll turn myself in when this is all over. But you mustn't give up. We can still get what we want."

"No," came Joshua Calley's deep voice. "This whole thing is over, Mrs. Carpenter. It was ridiculous from the start. We're turning you and Mark in to the authorities in the morning, as soon as we negotiate our surrender."

"Surrender?" Lois was almost shouting. "Are you fucking crazy? You'll have to go through my people first." She turned and urged Curt Smith and her other followers forward. They began to surround her, but then something happened that still sends chills down my spine. The temperature in the room seemed to drop as every other man in Merriam Hall lifted their own weapons and lined up behind Calley.

Lois's people were outnumbered three to one.

"You fucking idiot," Lois hissed at Mark. In a moment, she had damned herself in the eyes of everyone there. "Why didn't you trust me?"

"That's not why I did it," Mark said. "I…I just wanted to hear your voice."

Lois glared at him.

"Pathetic," Smith muttered beside her. He lowered his rifle and stepped away. And with that, it was over.

Or so we thought.

CHAPTER 56

BRAD PATTERSON

Before we went to the big meeting at Merriam Hall, we met in Lois's trailer. She seemed distracted. For once Mark Simons wasn't mooning at her. He sat there with a smug grin, and I wondered about that. It was hard to visualize those two together, but Mark was damn persistent, I knew that.

Of course, we found out pretty soon what *that* was all about.

We waited outside the trailer while Mark and Lois and that Smith guy had a private meeting. Everyone had ignored Jerry's crazy One Hundred Freedoms manifesto, except to make fun of it. I'd steered Jerry away from more than one group of men who looked ready to ridicule him. I've always had sixth sense about that.

Lois came to the door after the others left and asked the two of us in. I was nervous about it, but Jerry looked proud, so I kept my doubts to myself.

"Later tonight, I need you two to go stand guard on the eastern perimeter of the camp," she said.

The east perimeter was the one facing the desert.

"Why?" I asked. "There's nothing there."

But Jerry didn't question it; he just nodded excitedly, happy to be given a task.

"Some guys are coming in tonight, after midnight. Keep an eye out for them. Lead them to my trailer when they get here, but keep them out of sight."

Why? I wanted to ask. *What's going on?*

But Jerry said, "You bet, Lois. We'll be there."

Lois stared into his eyes, then patted him on the shoulder like he was a puppy dog. I was almost offended. She gave me a nod, and even though I knew what she was doing, I still felt a moment of validation, like it was important that she acknowledged me. Unbelievable how easy it is to be manipulated by someone who has no scruples.

She started to turn away.

"Who are these new guys?" I asked.

Lois glanced at Jerry as if to ask why he couldn't stop his idiot friend from asking idiot questions.

"Amateur hour is over," she said. "These men have trained for years for this. Not that you guys are amateurs, I can tell how dedicated you are, but most of the people in this camp are here because of the drama, not because of what we're trying to accomplish. Hell, half of them have left already. But I think we have a chance of really making a difference, Jerry…Brad." She hesitated and looked at me, like someone does when they're not sure they used the right name. *Yeah, she really gives a shit about me.*

"We can get the Ochocos back, turn this place into a working ranch, maybe even get rid of the Antiquities Clause. But it takes commitment. Men ready to sacrifice. Men like you."

I thought none of that was likely, but Jerry looked thrilled. He had a kind of shoulder flexing thing he did when he was really excited, and sometimes he even rubbed his hands together in elation like a cartoon villain. It was funny most of the time, but not now.

What could these new guys do that we hadn't done? I mean, we'd taken over a national monument, thumbed our noses at the federal government for weeks. According to Marston, they were even willing to reconsider the designation of the Ochocos as a monument (though with him arrested, I figured that option was gone). But that was the point, wasn't it? We were a ragtag bunch of ranchers and would-be cowboys, and the only thing that kept us from being swept up by the cops was the FBI's history of past confrontations, most of which hadn't ended well.

We'd made our point, and now we were just looking for a way out that wasn't humiliating.

There was really only one thing these new guys could be bringing to change things. Most of us already there wanted to go home; none of us wanted a shootout, now that the possibility loomed. Reality had finally hit home for most of us. The only thing these hard-asses could add was a willingness to go to extremes.

But I had a funny feeling that now wasn't the time to express doubts. With Jerry, you had to pick your moments to suggest things, to try to get him to think about the situation with a clear head. Right then, he was completely in Lois Carpenter's thrall.

So we went to that shitstorm of a meeting, and when it all came crashing down, all I felt was a vast relief. I was sad about Carver, but it appeared to be the breaking point for everyone. It was over. We could go home, at least until the FBI knocked on the door. Or maybe they'd arrest us at the barricades. I didn't care.

Most of us walked away from the meeting silently. It had been a gut punch to all of us that one of our own was dead, murdered by one of our own.

I put my arm over Jerry's shoulder. "Do you want to wait until morning or get out of here now?"

"What do you mean?" He shook my arm off.

"I mean, do you want to leave now, or try get a good night's sleep first?"

"Lois gave us a job, Brad. Did you forget that?"

We stopped in the middle of the crowd. Jerry's voice was rising, so I pulled him over behind some tents. "It's over, Jer. It's fucking over, don't you get that?"

"I don't care what the rest of these pussies think. I'm meeting the new guys. Leave if you want."

"Jesus, Jer. These hard-asses want a shootout. They want another Waco or Ruby Ridge."

"Would that be so bad?" Jerry asked. My heart sank when I saw the mulish look on his face. Once he sank into one of his pouts, it could take days to talk him out of it.

"Randy Weaver's wife and son are dead, Jer, and he's in prison. Waco? They're *all* fucking dead."

"Yeah, but we're talking about them, aren't we? Their sacrifice led to this."

I didn't answer for a long time, knowing I'd already lost the argument. Then I said quietly, "It also led to Oklahoma City."

"That's different. We aren't like that."

I didn't answer.

"I'm doing it, Brad," he said stubbornly. "Go ahead leave. It's all right with me. I know your heart isn't in it. You came along because of me. Really, no hard feelings."

I didn't believe a word of it. He'd hold it against me for months, if not years. I'd be one of the pussies.

I decided to stay with my friend. I knew how Jer thought. Never having been drunk in his life before coming here, he'd been drinking steadily at the camp. The night before, he'd gone on a drunken tear about how horrible the Oklahoma City bombing had been. "Those poor babies," he'd cried. I figured that underneath it all, he understood the danger, and given time, he'd come around.

If I had enough time.

Back at our tent, we drank a few beers, hardly talking.

At midnight, we made our way to the eastern edge of the camp. This was where the latrines and the trash dumps were. The smells were pretty overpowering, but Jerry stood on guard like he was at Valley Forge or something.

We didn't see the newcomers until they were upon us. I heard a rustle of fabric, looked into the darkness, and a shadow emerged, and then another. There were five of them altogether, big guys, and fit.

They were outfitted like a fucking Seal Team.

Oh, shit, I thought.

Jerry all but saluted them, and whispered to their leader that they were to follow us. We made it to Lois's trailer without anyone seeing us, or at least anyone making an issue of it.

The door to the trailer was locked, but one of the hard-asses stepped up and picked the lock within moments.

That was the real eye-opener for me, the way he made short work of that lock. Hard men dressed in fatigues and holding big guns—I'd run into a lot of guys who were into that bullshit, but most of them were wanna-bes and pretenders.

These guys were the real deal.

CHAPTER 57

HART DAVIS

We should have left that evening. Not leaving was just one more bad decision on top of all the others. But I admit I wasn't looking forward to going to jail. No way could I afford to pay bail—that is, if the authorities even bothered to give me bail.

One more night of freedom, I thought.

I didn't figure the cops would arrest all of us, at least not at first. But those of us who'd stood in front of the camera? The Strawberry Mountain Killer? Yeah, they'd make a point of it. I'd known that as soon as Marston and the others pulled out their guns.

So I stayed, hoping to get one last good night of sleep.

The visitor center emptied out pretty quickly, people rushing out like bugs spilling out of a rotted log. Most people went to their tents or trailers instead of leaving the camp. It was late, and they probably thought, like I did, that morning would come soon enough.

While Merriam Hall emptied out, Peter Sterns kept his gun leveled on Mark and Lois, but neither looked like they wanted to put up a fight. Mark kept glancing at her with sad puppy dog eyes.

"I didn't mean to—" he started to say.

"Shut up, Mark," she said. "Don't say another word, not to me, not to anyone. We're innocent. It was only a prank, and the recordings will prove that. Just keep your mouth shut."

"What are you going do with them?" I asked Joshua, who

was standing there like a statue, staring down at his two prisoners.

He stirred and looked around the now-empty room as if surprised to find himself there. "Do you think Nicole would let us use her office?"

"She's with Garth in the shed, so I think that'll be fine."

"Good," he said. He patted his belt and his pockets as if expecting to find his gun, but I'd noticed before that Joshua was rarely armed. His bulk and demeanor were usually enough to intimidate people. He turned to Peter. "Mind if I borrow your gun? I'll watch them tonight. No way am I getting any sleep anyway."

'Sure," Sterns said, handing over the Glock, which looked like a toy in Joshua's beefy hands. "But I think we should sur-render right now. Walk right on out of here."

In hindsight, his instincts were better than the rest of ours.

"Nah, I don't want to approach the FBI in the darkness with a gun in my hand. I'll march these two over first thing in the morning." Again, Joshua patted his pockets, looking frustrated. "Forgot my phone, my gun...my goddamn head. I thought this was going to be easy. You still got that direct line to Agent Adams?"

For a second, I thought he was referring to Perry Campbell's phone, which I'd left out in the desert in its hidey-hole. Then I realized he was talking about the phone we'd been publicly given to stay in communication with the FBI. "Marston had it last."

"Damn. Well, I guess any old phone will work. Call 911 or something and they'll patch you through. No...wait..." He transferred the gun from his right hand to his left and dug into his jeans. "Here... Adams gave me his card the last time I saw him. He told me to punch in this number direct."

I hesitated an iota before reaching for it. He noticed. "What? I wasn't going to use it."

"Not saying a thing," I said. "I mean, even if you did, who could blame you?" I examined the card and saw that there was handwriting on the back: *Extension #114.*

I sensed movement a few feet away and looked up, startled.

While Joshua had been distracted, Lois had gotten right up in his face.

"You black bastard," she said. "I should have known you'd turn on us."

"Being black's got nothing to do with it," Joshua said. He put out his hand and pushed her away. She leaned against his hand with everything she had but slid backward anyway. He looked like he was barely trying. I resisted the urge to laugh.

She cursed and turned away.

I said, "All right, I'll give Agent Adams a call, but he probably already knows what's happened tonight. I'm pretty sure a lot of people have already left."

"Wouldn't hurt to let the FBI know officially," Joshua said.

I pulled out Mark's phone.

"Don't use that," Joshua said, his voice sharp. "Leave it with me. I'll hand it over in the morning."

"OK," I said, not sure what else needed to be said. "I'll see you then." I began to turn away.

"Davis," he said. "If you see Jerry Johnson or Brad Patterson, make sure they're all right, OK?"

I nodded. It wasn't until I was out the doors that I realized I wasn't sure where to go.

Go back to your tent, part of me urged. *Get some sleep.*

Back at the tent, I pulled out my own phone and tried three times, in the dim light that came through opaque walls, to dial the number on the card. Luckily, I remembered the extension number from when I'd looked at it before.

Special Agent Adams answered before the second ring. "Mr. Calley, I'm glad you called. Is everything under control?"

"This is Hart Davis," I said.

The hesitation was hardly noticeable. "Mr. Davis, I'm glad to hear from you again. I was getting worried about you."

He was smooth. I'll give him that.

"We're coming out tomorrow morning," I said. "All of us."

"Come now, Hart. We promise you safe passage. We'll put you up in a motel tonight. How does a hot shower sound?"

I closed my eyes, so tired I was dizzy. Earlier in the evening, I would have taken him up on his offer. But now I realized that if I did, I might never see Nicole Nelson again, and no matter how much she despised me, I wanted one last glimpse of her.

"We're all very tired, Agent Adams. Don't worry. We won't cause you any trouble. However, there's been a complication."

"A complication?"

I wasn't buying his ignorant act. I was certain he'd heard all about the meeting by then from some of those who'd already left. But he wanted to hear it from me; maybe he hoped I'd incriminate myself somehow.

"There's been a death," I said. "We're pretty sure it was a murder. We've put Lois Carpenter and Mark Simons under citizen's arrest."

"Who's the deceased?"

"Agent Adams, do we have to play this game? You know damn well what's going on."

"That's why you need to get out of there," Adams said. "But if you aren't going to leave, I need you to send me the recordings on that phone."

"I don't know how to do that," I said.

"You still hanging out with Nicole Nelson? She'll know how."

"I don't have Simons's phone, Joshua Calley has it. He's guarding Mark and Lois tonight."

"How about we come on into the compound," Adams suggested, "and take them...and the phone...off your hands? Get Carver someplace where evidence can be preserved?"

"It's not a good idea," I said quickly. "Most of Lois's followers are still around. I'm not sure they'll take that lying down."

There was a long pause, and then a deep sigh. "All right, Hart, have it your way. We'll wait until morning. But no more delays, you hear?"

"I want out of here as much as you want me out of here," I said, ending the call before he could reply.

I headed for Garth's hut, eager to see Nicole, even if all she did was glare at me. Naively, I thought facing her was the biggest challenge I was going to have that night.

CHAPTER 58

MARK SIMONS

I was alone with Lois in the cluttered office, the door locked, but she wouldn't even look at me.

"I'm sorry," I said again.

She grabbed a pencil off the desk, marched straight up to me, and put the tip under my chin. "One more word and I'll shove this into your brain."

She was maybe three inches taller than me, but I had a hundred pounds on her. I could overcome her within seconds.

I couldn't help it. Tears sprang from the corners of my eyes. I desperately tried not to blink, knowing they'd roll down my cheeks and she'd see them. She turned her back on me, went around the desk and sat on the chair, swung around, and pretended to read the titles on the spines of the books.

I don't know how long I stood there, completely paralyzed by my humiliation. I was certain she would ridicule anything I said or did, any movement I made. I couldn't bear it. Finally, I plopped down on a box of papers, which threatened to collapse under me. I wanted to curl up and never move again.

That's the way it stayed for the next hour, me sitting like a mannequin, Lois swinging back and forth in the chair.

"How am I supposed to pee?" she exclaimed. She got up and walked to the door, right past me, as if I didn't exist. She raised her fist to pound on the door, then hesitated. She went back, got on the chair, and climbed up onto the desk. She pulled down her pants, turned her back to me (for which I was strangely grateful), and splattered urine all over the desk, soaking the papers and books.

She turned around and pulled up her pants. "What are you looking at? You ain't ever getting any of this again."

It should have turned me off, but even the thought of her gave me a hard-on. It didn't seem possible that my horniness could overcome my humiliation, but there it was.

I'm stronger than her, I thought. *We're going to be here all night.*

And then I was ashamed of even thinking it. I hadn't sunk that low, not yet.

She sat back down on the chair, but moments later, she jumped up, staring at the droplets of pee on her pants legs.

"Shit!" she hissed, and then louder, almost a scream, "Shit, shit, shit!"

She grabbed the back of the chair and tried to wheel it around the desk, but a wheel got caught on one of the boxes and it began to tip over. She threw the chair the rest of the way to the floor, screeching, waving her arms angrily and stomping her feet. It would have been funny if it weren't so terrifying.

I looked to the door, wondering if Calley would poke his head in. By the time I turned back, Lois was on her knees on the floor, eyes closed, her face in a silent scream. I started to get up, but without opening her eyes, she stuck out a hand and a long finger pointed at me. "Don't!"

She breathed heavily for a few moments, then rose to her feet with a determined air, her face composed. She looked around, picked up the chair, and wheeled it to the opposite side of the room from me. She sat back, closed her eyes, and didn't move.

Is she asleep? I wondered after a few minutes. *Is that even possible?*

But of course, now I know she was merely waiting, like a cat outside a mouse hole.

Minutes later, I caught myself dozing off, leaning so far over the edge of the box that I nearly fell off. I got up and shook my head, but it didn't help. Without really thinking about it, I got down on the floor and lay on my back.

All the fear and humiliation swirled behind my eyes, but beckoning just behind it was a black void, sleep so deep it promised oblivion.

I fell into it gladly.

CHAPTER 59

BRAD PATTERSON

The trailer felt crowded even though some of our nightly meetings had been larger. The newcomers were equipped with rifles, pistols, camouflage and flak jackets, and heavy boots, with kits bulging…and God only knew what else. Grenades? Nuclear bombs? I was in way over my head.

Sure, the five militia guys were bulked up with gear, but it wasn't just that. They jostled for space, squeezing Jerry and me into the corner of the kitchen. Most of them were shaggy, though the smallest of them was clean-shaven, and when he took off his hat and rubbed his head, I saw that it was shaved too. It was the only motion he made. He moved less than the others, almost disappearing into the fake wood paneling.

I didn't want to be there, and I didn't want Jerry to be there, but my best friend was vibrating with excitement. The more he was liking it, the less I was.

When Smith and Benson arrived, the trailer became claustrophobic.

Smith snapped off a military salute to the biggest of the newcomers, who had claimed an entire half of the couch for himself.

"Captain Marshall," Smith said. "Good to see you."

Marshall was heavily bearded, his hair in a ponytail, with mirrored glasses. If he shaved all that hair off, I wouldn't know him from Adam, which was likely the point. He saluted back, his motion seeming lazy to me, as if he was annoyed at the necessity. The captain turned to Jerry and me. "Maybe you two should wait outside."

I started heading for the door as soon as he said it, but Jerry balked. Smith said, "These men are solid, Captain."

Jerry stood at attention. "We'll do whatever you want, sir."

Marshall stared at us a few moments longer; especially, it seemed, at me. Then he nodded. "What happened here, Kadry?" he asked.

Smith...no, *Kadry* noticed me start at the name and raised his eyebrows once in amusement. Of course his name wasn't Smith. I should have known that. We all thought he was the Curt Smith who'd spent time in prison for looting Indian artifacts, but of course, none of us had ever actually met the man or seen pictures of him.

"Lois went a little off the reservation," Kadry said. "She, ah, took out John Carver."

"Took him out?"

"Poisoned him."

"Who is John Carver?"

"Apparently, someone she manipulated into killing her husband. I didn't know that. Did you?"

His tone was a little sharp at the end of that statement, which surprised me. Until then, I'd thought Marshall was in complete charge.

"I know that she is a hardnosed bitch," Marshall said, choosing to ignore the challenge. "It doesn't surprise me one little bit. Why did you let her go and do that, Kadry?"

"We didn't know what she was up to, sir," Benson, or whatever his real name was, broke in. "She convinced some loser to help her. The moron recorded the plans on his phone. There wasn't much we could do."

"Where is Lois now?"

"I don't think she left the main hall," Kadry said. "So I'm guessing they locked her into one of the back rooms. Joshua Calley is guarding her, or maybe Davis. He was still there when we left. We can take them out easy."

"I wouldn't underestimate Joshua," Benson said. "But I don't think Davis would shoot even if he was given the chance."

Marshall laughed. "He's the goddamn Strawberry Mountain Killer."

"I gotta say, that's hard to believe," Kadry said. "Besides, all he or Calley have is a Glock."

"Have you ever been shot by a Glock?" Marshall asked. "No? Neither have I, and I'm not planning on it."

"They won't be expecting anything," Kadry insisted.

"Draw me a map of the place," Marshall said. He turned and addressed the small, quiet guy, who I was startled to realize was standing mere inches behind me. "Carter, you think you can take him out?"

"You want him alive?" Carter had a deep voice for someone with such a small frame.

"Preferably," Marshall said. "The FBI is going to be looking for any excuse to storm the place. I'd like to delay that until we're ready for them."

"Taking him alive will take me a little longer," Carter said, "but it shouldn't be a problem."

"Good," Marshall said. "Meanwhile, the rest of you start setting up the booby traps." He stood, and the trailer got even smaller. He loomed over Smith—Kadry—who, until then, I'd thought was a big man. "Is the diagram of the camp you gave us still accurate?"

"A lot of the vehicles have left," Kadry said. "But the general outlines are the same."

"How many of the people here can we depend on to back us up?" Marshall asked.

"Other than Patterson and Johnson here, not many. Until yesterday, when he got himself killed at the roadblock, I would have said Jules Francisco was solid."

"Jules…fucking…Francisco," Marshall said, as if he was invoking Abraham Lincoln or someone. "He's the reason we're here. I wasn't sure Lois was right until then. But now, as the hippies used to say, the whole world is watching. Jules…fucking… Francisco." He shook his head in wonder. "What about the three park rangers?"

"Unbelievably, they're still here," Benson said, shaking his head in turn. "They're holed up in Garth Perkin's little shack. They really aren't expecting anything. Everyone was planning to turn themselves in tomorrow."

"Then we got here just in time," Marshall said. "Landstrom, Hanson, go stake out the shack. Don't let our hostages leave."

I felt my body go cold at the word *hostages*. This was really happening.

The two men saluted and left the trailer, but my claustrophobia didn't ease. That's when I realized that it wasn't the close quarters that was causing me to shake. I was scared. These guys were determined to kill or be killed. There was no negotiating here. A suicide mission; that's what it looked like to me. I mean, the entire USA and all its law enforcement and most of its citizens were outside this camp and against us. What the hell did these guys think they were going to do here but die?

I didn't much want to die with them.

I glanced at Jerry and could tell that none of that had even occurred to him. He thought we were Afghan rebels or something, going to fight the powers that be to a standstill.

Jesus.

I wondered if Lois had any more of that poison. Maybe a smaller dose, just enough to knock Jerry out of commission. I was pretty sure Vanessa and Harry would forgive me.

But Jerry would never forgive me, no matter how this turned out. No matter if everyone here ended up dead, he'd blame me.

I could just leave. What did I owe the Johnsons anyway?

Well…I pretty much owed them everything. I'd arrived at the Johnson ranch on a downward spiral, and it was a miracle that I'd pulled out of it. Being surrounded by teetotaling Mormons and good honest work helped. Truth was, I'd have been dead by then if not for them. So, thinking about it that way, I guess I owed them my life.

But that didn't keep me from shaking, my mind skittering over the very idea of what would happen if we stayed. I was dry-mouthed and sweating.

"What do you want us to do?" I heard Jerry ask.

With a steadily sinking heart, as if listening to someone in another room, I heard Marshall tell us.

CHAPTER 60

MARK SIMONS

It felt like I slept for hours, and for a blessed moment upon waking, I forgot everything that had happened. I'd dreamed, in fact, of Lois and me, together in the trailer, not making love yet, but laughing, eating, drinking, with sex promised in the near future.

I woke to something wet splatting against my cheek. I reached up, thinking it was a fly, and felt something small and moist plastered to my face. As I brushed at it, other small pieces dropped to the floor. I leaned on one elbow, staring down at the dried nuggets of paper, trying to make sense of them.

And then another one hit my forehead and I looked up to see Lois leaning back in her chair with an ugly grin, holding a straw in her hand. She was chewing something. Then she put the straw to her mouth and blew another spitwad my way.

I didn't even try to avoid it. It struck my nose, the spit splattering into my eyes. I closed them.

"Stop it," I said. My voice was so lifeless I wasn't even certain I'd spoken.

"Stop it," she mimicked.

I rose to my knees, then stood, and I was glad to see that she straightened up in alarm. She hadn't totally forgotten that I was a man. But then she read something in my posture and grunted. She tore another piece off the shredded notepaper in her lap and began chewing.

"Don't, Lois."

She stood up and threw the straw onto the ground. "You

were more fun when you were passed out," she said.

"Lois… Please listen. I didn't mean to—"

"For fuck's sake, quit saying that. I don't want to hear anything out of you, Mark. Nothing at all. Here's how this is going to play out, you pathetic asshole. I will admit to giving something to Carver to give him a little indigestion. But you…you took it too far. You took him into the desert and did something to him. That's the only explanation."

"We can *both* deny it," I said.

"We could, but I'd rather throw *you* to the wolves. You're the reason we're locked in here."

"But—"

"Shut up. You don't know how tempted I was to shove that pencil up your nostril while you snored and slobbered all over the floor. But that's the end of it. You are beneath my notice. From this moment forward, you are invisible."

For the next hour or so, I paced around the room. The desk was starting to stink. Somehow flies had managed to get into the room and were swarming; the kind of flies that seemed to have a death wish, that linger on your skin until you slap them dead.

Lois never even looked my way.

I went back to my spot, sat down on the flattened box, and tried not to fall back to sleep. Not because I was worried she'd kill me, that would have been a relief, but because I was afraid she'd do something more humiliating than that.

Besides, I was too hungry and thirsty to sleep. I didn't know what time it was, but I sensed it was still dark out. There wasn't the slightest sound anywhere.

A loud *thud* outside the door brought me to my feet. Lois stood up too, but she didn't seem confused at all. It was as if she was expecting it.

The door opened and I stepped back, expecting Joshua Calley's huge form to enter. Instead, a small man came in, doffed his hat, showing a bald head, and nodded to Lois. "Ma'am."

"Carter," Lois nodded. "They're all here?"

"Yes, ma'am."

"And they brought everything we discussed?"

"They're being deployed as we speak. What do you want me to do with your guard?"

"Is he dead?"

"No, ma'am. I choked him out. He'll be waking up soon. He's a big guy, so I suggest we do something fast."

"Drag him in here," Lois said.

The guy—Carter—went back out, and I heard scuffling, and then another *thud*. He poked his head in the door and looked over at me. "You there, help me pull him in."

Even with the two of us, it was an effort to move Calley's deadweight.

Lois went to the desk and started opening and closing drawers, reaching inside a few times. Then she grabbed a paperweight off the desk. It looked like petrified wood. She came over and displayed a dozen nails of varying sizes on her palm.

"Nail the bastard in," she said.

"He'll die of thirst if we leave him in here too long," I said.

She didn't bother to answer or even look my way. But Carter gave me a quick glance and said, "Ma'am?"

"Grab a case of water out of the pantry," she said, sounding annoyed.

"Food?

"Let him starve," she said. "It'll all be over before it hurts him, and if not, the bastard deserves whatever happens to him."

Lois left the room with Carter on her heels. I hurried to follow them, not at all certain they didn't intend to leave me too. Carter trotted across the reception area and came back lugging a pallet of water. He threw it inside. It landed with a loud thud.

He closed the door and started to hand me the nails and the paperweight.

"No, you do it," Lois said. "This guy wouldn't know how to nail his own ass to the floor."

Carter laughed at the absurdity. I almost walked away. Oh, God, how I wished I'd walked away. *This guy,* she'd called me. It struck me that Lois hadn't used my name since Davis produced the phone. It was as if she was trying to erase not only all memory of me, but my entire existence.

I thought maybe she'd turn and tell me to go away. But what

she did was worse. She ignored me. I was invisible to her. I followed along wherever she went, and I felt myself shrink, little by little. I had no will of my own anymore. I was a remnant of her willpower, unable to do anything but stand there and be degraded.

But underneath the humiliation, something was happening. A small part of me began to rebel. I started to see Lois for what she was, and as she ignored me, I didn't disappear, but turned into something else.

CHAPTER 61

BRAD PATTERSON

The hard asses had deposited their heavy packs outside Lois's trailer door between the flower beds. Benson picked up a satchel and handed it to me. I almost buckled under the weight and couldn't help but grunt. Benson smiled.

Kadry picked up another satchel and threw it to Jerry, who promptly dropped it with a thud.

"Jesus, Kadry!" one of the new guys said. "You trying to blow us up?"

"They're just lumps of metal until they're armed, Landry," Kadry said.

"You sure about that?" Landry asked, lifting his own satchel gingerly.

Kadry smiled. "Take Patterson to the west side of the camp and start laying down the charges."

Landry gave a lazy salute.

"Bannister, take Johnson and do the east side. If you wrap around, you should meet in the middle. Hurry. We don't have much time."

"What about the south?" Landry asked.

Kadry smiled again. He was enjoying this. "Benson and I are headed over there right now. That's gonna be the kill zone."

The kill zone? My mind couldn't quite take in the words.

This nightmare was getting worse. The more I wanted to get away, the more I was being dragged into the middle of it. I didn't trust myself to speak, certain I'd start babbling if I did.

Walk away, I thought. *Jerry is an adult. He can make up his own mind.*

But I couldn't do it.

Kadry pulled a couple of folded papers out of his pocket and handed one each to Jerry and me. They were maps, with Xes marking the spots. Spots for what, I wasn't sure, but nothing good.

It was colder than shit. I could see my breath in the light of the doorway. As soon as we left the lighted area, I stopped. "You got a flashlight?" I asked.

I couldn't see Landry, but his voice was surprisingly close. "We're doing this in the dark, buddy. Don't worry, I know how to arm them safely."

"I need to see the map again," I insisted.

"Shit, man," Landry said. He handed me a small flashlight. "Keep the light down and pointed at the map."

The Xes were all just outside the perimeter of the camp. I had pretty much figured out where they were from a single glance at the map, but I hoped to flash some light toward the FBI barricades, accidentally like.

I studied the map longer than I needed to. Handing the flashlight back, I pretended to fumble and dropped it.

The bastard caught it midair and snapped it off in one motion.

Damn.

"You done fucking around?" Landry asked.

"This way," I said. I didn't try to steer him astray. I figured he'd gotten a sense of the tactical boundaries, and he wasn't kidding about doing the work in the dark. He was obviously trained for it. The biggest X was right in the middle of the designated area. There were two more large Xes on either side, about halfway to the corners.

Landry brought out a handheld GPS unit, which took him closer to the marked spots than I could have. He handed the map and GPS to me and let me do the navigating. I wasn't sure what they needed me and Jerry for, except as mules.

He motioned for me to bring over my satchel. From it, he removed a large, square metal object, handling it gingerly. Then he removed some wires and a small square box from the bag.

"Stand over there," Landry commanded. "I ain't doing this part in the dark." He pulled out his small flashlight and put it in his mouth, then extended the scissor legs of the device and planted it firmly into the ground. In the flashing light, I read the large letters embossed on the front.

Front Toward Enemy.

Pointed right at me.

From the recesses of my adolescent mind (I had watched every war documentary I could find), a name came to me: Claymore. Detonated from a distance, it would blast out ball bearings for a hundred yards in a wide swath.

Landry leaned over the smaller box, adjusted something, then stepped back. Only then did he notice me frozen in front of the thing. He urgently motioned me out of the way.

Then he relaxed, handing me an entrenching tool and pointing me to where he wanted me to dig. We continued to lay down smaller mines, which were surprising light, made of plastic instead of metal. He placed these randomly, stepping forward ten paces, then back, then sideways. The smaller mines apparently didn't need to be very deep. A good wind would blow away the sand covering them, but then, they didn't have to be there for long. Landry always slowed down at the last moment, reaching down and pulling something and stepping back, then not moving for a time. I froze along with him and only started breathing again when he moved on to the next mine.

I marked the locations of each of the mines on the map, using the GPS, which was reassuring. I doubted that Landry or the other hard-asses cared if there were unexploded bombs if by some miracle this all ended safely, but I'd sleep better knowing that the authorities could find them.

When we reached the point where the next big X was on the map, Landry pulled out a cylinder. I almost dropped everything and ran into the darkness. The only thing that kept me from doing that was my awareness of the mines.

I recognized the new mine from Vietnam documentaries: a Bouncing Betty. Landry set it up quickly, then stepped back to admire his handiwork. I couldn't believe it. If the damn thing were triggered, it would be propelled a few feet into the air and detonate, blasting metal shrapnel for dozens of yards in every direction. Anyone near the thing would be shredded.

With growing dread, I followed Landry around to the north side, laying down the last of the mines. There was maybe ten feet between them, though every third or fourth mine, Landry would mix it up, burying them either closer together or farther apart.

The moon went behind dark clouds, and Landry resorted to using his flashlight a couple of times, but then seemed to decide it was too dangerous, so we laid down the last of the mines almost blind.

We nearly slammed into Jerry and Bannister in the dark. They were finishing off the installation of another Claymore.

"Can you believe this?" Jerry said excitedly.

"Keep your fucking voice down," Landry said.

"Sorry," Jerry said.

I didn't trust myself to answer. *No, Jerry, I can't believe this. This is scary as hell.*

The whole job didn't take long. I'd thought might take all night, but Landry and the other hard-asses knew what they were doing.

We finished up and headed back. Landry was humming some heavy metal tune, like he thought it was the apocalypse or something. Maybe it was.

The trailer was brightly lit. Through the window, I could see Lois Carpenter's slender shadow. Laughter erupted from inside. It was an alien sound. Laughter didn't belong in this new and dangerous world. It brought me up short.

Jerry followed Landry and the other guy right to the door.

"Jerry," I said.

He turned, still smiling in excitement.

"It's three o'clock in the morning, man. Let's get some sleep."

"Sleep? Are you kidding me? Seems like all I've done since I got here was sleep, because nothing was happening. But now? Hell no."

I wanted to pull him aside, to explain the implications of all this, but he climbed the steps and went inside the trailer before

I could say anything further. I stood out there alone, wondering how I'd gotten there.

There is no one watching me. I can escape.

It wasn't until I got to my tent that I realized I still had the map.

I imagined federal agents, state troopers, and sheriff's deputies like my Uncle Martin approaching the camp, unaware of the danger. I saw them mowed down, blown up. I saw the vengeance that would come down on those who'd done such a thing.

I shuddered, realizing my fingerprints were all over the mines.

Fingerprints? I'm worried about fingerprints? They'd be blown up, along with everything else.

My phone was in my backpack, along with my wallet and anything else I needed for a quick getaway. The pack was hidden in an empty cooler, though with the scarcity of beer lately, that had probably been a stupid place to hide it.

I reached for the phone, suddenly certain there'd be no power; it was low, but still in the green. I poked my head out of the tent and looked around. Most of the people who had been camped around us were gone, leaving behind piles of garbage, torn tents, and soiled sleeping bags. Jerry's tent was tilting to one side, abandoned.

I punched in a number.

"This is 911," came a businesslike voice. "What is your emergency?"

CHAPTER 62

PETER STERNS

Dear Ms. Fitzgerald,

The following is for your eyes only, for reasons that will become apparent. As my lawyer, you seem like a fair and honest person, and I'm trusting that you'll not show this to anyone else. Hart Davis has advised me to show my human side to you, so here it is, as foolish as it may seem.

Considering the mess we were in, it probably seems strange that Mich and I never really talked politics. Everything but, it seemed like. So when she followed me to Garth's hut, I wasn't sure if it was because she was sympathetic or because of me. Maybe it didn't matter.

Like I said, I was afraid to find out. I once had good friend, the kind of guy who bent over backward to be helpful, who was about as easy to talk to as anyone I ever met. Then one day, he just blurted, "I'm a Nazi." You know, not conservative or right wing or alt-right, but a flat-out Nazi.

After that, it was as if someone had thrown a swastika flag over him; I couldn't see him any other way. I don't think we spoke more than ten more words to each other.

The big problem we had with the takeover, as far as I could see, was that we were attracting these kinds of crazies. You didn't have to scratch the surface very hard before conspiracy theories and outright delusions popped up. The nuts weren't really the core of the protesters; in fact, they were disregarded. Foolishly, it appears now, because they were who the reporters talked to the most.

I liked Mich a lot. I was pretty sure she wasn't one of the loonies, but I couldn't be absolutely sure. I decided to maintain the illusion for as long as possible.

"Anyone got some champagne?" Garth asked.

"I'm not toasting my going to jail," Hart said. "But I'm relieved. Without Lois, I doubt any of the others will pursue this."

"So we can leave?" Perry asked.

"Any time," Hart said. He glanced at his watch, and I followed his example. It was after midnight. "I don't know about you, but I'm dead on my feet. Calley said something about it being safer to surrender in the morning, and I agree."

Surrender. The word seemed to suck the happiness right out of the air. We fell silent, and as the gloom settled in, we realized how quiet it was outside. The camp was already mostly abandoned.

I looked around for someplace to sit or stretch out. The room was crowded. Garth had claimed the cot; there was space for two or three more people on the floor, with some of the extra blankets. Nicole needed to stay, since her normal sleeping quarters had been commandeered, and I doubted that Perry wanted to leave his two people alone.

"I'm heading back to my tent," I said. "I'll see you in the morning."

"Me too," Hart said, glancing over at Nicole. She ignored him.

I started to head out and sensed someone following me. I expected Hart and turned to slap him on the back. It was Mich.

"Crowded in here," she said. "Mind if I join you?"

I sensed the others studiously ignoring us, just as I was trying hard to ignore the possible implications.

"Sure," I said. "I've got an extra sleeping bag." I turned to Hart. His tent was about five spaces east of mine. "You coming?"

He looked like he was trying not to grin. "Nah, you go on ahead. I'll see you tomorrow."

What the hell? Do they all know?

But I suppose we hadn't been keeping it secret. We'd been spending just about every waking hour together. The only time we hadn't spent together was our sleeping hours.

Believe it or not, I was still not sure about how Mich felt about me. She did dress a little like someone who wasn't interested in guys. But she also dressed like any commonsense woman in the High Desert.

Oh, I really did know. But not consciously. So I was still in suspense.

It was a beautiful suspense too, that anticipation of a first kiss, a first embrace, a first…

All the way back, my body was being flooded with endorphins. A moonlight walk. I'd never experienced anything so romantic. Neither of us spoke. Halfway there, Mich took my hand, and that's when I knew for sure. Another five paces and I turned toward her. She leaned toward me, and I pulled her the rest of the way. Then we were kissing as naturally as anything, fitting just right, her face tilted up to mine, my arms around her waist, her arms on my neck, pulling me against her even harder.

I don't know how long we stood there, at one with the universe, with the moon and the Milky Way and the crickets and the wind. It was as if all life condensed into that moment: not just mine, not just Mich's, but all life. Together in one.

"Get a tent," Hart said, walking past us.

Mich and I laughed joyfully, not embarrassed in the slightest. We made it to the tent, climbed in, and faced each other on our knees. We kissed for the longest time, and I was content. If she hadn't tugged on my shirt, I would have stayed there forever. I tugged on her shirt right back, and then both our shirts were off, and she reached back and took off her bra, and then we savored that for an eternity. Each little movement was the best thing I'd ever felt.

Her panties were dark in the diffused moonlight that came through the tent, but I knew they were purple, if for no other reason than she wasn't wearing anything else that color.

We slid into the sleeping bag, and I got on top of her, and we made love—not hurried, not slow, just a rhythm that felt right. There was nothing fancy, no gymnastics like with some of the girls I'd met at the dances, me trying to prove myself and them trying to seem cool about it.

No, this was as natural as breathing. We didn't speak after it was over. I could sense Mich smiling in the dark, and every few minutes, she leaned into me and pecked me on the lips, and when she wasn't doing it, I was pecking her on the lips. That said everything we needed to say.

The second time was more frenetic and noisy, and when we were done, I said, "We should be quieter. Hart will hear us."

She laughed. "You think he doesn't know?"

That seemed extraordinarily funny, and we started laughing and couldn't stop. In hindsight, it seems a little cruel to Hart. I knew what he was going through with Nicole. But at the time, there was only the two of us; only Peter and Michelle existed in all the universe.

"Have you written any more poems?" she asked.

I hesitated a little too long.

"You have, haven't you!" she exclaimed. "Let me hear one, please, please, please."

I'd told myself I'd never let her see my poems, but I had no doubt that she'd like it.

"Well, I don't know..." I teased.

"Nothing gets me hotter than a poem," she said.

"There once was a girl from Nantucket..." I began.

"Oh, my God!" she exclaimed, grabbing me and swinging her legs over me.

I was pretty sure she was joking, and besides, I was spent. I didn't move. She flopped over on her back with a pout.

"Well, I do have this one," I said.

"Brown-haired, purple Lady,
I waited, dreaming of you,
Knowing I could make you happy.
I had time to think
Of how it would be.

I waited, and began to doubt
Love existed,
Except in a lonely mind.

I waited, not unhappy,
Not happy,
Sometimes empty,
Sometimes full of myself
And my dreams.

I waited,
Afraid to look,
And discover you weren't there.

It seems so foolish,
Before I met you.
Love is real
Fantasies alive
And poetry true."

She took my head in her hands and kissed me deeply, her brown eyes staring deep into mine. And then I found out I wasn't spent after all.

Afterward, we lay back, this time too tired to even cuddle. "I'm going to be sore tomorrow," I said.

"You think *you're* going to be sore," she said.

Neither of us laughed, because the word *tomorrow* sobered us up. Tomorrow. We'd probably be going to jail; at least I would, being one of the original occupiers. Tomorrow we'd be in the real world, with real-world problems, and this idyll would be over.

Mich climbed out of the sleeping bag and started to get dressed.

"What are you doing?" I said. "You can stay."

"Peter," she said, then paused. "You can't talk about this to anyone, no matter what happens."

"Everyone is going to know," I said.

"No, everyone is going to *suspect.* Nevertheless, it's hearsay unless we confirm it."

"Confirm it?" I echoed. It seemed so cold, so official.

"Never talk about tonight, Peter. Or I can't help you."

"What are you talking about?"

A phone rang. I reached for my backpack, then realized that it was my old ringtone, the one I'd replaced with cowboy yodels. Mich reached for the lowest pocket of her cargo pants, which were halfway up her thighs.

"Yes, sir," she said. She stood and turned away from me.

"I understand, sir. Right away."

She hung up and turned back toward me. It was like she was a different person, one I'd never seen before. I could imagine her in some corporate office somewhere, dropping the hammer on some subordinate.

"Get dressed, Peter. We've got to get out of here."

"I don't understand."

"Please get dressed!"

I was so stunned I didn't move. She gave me an exasperated look. "Hurry up. When you're dressed, find Hart Davis. Tell him we're leaving...tonight."

She ducked out of the tent before I could respond.

CHAPTER 63

HART DAVIS

I heard soft rustling from Peter's tent. There was something about the furtive eagerness of the sound that told me what was happening. Not that I'd had any doubt. I'd passed them glued together on the path, and I'd debated taking a different route to my tent or passing by them with a small joke.

The second time they made love that night, there was no mistaking it. The tents around us were empty or had been removed, so I was the sole listener, I think.

So much for getting one last good night of sleep. I was happy for them, though. Something good had come out of this debacle.

I couldn't help but think of Nicole and what might have been. I could still see her face shining up at me from the floor of her office as she bent over, scribbling on the proclamation. It had taken all my willpower not to drop to the floor beside her, take her in my arms, and kiss her hard.

She was still mad at me, but I think she might someday have forgiven me—if I hadn't gone off with Lois. As I thought of her, Lois Carpenter's image rose up, a knowing smile on her face. *She's too good for you*, the apparition seemed to be saying.

I got up, put on my boots, and looked around the tent. Was there anything I wanted to take with me? Anything at all?

It was all stuff I could get more of. I felt a little guilty about leaving the mess, but the Feds would no doubt put me to work in prison, so I'd be paying for it one way or another.

As the lovebirds reached a crescendo, I unzipped the tent and started to step out. At the last moment, I went back and rooted around the bottom of my sleeping bag for the Smith & Wesson .38 revolver I'd squirreled away there. Unlike almost everyone in the camp, I didn't open carry as a matter of course.

I wasn't sure whether to leave it and perhaps have it accidentally fall into the wrong hands or take it with me and risk getting shot by the Feds. Finally, I strapped the holster to my belt, making sure it clearly showed. I'd surrender with my hands up. That ought to be enough.

I'd intended to go straight back to Garth's hut, maybe fix some coffee if I could do it without waking the others. But I meandered away from the path without thinking about what I was doing and soon found myself outside Lois's trailer.

It was brightly lit, and I could hear voices inside, more than one conversation going on, and the trailer rocked a little from heavy boots walking the length of it. Shadows passed by the windows, big, hulking shapes. I felt myself tensing up and had a sudden urge to get out of sight. I stepped back a few paces into the shadows of an empty trailer.

"They're up to no good," said a low voice behind me. "In case you're wondering."

I jumped and whirled around, barely holding back a cry of alarm.

"Sorry," the shadow said. "Didn't mean to scare you."

It took way longer than it should have to realize who it was. "Mark?" I put my hand on my pistol.

A rifle was leaning against the empty trailer, but he made no move for it.

"If it makes you feel better, you can draw your gun," he said. "I'll be facing my Maker soon enough, don't you fear."

I hesitated, then took my hand away from my .38.

"I didn't kill John," he continued. "Not that I'm not guilty of being a fool."

"How did you get out?" I finally said.

"I always liked you, Hart. I got nothing against you or the others. If you want to try to put me under arrest again, I won't fight it. But the others might."

"The others?"

"You need to get your friends out of here, Hart. Right now.

Like right this minute. A bunch of new guys have shown up. Bad dudes," he warned.

"We're leaving in the morning," I said.

"Too late. It may already be too late, but you gotta try. Believe me, you don't want anything to do with these guys."

As I hesitated, I heard a laugh from inside the trailer that froze me in place.

"Lois got free, too," Mark said. "By morning, she's going to be in complete control of this place. No one will get in or out without her knowing."

I nodded in the dark, then realized he probably couldn't see me. "I'll get the others, right now."

"You'll have to try to leave from the south," Mark said.

That made no sense. Anyone who was still around would see us. If Lois had posted any guards at all, and I had no doubt she had, they'd stop us. Heading out into the desert made more sense.

"They've booby-trapped the perimeter," Mark said.

"They've what?!"

"You don't realize how serious these guys are. Heavy-duty ordinance. You don't want to mess with that."

I let it sink in. After the first surge of fear, an amazing calmness came over me, as if the worst had already happened. I'd felt this way before—in the Strawberry Mountains. "Why are you helping me?"

"I'm fucked no matter what I do. I'm only staying because of Lois."

"Come with us, Mark," I said. "She doesn't give a damn about you."

"You don't think I know that? She hates me, if anything. But I can't help how I feel." He stepped away from the trailer, and I could see the determination in his round face. "Get going, man."

I turned and hurried toward Garth's shack.

CHAPTER 64

NICOLE NELSON

What did Hart expect me to do? Fall into his arms in forgiveness?

I ignored the mopey looks he kept sending my way. I was angry, but angrier with myself than with him. I'd been keeping him at arm's length, making him pay. And he'd given up on me.

In some ways, I couldn't blame him. Lois Carpenter was a good-looking woman, though I thought her politics were despicable. She had that tall, dark, and slinky look I'd always wished I could have, instead of being short, pudgy, and blonde. She was an adult, and I felt like an insecure little girl.

I'd decided to interact with Hart as little as possible. I'd make a clean break now, and when we left in the morning, never see him again. It had all been a big mistake. I'd felt him looking at me as he announced he was heading back to his tent, as if I was going to try to talk him out of it. I'd pretended not to hear him. Then he was gone, and instead of feeling relieved, I felt sad, suspecting I'd missed my last chance.

What made it worse was the obvious attraction between Peter and Michelle.

That could have been us, I thought as the couple left Garth's hut, trying to act cool.

It was too much. It was all too much. When this was over, I'd go back to my one-room studio apartment in John Day and try to forget everything.

Perry was slumped in a chair across from me, his head in his arms. He hadn't moved for quite a while. I figured he was asleep. As I looked over at Garth, he let out a snort. He was flat on his back on the cot, his mouth wide open, the long hairs of his beard blowing in and out of his mouth with each breath.

I slid off my chair, lay on my back on the rough wooden planks of the floor next to the cot, and closed my eyes. I'm not sure if I slept or not. The next thing I remember is the door flying open, missing my head by inches, a waft of air blowing through my hair. I sat up. Every bone in my stiff body hurt, and it hurt even more when I moved.

The hut was dark. Perry must have woken at some point and turned out the lamp. Whoever was in the doorway switched on a flashlight and zoomed the beam around the room as if counting the occupants. "Get up, everyone," said a commanding voice. "We're leaving."

The voice was feminine, and I couldn't make sense of it. I heard fumbling behind me and the table lamp came on, revealing Perry's hangdog, drooping eyes. He looked like a ghoul.

Garth groaned loudly. "Just let me sleep," he muttered. "Or go ahead and kill me."

Mich stood in the doorway, a pistol in hand, looking ten years older and three inches taller than the last time I'd seen her. The lovestruck look in her eyes was gone, replaced by something hard and flinty.

I stood up, fear sweeping over me, my skin tingling. Mich came toward me, bent past me, and pushed down on Garth's chest. "Get up, Garth. No malingering."

"Oh, Jesus. Don't use a word like *malingering* until I've had some coffee."

Perry tried to stand up, stumbled against the table, and then righted himself and moved to the center of the room. "What's going on, Michelle?" he asked.

"I'm ordering you to leave," Mich said. "All of you. No discussion. Let's go." She turned toward the door.

"Who are you to tell us what to do?" Garth said, finally sitting up, rubbing his eyes.

Mich made an exasperated sound. She reached down and pulled up her left pants leg, dug into the back of her boot, and pulled out a black plastic wallet with a small golden badge inside. Opposite the badge were the big blue letters "FBI." It was like something you'd buy at a toy store, but I could tell it was real.

"Special Agent Michaela Rodgers," she said. "You can still call me Mich. But right now, we have to get out of here."

I have to admit, of all the strange things that happened during the takeover, that was the most disorienting of all. I'm embarrassed to say now that I'd been rather protective of young Michelle, thinking she was an innocent. To see this hardheaded, competent woman taking charge was quite a wrench.

Garth was feeling the same doubts. "I told you all, I'm not—"

"Shut up, Mr. Perkins. You have no say in this. I'm ordering you out of here, even if I have to put a gun to your head."

"All right, all right," Garth said, heaving himself to his feet. "No need to get radical." He was wearing underwear and nothing else but a solid matt of hair all over the rest of his body. "Let me grab a few things."

"No time," Mich said. "Leave everything. We've got seconds, not minutes. I'm not kidding, folks. This is life or death."

Well, that finally got our attention, even Garth's.

"At least let me put on my pants," he said, looking around vaguely.

Perry reached down and flicked a pair of blue jeans in his direction. "Lead the way, Special Agent," he said. He started to head for the door. I fell in behind him. Garth struggled to get on his pants, hopping after us.

Someone loomed in the door. Mich whirled around, pistol raised.

"Whoa," Hart's voice said. "What's going on?"

"She's a Fed," Garth said. "Can you believe it?"

Mich—Agent Rodgers—looked over Hart's shoulder. "Where's Peter?" she asked.

"I don't know. I thought he was with you."

She shrugged it off with a visible effort. "We can't wait. We'll leave through the south corridor."

"And if they won't let us?" Hart asked.

She hesitated. "Then we fight our way out," she said in a low voice. "It's better than being taken hostage."

There it was—the word everyone had avoided since the beginning of the takeover.

"Why don't we go out the back?" Perry demanded. "There can't be enough of them to guard everywhere."

"They've planted mines around the perimeter," Hart said.

Mich gave him a sharp look. "How did you know that?"

"An unexpected friend," Hart shrugged. "How did *you* know?"

"A reliable source, was all I was told," Mich said. "All right, enough chitchat. Let's go. Walk quickly, but try not to draw attention to yourself. If we're challenged, keep walking. I'll deal with it."

"What about Peter?" I asked, still trying to reconcile this take-charge person with the woman who'd seemed to be in love with Peter Sterns.

"He can take care himself," Mich said. "I'm worried about you three rangers. You're the reason I'm here."

We emerged into the soft moonlight. It felt peaceful, not threatening. But my body was jangling. My footsteps felt like someone else was taking them. The camp seemed deserted. What few people were still hanging around were asleep. I didn't know what time it was, but I guessed it was a few hours before daylight.

Police all over the world picked this time of night to take down the bad guys.

CHAPTER 65

BRAD PATTERSON

It took some time to convince the 911 operator that I was calling from inside the camp and that I had vital information. "Please hang on, sir," the operator finally said.

"Better hurry," I said. "I don't have much power on my phone."

Maybe that lit a fire, because it wasn't long before Special Agent Rod Adams answered.

But during that short wait, I had time to wonder what I was doing. It felt kind of funny. I'd grown up watching cop shows, where they were the good guys. It didn't take much for me to revert back to that trusting feeling.

I was about to become a traitor to my friends; at least, that's the way they'd see it. But as far as I was concerned, I had a higher loyalty. I wanted them to survive, not to die for some useless cause that had no chance of success.

"What do you have for me, Patterson?" Adams asked.

I'd wondered what I was going to say, but his no-nonsense tone settled me down. I told him about the bombs and about the map. He listened all the way through without interrupting.

"Don't come in yet," I begged him. "I've got all the bombs marked on the map. If you try to come in the front, they've got a kill zone set up. Just give me a little more time."

"We can't wait forever," Adams said. "And we've got ways to deal with mines."

"But that would take time, wouldn't it? Slow you down? These hard-asses aren't joking around. I think they'd just as soon kill the hostages as get what they're demanding."

"What *are* they demanding?" Adams asked. He was obviously frustrated. "I mean, if they had anything rational to request, we'd at least have something to talk about. What do these new guys want?"

"Blood and fury," I said. "Blood and land."

"I can give them that," Adams said. "The blood part, at least. You need to understand, Mr. Patterson. I'm the reasonable one out here. I'm the good guy. I'm not just pretending; I'm trying to keep this from turning into a bloodbath. But the pressure from my superiors is increasing every minute. The next time we hear gunfire, we're coming in."

"Don't do it," I said. "You haven't seen what these guys are carrying. It isn't just the usual semiautomatics. They've got stuff I've never seen before. Military-grade stuff. Look...I think I can find people who will help me. We can give you guys enough time to get in here. But you've got to give me time to talk to them."

"Who?" Adams asked.

"Davis, for sure," I said. "Peter Sterns, I'm pretty sure. My friend, Jerry, he's a little enamored right now, but he's a good guy. I can talk some sense into him."

"Just leave, Patterson. Use the map and get out of there. We need that map, and it isn't safe."

"No," I said stubbornly. "I can't abandon my friends. I've got to try to talk some sense into them. I don't have much power left in my phone, Agent Adams. You need to listen to me. If you come charging in, the hard-asses will start shooting at anything that moves. You've got to let me work something out on the inside."

"It's going the other direction, Patterson. The time for talk is over. Now it's just a matter of timing; not if, but when."

"At least *pretend* to negotiate for a while. We'll try to save the hostages from the inside," I urged.

There was a long pause on the other end. My phone was blinking, about to shut off.

"I'll probably get in trouble for telling you this, Patterson. I'm trusting my instincts that you're on our side. We've...we've got an agent on the inside. The agent is bringing the hostages out tonight, *right now*, along with Davis and Sterns. You should join them."

"Tonight?" I echoed. "You realize the south exit is being guarded? I literally heard them call it a kill zone."

"Nevertheless," Adams said, "we've decided it is best to attempt an escape while this new crew is still getting accustomed to their surroundings. We're hoping they won't shoot cold bloodedly. Go with the hostages, Patterson. We need that ma—"

The phone went dead before he could finish the sentence.

I almost tossed the depleted phone into the sagebrush. This was all going to be over before I had a chance to recharge it.

I hurried toward Garth's shack, hoping I wouldn't be too late. I had a vague notion of distracting the two guards Marshall had sent. To my surprise, Garth and the others had gotten well beyond that point. They were parallel to Merriam Hall, moving at Garth's hobbling pace. I expected a burly FBI agent to be leading the way. Instead, the slim figure of Michelle emerged from the shadows, holding a pistol in the ready position. The three federal employees were in single file behind her, with Hart bringing up the rear, also armed. I was a little surprised that Peter wasn't with them.

Now that I was there, I wasn't sure what to do. I guess maybe I thought I'd approach Hart or the agent, hand them the map, and then disappear back into the camp. I still wasn't ready to abandon Jerry.

But as far as this bunch was concerned, I was one of the bad guys. I couldn't be sure they wouldn't shoot as soon as I showed myself. But there was no choice, except to leave the camp myself.

I was getting ready to step out with my hands raised over my head when the decision was made for me.

The two hard-asses Lois had sent to guard the shack emerged from the visitor center, rifles lowered. It was clear they'd decided to grab some of the warmth inside the building, and maybe to use the facilities. The hostages had almost gotten past them.

There was a motion detector light fixture over the entrance

of the building. It exposed the escapees, casting a wide beam of white light that made them look like ghosts.

The smaller dark guy was Hanson, if I remembered rightly. I tried to remember the other guy's name: a big blond guy, clean-shaven, Nordic looking. Landstrom. That was it.

"Where do you think you're going?" Landstrom didn't raise his voice, but in the deepness of night, it sounded like a shout.

There are so many ways it could have played out. I rerun it in my mind all the time, over and over again, wondering if the bloodshed could have been avoided. For instance, I could have stepped forward and said, "They have a right to leave." I mean, at least it would have given them pause. Or Mich might not have instantly raised her pistol and badge. It takes a lot to shoot someone in cold blood. I didn't know these new guys, but I wonder if Hart and the others had just kept walking, if they really would have pulled the trigger.

But the FBI isn't trained that way. Remove the threat with extreme prejudice, that's what Mich's response was.

"FBI!" she shouted, holding up her badge and raising her pistol.

As if in slow motion, I saw Hanson start to raise his rifle.

Mich fired three times point blank into his chest. He staggered but didn't fall. His returning gunfire climbed into the sky. Landstrom also started aiming his rifle. Mich whirled on him. It was obvious she wouldn't beat him to the trigger. Judging from her silhouette, she wasn't wearing a vest. It was an automatic rifle against a pistol. There was no way Mich was going to win that battle.

Out of nowhere, someone came flying through the air and slammed into the FBI agent at waist height. They tumbled backward and disappeared from view. By some twist of fate, they fell into the trench we'd dug, the one that had gotten us in trouble with the Indians.

But before they were completely out of the range of gunfire, Mich's left leg kicked upward, and I heard a *thump* and saw her leg shudder. A pained shout filled the night.

CHAPTER 66

HART DAVIS

I didn't recognize the two men who stepped into the light. People had been coming and going ever since the takeover began. I'd given up keeping track. A few people even showed up after the blockade was set up by the Feds, trickles of them coming in from the desert side, not enough for the FBI to worry about.

But there was something about the neatness of their camouflage outfits, their closely cut hair, and their general cleanliness and lack of tiredness that told me these guys were new arrivals.

Agent Adams had warned us.

Of course Lois's crew had posted guards. We'd known that. But until these two men raised their rifles, I'd hoped they'd let us go.

When Mich flashed her badge, I could tell where things were headed. I grabbed Nicole and pushed her down. Her knees buckled and she huffed, but she didn't object. I landed on top of her harder than I wanted to, and then spread myself out to cover her as much as possible.

My first impulse was to protect Nicole.

I looked up just in time to see Peter running into the light full tilt at Mich, who didn't see him coming. He slammed into her, and she bent double, her legs flying over her head. There was the *thud* of a bullet striking her. Blood flew into the air, though I'm not sure I haven't added that little detail to this memory. They were at the edge of the light glowing on the side of the visitor center.

Nicole said something underneath me, muffled but urgent.

"What?" I whispered, rising up slightly now that the gunfire had ceased.

"You need to get out of here, Hart," she said.

"What are you talking about? I'm not leaving you."

"There's nothing you can do. You'll just become one of the hostages. Get away. They can't have gotten a good look at you. You know your people. Find allies, Hart."

As soon as she said it, I knew she was right.

"I was stupid, Nicole," I said, my words rushed. "I don't blame you for telling me to get lost. But no matter what happens, remember this...I love you. Somehow I'll find a way to get you out of here."

My body cast a shadow over her, and I couldn't see her expression, but her sudden stillness told me she'd heard me.

She didn't answer. I didn't expect her to.

I looked over at our attackers, but they were approaching the trench, paying no attention to me. I started to get up.

Brad Patterson was staring right at me. As I started to walk away, I expected to hear him shout out, exposing me, but he stayed silent.

Find allies, Nicole had said. I wondered if I'd already found one.

CHAPTER 67

BRAD PATTERSON

Up to then, I'd thought of those men as hard-asses, but from that moment on, I realized what they really were—terrorists.

Mich had moved to one side when she'd confronted them, no doubt to remove her charges from the line of fire. Hart had tackled and covered Nicole. Garth and Perry were lying flat, their hands over their heads.

I was frozen through all it; mere seconds, though it seemed like forever. Peter Stern, coming out of nowhere, tackling Mich. The two of them falling into the ditch. Mich crying out in pain.

When I finally moved, I felt as though I was covered in concrete. I pulled my gun. To this day, I don't know if I would have shot anyone. I definitely wasn't going to shoot anyone in the back.

Landstrom and Hanson cautiously approached the trench, which gave me time to catch up.

Hart stood up behind them, reaching for his gun.

I got in his line of fire and stared him in the face. Hart stood there uncertainly for a few moments, then leaned down and whispered something into Nicole's ear. He turned and disappeared into the darkness.

It was the smart move. The terrorists had the upper hand. They hadn't gotten a good look at Hart and didn't know who he was. If Hart wanted to help Nicole and the others, he needed to not be part of this.

The terrorists reached the lip of the trench and aimed downward. I got to the trench. Peter Sterns was just starting to stand.

He held his hands up, palms out, to the two men. "I've got this!" he shouted.

He seemed to notice the blood on his hands for the first time. I could sense him taking inventory of his own body; then he looked down at Mich.

Blood soaked her leg, as if someone had poured a pitcher of red syrup over her. Her pants leg quivered, as if caught in a current, and I knew that blood was spurting beneath the cloth.

Peter dropped to his knees. Even in the dark, I could see his face turning pale. He unbuckled his belt and pulled it off, then wrapped it around Mich's upper thigh, cinching it tight. "Either of you got something to tie her hands with?"

The terrorists looked uncertain, glancing at each other. From their perspective, Peter had taken out an enemy. He would seem to be an ally. They wouldn't know about Mich and Peter's relationship.

"I'll tie her up with my belt," I said, dropping down into the trench. Peter gave me a worried look, as if wondering if I was going to rat him out. I shook my head so slightly that only he could see it. As my hand passed over my back pocket, I pulled out the folded map.

Peter turned Mich onto her stomach, more roughly than he needed to. She cried out, "Let me go, you bastard!"

I couldn't tell if she was really pissed or acting. The terrorists exchanged a long glance, and even in the dark, I could sense them relax.

I wrapped my belt around her arms, leaned over her, and slipped the map into her back pocket. "Make sure Adams gets this," I whispered.

"Why are you saying?" Hanson demanded.

"I told her that she'd be lucky to survive the night."

It was completely silent, as if the gunfire had shocked the darkness into stillness. I held my breath. Despite my pleas to hold off, I figured the FBI assault team was on its way in.

Hanson and Landstrom stood over us as, around us, people emerged from the tents and trailers. I was surprised by how many people were still in the camp. It gave me some comfort, though maybe it shouldn't have. These were the people who'd stuck around even after Joshua Calley had declared the occupation over.

And where was Calley, anyway?

They shouted questions at Peter and me, casting curious glances at the terrorists and their assault rifles. Lindstrom and Hanson were new faces to them.

Mich grew steadily paler, her skin glistening in the white light. The blood trickled onto the dust beneath her leg, but at least it didn't appear to be spurting anymore.

"She's going to die if she doesn't get to a hospital," someone said.

I was grateful it didn't fall to me point out the obvious. Trying to play both sides was a dangerous game. I needed to signal to one side that I was with them without letting the other side know it.

It was a moot point, I figured. At any moment, I expected gunfire to erupt from the south entrance or explosions from everywhere else.

"Where's the Fed's gun?" Lindstrom asked.

"I've got it, I've got it," Peter said, holding up the pistol and throwing it out of the trench into the dust.

Lindstrom didn't look reassured. "I say we kill her anyway. The Feds are going to execute us for this. Ain't going to be no trial for shooting an FBI agent."

"True that," Hanson said. He motioned with the barrel of his rifle. "Stand aside, you two."

Peter stood up. "I'll take the blame. I'll tell them I shot her. You don't have to do this."

"Get out of the fucking way," Hanson said, lifting his rifle to his shoulder.

It was clear to me that nothing was going to move Peter out of the line of fire. I saw him tense and begin to raise his pistol. I put my arm around him, trapping his.

It was the longest moment of my life.

"Who's been shooting?" Lois moved into the light.

She looked older, her gauntness and wrinkles accentuated by the shadows. Marshall and the other terrorists clustered behind her. My heart dropped when I saw Jerry standing at the fringe of the group, with that stupid rigor mortis grin he got when he was excited. He raised his rifle, no doubt sorry to have missed all the action.

Strangely, the tension in the air lifted. Finally, someone was there to tell them…us…what to do. I'm not sure what I expected. Clarity, I guess. One way or another, a decision would be made; fight or back down.

I realized to my surprise that I was calm, ready for either possibility.

"She's FBI, ma'am," Lindstrom said. "They were trying to escape."

"They?" Lois asked. "Who are *they*?"

"The agent and the three hostages," Lindstrom said.

"I think there was another guy with them," Hanson said. "I didn't get a good look at him."

Marshall peered doubtfully at Peter, who was short and scrawny, then at me. To him, everyone probably looked equally suspicious.

But Lois knew. She looked around the crowd as if looking for someone in particular. Hart timed it just right, I'll give him that, choosing that moment to step out from the tents. He was wearing a T-shirt and long johns. He was unarmed. He yawned and scratched his balls, as if he'd just woken up.

Lois frowned. I could tell she didn't buy his act, but she had no way of challenging it. I held my breath, wondering if she'd call him out.

She turned to her people. "Marshall, you and Carter take point. Make sure the south entrance is covered like we talked about. Benson, check the north perimeter, let us know if they're coming. Landry, take the west." She looked around as if frustrated that she didn't have more terrorists available to order around.

Jerry was all but jumping up and down, trying to get noticed.

Keep your head down, idiot, I thought. *You're going to get killed.*

"Johnson, check out the east side," Lois said.

"Yes, ma'am," he said, turning to go.

"Wait a moment, dammit," Lois said. She closed her eyes and took a deep breath, and I could almost see the calculations being done in her head. "Fire three quick shots if you see them coming."

"I'm amazed they aren't already here," Marshall said. "What's keeping them?"

"Good question," Lois said. "Do it anyway."

He nodded, waved to the others to get going, and trotted off. If I'd had any doubt who was really in charge, that dispelled it.

Lois looked down at Peter uncertainly. He was still standing in front of Mich. How much did Lois know about Peter and Mich? The two might have thought they were being careful, but that kind of infatuation is hard to miss.

"Step away from her, Peter," she said. "I can't be sure whose side you're on."

"Sterns took her out, ma'am," Lindstrom said. "I'd probably be dead if not for him."

"Really," Lois said. It didn't sound like a question.

Mich groaned. Her eyes rolled back in her head, the whites catching the light, looking ghoulish. Peter dropped to her side, scrambling to cinch the belt even tighter.

Lois frowned.

It was up to me to save Mich. Peter was too compromised. With a cold chill, I realized that if Mich stayed and the map was found, they'd know who'd placed it on her.

"She's going to die if we don't get her to a doctor," I said.

Lois turned to me curiously. I searched her face for signs of suspicion, but as far as she knew, I was loyal.

"An FBI agent makes for a lousy hostage," I continued. "A dead one makes an even lousier one."

"I would think she'd be the best kind of hostage of all," Lois said.

"No," I insisted, "the Feds will be all over us in minutes. Unless you're ready for that."

Lindstrom grunted. "He's got a point. It might buy us a little more time."

Lois said, "All right, Patterson. You and Sterns carry her out of here. And Sterns…you might want to think about not coming back if your heart isn't in it."

"I didn't know she was a damned FBI spy," Peter said. He

sounded convincing, even to me.

Lois examined him closely, then turned to the crowd. "That goes for the rest of you too. If you aren't in all the way, now's the time to leave."

She was addressing everyone, but she was staring at Hart. I could tell she wanted to challenge him, but she didn't quite have full control of the situation. Her cadre was still outnumbered by the original occupiers, most of whom considered her a murderer. I didn't have much doubt that her people could have taken out any opposition, but how would that look to the people she was trying to reach in the outside world?

To my surprise, no one left. I wasn't sure what to make of that.

"If you decide to leave," Lois said, "leave by the south entrance. Everywhere else is booby-trapped."

"Booby-trapped?" one of the men asked. I recognized him as one of the second wave of occupiers. Kerry Lawrence. One of the locals, who'd always been a little standoffish, as if they weren't quite sure about all this.

"We have to protect ourselves," Lois said. "If they're coming in after us, we don't want to make it easy for them."

"Screw this," Lawrence answered. "I didn't come here to fight the entire U.S. government. We can't win that battle."

"Then why are you here at all?" Lois said. "Go ahead, get out of here. You and anyone else who is a fair-weather patriot."

Hart stepped up beside Lawrence, still in his long johns. He put his arm around the other man's shoulders companionably. "I don't know about the rest of you, but I'm sticking around. Not because I want a fight, but because I want the Feds to know that not everyone here has given up on negotiation. Not everyone here wants to shoot it out."

Lawrence stiffened at Hart's touch.

Nicely done, I thought. *You've boxed them in.*

Lois's expression didn't change, but I knew her well enough by then to read her body language. She wanted to shoot Hart right then and there.

Lawrence nodded, and the tension broke. "You're right, Hart. We'll stay and keep the peace."

"You ready?" Peter said, at my side. "We need to hurry."

"Sorry, man. Let's go."

He bent down and took Michelle's legs. I took her shoulders and we climbed out of the trench, stumbling toward the south entrance, spotlights on us the whole way. I was thankful that Mich was passed out despite the dead weight. I saw the splattered black dots in the dust. It felt as if she was getting lighter with every step, as if all her blood was leaving her body.

Peter picked up the pace, and I staggered, trying not to drop her.

Then, abruptly, twenty yards from the barricade, he stopped.

CHAPTER 68

PETER STERNS

I could feel the life leaving Mich. I was so scared I was numb. I wanted to throw her over my shoulder and run toward the lights. Every spotlight was on us. I heard distant shouting, the whoop of a siren. The spinning red lights of an ambulance approached the barricades.

When she'd run off from my tent, I'd gotten dressed as fast as I could. So fast, I forgot to grab my pistol. I went looking for Hart, but he wasn't in his tent or anywhere else. Finally, I gave up and headed for Garth's shack.

I missed them. I was surprised Mich hadn't waited for me. Apparently, whatever had alarmed her had been too important to be delayed. I tried to make sense of the phone call, the half of it I'd heard. Mich had transformed before my eyes, no longer an uncertain girl but a hard woman, her face going grim as she listened.

I think that even before I heard her shout out "FBI!," I'd known. Part of me had always known she didn't belong here, that for some reason she was acting. I thought it was because she wanted the adventure or planned to write a book or something. Or maybe that she was an undercover journalist. It hadn't really mattered to me. I'd known she was way out of my league, that it was only because we were in the middle of nowhere, surrounded by men who rarely if ever picked up a book, that I looked relatively attractive to her.

I didn't care. I wanted as much of her as I could get for as long as I could get it. On that future day when she walked away, back to her regular life, I was determined not to regret it.

The two attackers, who I'd never seen before, had the drop on her. It was amazing that she'd gotten three shots off, dead center, at the first one before the other attacker turned his rifle on her.

I didn't think about it. I don't remember running. I just knew I wanted to get between her and the gunfire. It was pure accident that we tumbled into the ditch, and pure bad luck that a single bullet caught her in the leg.

I think it nicked the femoral artery. It didn't hit it smack dab in the middle, or she'd be dead by now, but it was bad enough that I knew we couldn't stop the bleeding.

Brad was carrying her under her armpits, the heavier part of the lifting, and he was obviously growing tired.

I was sure that the jostling Brad and I were doing to her was pumping more blood from her body.

Let them come to us.

The thought was small but strong, and I knew it was the right decision.

I stopped, dazed. The overwhelming disaster had blown my circuits. I wanted to take Mich in my arms and cradle her, close my eyes, and mystically transport us someplace else. Someplace where we'd wake up and this nightmare would be over.

"Why are you stopping?" Brad asked.

"If we get any closer, they're going to arrest us."

Brad didn't answer. Amid his silence, I heard shouts of "Get on the ground! Hands over your heads! On the ground, now!"

I cupped my hands around my mouth and shouted, "You've got a wounded agent here! Come and get her!"

I wasn't sure they could hear me, but I had no doubt they knew exactly what was going on. They'd been watching us since we left the camp. I didn't think they shoot me if I turned my back on them, but I backed up, my hands out from my body to show I was unarmed. Brad walked backward at the same pace. Then we turned and hurried away.

I heard the ambulance whoop again and start toward Mich, and I knew I'd done the right thing. She would get help that much sooner.

But there was one thing I couldn't understand.

"Why aren't they coming into the camp?" I asked aloud.

"'Cause the whole place is surrounded by bombs," Brad said.

I nearly stopped in surprise. "Bombs?"

"Booby-trapped and wired, man. Bouncing Betties and Claymores and other landmines and shit I've never heard of."

The names were vaguely familiar, as if I'd heard them before. They sounded menacing. "How do the Feds know?"

Brad walked beside me silently for few moments. I figured he didn't know. I was just thinking out loud. Then quietly, so low that I could barely hear him, he said, "I told them."

"*You* told them?"

"I never bargained for this," Brad said. "These people are nuts. If you want to fucking tell them, go ahead. I don't care anymore."

"Dude, they don't trust me one little bit," I said. "I'm worried Lois knows about me and…and Mich…" My thoughts scattered at my saying her name, and again, everything but my fear for her vanished from my mind.

"Lois may not trust you," Brad said, "but the others think you're a hero."

We were far enough from the spotlights that we were in shadow, maybe fifty feet from the south entrance. Somewhere in the darkness of the camp, two of Lois's new mercenaries were hidden, ready to catch any invaders in a crossfire.

As if Brad and I could read each other's intentions, we both stopped and faced each other. We were in no man's land. I could feel the pull from both sides. In one direction was safety, if only the safety of a jail cell; in the other, our friends and enemies. Yeats's words came to me, ones I hadn't realized I'd memorized: *Things fall apart; the center cannot hold; Mere anarchy is loosed upon the world.*

"What are we doing?" Brad asked. "Is this crazy?"

"I'm going back into the camp," I said. "I don't want what's about to happen to happen."

"No…yeah…I get that. I mean, how'd we *get* here, man?"

I looked into his shadowed face. I couldn't see his expression, but I realized that the old sarcastic Brad I'd always known, the one who rolled his eyes and mercilessly needled his friend Jerry, that guy was gone, rubbed raw by danger and reality. We weren't the same two men who'd arrived at the John Day Fossil Beds National Monument together.

I knew what he was asking. How had this come to pass?

We'd stumbled into it innocently, I think. Not really understanding the stakes. I'd come out of loyalty to my boss, Harry Johnson, not because I believed in the cause, whatever that was. I was guessing Brad had come along with Jerry out of comradeship.

"We've got to pretend we're on the hard-asses' side," Brad said, "because if we're forced out, we can't stop them."

"Stop them?" I said quietly. "How do you plan to do that?"

"Hell if I know. I just know that if I'm not with Jerry, he'll get himself killed."

"Deal," I said, holding out my hand.

He shook my hand and laughed shakily. "So…what side *are* we on?"

"Fuck sides," I said. "I just want me and my friends to get out of here alive."

"Damned straight," he said.

We turned together and walked toward the south entrance. There was no one around. No one had waited for us. Our resolute march faltered.

"What now?" Brad asked. "Head for Lois's trailer?"

"I'm going to check on Nicole and the others."

"I'll come with you."

The camp was deserted. It was hard to believe that just a few days before, it had been swarming with people. As we got to the main clearing, we saw that two of Lois's men were standing guard.

"No one's allowed any closer," one of them said.

"What's going on, Landry?" Brad asked. He apparently knew this guy, who I'd never seen before.

"Lois's called for a meeting, eight o'clock tomorrow morning," Landry said. "Go to bed, get some rest. You're going to need it. Shit's going down, boys. The real shit's going down."

CHAPTER 69

MARK SIMONS

I had no pride left. I was like an unwanted dog, ignored, and the more I was ignored, the more I hungered for Lois's attention. I don't think she ever looked at me again. Her eyes passed right over me as if I wasn't there.

Until that final moment.

I saw it in her eyes. She knew what was happening, realized that she'd made a mistake, that the cur she'd kicked every chance she got had turned on her.

But I didn't know for a while what I was going to do. I was still in love with her, or so I thought. Love had not yet turned to hate.

I followed Lois and her people around. I sat at the end of their table in the mess tent. I stood at the fringes of the group as she gave instructions. It was clear that she was in charge, not Marshall, despite his imposing presence. The newcomers gave me some curious looks at first, then someone must have told them about my disgrace; after a while, they took their cues from Lois and ignored me completely.

Her people claimed the many empty trailers surrounding hers. I tried to find a bunk, got flat stares, and left. I pulled up a tent from the abandoned tent city and set it up behind her place. From there, I could see the shadows of those inside through a small back window. I always knew when it was her who passed by; something about the movement, the silhouette.

I slept well, for some reason. My dreams were pleasant; in them, Lois still liked me, still smiled at me. And then I'd wake up and reality would be like a weight on my chest, keeping me ensnared in my sleeping bag, and it took much more effort than it should have to crawl out, to pull on some clothes.

I knew I looked like hell, which didn't add to my acceptance any. At breakfast, I came into the mess tent and sat down at the end of Lois's table.

"Jesus, you reek," Landry exclaimed. I'd left a couple of spots between the others and me, but apparently it wasn't enough. "There are empty tables all over the place, you freak. Grab one of those...as far away from us as you can get."

I got to my feet, casting a glance at Lois. It was as if she hadn't heard anything. I went to the corner and pushed some scrambled eggs around on my plate. I couldn't remember the last time I'd really eaten, though I must have. I must have been hydrating, and shitting, and all those things, but I remembered none of it.

If I'd walked away then, maybe I could have found a way to reclaim myself. But I was so lost that I couldn't see it. Lois was a lifeline to me, one that was tangled and torn and that she was trying to cut, but my own need kept it taut, kept me near her, as if I was on a leash, unwanted but still not free.

When she got up from the breakfast table, I waited until she and her entourage left. Then I followed them. I was unclean, an untouchable, ten paces behind the others. I was a ghost, I was a monster, too ugly to look at, too pathetic to even waste a kick on anymore.

All those who were still at the Fossil Beds were at the morning meeting. The media wasn't, and I didn't know why. I found out later that the Feds were keeping them out. I think Lois was pissed off about that.

When everyone was gathered in the reception area, the back door opened and the three hostages were led in. Their hands were tied. I think that shocked everyone. This was real; this was really happening.

In that moment of silence, loud banging came from the office, along with the deep and angry voice of Joshua Calley. Apparently he'd been locked in. It was impossible to make out the words, but not the message. It shocked those who didn't already know of the change in fortunes. I caught Kerry Lawrence looking nervously that way and then turning to his friends to say something.

To my surprise, it was Marshall who stepped forward to address us, not Lois. She stood to one side, looking innocent, as if she was a mere bystander.

"Things are going to change around here," Marshall said. "There will be no more communicating with the authorities by anyone but authorized personnel. We want you to give us your phones, right now. From now on, there will be only one spokesperson."

"I'm sorry," Kerry Lawrence said, "but I don't know *who* you people are…"

I saw the look that passed between Peter Sterns and Hart Davis. They were glad that someone else was taking point.

I knew that the two men weren't on our side—on Lois's side. I tell myself that what went down was an impulse, a moment of madness, but the fact that I didn't tell Lois and the others about the traitors in their midst…well, maybe I was already backing away.

Hart Davis and the other original occupiers would have accepted me back, I know this. But the pitying looks they kept giving me were worse than the disdain and snubbing I was getting from Lois and her friends. Strange to say, but I still had too much pride to crawl back to my old friends.

Marshall turned toward Lawrence, then gave Lois a sidelong glance as if asking if he was a problem. She shook her head slightly.

"We're *you*, man," Marshall said. "We've come to join you. We're *with* you."

Lawrence wasn't buying it. "But I don't know you, bud. You just got here. I don't see why I should turn my phone over to a stranger."

Marshall spread out his hands. "Look, we just think there needs to be a single spokesperson."

"Spokesperson?" Lawrence said. "Who would that be? As if I don't know."

"I'll be taking on that job," Lois said. "It's for the best, people.

We want a clear message when we deal with the Feds. Well-defined demands that no one can pretend they don't understand."

"I thought our demands were pretty clear," Lawrence said. "Just as clear as the fact that they ain't never going to meet them."

"That's because the cost hasn't been high enough," Marshall said. "Enough of this shit. Put your phones on the table. If you don't want to do that, leave. We won't stop you. But if you stay, you have to live by our rules."

It was one of those moments when everything could have changed. If the others had refused, maybe none of the rest would have happened. Everyone looked to Lawrence. He shrugged, pulled out his phone, and threw it on the table. "I hate the damn thing anyway," he said.

One by one, the rest of them followed his example. I could tell that Marshall was almost surprised. He seemed to relax a little.

Then he went too far.

"We also need you to turn in your weapons," he said.

Total silence. Merriam Hall was half full, yet there wasn't the slightest noise. Nothing could have shocked the occupiers more than being asked for their guns.

Marshall put up his hands. "You'll get them back, but we want an inventory. We want to make sure that we have maximum firepower, with the right guns in the right hands."

Again, there was dead silence. Again, one by one, everyone looked at Lawrence. He didn't change expression; you could hardly see his lips move, but you could hear him loud and clear.

"That makes you no better than the Feds. I'm not handing over my firearms to anyone."

Marshall straightened up, his eyes narrowed. His hand went to the strap of his rifle. I think the son of bitch was itching for a fight, any fight.

Lois stepped to the big man's side and put her hand on his arm. He gave her a reluctant glance, then dropped his hand.

"I'm sure it will be fine, Marshall," Lois said. "Of course they can keep their weapons." She reached into her pocket and pulled out a small blue phone. Behind her, Perry Campbell started in surprise.

Lois turned to him. "This will dial Special Agent Rod Adams directly, won't it, Mr. Campbell?"

"How…?"

"Did you think we weren't watching you every minute?" she said. "As long as you're all here, it's time to start the real negotiations." She ambled over to Campbell and waved the phone in front of him. "Where's the speaker on this damn thing?"

Campbell pointed to one of the buttons, which Lois pressed.

"Perry, what's happening?" The voice was distorted, but there was no disguising the worry in it.

"This is Lois Carpenter, Agent Adams. From now on, you'll be talking to me and no one else. Do you understand?"

"What do you want, Mrs. Carpenter?"

"We have three simple demands. Are you listening? Do you want to grab a piece of paper to write them down?"

"Quit screwing around, Lois."

"Lois now, huh? Well, I guess the negotiations have really begun. Here they are: One, we want a presidential pardon for everyone involved in the takeover…in writing. Two, we want that fact broadcast to the world. Three, we want the president to rescind the John Day Fossil Beds designation as a national monument, returning it to private ownership."

"You people can't keep moving the goalposts."

"You were negotiating with Marston," Lois snapped, "and see where that got him. Have you understood our demands?"

"Maybe you should have been paying more attention, Lois," Adams said, sounding tired. "We've been talking about variations of these terms for days. What's really new here?"

"Make up your mind, Agent Adams," Lois said. "Are we moving goalposts or is there nothing new? Here's all you need to know…*we have your people.*"

There it was. Until then, everything might have been explained, or rationalized, or covered up. But once Lois affirmed that the rangers were hostages, there was no forgiveness, no way to sweep it under the rug.

There was a long silence, and then, "What's *that* supposed to mean?"

"What do you think it means? I'm just the spokeswoman

here. You have twenty-four hours to comply or…"

"Or what?"

"I think it's best if we aren't specific, don't you? Let's just say there will be severe consequences."

There was another long silence on the other end. I figured Adams had switched off his speaker and was conferring with his bosses.

When he came back on, he was all business.

"You've given me specific demands, and I appreciate that. We can work something out. But I can't do anything in one day, Lois. That is just not possible."

"You have twenty-four hours. No more, no less." She looked at her watch. "That would be…let's round it off…eight o'clock tomorrow morning. This is not a negotiation anymore, in case you haven't figured that out yet. Give us what we want or…"

"Let me talk to the hostages," Adams said.

"Hostages?" Lois echoed. "They're our guests, Agent Adams, that's all. They're right here listening."

"Are you people OK? Have they harmed you?"

Campbell stepped forward and leaned toward the phone. "Our hands are tied and we're guarded twenty-four/seven. We *are* hostages, no matter what they say."

Marshall stepped toward Campbell, rifle pointed at him, motioning him back.

Lois held the phone up. "So do we understand each other, Agent Adams? You have until this time tomorrow."

"Wait!" Through the phone speaker, Agent Adam's shout was distorted. "If the rest of you are listening, I'm ordering you to leave, right now, or we will consider you enemy combatants."

"Who said anything about enemies?" Lois said. "Are you declaring war? Those are your words, Adams. Not ours. We aren't keeping anyone here against their will except those who have actively worked against us, who are tools of the tyranny of the federal government."

"Lois, they're park rangers; all they do is talk to tourists. They aren't your enemy. We can work something out as long as you don't do anything you can't take back. You've got to give us time."

"I am giving you time…till eight o'clock," Lois said. "Call me back when you have something."

She hung up and looked out at the crowd. "Like the man said, you're free to leave if you don't agree with this course of action. But if you stay, you will be given guard duties. Check in with Marshall and Landry, and they'll give you your assignments. That's it, people. This is all going to be over in twenty-four hours, one way or another."

I was sort of amazed that there wasn't an immediate exodus. Lois would have preferred that. She'd wanted only her loyalists there.

The occupiers trailed out of Merriam Hall, some stopping by the counter where Landry was assigning duties, others not. I wanted to shout at them, *She doesn't care if you live or die! Don't you get it?*

As if she could hear my thoughts, Lois turned and looked at me. I felt my heart leap, and then she looked away as if it had never happened.

But she'd given me just enough of her attention to know that I still existed, that I wasn't already a ghost. She'd noticed me, if only by accident, and that was enough for the leash to tighten around my neck again.

I was hers forever. I was never going to escape.

CHAPTER 70

VANESSA JOHNSON

I was going to get my son, no matter what. The cops weren't letting anyone in. Jerry wasn't going to come out. I'd asked Bradford to take care of him, but Bradford was always an idiot. I couldn't trust him to protect my son, not really.

So I figured I'd go in and get Jerry myself. Or join him. I still wasn't sure.

What really decided me was when I saw the tanks. There were three of them, huge things, like giant bugs with all sorts of weird attachments on them. I'd seen what the tanks had done in Waco, setting fire to the compound. The Feds wanted us to believe it was an accident and that the Davidians had set down torches and lamps where they could be knocked over. But those who understood the truth, we knew that they'd done it on purpose. Oh, maybe not to kill everyone the way they did; maybe they expected them to try to escape. But the results were the same.

We walked as far into the desert as we could. Well, as far as *I* could. It's not like I didn't know I was middle-aged and over-weight, but I had no idea I was a near cripple. What did I expect, since I rarely left the ranch kitchen much those days? I thought that because I was on my feet all day long, feeding the ranch hands breakfast, lunch, and dinner, somehow I was healthy.

I was dripping sweat before we went a hundred yards. I fell flat on my face in the sand. Derrick pulled me to my feet. I got angry at him, slapping his hands away. That was the last time I touched my son. Slapping his hands. I will never, ever forgive myself.

But more, I'll never forgive the FBI for not letting me get in there through the front entrance like a free person. If they hadn't forced me to go around, none of it would have happened. Damn their souls.

Damn *your* souls. I know you're reading this. May you rot in hellfire for ever after.

I spit out dust for what seemed miles, and a grain of sand got in my left eye and it kept watering and watering, streaks running down the dust on my cheek.

But I was determined. I kept moving, even if I had to rest every few hundred feet.

Derrick was so patient with me. He was always the kindest of my boys. Jerry was the hothead, but Derrick, he was happy wherever he was. He only came along because of me.

He talked three of his friends into coming with us. To be honest, I didn't pay much attention to them at the time. I'm not sure I even knew their names, though I do now. Justin, Jared, and Cameron, may their memories be forever blessed. They were martyrs to the cause, all of them, especially my Derrick.

The FBI couldn't even do a blockade right. They left a corridor between the lava rocks and juniper trees, out of sight in a gully. Derrick's friend, Cameron, saw it in his binoculars, which was what gave me the idea. If the damn FBI had done their job and stopped us, none of it would have happened.

We emerged out of the gully with only a few hundred feet to go. The second we stepped out onto the flats, we heard yelling, both behind us and in front of us.

"Go!" I shouted to Derrick. "Go get Jerry!" I wasn't sure the Feds wouldn't catch up to me, and I didn't want to slow down the boys.

The boys took off like a shot. I stumbled after them, trying not to fall on my face, and within seconds, they were dozens of feet ahead of me. I wasn't even halfway across before the boys came up on the camp.

The shouting was loud on both sides, but even louder from inside the camp. I thought they were cheering us on. I couldn't make out the words.

The first bomb blew Jared and Cameron into the air.

I couldn't make sense of it. Bodies flying, and parts of bodies, the heads seeming to fly farther, Cameron's body falling flat, Jared's sliding in the dust. I see all this in my memories, but I couldn't understand what I was seeing when it was happening.

Justin kept running and hit the second mine. He disappeared in a red mist, nothing left of him but bones and shattered meat.

My boy Derrick stopped dead in his tracks. He turned toward me, his face white. He was so scared. I'd seen that look before, when Harry had made him jump off Pinnacle Rock into the Round Butte reservoir. I remember that same fearful face when that mangy dog next door had rushed him (I got there first with my butcher knife. Never got bothered by that mutt again!).

I kept running. I didn't care about myself. The FBI was blowing us up, that's what I thought. I found out later it was our own people who laid the mines, but considering what happened, how can I blame them? They had a right to protect themselves.

I wish I'd known, that's all. I wish someone had told me.

Derrick started moving toward me, and I knew. The second he took that first step, I knew.

"Stop, Derrick!" I screamed. "Don't move!"

I was still twenty yards away when the bomb went off under my son. At almost the same moment, my legs went out from under me. I screamed and didn't stop screaming. Not because of the pain, but because I knew.

My son was gone.

I don't remember anything after that until I woke up in this hospital bed. There were a few blessed moments when I forgot, and then...I screamed and screamed.

They must have given me a shot, because I dropped into a red sleep, filled with blood, until I woke again. I managed not to scream this time, except inside. I wouldn't let them put me to sleep again. I needed to remember.

I'll never wash that blood off, the blood of my youngest son. I feel it on my hands, I see it in the mirror, I dream of it flowing down my cheeks, the texture of syrup, the smell of iron.

I never saw his body. Maybe it was a blessing, but I still wish

I could have seen him one last time. I thought my legs were gone, but though shredded by shrapnel, they made it through. I won't ever walk again without a walker, but I'm alive.

I'm alive to carry on the fight. I'm more determined than ever. You hear that, you bloodsucking leeches? I'm coming after you. I had six sons, and now…

I will sacrifice them all, and myself, because they aren't free. They're slaves to the deep state.

Live free or die!

My husband, Harry, says to stop saying that, but I don't care.

Live free or die!

CHAPTER 71

HART DAVIS

I moved out of my tent into one of the nearby empty trailers. The camp was quiet, dark except for a sliver of moonlight. Everyone was in shock over what had happened to Vanessa Johnson and the boys who'd tried to get into the camp. You'd have thought that would have ended the occupation, but instead, it was as if it was the first battle of a new war.

The trill of crickets and the croak of bullfrogs, which had filled the previous nights with their mating calls, were strangely absent. When clouds passed overhead, the darkness was complete.

The bombs going off had been the final straw for most of the original occupiers. Throughout the afternoon, one by one or in small groups, they walked out the south entrance with their hands held high, hunched over as if they expected to be shot, though by which side it was hard to say.

They were lucky. They were gone before Lois made her announcement, damning everyone who stayed. I wondered if any of us would survive if she carried out her threat or if the Feds would make a clean sweep of us. I doubted we had many sympathizers left out there in the real world. Threatening the rangers, making them hostages, was a step too far for most people. That was ISIS kind of behavior.

They wouldn't dare choose Nicole to punish, I told myself. If I'd believed that they would, I would have headed straight for Garth's shack, where the hostages were being held, and I would have shot it out right then and there.

By then, Lois's people were in complete control. Only a few others remained at the Fossil Beds Monument. Kerry Lawrence was still around, and a couple of his friends, whom I didn't know. They'd been ready to leave with everyone else, but I'd gone to Lawrence and asked that he stay.

"We're the only ones who can stop this, Lawrence," I told him.

He wouldn't look me in the eye. "I want to help, but we're outnumbered. I don't think there's much we can do."

"If we're here, Lois won't be as likely to do anything too extreme."

He gave me a skeptical look but told me he'd think it over.

I didn't try to argue further, but I figured "think it over" was an easier way to say "no."

That left Peter Sterns and me, as far as I knew. That was about it. The only sane ones still in the camp. Not enough to stop Lois and her people.

I wondered if we'd even have a chance to change what was about to happen, or whether her people would come in the middle of the night to take us out. Then only the terrorists would be left. I tried to imagine how scared Nicole must be, then realized she was probably braver than I was, huddling in my little trailer, uncertain what to do, trying hard to come up with a plan, any plan, that had a chance of success.

At midnight, a time of night when I was usually dead on my feet, I was still wide awake. There was no way I was going to sleep, I thought. The eight o'clock deadline seemed both years and mere moments away.

A soft knock on the door shook me awake. I'd nodded off sitting up. There was something about that knock, something inexplicably feminine, and I quickly opened the door, thinking it was Nicole, as impossible as that would have been.

Lois stood there looking up at me with a strange smile. She was wearing makeup, clean clothing, and looked as good as she'd ever looked.

"You gonna to ask me in?"

I looked over her shoulder, trying to catch movement in the darkness, to see if she had an escort of guards, but she was alone.

"What are you doing here, Lois?"

"I thought we might have a chat, that's all," she said. "Now's your chance to talk me out of this."

I swung the door all the way open, then turned on the lamp on the table and sat down on the bench seat. Damned if I was going to offer her a drink. She sat across from me. She'd obviously spent some time trying to look good. Did she think something could happen between us?

"Do you really think the Feds are going to give in?" I asked.

She shrugged. "Why not? They can give us federal pardons and then hit us with state or local charges later. That would be the smart move. They can rescind the Ochoco Monument status and then rescind the rescinding. That's what I would do. Either way, we can't lose. People will see that they tricked us, and we'll win."

"You're willing to go to jail?"

"I don't think it will come to that. You know that almost none of the Malheur occupiers went to jail, except the idiots who pleaded guilty? But even if that happens, we'll be in the news for months, maybe years. I'll be interviewed on every network, every talk show."

I laughed. I couldn't help it. It seemed so ludicrous to be mentioning talk shows after everything that had happened. "You're playing with people's lives so you can get on TV?"

Lois didn't answer, as if the question was rhetorical.

I snorted. "You planning to write a book or something?"

She stared back at me without changing expression. "Why not? Would that be so weird?"

"That's not going to happen, Lois. The Feds are afraid of setting a precedent. They can't afford to give in or every nutcase in the world will start taking hostages."

She didn't say anything. I realized that she already knew that. The other stuff, her being interviewed on TV and writing a book, that was fantasy.

"What are you going to do, Lois?"

She gave me a knowing look.

Nicole. The thought of her being at the mercy of this cold-hearted woman was like body blow.

Take Lois out now, I thought. Without her, maybe the others wouldn't follow through. But the moment I considered it, I realized that Marshall and the other men he'd brought were different. They'd execute all the hostages if they had the chance.

"Don't worry, Hart. I'm not going to pick Nicole. At least, not as the first one," Lois said.

"The Feds aren't going to let you execute a hostage, Lois."

"Of course they aren't. They're probably coming in within the next few hours." She glanced at her watch. "I figure either four or five o'clock. What do you think? Any bets?"

"How can you be so casual about it?" I wanted to shout, to wake up the few remaining occupiers, to point at Lois and tell them how nuts she was. Instead, I said quietly. "Why, Lois? What's the point?"

"Did you know that the militia movement grew tenfold after Ruby Ridge? After Waco, it grew tenfold again. If that idiot Timothy McVeigh hadn't gone and blown up babies, who knows how much more it would have grown? But you can't keep freedom down long. People come around; they see what's happening."

"Chances are you're all going to get killed," I said.

"You ever heard of the Battle of San Jacinto?"

"Of course. Sam Houston and the Texans defeated Santa Anna's army."

"Well, I'm betting almost no one else in this camp could tell you that, but every damn one of them knows about the Alamo."

I stared at her, trying to see if she was serious. "You don't strike me as the martyr type, Lois."

"Santa Anna let the women go," she said, sitting back. "I plan to leave my guns behind tomorrow. I don't think the Feds will shoot an unarmed woman."

"Jesus, you're willing to let your people die just so you can get the glory. You are one narcissistic bitch."

I don't know what I expected. I guess for her to get angry, to slap my face, or to stomp off.

She laughed. "You just figuring that out?"

"Why? I don't get it. What's in it for you?"

She put out her hand and covered mine with it. I pulled

back as if a scorpion had landed on me. She frowned. "You like Bigfoot Ranch, don't you, Hart?"

"Of course."

"I *hate* ranching. Every minute of it. You know that most of the Eastern Oregon ranchers are rich. Land rich, at least. But Mathew wouldn't sell any of his land. He was like you. He liked the whole lifestyle. I thought when he died, I could sell his land and live the way I wanted to live, but the son of bitch had mortgaged the property to the hilt. At a time when just about every other rancher was getting rich developing subdivisions, he was pouring money into his damn cattle. Worse, he'd reduced his life insurance without telling me. When everything was settled, I had less money than when I'd started."

She knew that I knew that she'd murdered her husband. Was she asking for sympathy?

"I take it back, Lois. You aren't a narcissistic bitch. You're a *murdering* narcissistic bitch."

"Guilty," she said, amused.

"Get out," I said.

She stood up but didn't move toward the door. "I thought maybe, you know, we could comfort each other tonight. You know, physically. Doesn't have to mean anything."

I grabbed her elbow. She cried out, and I loosened my grip. Even then, I couldn't hurt her. But I also wanted nothing to do with her. I pushed her toward the open doorway. She stood there stubbornly while I motioned for her to leave.

"You might want to stay in the trailer, Hart," she said. "Until it's over. You wouldn't want to get caught in the crossfire."

"Get the fuck out."

She stepped down the stairs and into the darkness as if she didn't have a care in the world.

CHAPTER 72

PERRY CAMPBELL

I didn't sleep the night before the shootout. Garth snored loudly, Nicole tossed and turned, but I didn't feel an ounce of sleepiness. I sat at the table, staring at the wood grain and remembering my wife, who'd been gone for twenty years, and my two daughters, who rarely got in touch. Were they out there in the world, worried about me? Or were they shaking their heads, thinking, "We always knew he'd get in *someone's* way."

I was certain this was going to end with one of us rangers being hurt.

I'd never seen anyone shot before.

When it finally happened, the shattering sound of the first shots was enough to send me sprawling. I swear, my heart stopped, and it took its time about deciding to beat again.

Looking back on it, I realize that might have been a good time to try to get away, but I lay there in the dust, seeing in my mind Mich flying backward, blood spraying into the air.

And then listening to the attackers calmly discuss shooting her in cold blood.

I tried to convince myself that what Lois hinted at by "severe consequences" wasn't what I thought it was. But the fear in the pit of my stomach, which grew with every hour until I felt hollowed out by it, that fear told me something else.

They are going to kill us.

My mind skittered across the idea of execution. Ever since I was a child, the idea of the cold-blooded execution of another human being had creeped me out more than anything. *Why don't they fight?* I'd wondered. *Wouldn't it be better to die fighting or trying to escape than being slaughtered?*

As I grew older, I came to understand that it wasn't that simple. People did try to escape, to fight, and were killed for the effort. Others never had an opportunity. But most of all, there was that final hope that someone, something, *anything* would come to save them.

I felt that hope all night long. I knew I wasn't immortal, I knew I could easily die, but somewhere deep down, I didn't believe it. Even though I was afraid, I was convinced something would save me.

I say "me" because I was sure I would be the one they picked first. I was the highest ranking and represented the federal government. They wouldn't pick Nicole, I was pretty sure.

I'm not sure why I never thought about Garth. Maybe because I knew what a kind and gentle soul he was, despite his rough ways. I knew him as a genial presence, someone uncomplicated and direct. Me? I'd been through enough bureaucratic fights in my career to know I wasn't universally loved.

Though why that would matter to the terrorists, I'm not sure I even considered.

Terrorists were how I thought of them then, and it was what they were. I'd been stupid and shortsighted to see them as anything else. What is it they say about liberals? That they're only liberals because they haven't been mugged yet?

The two guards chatted outside all night, laughing, groaning at bad jokes, having an earnest argument about politics. They were the same two men who'd confronted us, who'd shot Mich. I couldn't make out their words, but I sensed them cursing the government. I felt their unreasoning hate. Smoke from their cigarettes trickled through the cracks in the wall.

When daylight started filtering through those cracks and under the slit in the door, I tried to deny it. The night had been both endless and brief. It couldn't be over yet.

Suddenly, I was sleepy. I knew I could lay my head on the table and be out like a light. Deep voices shocked me into alertness, my mind trying to grab hold of something solid, to make sure I wasn't in some kind of dream.

Garth stirred, cursing, and I was back in the real world, and the daylight did nothing to dispel the nightmare.

The door flew open. Against the morning sun, I could see only shadows. They stood still and threatening.

Nicole roused herself from her sleeping bag on the floor. Garth sat up, wiping spittle from his beard.

I stood up to face my fate. My legs could barely hold me. It wasn't that I felt heavy; it was more like I was fading. It was as if I was looking at myself from a distance, as if I was watching myself in a movie.

But they didn't come for me. They pushed through the door and went to Garth, pulling him off the cot.

"Let me get dressed at least," Garth said. He sounded calm, as if he'd expected this.

"No, not him," I heard myself say. "Take me, I'm the boss. Forty years of service, SES level, which in case you don't know is pretty damn high. Garth is just a G5."

They looked at me like I was speaking Greek. I forced myself to say something more. "I'm the government you hate, not Garth."

The media has tried to make me out to be a hero. But I can tell you, I didn't *want* to say that. Every part of me was screaming *Take him! Take him!* I had to force myself to say those words, one by one. At each word, I almost faltered, almost didn't get it said. I was a fake and a fraud. I was scared and witless.

But I forced myself to say the words, and then I forced myself not to take them back.

Some hero.

"I don't really give a shit," Smith said. I've learned since that that was an alias, that he was really Robert Kadry. "Garth here pissed me off. He's the same asshole I've run into every time I've had to deal with the government. He's the asshole at the DMV or the Social Services office, taking his lunch break while we peons sit out in a crowded waiting room on rickety chairs in stinky air. He's the guy I've wanted to shoot a hundred times."

"I gave him his instructions," I said. "I'm responsible."

"Hey, I admire your balls, Campbell. I'd have never expected it from you. But Garth is the one we want. He's the one everyone is going to miss. I just know it. He's got buddies from college all over the country, old girlfriends, doting parents…what do you want to bet?"

I lunged toward the man. I don't know what I thought I could accomplish. His open holster, I remember seeing that. I had some quixotic notion of grabbing his gun Rambo-style and shooting them all down.

I didn't even get halfway there before someone tripped me. I landed on my shoulder on the concrete floor and slid the rest of the way into Kadry's boot.

That's the last thing I remember until waking up in the hospital.

CHAPTER 73

HART DAVIS

Lois had been gone for only a few minutes when I heard a light tap on the trailer door. My heart sank. I really didn't want to talk to her ever again. She was crazy. It wasn't about the money, no matter what she told herself. She loved the violence and the chaos. Most of all, she reveled in being the one who instigated it.

I opened the door a crack, intending to tell her to go away, that we had nothing left to talk about.

It was Brad Patterson. Of all of those who'd come in the first wave of the takeover, I knew Brad the least. He and Jerry Johnson were always together, and they interacted more with each other than they did with the rest of us.

"What do you want?" I asked. I cursed myself for opening the door without my .38 in hand. Were they coming to take me away? To lock me up, or...

Someone was behind him, and I almost slammed the door shut. I wasn't sure how the lock mechanism worked, but it might give me time to get to my weapon.

"Let us in, Hart," I heard a familiar voice say.

Peter Sterns stepped out from behind Brad's shadow. "Brad's on our side. We've come bearing gifts."

I opened the door all the way. Brad leaned down from the steps and picked up a duffel bag that, judging from his grunt, was heavy. Peter also had a bag, draped over his shoulder, his fingers white from holding onto the straps.

They clunked the bags down in the middle of the trailer and

opened them. Each bag held an AK-47, magazines, camouflage clothing, and bulletproof vests.

"Where did this all come from?" I asked.

Brad snorted. "The terrorists brought in enough gear for a war. They won't miss a few things."

I took a vest and a rifle, but eschewed the camouflage. Peter, I noticed, had made the same decision. Brad, meanwhile, now looked like one of the men he called hard-asses.

"So," Brad said, sitting down. "We saw Lois leaving. What's up with you two?"

"A mistake," I said. "Not one of my prouder moments."

"She's got something about her, for sure," Brad said. "In a psycho bitch sort of way. I'd do her."

"Trust me, you don't want to."

"So, what's the plan?" Peter asked.

"We have to get the hostages out of here."

"No shit. But how do we do that?"

"We take down the guards and make a run for it?" I said.

Brad shook his head. "We might be able to spring them from the hut, but what then? We can't get through the minefields, and the only exit is to the south. Carter and Hanson have a crossfire zone set up. We wouldn't get ten feet once we entered it."

"So we take them out," Peter said.

"Those guys scare me," Brad said. "They're pros. Ex-military or some shit like that. They'll be well hidden and somewhere we can't approach without being seen."

"We'd have surprise on our side," I pointed out.

"Yeah, well..." Brad shrugged.

"I take it *you* have a plan?" I asked.

"Not much of one, I admit. Just the idea that we need to wait until the shit starts going down before we make our move. Wait until everyone is preoccupied doing something else. I say we strike at eight o'clock, when whatever Lois is planning happens. We use the chaos as cover."

"Why aren't the Feds here yet?" I asked. "I don't understand it. I can't believe they're going to let Lois have the upper hand."

Peter answered. "Brad sent a map to the FBI that shows where the mines are located. My guess is that they're trying to figure out a back way in. But yeah, if they don't show up soon, who knows what will happen?"

Hanging in the air was the dread we were all feeling.

"I think Lois is going to execute one of the hostages," I said.

They fell silent at that, but neither of them contradicted me.

"I say we wait until it's all about to happen, then strike," Brad said. "I'm betting they'll have everyone gathered for…for the thing. The hut will probably be minimally guarded. You two should stake out the place, and when the shitstorm happens, you strike. By that time, I'm guessing, the Feds will be on their way."

"And what about the hostage they choose?" Peter asked.

"I won't let it happen," Brad said. "I promise you, I'll take out whoever holds the executioner's axe. I've talked to Lawrence and his people. They're staying."

"That's a surprise," Peter said. "Hopefully, they'll do the right thing when the time comes."

"Doesn't sound like a much better a plan than shooting it out now," I said.

Brad stood up and went the door. Dawn glimmered on the horizon. "Too late for that anyway. If you're going to stake out the hut, you'd better get going before all darkness is gone."

Peter and I looked at each other. He nodded. I reached down for the rifle and examined it to make sure I could operate it. Brad came over and gave me a few pointers, and then slapped me on the back.

"When you hear something going down, that's when you strike," he said, then turned and left.

Peter and I followed him out the door, but he was already out of sight. We hurried to the line of trailers that marked the edge of the takeover camp. Garth's hut was just a few feet beyond.

We moved to the edge of the nearest trailer. I slowly peeked around the corner. There were two guards. One was standing, alert. The other was leaning against the door, apparently half asleep. I motioned for Peter to go around to the other side of the trailer.

Then we waited.

Time moved slowly, stuck in a loop of light glimmering

but never quite brightening, and then, suddenly, it was day. I glanced at my watch. Seven o'clock.

As if on cue, I heard voices. From the main corridor between the trailers, four men appeared, three terrorists and Jerry. Even though he was dressed and armed the same as the others, Jerry stood out with his unkempt hair and slouching posture. He trudged while the others marched.

As they neared the hut, I couldn't help but second-guess our plans. Here was our chance to take out three of our enemy. I left out Jerry, because chances were he would be useless in a fire-fight. He might run, he might fall to the ground, he might stand frozen, but I didn't think he'd shoot back.

But even though they were right in our sights, I had no way to signal Peter or Brad of the change in plans.

Then the moment passed. They went inside the hut. I heard Perry's shouts, then silence. A little while later, they pulled Garth out of the shack.

The ranger had managed to pull on a pair of jeans, but he was bare chested and barefoot. His beard and hair were wild, pointing every which way. He wasn't making it easy, either. They were practically dragging him out. His head was high, and he looked defiant.

I felt a flash of guilty relief. I'd been pretty sure they wouldn't pick Nicole, but Lois was so crazy, who knew for sure? I'd thought it would be Perry, but once I saw Garth, I realized it was inevitable. He'd butted heads with Smith and Benton too often.

The two guards stayed behind, unfortunately. I'd hoped they'd take one or both of the guards with them, but no such luck.

The next hour was even longer than the previous night had been, every second a minute and every minute an hour. I kept looking at my watch, then forced myself to quit looking.

Nicole was less than twenty yards away. I could sense her. I can't explain it, but it was as if she was right there and I could almost touch her and smell her. I sensed her presence and her soul, but I had no way to let her know I was watching over her.

No one was going to take her away. No one was going to open that door.

As I stood there, eyes closed, there was a single shot in the distance. A few moments later, the world erupted with the sound of thunder. I looked up, startled, saw blue skies, and realized it was automatic weapons fire punctuated by explosions.

I stepped out from behind the trailer.

CHAPTER 74

BRAD PATTERSON

It was a bright morning, with a nip in the air. Everyone showed up by 7:30 in the central plaza, between the mess tent and Merriam Hall. The few remaining occupiers waited, wondering, hoping or fearing, I suppose, what was about to happen.

When they marched Garth into the clearing with Smith on one side of him and Benson on the other, I knew. I'd seen the look in Smith's eyes when Garth confronted him at the dig.

Of course they'd picked him.

But were they really going to go through with it? Even when it was happening in front of me, I couldn't believe it, even though I'd seen how they were willing to lay down traps that would kill anyone who approached and that had already killed four innocent boys. But a cold-blooded execution seemed like something out of a faraway war, from an old newsreel.

Garth faltered at the sight of the onlookers. His defiance melted and a slack expression came over his face. He looked like a man being marched to the gallows—which he pretty much was. Someone pushed him roughly from behind. Garth stumbled, fell to his knees, and didn't get up.

Jerry stood behind him, an ugly look on his face.

That expression has remained with me to this day. Part of it, of course, is that cameras were filming the whole thing and the record is permanent. *The look of hate*, the headlines said. *The face of fanaticism*. At the time, the media was so far away that I didn't realize they were filming or that they could get such clear pictures. It didn't occur to me then. Maybe if it had, I would have tried to pull him away.

Marshall stepped forward, pistol in hand. I expected him to make a speech. Lois would have, but Lois was nowhere to be seen. My stomach dropped. When I saw that she was missing, that's when I knew it was really going to happen.

Marshall turned to Jerry and handed him the pistol.

I was frozen in place. I couldn't move, I couldn't think. I'd promised Hart and Peter that nothing would happen to the hostage the terrorists chose. I'd fully intended to kill whoever made that move.

But Jerry? He was my best friend, maybe my only friend. This was a moment of madness, that's all. It wasn't really him.

"Jerry!" I shouted. I don't think he even heard me. He didn't look reluctant in the slightest. He looked proud of himself.

I raised my rifle, intending to shoot at Jerry's feet or perhaps at his legs or arms, something other than a killing shot. Kadry noticed my movement and motioned to Benson, who raised his rifle toward me.

Jerry stepped forward, extending the barrel of the pistol until it touched the back of Garth's head.

Jerry's head disappeared in a spray of blood, followed milliseconds later by the sound of a shot, echoing through the camp.

Standing next to Kadry, Lindstrom stiffened for a moment, a look of surprise on his face, then dropped straight down, landing face first in the sand. He didn't move.

Again, the sound of the killing shot took an extra moment to reach the clearing. The FBI had trained their snipers on us and were taking us out.

Benson was distracted long enough for me to move. I dove behind the rocks that lined the central campfire. A spray of bullets ricocheted over me.

Kadry crouched and his hat went flying, a bullet missing a killing headshot by inches. He swung his rifle to his shoulder and aimed it down at Garth. But Garth wasn't on his knees anymore; he was rolling into Kadry's legs. Kadry jumped back, almost lost his balance, then aimed once more at Garth, who was still coming at him.

I put a bullet into the middle of Kadry's forehead. The top half of his head went flying behind him.

Benson ran toward me, firing. Before I could train my gun on him, he shuddered as a spray of bullets hit him midchest. One of the bullets chewed into his throat; another blew away his jaw. He tumbled backward.

I couldn't see who was firing, but realized it had to be Lawrence or one of his men.

I looked for Landry, but he'd disappeared into the tent city behind them.

"Stay down, everyone!" I shouted. I wasn't sure the FBI wouldn't shoot us all and be done with it. Garth was on his hands and knees, scooting for the cover of Merriam Hall. No one took another shot at him.

Then there was a moment of silence. I looked around. Lawrence was in a kneeling firing position, swinging his rifle around, looking for more of the hard-asses. But the terrorists who had accompanied Marshall were down. The rest of them were guarding the perimeter of the camp. I winced, certain that the FBI snipers would take Lawrence out, but the silence continued. Carefully, I poked my head out from behind the rock circle. I raised my hands.

Lawrence lowered his rifle and stood up, raising his hands, following my example. If Landry or any of the others were behind cover, we'd be easy targets, but I estimated that the snipers were the bigger danger.

Then, from both the front of the camp and the back, a flurry of gunfire filled the silence, followed by a huge explosion. A black cloud rose above the camp, and as the echoes receded, the grinding of tank treads took their place.

CHAPTER 75

HART DAVIS

As soon as I stepped out from behind the trailer, I realized that I hadn't thought things through. Both guards were facing south, listening to the gunfire. They were on high alert. The green shack was in the line of fire behind them. The plywood walls would shatter under gunfire, and whoever was inside would be cut down.

Peter stepped out from the other side of the trailer, but his line of fire was no better than mine. He must have had the same thought, because he didn't shoot either.

I realized I couldn't just shoot someone down without a warning.

"Drop your rifles!" I shouted. But even as the words left my mouth, the two guards were doing the opposite, raising their weapons to their shoulders. I ducked back behind the trailer, stumbled and fell, and it probably saved my life. The trailer's aluminum side was shredded under the gunfire. My head was near the tires, and as I lay there, stunned, bullets thudded into them, and the tires sighed and deflated. Dust was kicked up near my legs, but the shots miraculously missed me.

I started to get up and was slammed against the side of the trailer by something striking my chest. It was as if someone had swung a two-by-four at full force into my ribs. The bulletproof vest stopped most of the bullet's momentum, but if it hadn't been for the trailer wall in between, I doubt it would have stopped the full impact.

I got back down, crawled to the corner, and poked my head

around it. The two terrorists were charging my position, but the shack was still behind them. I hesitated again, but I knew that I had to take a shot if I wanted to survive. I had to hope that Perry and Nicole had hit the deck.

A sudden certainty struck me that they had done exactly that. I aimed for the first man's head and fired. I guess I'd expected a single shot, not remembering that the AK-47 had been converted to automatic. Bullets slammed into my opponent at chest height, and my rifle jerked down from the recoil, not upward, because of my position on the ground. It was as if I could follow the trajectory of the bullets in slow motion as they struck the man in the groin, just below his vest, and then marched down his right leg.

That leg flew to one side at a strange angle, and he tumbled down after it.

The bullets keep stuttering until the gun jammed or the magazine was exhausted, I never learned which. The final round hit the terrorist square in the top of his head as he fell into the stream of bullets.

The other terrorist was untouched, but by that time he was far enough away from the shack that Peter was able to get an angle on him. Peter stepped back out into the open. The terrorist tried to change direction, tried to turn his rifle toward this new opponent, but Peter's gunfire struck him in the neck and head and he dropped, thudding to the ground.

I started to stand up. My right leg went out from under me, and I felt a sharp pain in my side. I looked down. Blood was flowing down my pant leg. The bulletproof vest hadn't stopped the bullet completely. I put my hand to the wound, which was near my right hip, and realized that it had taken out an inch-wide chunk of my side but no more. Didn't make it hurt any less.

I got to my feet this time, tossed the rifle aside, and reached for my revolver. Peter was just standing there as if not believing what he'd done.

"You good?" I shouted.

He looked at me, dazed, and then nodded.

Both guards were unmoving, but I wasn't taking any

chances. I approached slowly, stood a few feet away, and examined them. There was no doubt that they were dead. One man's neck was severed, and the other man was missing most of his leg and part of his skull, and his blood trickled instead of flowed.

The door to the hut opened. I whirled, raising my .38. Was there a third guard? I doubted they would have left the door unlocked.

Nicole came out, saw me with my gun extended, and raised her arms. She didn't quite smile, but she took in the sight of the two slain guards, and then looked at Peter and me and said, "Don't shoot. I surrender."

I found out later that she'd spent most of the time after they'd taken Garth away trying to pick the lock. When the gunfire erupted, she'd dropped to the floor. After a few moments of silence, she went back to the door and tried it again. In frustration, she pushed against it, and to her surprise, it popped open.

"Nicole," I said. I didn't know a single word could be uttered with so much meaning, as if everything I'd ever said and done up to that moment was punctuated by that one name. She walked straight into my arms.

I don't know how long we stood there. Finally, Peter cleared his throat. Nicole gently disengaged from me and gave him a hug too.

"Perry?" I asked.

She nodded. "He's inside. Hurry, he's hurt."

Perry was lying on his side, his arms cradled under his head. There was a nasty bump over his left eye.

"I think he's got a concussion, but I don't think it's worse than that. I mean, that's bad enough," Nicole said.

Gunfire erupted to the south of us, and I knew that the real fight for the camp had begun. Then the hut shook on its foundations. A shock wave pushed against our ears and eyes, and then it passed. Someone had set off a mine, one of the big ones. Seconds later, there was second explosion, and then a third.

Trying to get away from the camp was out of the question. There was no way we could carry Perry out of there and still protect ourselves.

"We should wait outside the hut," Peter said at the doorway.

"And look as harmless as possible."

"I'm not disarming until I know this is over," I said.

"I'm not telling you to. But let's make sure it's the enemy before we raise our weapons."

"Shouldn't we help the others?" I asked.

"The gunfire and explosions are coming from the north and south perimeters," Peter said. "The gunfight inside the camp is going to be over soon, one way or the other."

Nicole said, "Peter's right. The FBI will know where we are and who we are. They won't shoot at first sight. We just have to hope they get here before the terrorists do."

And so, while it sounded as if World War III was being fought a few hundred yards away, we sat down, leaned against the hut and waited, guns in hand.

CHAPTER 76

JOSHUA CALLEY

I wasted the first day raging against my imprisonment, drinking too much water and planning how I was going to throttle Lois Carpenter and her people. I had no doubt it was her followers who'd taken me down.

The last thing I remembered was an arm going around my throat. The arm was covered in rough camouflage, and there was a red symbol stitched on the sleeve. It wasn't until later that I remembered what it was: a swastika.

My attacker was smaller than me, which was maddening, but he was more than strong enough to squeeze my throat, to cut off the blood flow to my brain. I smashed him against the wall once, but the pressure didn't ease, and then darkness swarmed my consciousness.

I awoke in the middle of a room that was completely dark. Worse, it stunk to high heaven. I shouted and roared for a time, until my voice was fragged. Finally I shut up, deciding that I needed to wait for my moment, that I needed to be smart about this.

Stumbling around in the pitch dark, I found the light switch.

In the dim light of a single low-watt bulb, I saw that the office was a wreck. Lois and Mark had trashed the place. Nearing the desk, I recoiled from the smell of urine. It enraged me. Pointless vandalism. I smashed against the door again and again, until pain splintered down my shoulder and into my arms.

Though I sensed the door was unguarded, it was solid. There was no way I was going to force a way out through brute strength.

The water bottles I discovered by stepping backward and tripping over them, landing on my tailbone. Apparently, Lois wasn't going to let me die of thirst in here. The case of water seemed more than enough…at first.

Landing on my ass hurt worst of all. The humiliation, the stupidity of it all was enough to make me scream again, in a wordless rage against the world. Sometime later, I found myself sitting on the floor, staring at the concrete, breathing heavily, my mind a blank.

I looked around for tools. There was a cheap pair of scissors and a small Phillips-head screwdriver in the desk. I hacked at the metal door's lock for a while, but probably only succeeded in permanently freezing it into locked position.

Pacing around the room, I examined the cheap wood paneling, hoping there was Sheetrock underneath and I could punch my way through. But beneath the thin wood were cinder blocks.

I sat down on the cot, frustrated. The cot was all of about five feet long, good enough for Nicole Nelson, perhaps, but when I lay back, my legs dangled off the edge. In spite of everything, I napped for a time. I remember a dream of concrete being poured around my boots, of me escaping by pulling them off.

When I awoke, I went back to the cinder blocks and re-examined them. I pried at the mortar around one with the screwdriver, and a chunk an inch long skittered to the floor. Excited, I smashed again and again at the mortar, and it crumbled away.

I stepped back, looked around, grabbed a chair, and smashed it against the floor until I freed one of its legs. I picked the leg up and rammed it against the block. It shifted outward a good half inch.

Thank God for cheap federal contractors.

That's all it took. I don't know how many times I battered the cinder block, but it finally dropped outward. Light streamed into the room, the sunlight so much brighter than the single bulb that it seemed like dawn had broken.

How long had it taken? I sensed that as engrossed as I was in the task, it had taken longer than it seemed. My knuckles were bleeding, the blood covered by gray grit.

I picked up the screwdriver again, planning to attack the second block.

Voices filtered through the door. It sounded like more than one or two people. I went to the door and started pounding, shouting. I suppose I hoped it was the FBI and that it was all over. When minutes passed and no one responded, I knew that the terrorists were still in control.

I went back to the concrete and hacked away with renewed diligence. Halfway through the second block, the screwdriver bent in half. I tried to keep using it, but it was so awkward as to be useless.

I picked up the scissors, which seemed even flimsier, and tried to leverage the mortar out. To my surprise, this was much more effective, and a second block fell away.

My hands were sore, with blisters on three of my fingers; my arms were heavy. I estimated that I needed to remove at least four cinder blocks before I could squeeze my way out. The water was gone by then. I'd thoughtlessly guzzled it early on, and now, on the second day of my imprisonment, the thirst crept up on me little by little, a nagging worry at first, slowly pushing its way to the front of my brain until every thought I tried to form was blocked by my thirst.

It grew dark, and a breeze blew in through the opening, and I inhaled the promise of freedom.

I forced myself to keep chipping away. I was halfway through the third block when the scissors snapped in half. My big fingers simply couldn't get a grip on the smaller pieces.

I roared in frustration. My voice echoed in the room, and when it died away, the deep silence that answered told me I was alone.

I sat back down on the cot, ready to give up.

A single gunshot brought me to my feet. Moments later, automatic gunfire erupted, and in the distance, there was an explosion, and a shock wave shook the room. Fragments of mortar around the brick I'd been working on sprinkled to the floor.

I don't remember much about the next few minutes. I used the chair leg as a battering ram at first, but then, in frustration,

I ran at the wall. I bounced off, fell backward, and did it again. The third cinder block dropped away. I remember kicking at the fourth block again and again.

Judging by the pain in my legs and shoulders the next day, I must have gone berserk.

I tumbled outside, covered in white concrete dust, staring up at the morning sky. I looked down. I looked like a ghost, a few patches of my dark skin showing underneath the white dust.

I stumbled to my feet. The gunfire from the front of the visitor center had died away, but the explosions from the back of the camp were increasing, a steady *thump, thump, thump.*

From the south, the automatic weapons fire was continuous. I'm not sure why I turned in that direction. I guess I sensed it was where I could be the most effective. There wasn't much I could do against explosions.

I kept to the cover of the trailers and tents, making my way through the camp, seeing glimpses of other people and avoiding them, unsure if they were the good guys or the bad guys. I decided that Lois and her mercenaries were the bad guys and everyone who opposed them—whether it was the other occupiers like me or the damn Feds, it didn't matter—were the good guys.

Halfway through the camp, I realized I was still holding the chair leg. I swung it through the air a couple of times, satisfied by its weight. Wouldn't do much good against a bullet, but the terrorists weren't expecting anyone to come up behind them.

The gunfire was deafening, but in the microseconds between each explosion, I heard the heavy treads of an armored vehicle approaching. I almost stopped, thinking that whoever was doing the firing was about to have their heads blown off.

But the gunfire didn't stop, and as I crouched, I was suddenly certain that the terrorists were prepared for this. I crept toward the sound of gunfire.

The shots were hard to pinpoint. I slowed, looking for any sign of movement. It was only because one guy reached down and lifted a bulky-looking weapon to his shoulder that I noticed him.

The flash of red on his sleeve was all it took. A swastika. I ran at him full blast, covering the open area between us in seconds. It was crazy, and I was lucky that he had put down his automatic rifle and was encumbered by the bulky RPG. I was even luckier that the FBI snipers didn't take me down.

The little bastard sensed me coming at the last second and turned with the RPG, and I saw his finger tighten on the trigger. The shell flew past me, nearly blowing me off my feet, but nothing was going to stop me now. I never did hear the explosion from the missile. I think the damn thing somehow threaded its way through the trailers and tents and outbuildings and went out into the desert.

I swung my club down on the creep's head and felt his skull give way, then heard the *thud* of the rocket launcher falling to the ground.

My momentum carried me past him, and I rolled into the open.

From my left, a man rose up and turned his rifle toward me.

He seemed to bow to me, a stitching of red opening across his belly, and he lurched head first into the dirt, his ass pointing in the air.

The tank came into view and stopped, its turret pointed at me.

I dropped the club and raised my hands.

The silence was shocking. The air was vibrating with the sound of the tank's heavy engine, but it was almost soothing compared to the explosions and rifle fire of moments before. Seemingly out of the desert floor, two men rose up, rifles at their shoulders, and started shouting at me.

I couldn't hear them. I was deaf, but I knew what they wanted. I lay down in the dirt and put my hands behind my back.

As I sensed their footsteps near my head, a single gunshot rang out. It was muffled but distinct even to my deafened ears. The two agents dropped down into my line of sight, looking over me. Moments later, there was a second shot.

We waited, none of us moving, for what seemed like forever. Finally, one of the agents rose and crawled toward me. I felt bands being wrapped around my wrists, then cinched tight.

"You're a big guy, aren't you?" the agent whispered.

I shrugged in the dirt.

"Well, big guy, thank you. We would have walked right into an ambush. Whatever happens from now on, you've got my gratitude."

CHAPTER 77

MARK SIMONS

I sat at the window of my trailer that last night, watching the comings and goings across the way. I wasn't surprised that Lois stayed behind. When the heavily armed thugs left her trailer, I watched as she stood at the doorway with a smile, waving at them.

Then the smile dropped away and a triumphant look came over her face.

This was the true Lois Carpenter. The smile was never real, never had been.

I was determined to drink the last of my beer, even though I was already unsteady on my feet. Liquid courage. I was going to tell Lois exactly what I thought of her.

When I was certain no one was coming back, I staggered to my feet, stumbled down the steps of my trailer, and lurched over to her door. She answered it with a smile, which dropped off her face instantly upon seeing me. She tried to close the door, but I got my boot wedged inside. She slammed the door even harder, and I smothered a cry of pain.

"I'm coming in," I announced.

Lois looked up and down the clearing to make sure no one was watching. Then she shrugged and let go of the door.

By the time I limped up the last step, she was already sitting at her table, an open bottle of vodka in front of her. I went to the cupboard, snagged a coffee cup, and sat down across from her.

She kept her hand on the bottle as if signaling that I wasn't welcome to it. I pulled it out of her grasp and poured vodka into the mug until the clear liquid sloshed over the rim. Though I rarely drink hard liquor, I took a deep gulp, and started coughing.

Lois laughed as if amused. So I took another gulp, and this time it went down smoothly. I think she sensed that there was something different about me, but she didn't quite realize how much I'd changed over the last few days.

"Why do you hate me so much?" I asked.

"Hate you?" she said. "I don't think anything about you, Mark. You're beneath my notice."

"So why treat me like a dog?"

"Because you're weak, Mark. I can't stand weak men."

"But you'll fuck Hart Davis?"

"Are you a stalker now, Mark? Have you sunk even lower?" She took a small sip of vodka. "Hart and I may be on opposite sides, but he isn't weak. I respect that. What I can't respect is a man who does shit because some woman tells him to."

"And yet that's what you demand," I said. "If you surround yourself with weak men, how do you expect to win?"

"There's no winning, Mark. There's only survival."

"So you send them into harm's way while you sit here having a cocktail?"

She looked down at her cup of vodka. She lifted it and drained it, then poured a second helping to the rim. "I didn't tell those men what to think. They were already stewing in resentment. I'm just the one that helped them do something about it."

A single shot rang out in the distance.

Lois smiled and took a sip.

Someone had just died. I could feel it. Someone had been executed, and Lois's response was to smile.

I started to say something, I don't remember what, because for the next few minutes it was impossible to say anything and be heard. The trailer rattled again and again from explosions, and the gunfire was so heavy that it was a steady roar. There was a lull, then another explosion and another wave of gunfire, which dwindled slowly, until finally individual gunshots could be heard, until I could count my heartbeats and then my breaths between each shot.

Lois was vibrating with excitement, as if she was floating above her chair. Her hands were steady, her face calm, but the electricity in the air was almost sexual. I wanted her, and I put out my hand, intending to take hers.

She slapped it away.

I muttered, "'All my beautiful wickedness.'"

"What's that?" She was annoyed, but I was pretty sure she'd heard me.

"I said, behold your beautiful wickedness."

"Jesus, Mark. Grow up. This isn't Oz, this is the real world."

"No, Lois. None of this is real. I used to live in the real world. Going to work every day and worrying about bills, and once in a while having a good meal, and maybe if I was lucky, a little sex, and if I was even luckier, a vacation once in a blue moon."

"You really are pathetic, Mark."

I pulled out my pistol and laid it on the table, my finger on the trigger.

"What are you doing, Mark?

"I was going to blow my brains out in front of you, but you're right...that's just pathetic."

"Mark, you don't have to do this."

"Do what?" I asked. God help me, the power I felt at that moment *was* wicked. I got a glimpse of how Lois must have felt every moment of every day. It was intoxicating and scary.

"Mark..." Lois put her hand out, her face softening.

I shot her in the heart.

She had time to look down at the flower of blood blooming on her shirt. Then she sighed, laid her head down on the table, and stopped moving.

I had one bullet left.

I put the gun under my chin and felt the barrel burning into my skin.

I pulled the trigger.

Mark Simons (Suicide Note)
I couldn't even do that right. I blew off my lower jaw, my left cheekbone and eye, and half of my scalp. But I survived. I remember waking up from surgery, willing myself to die,

feeling my heart give out, then a shock as I was brought back.

I went to hell for a time—it seemed forever—voices screaming at me, every nerve in my body on fire, replaying every bad memory I ever had.

The rest of my life is going to be spent in solitary, in protective custody. I wouldn't last a minute in the general population, so I'm told. I'm the traitor, the Benedict Arnold of the Sagebrush Rebellion, apparently.

The rest of my life won't be long, because I intend to kill myself the first chance I get. I don't see how they can stop me.

Shrinks can read these notes and try to figure out what made me tick.

But I was just an ordinary guy who fell in love with the wrong woman.

CHAPTER 78

NICOLE NELSON

I have refused all interviews. My bosses are fine with that, because I'm more ambivalent than they prefer. I believe that those who took over the John Day Fossil Beds National Monument with guns should pay the price, and those who used violence to advance their ideology should be thrown in prison and the keys to their cells melted down so they can never be used again. But my superiors are correct that I would like to point out reasons why this takeover happened, reasons that don't always coincide with official policy.

Hart Davis has cooperated fully with the authorities. He feels responsible for what happened, as he should. I respect him for it. Once again, the media has come over to his side after initially vilifying him as a bad guy. Like his confrontation three years before with the mercenaries up in the Strawberry Mountains, he has gone from villain to hero. There's a good chance he won't be charged at all.

We haven't promised anything to each other. It's been left unsaid.

Peter Sterns and Jim Marston both got two-year sentences, mostly for having pulled out weapons during the initial takeover. The other original occupiers have pleaded innocent, and there is a good chance, based on previous trials in previous, similar takeovers, that they'll be found innocent, or at least have a hung jury. Here in the West, it is hard to assemble twelve jurors who feel the same way about the federal government, no matter how much they are vetted in advance.

The terrorists who came in at the end? There were only a couple left alive. If they are found innocent, then there is no justice.

Will this be like the Oklahoma City bombing, when the militia movement receded and went underground? Or will this be like Ruby Ridge and Waco, which lit a fire that is burning to this day?

Or will it sputter out, neither a win or a loss for either side?

It doesn't matter. The government will never stop going after them. If they are found innocent of one crime, they will be charged with another. If a hung jury is the result, they will be retried. But then, the trials give these fanatics a chance to espouse their ideology, and they won't forego that opportunity.

In the end, I think those who pleaded guilty are probably the wiser ones.

CHAPTER 79

SPECIAL AGENT ROD ADAMS

FBI ACTION REPORT EXCERPT

I understand that my decision not to infiltrate and implement a rescue mission earlier may come under criticism, but I judged that the danger to innocent lives was greater taking precipitous action than waiting for the situation to play out. We had assets within the camp; our informers and our agent were in danger. I judged it better to let those assets attempt to prepare the way.

It should also be noted that we had significant inside information, as well as utilizing surveillance techniques to gauge those whom we thought were a danger and those whom we believed were *in* danger. At no time in those last few days of the takeover were we unaware of the location of any of the occupants of the camp. Moreover, we had solid intelligence on their intentions.

The outside terrorists did surprise us, but once we realized they were there, we quickly identified them.

When our assets went silent, I did almost order the rescue mission to proceed. But the map provided by Brad Patterson showing the coordinates of the mines was still being examined and the best approach was still being worked out.

I take full responsibility for the delay.

Fortunately, as events unfolded, we were able to use mine-exploding equipment and make a safe approach to the north perimeter. Just inside this perimeter, we found two of the hostages, Perry Campbell, who was unconscious from a concussion, and Nicole Nelson, who was unharmed. Two of the occupiers, Hart Davis and Peter Sterns, were standing guard over her and immediately surrendered. (In the addendum, you will find my recommendations for leniency for Mr. Davis and Mr. Sterns. Both of these men were helpful in resolving the situation without greater bloodshed. However, Mr. Sterns was also among the original occupiers and is therefore partly responsible for the takeover happening in the first place.)

The greatest threat was our approach to the south. We knew that Virgil Carter and Moses Hanson were positioned to create a kill zone, and they had moved and taken cover several times, so our spotters weren't certain where they were. Obviously, this professionalism worried us, and we needed to plan our approach carefully. Over the previous day, three of our agents had managed to conceal themselves within a few hundred feet of the entrance, but we were still uncertain of the exact location of the sentries.

Our hopes were that upon gunfire commencing, we could ascertain their locations and they could then be neutralized. The problem, of course, was that we had to expose our own personnel to draw the fire.

Again, the decision to delay proved to be beneficial, because Joshua Calley's actions flushed out the snipers and they were dispatched. (See addendum for my recommendation for Mr. Calley, who I believe saved many lives.)

The events that took place within Lois Carpenter's trailer were unexpected, but the situation was resolved satisfactorily.

We were lucky. We lost none of our own people, and most of the occupiers survived. And of course, most importantly, the hostages were rescued. I believe that attempting a rescue earlier would have been a mistake, and I am convinced that it was only by wearing down the resolve of the original occupiers that the action turned out fortuitously.

The following recommendation is perhaps outside the purview of this Action Report, but nevertheless, I feel it must be made. I believe than in our pursuit of foreign terrorists, a commendable goal, we have neglected a homegrown danger.

I do not believe this will be the last of the takeovers and

therefore recommend that greater resources be dedicated to this problem.

The very foundation of our liberty is at stake, and whether one man's liberty becomes another man's tyranny. This threat should not be taken lightly.

EPILOGUE

HART DAVIS

In the end, they let me go. The investigators could find no pictures or videos of me carrying firearms—until that final day. Marston swore that I wasn't part of the planning, though whether he did so because he was trying to help me or damn me, I've never been sure.

Marston was a hero of the movement now. As were Peter Sterns and Brad Patterson. They were presented as examples of peaceful protesters who in their idealism had brought to light the abuses of the federal government, especially since they had then shown that they were good and true citizens by fighting the terrorists who'd invaded the John Day Fossil Beds National Monument. Lois Carpenter and her crew had been revealed as white nationalists, a violent splinter movement that everyone was ready to disavow.

Nicole was waiting for me on the steps of the Deschutes County Courthouse in downtown Bend. She took my arm silently, and we crossed kitty-corner from the courthouse to Brother John's restaurant. To my surprise, Nicole ordered a Deschutes Ale to go with her hamburger.

She smiled at my reaction. "I got in the habit of having a beer after work with Garth."

I looked down at my plate and carefully picked up a French fry, trying to keep my hand from shaking. "So...you like him?"

Nicole put out her hand and covered mine. "He's funny. I thought about it for a few seconds, but no, I don't like him that way."

I looked up into her eyes, and she was smiling—all the way down. For the first time in a long time.

"I've been assigned to Crater Lake," she said. "I don't know if it's punishment or reward. Not a whole lot of paleontology going on there. But it is the big leagues."

"They probably just want to keep you safe," I said.

I let a little time pass before I said, "I can try selling Nelson/Davis Wilderness Tours, join you up there."

"No," she said. My heart dropped, but she squeezed my hand. "No place for you to stay. Besides, we can see each other on our off days—and during the off-season. It's not so far away that we can't drive back and forth."

"I'm willing, Nicole. I'll follow you wherever you go."

"Why don't you keep the business going for now, Hart? I'm still not completely ready to make a commitment."

"I understand," I said, a little too quickly.

"Hart, I do love you. I can't really imagine a future without you."

"Really?"

"Besides," she said, laughing, "you do tend to get into some interesting situations. I want to be around for the next one. So let's just see how it goes. Not make any drastic decisions."

I took a bite of my hamburger, the juices squirting out of the side of my mouth. I wiped off my chin with the napkin.

"I'm good with that. Whenever you're ready, I am too."

She looked over at the waiter. "A couple more beers, please."

ABOUT THE AUTHOR

Duncan grew up and spent most of his life in Central Oregon, the dry side of the Cascades, and whose terrain is featured in many of his books. He wrote several books out of college, including the heroic fantasy novels *Star Axe, Snowcastles,* and *Icetowers*. In 1984, he and his wife Linda bought Pegasus Books in downtown Bend, Oregon, which they still own and operate. They also ran a used bookstore, the Bookmark, for 15 years.

In the last five years, he's been able to get back to writing again, and found that he has a lot of pent-up creative energy. He's written numerous books for several different publishers, mostly in the horror or dark fantasy genres, though recently has been branching out into fantasy again, as well as thrillers.

Duncan grew up and spent most of his life in Central Oregon, the dry side of the Cascades, and whose terrain is featured in many of his books. He wrote several books out of college, including the heroic fantasy novels Star Axe, Snowcastles, and Icetowers. In 1984, he and his wife Linda bought Pegasus Books in downtown Bend, Oregon, which they still own and operate. They also ran a used bookstore, the Bookmark, for 15 years.

In the last five years, he's been able to get back to writing again, and found that he has a lot of pent-up creative energy. He's written numerous books for several different publishers, mostly in the horror or dark fantasy genres, though recently has been branching out into fantasy again, as well as thrillers.

Curious about other Crossroad Press books?
Stop by our site:
http://store.crossroadpress.com
We offer quality writing
in digital, audio, and print formats.